THE OUT POST

A Jamison Valley Series Novel

DEVNEY PERRY

THE OUTPOST

Editor: Elizabeth Nover, Razor Sharp Editing

www.razorsharpediting.com

Cover Artwork © Sarah Hansen, Okay Creations

www.okaycreations.com

Proofreader: Julie Deaton

www.facebook.com/jdproofs

OTHER TITLES

Jamison Valley Series

The Coppersmith Farmhouse

The Clover Chapel

The Lucky Heart

The Outpost

The Bitterroot Inn

The Candle Palace

Maysen Jar Series

The Birthday List

Letters to Molly

Lark Cove Series

Tattered

Timid

Tragic

Tinsel

Tin Gypsy Series

Gypsy King

Riven Knight

Stone Princess

Noble Prince

Fallen Jester

Runaway Series

Runaway Road

Wild Highway

Quarter Miles

Forsaken Trail

Dotted Lines

Calamity Montana Series

Writing as Willa Nash

The Bribe

The Bluff

CONTENTS

PROLOGUE

"Ms. MacKenzie? They're ready for you."

I nodded at the woman who had come to fetch me from my dressing room, then slid off my tall director's chair. As I followed the woman through the labyrinth of hallways in the studio, I studied her clothes. Her all-black ensemble made me jealous and even more irritated with my colorless outfit. With my stark-white blouse and beige pencil skirt, the only color I had on was the fire-engine-red soles of my patent white Louboutin heels.

My stylist was getting an email the second I was done for the day. No more light colors for public outings. Or anything, really. The bright clothing contrasted too much with my mood.

Black.

We needed to incorporate more black.

"Can I get you anything?" my escort asked over her shoulder.

"Water, please."

She smiled before taking a sharp right turn, leading me

1

out onto the television set where I'd be spending the next two hours taping an interview. I winced and held up a hand to shade my eyes as they adjusted to the beaming spotlights overhead. Why did they always keep these sets so hot? Ten seconds and sweat was already dripping down my sides.

My escort left me with another woman, a pretty brunette, as she went to fetch my water.

"Sabrina MacKenzie," the brunette said. "It's so nice to meet you. I'm Bryce Ryan."

"Oh, uh, hi," I stammered, reaching out to shake my interviewer's hand.

She grinned. "You were expecting a man, weren't you?"

"Guilty." My exaggerated frown made her laugh.

She turned, and I followed her to a pair of seats staged opposite one another and sat down. "It happens all the time. I've grown to enjoy the shock on people's faces when they realize I'm a woman."

That was a bit twisted, but I just smiled and left that comment hanging. My escort returned with my water and I sipped it while Bryce thumbed through her interview cards. I was reserving judgment on Bryce's journalistic skills until after the interview, but I had a feeling those cards contained nothing but predictable questions.

How does it feel to have taken down a criminal empire?

Were you surprised when you were nominated for the award?

Are you actually considering giving up your career as an investigative journalist to keep writing smut?

Eleven interviews and no one had bothered asking me anything unique. I'd been praised for my investigative journalism and judged for my fiction. Heaven forbid I author something that women might actually enjoy reading. And to include descriptive sex scenes? Scandalous.

"Romance novels?" Bryce asked.

Oh, boy. Here we go.

I smiled sweetly. "I do love a good romance novel. Especially if there's a little erotica mixed in too."

She grinned. "Sounds like I'll be buying your novel tonight."

Maybe being interviewed by Bryce wouldn't be so bad after all.

"Bryce," the producer called from behind the row of cameras. "We're all set."

"Thanks." She waved over the hair and makeup team. My blond hair got fluffed and placed while her skin was dusted and blushed. With both of our lips recolored, we settled in for the interview. The cameraman gave us his countdown and then Bryce did her introduction before turning to me.

"You've had quite the year, Sabrina. Just a little over one year ago, you wrote an article for *The Seattle Times* that shut down the biggest gun-smuggling operation on the upper West Coast. Then you disappeared for six months, only to reemerge as a best-selling romance novelist. You've just won a Pulitzer Prize for investigative reporting and I've heard that there are talks of making your book into a blockbuster. How does it feel to have reached such success in your career?"

"Thank you. It's been wonderful, albeit very busy." I smiled and glanced at my lap to hide the flash of pain that crashed through my heart. Nothing about my successes gave me joy. Talking about my accomplishments just reminded me of how much I had lost.

"You've made some major achievements since you came

back to Seattle," Bryce said. "Most journalists, including this one, would kill to be in your position. How does it feel?"

I gave her my rehearsed answer. "It's been incredible. Surreal, really. I'm still in shock at how much has happened over the last year."

"I can imagine." She flipped to a new note card. "Let's talk more about the article."

My cheerful face belied my true feelings. I was miserable on this television set. I was exhausted from talking about that damn article. I was done having people fuss over its success.

Everyone thought it was the article that had changed my life.

It wasn't.

It had been the six months I'd spent in Montana.

It had been the six months I'd spent with him.

CHAPTER ONE

SABRINA

T*hirteen months earlier . . .*

Heroines and Villains
The Seattle Times
April 3
By Sabrina MacKenzie

When I was 16, my father took me with him to the DMV to
get my driver's license. I remember the heat radiating off the
black parking lot as we walked inside the courthouse. I
remember the caustic smell of hot tar and worrying that my
flip-flops would melt if I stood still for too long. I remember
my thighs burning as I jogged up the 18 stone steps that led
to the imposing building's front doors. The DMV was
located on the top floor of the courthouse and Dad asked if I
wanted to take the stairs or the elevator. I chose the elevator,

not wanting to be sweaty or red-faced when I took my picture.

We got stuck in that elevator.

For 45 minutes, Dad and I were trapped inside that hanging box with three cops. A good-guy trifecta. Sitting on the cramped elevator floor, Dad chatted with the three uniformed men about their careers while I sat in silence. For 45 minutes, I was in awe, not even slightly panicked that we were stuck in the elevator. Why? Because I was with heroes. Because I couldn't get enough of their real-life adventures. Because their actual accounts were far more entertaining than any fictional tale I'd ever been told.

By the time the elevator jolted to life, a reporter had been born. I craved more of their stories. I craved a story of my own. I've long since admired the men—and women—in uniform who fight to protect us from danger. And although a career in law enforcement or the military was not part of my destined path, I have dreamed of doing my part.

This is my story. As you may have guessed, its heroine is me, and this past fall, I set out to catch a villain.

———

SWIPING the steam off the bathroom mirror, I took a hard look at myself. The grime had been scrubbed from my hair, and my fingernails were no longer caked with dried blood, but I was still a complete mess. The angry red bruises around my throat would take weeks to disappear and the gash on my lip was likely going to scar.

"What the hell did you do, Sabrina?" I muttered, my voice scratchy and rough. The woman in the mirror didn't answer, not that she needed to.

What had I done?

I had written an incredibly condemning article vilifying a prominent Seattle family tied to the Russian mafia. Basically, I'd waltzed right into the middle of a hornet's nest and started poking the wasps.

It was no surprise that I'd been stung.

Gently pulling and prodding my face, I inspected my injuries. Anton Federov, my "boyfriend," had done a number on me. Both of my eyes were red and swollen. I had a gash on one cheek and another by my hairline. My bottom lip was huge and split on one side. My face felt five times its normal size but what hurt the worst were my ribs. Anton had landed one good kick to my right side, and even the smallest movement sent sharp, stabbing pains through my torso.

The fact that I'd been able to escape before Anton had been able to rape me was nothing short of a miracle. That I'd made it out of my apartment before he could beat me to death could only be credited to divine intervention.

I just hoped that my lucky streak would continue and the evidence I'd sent to the FBI this morning would be enough to keep Anton behind bars for the rest of his miserable life. Because until he was put away, I would be hiding out with my best friend, Felicity, in her small hometown of Prescott, Montana.

Shaking off thoughts of Anton, I averted my eyes from the mirror and went about blow-drying my light-blond hair. With it floating down my back, I rubbed on some lotion and dressed in a pair of black leggings and a gray hoodie. Then I took one last glance in the mirror, wincing again at how awful I looked, and limped out of the bathroom.

Two steps out the bathroom door, I froze. A crowd of strange faces was all aimed my way. Faces that had not been here when I'd gone into the bathroom.

Ignoring their eyes, I hobbled down the hallway, keeping my eyes pinned to Felicity's as the five people in the kitchen watched my labored steps.

Felicity's ice-blue gaze was full of worry and concern. Her hair was all puffed up, likely from running her hands through her long blond tresses. I hated that I'd caused her stress by coming here but I hadn't had anywhere else to run. Montana had seemed like the best place to hide out from the Federovs, and even though it was the middle of the night and I'd just met her boyfriend, Silas, I felt safe in his home.

That was, until three strangers showed up.

I was trying to stay under the radar here. The fewer people that knew I was hiding out here, the better. What were Silas and Felicity thinking, bringing others into this mess?

Before I could ask, Felicity started introductions. "Sabrina, this is my brother, Jess. Remember I told you he's also the Jamison County sheriff?"

What the hell! She'd called in a cop?

"Hi." I dismissed the sheriff and frowned at Felicity. "Did you forget I was in hiding? Who are these people? And you brought in a cop? We can't report any of this."

"Don't worry," Jess said, stopping my rant. "I'm off the record."

I gave him a wary glance, then relaxed at his obvious sincerity. Jess would keep my whereabouts a secret. I took a brief moment to study my best friend's brother. I'd seen a picture of Jess once, years ago when Felicity and I had been in college, but he was all grown now, not the teen from the photograph. Jess's light-blue eyes were honest and matched Felicity's, but that was where their similarities ended. Though, he was just as attractive as his sister was beautiful.

"This is Maisy Holt," Felicity said, directing my attention to the woman standing between Jess and Silas. "She used to be a nurse, so she's going to take a look at your injuries."

"Thanks," I told Maisy. "I'd appreciate that." When I'd gotten to Silas's ranch, Felicity had insisted I go to the hospital, but I'd refused. Hospitals asked questions and made records. I couldn't take that chance, but I needed someone with medical experience to look me over. I knew my face would heal but my ribs and ankle were a concern. The last thing I needed was a broken bone.

Maisy gave me a tiny wave and a gentle smile that lit up her face. Her big doe eyes were a beautiful mixture of gray and blue that complemented her white-blond bob perfectly.

"And this is Beau Holt, Maisy's brother," Felicity continued. "We were in high school together."

My eyes raked over the other man in the room. He stepped away from the counter he had been slouched against and stood to his full height of *seriously tall*. My eyes traveled up and up, finally finding his, and once they did, I couldn't tear them away.

Beau's eyes were like the color of the ocean during a storm. My face flushed and my heart beat like a bass drum as I stared into his blue-gray gaze. Attraction mixed with fear and pain and stress. I had so many emotions whirling that I stood frozen. Brain-blanked. Mesmerized.

Those eyes were a beautiful distraction from the mess that was my life.

He took another step, his mass looming closer, and I flinched. The trauma from this morning's attack was too fresh to stop my knee-jerk reaction. Beau's dark lashes narrowed and his stern look hardened to a scowl as I snapped out of my trance.

Forcing my eyes away from his, I took in the rest of his face and enormous body. He had dark-brown hair, messy and a little too long on top. His angular jaw was covered in a thick beard. He had a straight nose that sat dead center between his high cheekbones. *How tall is he?* I was five seven and he looked to be almost a foot taller.

Beau's features reminded me of a Spartan warrior. Long, long legs with beefy thighs. Broad shoulders and bulging arms made of muscles layered upon muscles. I'd bet my life's savings that underneath his faded jeans and simple black thermal he resembled King Leonidas himself.

Scowl and all, Beau Holt was gorgeous.

The flame in my face burned hotter and I swallowed hard, pulling myself out of momentary lust to find my voice. "Nice to meet you." His face didn't soften and he didn't respond so I assumed my own scowl. "I get why the cop and the nurse are here but what's your role in all of this, Goliath?"

"Sabrina," Felicity hissed.

"What?" I pretended I didn't know how much my tendency to nickname everyone embarrassed my friend.

She opened her mouth, likely to scold me, but Silas interrupted. "Beau's here to help figure out where we can stash you for a while."

"Stash me? I thought I could just hide out at Felicity's place for a while."

Jess and Beau declared "No" at the same time Silas scoffed "Not happening."

Before I could ask why not, Felicity pulled me further into the kitchen and slid out a stool from underneath the granite island. "Come sit down. Maisy can get to work on you while we all brainstorm what to do."

I wasn't sure why we needed to brainstorm. What was so complicated about me camping out in front of her television for the foreseeable future?

"How about we get the full story first?" Jess asked. "I'd like to hear this from the beginning."

I took my seat, glad to have the weight off my ankle. I'd already given Silas and Felicity the whole story but Jess's tone was firm. I'd be telling my tale again. So I filled my lungs as best I could with aching ribs and wasted no time summing up the mess I'd made of my life.

"I'm an investigative reporter for *The Seattle Times*. Last fall, I took an assignment to dig into a well-off family suspected of smuggling weapons into the U.S. through their shipping company for the Russian mafia."

"You're messed up with the Russian mob?" Jess asked.

I nodded and waited for his inevitable mutter of "Fuck me." I'd gotten that a lot tonight.

At the time I'd taken the Federov story, it had seemed like such a brilliant idea. I'd thought it would be my one big chance to make a difference. To make the world safer by uncoupling a link in a chain of organized crime. I'd have the chance to keep guns out of the hands of innocent children.

For months, I'd never once regretted my decision or my actions. Today, I'd learned that old adage was true: *What a difference a day makes.* Now that I'd been beaten and forced to run away from my home, regret was settling in my stomach like day-old Chinese food.

"Keep talking," Beau rumbled in his rich baritone.

I took another semi-deep breath, flinching when my ribs stung. "Long story short, I went undercover and started dating a man named Anton Federov. His family owns the shipping company I was investigating. His father, Viktor, is the CEO. Anton and his brother, Ivan, run all of the operations. I had seen Anton casually a few times before I started on the story, so I decided to use my connection in hopes of getting inside information."

Grumbles from the men filled the air.

"Does this hurt?" Maisy asked, pausing my story. She was palpating my ribs but even her slight touch caused me to wince.

I sucked in a sharp breath and nodded.

"And this?" she asked, moving further up toward my breasts.

I nodded again.

"I think you may have a cracked rib or two. Since you can't exactly go to the hospital, let's wrap them up and see if they heal. We just want to make sure you can still take deep breaths. But I'll warn you, ribs take a long time to heal on their own. Sometimes a month or longer."

I sighed. "Okay."

When I turned my eyes back to the men, they were all waiting for me to continue my story. "My boss had been sent an anonymous tip with evidence indicating the Federovs' international cargo ships were carrying guns. He asked if I'd take the story and run with it."

And run with it I had.

Sitting in my boss's office, he'd handed over the anonymous file and I'd started flipping. Pictures. Memos. Nothing unexpected until I'd come upon a photo of Anton and nearly fallen out of my boss's uncomfortable desk chair. Color me unhappy to realize that my two-time sexual partner from the previous summer was a criminal. I'd felt like a dunce and a slut for having had sex with him just because he'd been crazy hot.

Not that I'd known he was a criminal at the time. Regardless, I'd been so mad at myself for my extraordinarily bad taste in men that I'd immediately agreed to take on the story. That anger, coupled with the chance to take out one of the wealthiest criminal families on the West Coast, had motivated me to dig my claws in deep.

"So, you start dating this guy, what did you find?" Jess asked.

"Not much at first. Mostly I worked to find out who had sent the anonymous file to my boss. It turns out it came from one of the dock managers at the Federovs' pier. He'd noticed some suspicious shipments. Weights coming in higher than was planned. Extra containers that weren't documented on their manifests. We were able to collect enough evidence to prove that smuggling was occurring but not enough to directly tie it to the Federovs themselves."

Everything my source and I had uncovered had just led to shell companies. I could have run with it, but in the end, the bad guys would have gotten away with their crimes. The port authority would have gotten a slap on the wrist and the Federovs would have been under a microscope, but eventually, they'd have been free to find a new way to keep bringing in guns.

The evidence from the pier hadn't been enough for the ruthless takedown I'd craved.

Enter Anton.

He held the key to locking the door on the Federovs' jail cell.

"Let me guess," Jess said. "You used your fake relationship with Anton to get proof that he knew about the gun shipments."

I nodded. "I found enough to incriminate him, his brother and his father."

From everything I'd gathered, I'd deduced that almost every international cargo shipment over the last ten years had included at least one illegal container. Hundreds of thousands of banned weapons had been pouring into the country because of the Federovs. Viktor and his sons had pocketed hundreds of millions of dollars.

"Time for a break so I can work on her face," Maisy announced. She started rifling through a rather large first-aid kit to find some antibiotic ointment and butterfly bandages.

"Does she need stitches?" Beau asked.

I'd been averting my eyes from Beau while retelling my story—mostly so I wouldn't get flustered by my intense attraction and forget what I was talking about—but now that all I had to do was sit quietly, I let my eyes rake up and down his huge body again. I hoped that Maisy's arms would obstruct his view of my blushing cheeks.

"No stitches," Maisy said.

I looked into her eyes and saw her small grin. Her brother might have missed my blush but Maisy had not.

As she cleaned the gash in my lip, Silas took the initiative to continue telling my story. "Sabrina had been using a fake last name but somehow Anton figured out who she was. He came to her apartment this morning and beat the piss out of her. She was lucky and got away. Paid a guy to bring her straight here, so she doesn't think the Federovs could have followed her."

I shuddered. This morning felt like a lifetime ago. I'd been drinking my morning coffee, enjoying the feeling of a job well done. I'd sent my boss my story to publish in tomorrow's paper and a huge file of evidence to my FBI contact. And the best feeling of all, I'd been done with Anton Federov.

At least that's what I'd thought until my front door had burst open and an irate Anton had stormed in.

After three punches to my face, I'd fallen to my living room floor. He'd taken the opportunity to kick me in my ribs before coming down on top of me and wrapping his hands around my throat.

I'd squeezed my eyes shut, not wanting his monstrous face to be the last thing I saw in this world. When the pressure had left my throat and I'd no longer been able to feel his weight on me, I'd thought I had died.

At the sound of his unbuckling belt, my eyes had flown open. I'd summoned all my strength for one excruciating kick to his balls before scrambling up and sprinting out my broken front door. Rushing down the staircase to the back-alley exit, I'd twisted my ankle in the descent.

From there, I'd hurried to the corner CVS and begged the clerk to call me an Uber. It was another stroke of luck when the driver had been willing to take me the twelve hours to Montana in exchange for five thousand dollars under the table.

Thankfully, the kid had been short on money and needed the fare. I'd lied and given him a fake name before curling up in the back seat and making the long journey in almost complete silence. For twelve hours, all I'd thought about was how fortunate I was to still be alive. I'd done everything in my power not to picture Anton's face looming over me as he'd nearly strangled me to death.

"Are you okay?" Felicity asked quietly.

I snapped out of my thoughts and sniffled, willing the tears not to fall. "I really hope he's in jail," I whispered.

"Me too."

"Even if he is, they could still come after me."

"We'll find a way to keep you safe." The confidence in her tone settled some of my nerves.

"I'm in deep on this one." Saying the words made the reality of the situation even heavier. "You know as well as I do that the mafia doesn't just let their enemies go free. I should have done more to protect my own identity. I was so caught up in the story and keeping my source hidden, I didn't do enough for myself."

"What about your source?" Jess asked. "Did you tell him that Anton figured out who you were? He could be at risk."

"No one but me knows who he is, not even the FBI. He only came to me in exchange for the promise never to reveal his name. That way he can never be asked to testify and expose himself to retaliation from the Federovs."

I had spent weeks convincing Roger Anderson to be my source. He had been terrified that the Federovs would learn he'd been the whistleblower, but finally, he'd agreed. Roger was a good man with a young family and I'd take Anton's hits all over again if that meant keeping his identity a secret. No one, not even the people in this kitchen, would ever learn he'd helped me collect evidence.

"All right, I'm done," Maisy said. "Rest your ankle. Keep

your ribs wrapped tight until they start to feel better. Take it easy on your face. Use this ointment every day and it should help with the scarring."

"Thank you."

"You're welcome. I'm going to collect Coby and go home. The less I know the better."

I couldn't fault her for wanting to escape this fucked-up situation. I'd do the same in her position. She disappeared further into Silas's loft for a moment and came back down with a sleeping toddler in her arms.

"Do you need any help?" Beau asked her.

"I've got him. Good night. And good luck, Sabrina."

I nodded and watched as she carried her little boy outside into the night. The minute the door closed behind Maisy, Jess started in with more questions.

"You're sure you got enough evidence for a conviction to stick?"

"I'd be shocked if it didn't." Anton had been a bit too trusting of his pretend girlfriend. "I was able to get into his safe and his computer. I found the gun shipment schedules and evidence that his family had approved them all. The FBI should have taken down an illegal handgun shipment," I glanced at the clock on the oven, "six hours ago. With my intel, Anton should currently be sitting in a jail cell."

"You trust the federal agent you contacted?"

More than any police officer I'd ever met. Henry Dalton was as honest as they came. "I've worked with him for years. He's a good guy and an even better cop. He's solid."

"If he's such a good cop, why'd he let a reporter do an investigation meant for the FBI?" Jess asked.

"You kept it a secret, didn't you?" Felicity guessed right away.

"No one knew what I was doing." No one.

"Reckless," Jess huffed. "Just like coming here. You should have gone to your FBI guy instead."

He was right, but it didn't make it easier to hear. "Probably, but I panicked and my first thought was to run. I'm not all that confident in protective custody and really don't want to enter witness protection."

Jess shook his head. "The Federovs aren't going to stay in jail for long. They'll be after you if they aren't already."

"I know but as soon as my story breaks tomorrow, they'll be hounded by the press. They won't be able to go anywhere without an audience."

"That still doesn't make it safe for you to go back to Seattle," Felicity said.

"And you can't show your face in Prescott," Silas added. "The first place they'll look for you is with family and friends."

If the Federovs wanted to track me down, this would be one of their first stops. My family all lived in Florida and we had a distant relationship. I was a work-a-holic and didn't have many friends other than Felicity. It wouldn't take Anton's men long to realize I was no longer in Seattle and start their woman-hunt.

"You need to be off the grid," Beau rumbled.

Off the grid? I was in Montana. How much more off the grid did it get?

"That's what I'm thinking," Jess said. "You got any ideas?"

Before I could tell them that this wasn't their problem, Beau talked over me. "Maybe one of the outposts? The one on the north side of Fan Mountain? I could take her up there and get her settled. Stick around for a while and clean the place up, then make trips up and down to keep her in supplies."

Jess and Silas shared a look that snapped my spine straight. What about this was amusing? Was my life being in mortal danger really that entertaining?

"I think that would work," Silas said.

"What's an outpost?" Felicity asked. She seemed as annoyed by their inside joke as I was.

"Think of it like a cabin in the woods," Jess said.

"Wait a minute." The color drained from my face. The woods? No. *Hell no.* "I don't think that's necessary. I'll just promise not to go out in public, stay tucked away in Felicity's closet or something. I'll be like Harry Potter living in my tiny cupboard."

"I'm sorry, Sabrina," Silas said gently, "but I'm not having you anywhere near Lis."

How could I argue with that? He was going all alpha-male protective for his woman. I loved him for her. Felicity deserved nothing less than a man that put her safety and well-being above all else. She'd dealt with enough assholes in her life. Not only was Silas handsome, with his tall frame and killer brown eyes, but he looked at Felicity like he loved her more than anything in this world.

And there would be no point in arguing with him. No matter how much Felicity or I protested, he would put her above all else.

I nodded. "I can understand why you'd say that. I don't want her in harm's way either, but I'm not going to disappear into the wilderness with a strange man."

A strange yet unbelievably attractive man. Unless Beau was married, my new vow to refrain from the male species would be short-lived if I was confined alone with the mountain of sexy standing across from me.

"Then what are you going to do?" Jess asked.

My fingers moved to my hair, twirling a lock as I ran through my options. Seattle was out. There was no way I'd be safe there. I wouldn't take my troubles to my family in Florida. Maybe I could embark on a massive road trip around the country?

"I don't know. I need a new ID. Maybe a car. Can you lend me some money?" I asked Felicity. I already owed her five thousand for paying my Uber driver, Kenny.

She nodded. "Sure."

"Okay. What else?" I muttered to myself. Sliding off my stool, I slowly paced across the living room to stare out the large windows.

I'd need some clothes and something to change my appearance. I winced at the idea of cutting and dying the long hair I'd had for decades, but if I was going to evade the Federovs, I'd need to do something drastic. I wouldn't put it past them to hack into cameras and security systems. They were filthy rich and extremely powerful. Basically, the worst possible enemy a girl could ever ask for. My nerves peaked as I stared into the dark night.

Stupid, Sabrina. So stupid.

When Felicity slid up beside me, I leaned my shoulder into her side as we stood quietly together. I hoped she had an answer to my dilemma. My brain was fried and I was too tired to think of something creative.

"I think you should go with Beau," she finally whispered.

"No way."

"Please, hear me out? They'll track you down if you're using my credit cards. The five thousand dollars I gave

Kenny is going to show up as a huge red flag. They could find you here in the time it would take you to get a fake ID. It's not like you can jump on an airplane. So what does that leave? You driving around the country like a vagabond, living out of the back seat and cheap motels?"

"That sounds better than living in a shack in the mountains."

"Really? Are you sure about that? I've heard three out of ten motels have bed bugs."

I smiled at her reflection in the glass. Leave it to her to make up some ridiculous fact about bugs to persuade me. She knew I hated all insects and ninety-nine percent of animals.

She smiled back but worry etched her face. If my staying in a repulsive wilderness hideout eased some of her worries and would keep me safe, I'd give it a shot. It wasn't like I had other options.

My forehead fell against the cool glass as I reluctantly agreed. "Fuck. You're right. I'll go with Goliath."

"Thank you." She pulled me off the window and into a gentle hug. "He's a good guy and I know he'll keep you safe. Think of it like a rustic adventure. Maybe write a story about it."

That would never happen. I'd written plenty of stories, and more often than not, they'd landed my ass in trouble.

Writing a story about being trapped in an "outpost" with mountain-man Beau was just asking for more headaches.

CHAPTER TWO

BEAU

"Do you think this is going to work?" I asked Jess and Silas, standing by the tailgate of my truck while Felicity and Sabrina climbed into the back seat.

"I think it's the best chance she's got," Jess said.

"What about you, man?" Silas asked. "We're asking a lot and your plate isn't exactly empty."

No shit. A headache formed between my eyes.

My desk was buried under a stack of paperwork, a search and rescue case could come up at any moment, fire season was right around the corner, and I had obligations to my family that I couldn't shirk. Putting my life on hold for two or three weeks was going to cause a lot of problems.

Sabrina wasn't the only one disappearing into the mountains. I'd need to spend some time there to make sure she was settled and comfortable. Once she'd agreed to go to the outpost, I'd started making a mental list of all the things that needed taken care of.

I blew out a deep breath and rubbed my beard. "I don't know. Shit's going to have to just wait, I guess." Which meant I'd come home to a clusterfuck.

"What can we do?" Jess asked.

"We need to decide what to tell everyone." The outpost had zero cell service and no way to communicate with anyone in town. People were going to wonder why I'd vanished and why I wasn't answering my phone or email.

"What if we told people that you got called out of state for an emergency search and rescue?" Silas suggested.

I nodded. "That could work. You'll have to keep the details vague."

"Done. We'll spread the word that it's confidential. What else?" Jess asked.

"I'll send an email to the office tonight and let them know I'll be out for a few weeks. Maybe you could swing by next week and check in?" I asked Jess.

"You got it."

My only saving grace would be my office manager, Rose. She knew the drill when I had to leave for emergencies. She'd step up and be the boss until I returned. "Rose should be able to keep the staff organized until I come back. My biggest worry is if a case comes up. You'll have to lead the search and rescue team if one does."

Jess nodded. "Will do."

I turned to Silas. "Would you let Maisy know I'll be gone and have her check in on my house? Tell her the truth about where we're at, just in case, but have her give my family the story about the search and rescue case."

"No problem. What if we need to get ahold of you?"

"One of you will have to drive up." I frowned. "Damn it. I wish there was a phone up there." It wasn't the first time I'd thought that all of the outposts in my jurisdiction needed telephones. Some of the bigger outposts had phone lines but the smaller ones had never been upgraded.

"Anything else?" Jess asked.

I shook my head. "I'll pick up the pieces when I come back."

"Thanks for doing this. It means everything to Felicity." Silas reached out for a handshake.

I took his hand. "You're welcome."

I wouldn't admit it now, but I wasn't just doing this for Felicity.

I admired the hell out of Sabrina. That woman had more guts than most people I knew. To infiltrate a gun smuggling operation and take them down was fucking impressive. Her loyalty to her source was a testament to her character. Her bravery and spirit called to my heart.

Unfortunately, her beauty called to an appendage a little farther south.

Even beaten to a pulp, she was stunning. Her blond hair, brilliant green eyes and supple lips were going to get me in trouble. But this was the right thing to do. I had the skills to keep her safe, and the place.

And if that meant making a mess of my own life, then I'd do it without hesitation.

———

SABRINA

I'd been introduced to the town of Prescott in the dark of night.

The sparse light from old-fashioned lampposts had given

me hints of the town's small downtown shops. The only signs still illuminated at that hour were those for two bars on Main Street. The narrow roads had been deserted and eerily quiet with the exception of the truck's humming diesel engine.

Even in the dark, I could see Prescott's appeal. It had a quaint and charming atmosphere with its Western décor and small-town flair. The community fishing pond, one-room theater and soda-fountain café seemed wholesome and family friendly. There wasn't a single similarity to Seattle, not even a McDonald's.

"I can see why you like it here. Why you'd want to move home," I told Felicity. She was sitting by my side in the back of Beau's truck while Beau and Silas were outside loading up supplies.

"There are some things I miss about Seattle," she said. "The Thai restaurant that was below our apartment when we were in college. The little salon where we used to get pedicures on Sundays. Mostly, all the places where we went together, but I'm happy to be home. I've missed my family."

Right before I had taken on the Federov story, she had moved back to Montana. Felicity had fit well into city life, but even after sixteen years, her country roots had never stopped pulling. That and the feelings she'd had for Silas since she'd been a teenager.

I grinned. "And you missed Sexy Silas."

She tried but failed to hide a smile. "And Silas." She turned to look out the back window where the guys were loading boxes.

We'd been running around Prescott for nearly two hours. Our first stop had been the grocery store. The men had gone inside the store and come out one minute before closing time, each pushing a shopping cart piled high with overflowing plastic bags. From there, we'd gassed up Beau's truck, then stopped by Felicity's house to collect toiletries, clothing and linens.

Now we were backed into Beau's driveway, waiting for him and Silas to finish packing.

When we'd pulled up to Beau's house, I'd thought he'd just be picking up his own personal articles. When I saw that he was loading a chain saw and an ax, I'd asked Felicity if Jess would just let me live out of a jail cell for a few months. She'd laughed but I hadn't been joking.

The idea of a jail cell had become even more appealing when Beau had welcomed a dog into the truck. Boone, some sort of red hound dog, was currently panting in the front seat, infecting my air with his hot breath and getting short hairs over everything. Most people would think he was adorable, with his floppy ears and wrinkled forehead, but animals were not my thing.

With the supplies loaded and our last stop complete, the men jumped back into the truck and we all rode in silence back to Silas's ranch. Emotions were swelling and I struggled to breathe past the lump in my throat. My hand instinctively found Felicity's, and I squeezed tight, drawing from her strength for these last few moments before she went back to her life with Silas and I was whisked away to a nowhere forest hideout with Beau.

When the truck was parked next to Silas's wooden barn, I swallowed the urge to heave. Felicity's door opened and Silas stood at her side. "All set. Time to head out."

We slid out of the back and stood next to the barn, instantly locking in a tight embrace. "I love you," she said. "Watch your back and listen to Beau."

"Love you too, lady. Be safe."

If I could have just one more wish come true, it would be for Silas and Felicity not to suffer any repercussions from me bringing this mess into their lives.

"Take care of her," I said those words to Silas at the same time Felicity said them to Beau.

With one last hug, I turned and marched to my doom.

Wherever Beau was taking me, I knew for certain the creature comforts I'd taken for granted would be missing. There would be no more quick trips to the mall for new shoes. No pizza delivery on Friday nights. No more phone calls with Felicity to gossip and hear her voice.

The clock on the dash showed 12:42 a.m. Not twenty-four hours ago, I had been celebrating a job well done in my tenth-floor apartment. Now I was sitting next to a *dog*, about to drive into the wilderness with a modern-day mountain man.

The reclusive life I had always feared was about to become my reality. My heart ached as I mourned the loss of my freedom and independence.

My eyes stayed glued to my lap as Beau settled into the driver's seat and pulled the truck into the black night. Every bump on the gravel road hammered down my spirits. Not even the prospect of spending time with a ruggedly handsome man could cheer me up. A charcoal cloud settled over my heart.

"It's a long trip," Beau said. "You should get some rest."

That wasn't going to happen. I was keyed up and on the verge of tears. "Tell me why we can't just stay here tonight." The idea of setting off into the forest after midnight seemed ludicrous. I didn't understand why we couldn't rest and get a fresh start in the morning. The lovely motel I'd spotted during my brief tour of Prescott had looked warm and inviting.

"I don't want to risk the chance of you being seen in the light of day," Beau said. "People around here talk. A lot. If someone sees you walking around with a face that looks like tenderized meat, the old gossips will be jabbering on about it for months. If the Federovs do come here, let's not give them any chance of overhearing. Okay?"

"What if I promised to wear a paper bag over my head?"

The vibrations of his rich chuckle hummed through the cab.

I guess that means no. My shoulders fell as I looked out the side window. The control I had over my own destiny evaporated with every mile we went. Who was I kidding? I had lost control the moment Anton realized I'd been playing him.

The darkness of night settled into my bones. The moon was blanketed by clouds and the only thing lighting our way was the truck's high beams. I'd never experienced such an empty night. There wasn't a light to be seen, not in the distance and not in the sky.

Beau navigated through a maze of county roads through the prairie, inching us closer to the mountains in the distance. We hit the tree line like a wall. The forest didn't slowly blend into the flatlands but instead drew a harsh line between the tamable and the wild.

As we eased into the forest depths, my anxiety reached new heights. Every muscle in my body was taught as my eyes darted between the trees, searching for signs of movement. At any moment now, the boogeyman was going to jump out from behind the wall of evergreens and attack us. We'd be completely at his mercy, unable to veer off our two-lane road due to the walls of thick, brown trunks at our sides.

"How much longer?" My knee was bouncing up and down as my fingers drummed on my thigh. The towering buildings of the city had never made me feel as trapped as the looming trees in this dark forest.

"About two and a half hours if we don't hit any roadblocks."

Hours? Where was he taking me, Siberia? And what did he mean by roadblocks? "What kind of roadblocks?"

"Fallen trees mostly. There are a couple places where the road runs along a creek. It flooded this spring and I don't know if the road was washed out."

I crossed my fingers in my lap, praying we didn't hit a roadblock. It was a sad fate that I actually looked forward to our arrival at the outpost just to get off this creepy road.

But since we had hours, I took in a fortifying breath, willing myself to relax as I counted down from one hundred. It was starting to help, my nerves settling with every number, but when I got to thirty-four, I saw a pair of yellow eyes peek out from behind a tree in the distance.

Was it a wolf? Or a grizzly bear? Maybe a cougar waiting to pounce on our truck as we passed? My entire body froze when the eyes disappeared. I searched frantically for signs of other animals hidden behind the veil of darkness. The swaying bushes had me jumping with every movement.

Oh my god, I hate this. Every cell in my being hated this. My heart was racing and my hands were gripping my thighs so tightly I'd have bruises tomorrow.

"That was just a deer," Beau said, sensing that I was on the verge of a panic attack. "We'll probably see a bunch of them as we go. They're nocturnal, raccoons and owls too, but totally harmless."

"What about the ones with big teeth and sharp claws? The not-so-harmless ones?"

"They aren't going to come anywhere near this truck."

"Are you sure?"

He chuckled. "I'm sure. You're safe with me, Sabrina."

That statement, coming from his soothing voice, settled some fears. "Will you talk to me as we go? I'm way out of my element here and, as you can probably tell, freaking way the fuck out."

He laughed again, the warm tone calming my erratic heartbeat. "What do you want to talk about?"

Before I could answer, Boone shifted from Beau's side to mine, laying his head on my lap. I stilled, unsure what to do, until he looked up at me with gentle eyes. Relaxing my frown, I hesitantly placed one hand on his neck. *Okay. Not horrible.* And at least he didn't stink. Instinctively, my fingers stroked his soft coat. It was kind of nice, petting this dog, but I'd still be washing my hand at the soonest opportunity.

"How long have you lived in Prescott?" Maybe asking questions would help occupy my mind.

"My whole life," he said. "I left for college but came right back after graduating."

"What do you do?"

"I run the U.S. Forest Service office and the Jamison County Search and Rescue team."

None of this was surprising. If I'd had to guess at his career, I would have picked an outdoor occupation. The rustic scent of pine filled the inside of the truck's cab, and it wasn't coming from those little Christmas-tree air fresheners.

It was all Beau.

Oddly enough, it was remarkably appealing. An hour ago, I would have said a salty ocean breeze was my favorite natural scent. Now it was a toss-up.

We sat quietly for a while, me gently stroking Boone while stealing glances at Beau from the corner of my eye.

His large frame fit well in his oversized green truck. I was swallowed up by the large seat but I doubted Beau would have been able to fit comfortably in anything else. His square and angular hands made the steering wheel look like a child's toy, spanning three-quarters of its entire diameter. I tried to force my inappropriate thoughts aside but all I could imagine were those big hands on my curves.

I had always worked hard to maintain my trim figure but my preference for pizza and beer meant there was always a little extra around my hips and tummy. I thought it was damn sexy when a man's hand roamed those areas and explored my softer places. The idea of Beau's mammoth, calloused hands spanning and kneading my ass created a dull throb between my legs.

What was wrong with me? How could I be fantasizing about sex at a time like this? I'd been a fiend all night about Beau.

Maybe it was my mind's way of preserving my sanity. Sex had always been my escape from reality, the one thing that I'd never taken too seriously. Tonight, I'd cut myself a break. Tomorrow, I'd eliminate sex from the mental roster.

"Did you grow up in Seattle?" Beau asked, tugging my thoughts back into the safe zone.

"No, I'm from Florida. I moved to Seattle right after graduating high school."

"Did you and Felicity meet in college?"

I grinned. "Sort of. We both went to the same school but

that's not where we met. She and I were both on the short list for a coveted apartment near campus. The landlord was a real piece of work. I'd been trying to bribe him with baked goods and gift cards for an open studio. Turns out Felicity was doing the same and the asshole was just stringing us along. When we put all the pieces together, we found a two-bedroom apartment managed by someone who didn't take advantage of two naive young women."

Felicity had been my roommate and best friend for nearly ten years. She had only moved out once we'd become established in our careers. She'd moved into a classy downtown condo while I'd stayed in the run-down apartment we'd shared. But when I'd inherited some money from my grandmother's estate, I'd splurged and used it to rent a place three blocks away from Felicity.

She was more family than friend.

Felicity was the one person I'd let into my life since high school. She was so strong and self-confident. She never let me push her away, even when I tried. It had taken some time, but I had learned that I didn't have to fear her friendship would end. She was in it for a lifetime.

When Felicity had moved to Montana, I'd needed something to fill the void of her absence, a reprieve from the loneliness. It was probably one of the reasons I'd thrown myself so completely into the Federov story.

But Beau didn't need to know any of that.

"Do you have other family in Prescott besides your sister?" It felt better to ask Beau questions than answer his. The reporter in me was always more comfortable gathering information than revealing.

"Yeah. Pretty much my whole family. I'm a fourth-generation Montanan. My parents are still in my childhood home.

My younger brother, Michael, lives two blocks away from me. My mom's parents live in the same place they have for thirty years. My other grandma is in the nursing home. Aunts, uncles and cousins are all close too."

"That sounds a lot like how things are with my family in Florida. I'm the only MacKenzie to move out of Florida in the last twenty years. Do you like having everyone close?"

"I do. I'm tight with Michael and Maisy and I try to spend as much time with Coby as I can, since he doesn't have a dad around. But having everyone in my business gets old at times. None of the women in my family can understand why I'm not married yet. And they hate that I won't let them set me up."

Unmarried. Good to know. I had assumed that was the case from his bare ring finger but now my hunch had been confirmed—not that I was ever planning on pursuing Beau. I was sure the attraction I had for him would fade in a few days. This was just hey-look-a-hot-guy flutters. Right?

Right.

Besides, what on earth would he want with me? I was a fucking train wreck.

"So why doesn't Coby have a dad?"

"Damn, you are nosy, aren't you?"

"Hey, now! I'm a journalist. It comes with the territory." I glared at his profile but softened at his wide smile full of straight, white teeth.

Now that was a good look.

Beau's resting expression was stern. His dark eyebrows and straight nose were such serious features. But smiling? *Hot damn.* It might take me a couple of weeks instead of a couple of days to get over my crush.

The twitterpation would eventually fade, just like it

always did. No man had ever captivated me for long. The most serious relationship I'd ever had had only lasted four months—that was if you didn't count my torturous farce with Anton, which had lasted almost six.

Don't go there.

My brain had enough to process tonight without my self-loathing playing into the mix. Later, after I was safe and settled into hiding, I could start to process how far I'd gone to get my story. I could think about how many orgasms I'd faked with Anton. How many times I'd held back a cringe as he'd kissed me. About how I'd used my body to get my story and become famous.

About how I'd lost sight of why I'd started all of this in the first place.

Those things I'd think about later, but not right now. Tonight, I'd focus on learning more about Beau Holt.

"So, are you going to answer my question?"

He sighed. "It's a long story."

"Don't we have a while until we get to the outpost?"

"All right." He nodded. "I'll give you the gist. Coby's dad was a doctor at the hospital where Maisy was a nurse. They started dating; she got pregnant. He didn't want to be a father so they broke up. Turns out he was a crazy fucker who was skimming prescription pills from the hospital and selling them to high-school kids in town. He kidnapped Jess's wife, Gigi, and Maisy and almost killed them."

"Wait. That was your sister?" I stared at him, my jaw flapping open.

"Yeah, that was Maze. The doc tried to kill her because she wouldn't have an abortion. He wanted to kill Gigi because he thought she'd figured out he was dealing. In the end, they were able to escape but only because Maisy stabbed him in the throat with a scalpel."

"Oh my god. I remember reading about that. It was so crazy it even hit the Seattle news. My paper wrote an article on it and everything." The article had said that she'd been forced to kill him but it hadn't gone into that much detail. "Wow."

"Yeah. Wow," he muttered.

And I thought I had problems. At least I hadn't been forced to take another human's life.

I'd only met her briefly but Maisy had been sweet and gentle. Her personality was a testament to her strength. A traumatic event like that could ruin a person, leaving them bitter and cold, but she spread warmth and happiness to those around her.

"I'm glad that everything turned out okay for her."

"Yeah. It took a while but she's worked through her bad days. Now we're all just focused on making sure Coby grows up with men in his life, that he doesn't feel like he's missed out because his father is gone. I mean, it isn't his fault his biological father was deranged. He's an amazing kid and deserves the best life we can give him."

Coby was a lucky little boy to have such a dedicated uncle. The pride and joy in Beau's voice was unmistakable. On top of everything he was doing for me, the love he had for his nephew endeared me to him even more. He wasn't just absurdly handsome.

He was also a good man.

Which meant if he showed even the slightest interest in me, I was screwed. Could someone like him ever want someone like me? We were from two different worlds. But what if—

I refused to go down that "what if" road. The one I was on was bumpy enough.

"It's wonderful that you and your family are there to support your sister. Has she dated anyone since Coby's dad?"

He growled. Actually growled, like a jungle cat.

Who did that? I struggled to choke back my laughter. "Did you just growl at me?"

"Maisy has enough going on without a man in her life. She runs the motel and she has Coby. If she needs anything, she's got her family and good friends. She doesn't need a guy coming in and messing any of that up."

"I'm not saying she needs a man. I'm a firm believer that women are fully capable of taking care of themselves. I'm just asking if she's dated. She might not need a companion but maybe someday she'll want one. Have you ever thought of that?"

He growled again, and this time, I couldn't keep my laughter at bay—though I quickly learned to try harder. My ribs and bottom lip screamed in protest.

"No more growling," I said. "It makes me laugh, which hurts. You promise to use your words from now on and I'll promise to never bring up Maisy's dating life."

"Agreed," he rumbled.

I grinned and turned my eyes back to the road. Beau's protectiveness of Maisy was another appealing quality. He was the defensive big brother and no one would ever be good enough for his little sister. My older brothers had tried to give me that. What would my life be like had I let them in?

I'd never know. I doubted I'd ever be close with my family again.

As Beau maneuvered the truck through a series of

sharp twists and bends in the road, I sat silently, staring out into the darkness. The events from the day were catching up with me. My body's aches and pains were becoming insistent and my head was fuzzy with exhaustion.

With Boone's warmth at my side and Beau's comforting smell filling the air, I started to drift off. I fought it for as long as I could but the gentle swaying of the truck lulled my weary body to sleep.

"Sabrina." Beau's voice echoed in my dream.

His thick fingers brushed my hair back and trailed across my shoulder. I hummed as his touch sent tingles down my arm. If only I could feel those fingers against my bare skin. I willed Dream Beau to pull back the cotton of my shirt and trace my collarbone.

"Sabrina, we're here," Dream Beau said again.

Wait. Not a dream. I jerked awake and winced at the sudden movement.

Curses.

I hoped I hadn't been snoring. Or, worse, moaning Beau's name.

"Sorry, I fell asleep." I looked toward my window and wiped away the drool at the corner of my mouth.

"No problem. I bet you're wiped."

"We're here?" Ahead of us, I saw a clearing but no sign of an outpost, just a tiny shed at the end of the road.

"Yep."

"Where's the outpost?"

His finger pointed to the shed. "Uh, right there."

"That little tiny building?"

"No. That's the biffy. The outpost is right in front of us."

My stomach dropped. I had no idea what a biffy was but

it didn't matter. Beau's words were clear. The outpost was the shed and my new, dreaded home.

Even in the dark and from a distance, I could tell there was only one room. Did that mean one of us would be sleeping on the floor? What about a bathroom? And laundry? I wasn't a gourmet cook by any means but would there be some place to prepare my meals?

For once in my life, I had no idea which question to ask first.

I tensed as Beau parked by the front door. I stayed in the truck, per his instruction, as he went to turn on the power.

When he was done, he came and opened my door. "Ready?"

"No." My honest answer got me a look of irritation mixed with pity.

He held out a hand to help me down from the warm truck and into the cold night. Underneath my clothes, my skin prickled with goose bumps. I followed closely behind Beau as he walked from the truck to the outpost. Shivering on the square cement pad, I waited for him to unlock the padlock on the brown wooden door.

He pushed inside first and I braced before forcing my feet to move. The musty smell assaulted my nose before Beau flipped on a light, revealing my new home.

There was no doubt about it now. I hadn't just messed up my life with the Federov article.

I had completely fucked it up.

CHAPTER THREE

SABRINA

"I can't stay here."

"I know it's not much," Beau said, "but we'll make it comfortable for you."

Not much? Talk about the understatement of the century.

The overhead lamp cast a dim glow through the open room but I could see enough to know that I'd never be comfortable here. Beau's footprints were visible in the thick layer of dust coating the floor. Every one of his steps sent echoing creaks and squeaks through the uneven floorboards.

On my left was a small kitchen circa 1972. The pea-green counters clashed fantastically with the mustard-yellow refrigerator and stove. Dead-fly carcasses were scattered across the counters. The fridge's door was opened slightly and there were suspicious brown droppings in the bottom.

In the back corner was an old, black wood stove with a pile of wood blocks at its base. Next to it was a log chair that looked about as comfortable as sitting on a gynecologist's exam table with your feet in the stirrups. Besides the chair, the room was empty.

"If you need to use the bathroom tonight, you'll have to go in the biffy," Beau said. "I'll get the well pump running in the morning so the water works."

"Biffy?" I asked.

"Outhouse."

"Oh my god." I was going to faint, and if not for the fear of touching the floor, I would have. I had walked right into my own personal hell. Prison inmates were given better accommodations than this. I didn't know whether to start laughing or crying.

In a nightmare flash, I pictured myself in six months, wearing the same clothes I was in now. My hair had become ratted in dreadlocks and I had befriended the mouse that came in and out through the gaping holes in the dirty floor-boards to share my moldy bread.

"I can't stay here," I repeated, my voice cracking.

Beau grumbled something before running a hand over his beard. "Let's get some shut-eye and worry about the place in the morning."

I didn't care that he sounded annoyed. I'd dealt with a lot today and wasn't going to try and hide my objection to living in this hovel. There was only so much this girl could put up with before she broke.

Tears filled my eyes and I looked over my shoulder to the truck. If I begged and pleaded, would he take me back to town?

Probably not.

"Listen." Beau's tone softened. "I know this isn't your thing. Tonight will be the worst. I promise tomorrow we'll get it all cleaned up and livable. Just think of it like camping for one night. Haven't you ever been camping before?"

I shook my head. The closest thing to camping I'd ever done was a stay at a beach cottage on the Oregon coast.

"Camping is fun." His smile held actual magical powers. One flash of those pearly whites and the angry bees swarming in my stomach returned to their hive. Beau should model for Colgate. He'd sell more toothpaste than Michael Phelps sold Wheaties.

I can do this. I took a breath. Then another. *Don't be a baby, Sabrina.* "Okay," I whispered. My head and shoulders fell as another wave of exhaustion crashed against my battered body.

"Hey." He crossed the distance between us. My eyes stayed on our feet. His brown boots looked at least twice the size of my size eights. With a finger hooked under my chin, he tipped my head back so my green eyes were locked on his stormy blues. "I wouldn't have suggested this place if I didn't think you could cut it. You took on the mob. A cabin in the woods will feel like child's play."

"You don't know me well enough to say that."

His finger left my chin to slide a lock of fallen hair off my forehead. "Oh, I think I've got a pretty good read on you."

My pulse quickened and my chest swelled, the wrap around my cracked ribs compressing even more tightly. When his hand dropped, I wasn't sure if my sigh was from relief or disappointment. My life was such a cluster right now. Starting something with Beau was the epitome of stupid, but damn, his fingers had felt good against my face. And that spark in his eyes was a beacon calling to my soul. Telling me to dock my fucked-up ship in his port and he'd make sure it didn't sink.

He took a step back, clearing his throat and breaking our stare. "I'll start unloading supplies."

Right. Time to move into my new home.

"I can help." I spun to follow him out the door but he held up a hand.

"I've got it. Take a load off that ankle."

Beau disappeared to the bed of the truck while Boone bounded out and ran inside. The hound plopped down next to the chair and I hesitantly followed. Doing my best to clear the dust from the seat, I eased onto the log chair.

"Not as uncomfortable as I'd thought, Boone." Lovely. I was talking to the dog now. "This doesn't mean I like you."

Boone dropped his head to his paws and ignored me as he watched his master bring in load after load, setting bags, coolers and boxes on the dirty floor.

When the truck was unloaded, Beau worked with efficiency to start a fire in the stove. "The heat is set pretty low, just enough to keep the water pipes from freezing. I'll get it all checked out in the morning and we can crank it up. For tonight, this will have to do. Hope you can sleep with the light and noise from the fire."

"Sure." I doubted I'd get much rest anyway. Between my aches and anxiety over the new location, I was in for a fitful night's rest.

"Let me make sure this won't smoke us out and then I'll set up your cot."

I watched him quietly, listening to the cracks and pops from the fire. It was the first time I'd ever been around a real wood-burning fire. The only fireplaces I'd ever seen were run by gas and fake logs. The smell of smoke and burning wood filled the outpost and chased away the must.

"So what do you use this place for anyway?" I asked.

"Besides hiding reporters who are on the run from gun smugglers."

He grinned and tossed another log on the fire. "These were set up mostly for forest fire crews. Biologists sometimes use them if they're doing field study. If there are public access trails, crews will use these while they do trail maintenance. Actually, there are outposts like this scattered throughout the mountains. The government built a bunch of them in the seventies, ran power lines and dug each one a well, so they're pretty self-sufficient."

"Is there a chance we'll get unexpected visitors?"

He shook his head. "There's a bigger station just south of here that's easier to get at from town. Since there hasn't been a forest fire on this side of the ridge in years, no one comes up here but me."

"Why would you have to come here?"

"For my job. I make sure all the outposts in the county are in good shape. Basically, that the power still works and the pipes haven't busted. Jess and Silas came up with me once to go hunting, but that's about all the traffic this place has seen in five years."

His definition of "good shape" was different from mine, but at least I was hidden. When he'd said that I'd be off the grid, he hadn't been kidding.

"There." He stood from the floor and swiped the wood bits off his hands. "That should keep us warm tonight. Let's head on out to the biffy and then I'll set up your cot."

Outhouse? No, thanks. "I'll just hold it."

He bent low and captured my hand, pulling me up from the chair. His tug was gentle but firm. I was going to the "biffy" whether I liked it or not.

43

"Fine," I grumbled. I needed to pee and would be even more uncomfortable if I tried to hold it all night.

He didn't let go of my hand as we walked across the room. My fingers looked dainty and childlike in his meaty grip. Nabbing a flashlight from the kitchen counter, he led me into the night, pulling me behind him as he followed a narrow footpath toward the outhouse.

The foul odor hit me when we were five feet away and my free hand flew to my nose.

Just get in and get out. Pee faster than you've ever peed in your life.

Beau dropped my hand to open the door and handed me the flashlight. Breathing through my mouth, I stepped into the small wooden room and lifted the lid on the hole.

"Oh my god." I gagged. "I'm in an outhouse."

I set down the flashlight, hovering over the seat to do my business. Mortification turned to horror when I realized that Beau could definitely hear me peeing. Men were so lucky. I'd kill for the ability to pee standing up right now.

I finished, foregoing the nasty toilet paper by the hole and yanked up my leggings before bursting out the door, walking back to the outpost as quickly as my ankle would allow.

Behind me, Beau chuckled.

"I'm so glad you find this entertaining."

"Don't get all riled up. I'm not *trying* to torture you."

But torture was exactly what this was. The back of my throat started to burn as my eyes filled with water. A hiccup escaped and I swallowed hard, forcing down others. I'd never felt so embarrassed. Anton had beaten away most of my self-confidence this morning. I'd been holding on to one last remaining sliver but Beau's laughter at my outhouse reaction had just shredded it to pieces.

"Hey," Beau said softly, clamping a hand on my shoulder and stopping me on the trail. The heat from his broad chest was at my back. "I'm sorry. I'm not laughing at you, just the situation. I'm used to this type of stuff and I've never really been around someone who wasn't. I apologize if I hurt your feelings."

I was grateful for his apology but it did little to lift my spirits. He saw me as a foolish city girl who would never fit into his raw and rugged world. I was the spoiled princess who required indoor plumbing and a dirt-free abode. He was the rough and tough guy who would be the only man standing after a zombie apocalypse.

Of course he would laugh at me. Of course he would pity me. I was ridiculous here.

"Please," I whispered. "Can we just go inside? I want this awful day to end."

He squeezed my shoulder. "Sure."

Back inside, he worked quickly to set up a metal-framed camping cot and roll out a thick canvas sleeping bag for my bed. From my duffel bag, I tugged out the pillow I'd borrowed from Felicity and pressed the fluffy down against my face. Her familiar scent brought back the lump in my throat. The floral smell would soon be replaced with campfire, the clean white cotton soon smudged with dirt. The good tainted with the unfamiliar.

I contemplated changing into pajamas but quickly dismissed the thought. I barely had the energy to sink onto the cot and toe off my shoes. Tucking myself into the sleeping bag, I burrowed deep, taking a few long inhales of Beau's woodsy scent, which lingered on the red flannel lining. Hugging my pillow tight, I watched as Beau laid out his own sleeping bag on the floor.

"Don't you have a cot? Or a pillow?" I asked.

"I'll be fine."

Silly me. Mountain men didn't need trivial things such as cots and pillows.

Beau stoked the fire one last time before settling into his bedding and crossing his arms behind his head.

"Night," he said.

"Good night." I closed my eyes, willing sleep to find me quickly. Maybe with some rest, I wouldn't feel the urge to curl up and cry for days.

"Tomorrow will be better, Sabrina," Beau whispered.

I believed him.

Because really, how much worse could it get?

———

A LOUD CRACKING sound caused me to jerk awake. The sudden movement sent blinding pain through my ribs and I collapsed back onto my cot, clutching my side. When the white spots in my vision cleared, I opened my eyes to see the sunshine trying to peek inside. There were only a few windows in the outpost, one in the kitchen and two high up in the pitched roof, but all three were filthy. Their heavy coating of dirt blocked out more light than it let in.

Beau's sleeping bag had been rolled up and stowed by the stove. Neither he nor Boone were anywhere in sight.

Slowly, I pushed myself up to sitting and did a quick assessment of my injuries. My face was puffy and no doubt an alluring shade of bluish purple. The lack of a mirror wasn't overly upsetting since I really didn't want to see how hideous I looked. My ankle was stiff and incredibly sore. The pain radiating from my ribs was excruciating and would likely kill me within the hour.

But if I died, at least I wouldn't have to use the outhouse ever again.

I sucked in a fortifying breath and stood from the cot. Another loud crack sounded outside and I shuffled across the dusty floor to squint out the kitchen window.

Oh, boy. Beau, the sexy lumberjack, was outside chopping wood. The vision was swoon worthy. His white T-shirt strained against his cut biceps as he swung the ax above his head. When it came slamming down to split the log, his thighs strained against his faded jeans. The only way to describe his legs was beefy. Those thighs could no doubt thrust with incredible force and I bet he could fuck a girl into oblivion.

"Phew." I leaned back from the grimy window and fixed my ponytail, giving my hormones a few seconds to settle before I went outside. I'd told myself last night that I'd eliminate sex from my thought loop and I had every intention of trying. But with him looking all manly and sexy? The struggle was real. When I was sure the flush had left my cheeks, I pushed out the door.

"Hi," I called.

Beau's ax stopped mid-stroke and he set it against a big stump. "Hi. Sorry if I woke you."

"It's okay. What time is it?"

"A little before noon."

Whoa. I'd slept a lot longer than I'd thought I could. Once I'd gotten settled into my cot, it had been surprisingly comfortable. The heavy sleeping bag combined with the warmth from the wood fire had created a cocoon-like bed.

That, combined with my exhaustion, had made me dead to the world for almost nine hours. I hadn't slept that long in years. Six hours was usually my max.

"Have you been up for long?" I asked.

He nodded. "A few hours. I turned on the water pump so the bathroom should be working for you now."

"There's a bathroom?" I asked in shock. Last night, he'd said there was water but I'd assumed it was only for the kitchen sink.

"Yeah. Didn't you see the door in the back corner?"

I'd thought that was another exit. The prospect of an actual toilet that flushed had me turning and practically sprinting inside. Ankle and rib pain be damned, this bathroom I had to see immediately.

Beau's thudding footsteps followed and Boone appeared from somewhere to trot at my side.

"It's not much," he warned as my hand reached for the bathroom's doorknob.

"Who cares? It's not an outhouse."

His chuckle echoed off the log-wood walls.

Pulling open the door, I stuck my head into the outpost's bathroom. The toilet was old and the once-white porcelain had yellowed. The shower was no bigger than a standing coffin. The mirror above the pedestal sink was warped and cracked in one corner. The green tiles were about as clean as you'd expect to find in a dive bar.

Tears of joy filled my eyes. It was the most beautiful bathroom I'd ever seen.

"Thank you," I said, turning around to Beau.

His face softened. "Not a problem."

"I'm sorry about last night. I know you've sacrificed a lot

to bring me up here and keep me safe. I don't mean to be ungrateful. It was just . . . a shock."

There were very few people in the world whose opinion of me mattered. In just one night, Beau had added himself to that list. The last thing I wanted was for him to think I was an ungrateful brat.

"You had a rough day," he said. "I get it. Coming here couldn't have been easy for you. I should have done a better job explaining what you'd be getting yourself into."

He was *such* a nice guy. The anti-Anton. "Well, thank you for all you're doing for me."

"You're welcome." His eyes locked with mine and I fought the urge to move into his arms. To press my nose against his damp shirt and pull in an intoxicating breath. His broad chest was so tempting. I could just make out a smattering of chest hair beneath the white cotton. I was a sucker for chest hair, that one defining trait that separated the men from the boys.

I was just about to inch closer, to give into the tractor beam that was his body, when Boone started licking my fingers. I gasped, yanking my hand away from his tongue's reach.

"Boone." Beau snapped his fingers and the dog instantly retreated to his side.

"He's fine. Sorry. I'm just not used to pets."

"It's okay." He rubbed the back of his neck before bending to scratch behind Boone's ears.

I shook off the haze of attraction and summoned up a smile. Beau and I had electricity, no doubt about it, but acting on our chemistry would only court more complications. I needed to keep reminding myself of that until the lust faded.

The giant backward step he took told me that he must have been thinking the same thing.

"All right, Goliath. What's the plan for today?"

He rolled his eyes.

Why did everyone react so negatively to my nicknames? Didn't they realize I was kidding? Well, I was kidding when it was someone that I liked. My nicknames for assholes tended to be a little on the evil side. Felicity's ex-boyfriends had received some of my more creative monikers.

"The plan is you're going to eat while I clean out the bathroom," he said. "Then you can take a shower if you'd like. The water should be heated up by now."

"I can clean the bathroom," I offered.

"You can, but you're not going to. In case you hadn't noticed, there's more to do than just the bathroom. Never fear, you'll get your chance to clean in there, but I don't want you on your hands and knees scrubbing the floor with cracked ribs. Let's take it easy. You can help me with the lighter stuff today."

I decided not to protest. My ribs were so sore that it hurt to breathe. I didn't think I'd physically be able to clean behind a toilet and in the cramped shower.

"Okay. Food sounds good."

"What do you feel like?" he asked. "The menu's limited until we can get the kitchen cleaned out and dishes washed. Today, your choices are granola bars or Pop-Tarts."

I chose a granola bar and followed him toward four huge plastic tubs, watching as he rifled through the dry goods he'd purchased last night. Next to the tubs were three large red coolers.

"How long will all of this last?" Beau's superhuman physique must require at least four thousand calories a day.

"Probably three weeks with the two of us."

"Then what?" My hopes soared at the prospect of going into town to refill foodstuffs. Even if it was just a day trip, I would gladly welcome a quick reprieve into civilization.

"Well, that gives us three weeks to teach you how to hunt and fish. I'll give you the quick and dirty about which berries and roots you can eat. I'll head back to town and you'll be on your own. I should be able to come back before winter though and bring you some supplements."

My mouth fell open as panic seized control of my major organs. He wanted me to become a hunter-gatherer? That was *never* going to happen. I'd rather take my chances with the Federovs. I started mentally calculating how long it would take for me to walk back to Prescott.

"Relax, Sabrina. I'm kidding."

I closed my mouth and frowned as my heartbeat went back to normal. "You should have taken up a career in politics. I've never heard anyone deliver such a convincing straight-faced lie."

The fact that Beau had all but convinced me I'd be scrounging through the wilderness for my own food was quite the feat. In my job, I'd learned quickly to sniff out a bluff.

"So really, what happens when all this stuff runs out?"

"You are going to be on your own at times. I'll have to get back to town for work but I'll come up every other week or so and bring you groceries."

"Right." An uneasy feeling rolled in my stomach. I knew Beau couldn't hide out with me forever but the reality that I'd be alone here was unnerving.

"Here," he said, handing me my breakfast. "Eat that and stop worrying. You won't be alone for long."

"Uh-huh." One day alone would be too long. A couple of weeks? I'd be crawling out of my skin. What I really needed was the internet. If I could just find out whether the Federovs had been immobilized by the FBI, then this nightmare would end and I could go home.

Beau left me to my granola bar while he disappeared into the bathroom with some cleaning supplies he'd unearthed from under the kitchen sink.

When he was done, he offered me the shower but I opted to help clean first. We spent the afternoon working our way from one side of the outpost to the other. Though the space was small, it took a while to sweep and mop the dusty floors, wipe down the windows and sanitize the kitchen.

But once it was clean, the place wasn't all bad.

While Beau stocked the refrigerator and freezer, I washed the pots, pans and dishes that had been collecting dust in the kitchen's cabinets. While everything was drying, Beau and I started unloading the dry goods.

"I don't suppose there's a washer-dryer hiding somewhere around here?" I took the box of rice Beau was handing up to me from his crouched position by a plastic tub.

He shook his head. "You'll have to hand-wash your stuff. I can take laundry back and forth to town though."

"Okay. I'm gaining a new appreciation for modern appliances."

"That's not a bad thing." He tossed me a loaf of bread. "I like that about roughing it from time to time. Makes you glad to be home."

I missed home. "Once I get back to the city, I don't know if I'll ever leave again."

Holding out my hand while shuffling boxes in the

cupboard, I waited for Beau's next deposit but it never came. He was staring, unfocused, at a bag of pasta.

"Beau?" I called.

His eyes snapped to mine and he shook his head out of wherever his thoughts had gone. "Here." He set the last few items on the counter and stood, disappearing outside with the now-empty tub.

"Ooh-kaay." What had that been all about?

I went back to unpacking, organizing the cramped kitchen as best I could. Beau came back inside and dragged over another tub, setting its contents on the counter in silence. I decided to give him a bit more space and turned to leave the kitchen but my bad ankle gave out.

Stumbling to the side, I braced for a hard collision with the floor but Beau rescued me first. He caught me around the waist and spun me so quickly I ended up cradled between his knees. My heaving chest pressed up against his. His soft beard just centimeters away from my forehead.

Tipping up my chin, I looked into his eyes but didn't make a move to leave his lap or strong arms. I just wanted to savor this fleeting moment for a few more seconds. Then I'd let him go and resign myself to putting some barriers up to block our magnetic connection.

"Are you hurt?" he asked.

I shook my head but couldn't break from his gaze. Those stormy ocean pools were as dangerous as the undertow.

The intensity of his stare snapped and in one powerful movement, he picked us both up off the floor. When I was steady on my feet, he took a step away, running a hand over his beard and then raking it through his hair.

"I'm just going to lay it out there," he said. "You're beautiful."

Those words, ones that should have elicited a beaming smile, made me brace. His tone was dreadfully serious. The next statement was certain to ruin his pretty words.

"We're from two different worlds. Let's not get wrapped up in this physical connection, or whatever this is, and do something stupid."

"Sure," I said, swallowing my disappointment. "I agree."

He was right, obviously. Beau was the type of man who needed someone with much less baggage than I was carting around. Nothing could happen between us. A fling would certainly lead to disaster.

But somehow, his rejection hurt worse than the kick Anton had landed in my side.

CHAPTER FOUR

SABRINA

Day seven.
I'd started keeping a tally on a scrap of paper in the kitchen, otherwise, the days would have blurred together.

Why? Because I was bored out of my damn mind.

Every day was the same. Wake up. Take a shower. Do my very best to style my hair without a hair dryer, straightener or curling iron. Eat breakfast. Read. Eat lunch. Read. Eat dinner. Read. Sleep.

Without the company of Felicity's Kindle, I would have gone mad by day four.

I had enjoyed the relaxed and sleepy pace at first. I'd lost myself in a few amazing romance novels and time had flown by, but then I'd started getting antsy. This girl was not made for sitting idle. My fingers were in a continuous state of twiddling, and every time I sat down, my legs started bouncing involuntarily.

I missed my job. I missed my city. I missed my apartment.

I missed my phone.

The phantom pains from its amputation were no joke. I reached for it constantly. Social media had never really been my thing but I'd gotten in the habit of checking it periodically throughout the day. I had used it to keep tabs on my brothers' lives in Florida. To see what rumors the gossip rags were spreading about my favorite celebrities. To stalk enemy reporters at competing newspapers.

Now I was completely disconnected.

No texting. No Google. No online shopping.

Since my ankle had mostly healed, I'd resorted to pacing to pass the time.

That's what I was doing now. Pacing. Eight steps to one wall. Eight steps back. If I went from the bathroom to the front door, it took fifteen.

And where was Beau, my so-called companion, during all these jittery steps?

Avoiding me.

He'd disappear first thing in the morning and come back right before dinner. Our evenings were spent mostly in silence. I'd read—or pretend to read while watching him from the corner of my eye—and he'd tinker around the outpost until he set up his bed on the floor and fell asleep.

Ever since his declaration that he had no interest in exploring our chemistry, things between us had become miserably awkward. Whenever he was around, I was so focused on avoiding his personal space that I could barely carry on a normal conversation. Beau must have sensed my discomfort too because for the last few days he hadn't even tried to make small talk.

I had to break this silence.

Maybe tonight I should clear the air. Tell him that I was attracted to him but had no desire for a romantic relationship. Tell him that all I wanted was the elusive male/female friendship. Surely by day fourteen, my attraction for him would fade and I'd be back to normal. Friendship would be easy then. Right?

Right.

"Hey." Beau's deep rumble startled me. I spun toward the front door, clutching my hands to my pounding heart. "Sorry." He stepped inside. "Thought you heard me come up."

I shook my head. "I was thinking. What's up?" I tucked my hands into the kangaroo pocket of my green hoodie to keep them still.

"I just finished with a project. I was wondering if you wanted to come out and see what I've been working on."

"Uh, sure?"

His eyebrows went up. "Is that a question or an answer?"

"An answer? I mean, sure. I'll go out," I gulped, "there."

I'd spent these last seven days inside. I wasn't a nature lover, and without Beau around, I hadn't wanted to go exploring on my own. The only time I'd ventured out the door had been to take a bag of trash to the burn barrel. Afterward, Beau had told me to make sure I locked the lid up tight to avoid attracting raccoons or bears. That had terrified me so much that I'd made it my personal mission in life to avoid creating garbage.

"Come on out when you're ready. I'll split a few more logs."

I nodded and went to dig out my tennis shoes. The sound of Beau's ax cracking through wood echoed off the walls as I bent to tie my shoes, breathing through the tenderness in my still-sore ribs.

"Ready," I called, stepping outside and shielding my eyes as they adjusted to the bright afternoon light.

He took one last powerful swing and I struggled to ignore the flutter in my belly. I fell in step beside him as we walked away from the road and outpost, his long strides slower than normal and mine doing double time to keep up.

"So, are you done acting weird?" Beau asked.

My chin fell and I gaped at him with huge eyes. "What?"

"I asked if you were done acting weird."

I narrowed my eyes at the smirk on his face. How could he pin this all on me? He had been acting strangely too. Well, maybe his behavior had been more in reaction to mine. *Whatever.* This was the last topic I wanted to debate.

"I'm not even going to acknowledge that remark." I held my chin high and picked up my pace. His chuckle elicited an eye roll.

We walked past a grouping of trees and into a long, wide clearing of lush, green grass. I tipped my chin up, the sunshine on my face incredible. My spirits instantly perked up. I needed to force myself to go outside more and boost my vitamin D levels.

I felt better now than I had all week.

Dropping my chin, I looked around. The outpost was situated in a mountain valley. The meadow we were walking through was surrounded by evergreen hills that turned to blue mountains as they rose into the sky. About halfway up their steep slopes, the trees were still dusted with snow. Standing out in the open, I felt so small compared to their majesty.

"This is beautiful." The grass was the bright, neon green

of spring and its clean smell was a welcome change from the woodsy aroma in the outpost. The air was still cool but not sharp. A breeze rustled through the evergreens, filling the air with a gentle whisper.

"Believe it or not, this is an airstrip," Beau said. "I've been working to clear trees that started growing too far into the meadow." He pointed to a few big piles of fallen trees around the edges of the field.

"Why is there an airstrip in the middle of nowhere?"

"In case a small plane needs to do an emergency landing. There are a bunch of these little strips throughout the mountains. Usually they're located by an outpost so there is shelter. Part of my job with the forest service is to make sure the fields are clear and the tree line doesn't encroach too much."

"That sounds like a lot of work."

"I don't do it all myself. I've got a crew that goes around to the larger places. A couple of the bigger outposts have full-time residents that live there year-round. But since this place has always been my favorite, I usually come up here and clean it up myself."

That didn't surprise me at all. Though Beau hadn't been overly chatty with me this week, he had seemed happy and content.

"You really love it out here, don't you?"

He nodded. "Yeah."

"Why?" My question wasn't judgmental, just curious. I had been plopped down in the middle of a different culture, a different world. Maybe if I understood what Beau found so appealing, the strange things here wouldn't frighten me as much.

"I guess it just suits me. It speaks to my soul. I've always felt at peace in the woods, and life just seems . . . simpler out here."

"Is your life in town complicated?"

He shrugged. "No. Maybe."

We walked in silence for a few moments as I waited for him to elaborate. When he didn't, frustration bubbled up in my gut. My inquisitive nature had been deprived this week. I missed being in reporter-mode and asking questions whenever they popped into my head. My boss had always compared me to a little kid, bouncing on my feet, asking "why" a million times until I was satisfied with the answer.

I needed more from Beau than a two-word response. "Come on, can't you give me a better answer? Humor me. Please?"

"Nosy." He looked down at me and grinned.

I gave him my "I'm waiting" look and he smiled wider.

"I wouldn't say life is complicated," he finally said, "it just gets busy. I could use about three more employees than I have. If there's a fire in the area, that number becomes more like ten. And lately we've had some tough search and rescue cases. Plus I do my best to help out with family and spend time with Coby so he's got a dad-type figure in his life. I've just got a lot of balls in the air and don't want to drop any."

On top of all that responsibility, he was taking on my troubles too. Beau was the type of man that everyone around him leaned on. And instead of seeing to his life in Prescott, he was stuck here. His absence from town could not be helping his stress levels.

Sabrina MacKenzie, you've been selfish. I had been so consumed worrying about my own life that I hadn't taken into consideration what this setup was doing to Beau's.

"I'm sorry, Beau. The last thing you need is to babysit me."

"I don't mind. Really. I needed to come up here anyway and do some long-overdue cleanup."

"You're sure?"

"I'm sure. Though, things would be even better if you'd stop avoiding me."

I nodded. "All right."

The least I could do for Beau was make our temporary living arrangement comfortable. I'd do my damnedest not to let my intense attraction get in the way of friendship. Beau had been right in drawing that line in the sand between us, and I'd overreacted, making things more awkward than they had to be. We were adults. He was acting like one. It was time I did too.

We strolled across the clearing, enjoying the fresh spring air and the sound of birds chirping in the trees. In the distance, Boone bounded through the grass, his tail wagging constantly while his nose discovered and dismissed different smells. Just like Beau, Boone was in his element here.

"Look there." Beau pointed to a bunny.

"Cute! A wildlife creature that doesn't scare the shit out of me." My appreciation of the animal was cut short when Boone came out of nowhere and barked, chasing the rabbit away.

By the time we hit the far end of the meadow, the awkwardness of the last week had all but vanished. When we turned to start back to the outpost, Beau asked, "What do you think is happening with the Federovs?"

I shook my head. "I don't know. Without the internet to check, I can only guess. I've been keeping my fingers crossed that the FBI stepped in." If they hadn't, then I didn't know what I'd do. Anton would be free to seek me out and finish what he'd started in my apartment. But I had faith that Henry, my FBI contact, wouldn't let me down.

Beau hummed and rubbed a hand over his bearded jaw. I'd learned this week that meant he was mulling over something. "What about your family?"

I hated to think of how my disappearance was affecting my parents, so much so that I'd been trying not to think about it. "What about my family?"

"They've got to be worried. I'm sure they know by now you're missing."

My shoulders fell. "Yeah. I'm sure they are."

The idea of causing them pain made my stomach ache.

My mom was probably in a perpetual state of motion—I'd inherited my pacing habit from her. While she was a frantic and active worrier, my dad was sullen and withdrawn when stressed. He'd had two ulcers already because his fears ate at him from the inside out. I just hoped that my brothers, who were the most levelheaded of us all, could keep them from panicking.

"Are you tight with them?" Beau asked.

I shook my head. "Not really. My parents are much closer to my older twin brothers. And work was always so busy for me I didn't make the trip home much."

My parents had only visited me in Seattle twice in all the years I'd lived there, once for my college graduation, and once when I'd received an award at the paper. My brothers had only come out for my graduation.

They'd offer to visit, and I'd tell them I was busy with work. They'd ask me to come home, and I'd suddenly have an idea for a story that just couldn't wait. The last time I'd seen my family was three years ago, when I'd flown home after Mom had begged me to be there for Christmas. We'd all spent an awkward week together, not having much in common anymore and all loathing the forced small talk, until I'd retreated back to Seattle.

But just because I wasn't close to my family didn't mean there wasn't love there. I knew my parents loved me, even if we didn't talk often. I was sure they were going out of their minds wondering if I was alive.

Twirling a lock of hair in my ponytail, I started thinking about all of the other people in my life. Was my boss worried that the Federovs had gotten to me? He always pushed me to test the limits during my investigations but he also always reminded me to be safe, first and foremost. He'd never forgive himself for assigning me this story once he learned how Anton had beaten me. I couldn't imagine how my boss was feeling if he thought I was dead.

Besides him, there was my doorman, who was more like a favorite uncle. He was undoubtedly concerned about my whereabouts and probably calling the police hourly to see if they had any updates.

But at least Felicity knew I was okay.

"I didn't mean to freak you out." Beau tugged my hand away from my hair.

"It's okay. I just wish there was a way for me to secretly alert people that I was alive. Everyone probably thinks I'm swimming with the fishes and wearing concrete boots."

"Hmm," he said. "Let's brainstorm that a bit. Electronic communication is out. That's easy to trace. Phone calls are a no-go too. What about mail? I doubt the Federovs are monitoring the postal service. What if you sent your family a letter? Prescott is just a couple hours from Wyoming. When

I go back, I could drive over the border and mail it just so we wouldn't have to worry about the postmark."

"That could work." My spirits lifted instantly. Easing my parents' worry would go a long way to easing my own. "You wouldn't mind?"

"Not at all. And you might as well get word to your FBI agent while you're at it. There's no reason for them to spend man hours trying to track you down when they could put those toward nailing Federov to the wall."

I smiled the first genuine smile of the week. "Agreed. Good idea, Goliath."

He grinned. "Thanks."

This plan settled some nerves but not all. Even if I notified my family and the FBI, there were still plenty of things still up in the air. Depending on how long I was here, the life I returned to in Seattle could be very different from the life I'd left.

Would my landlords hold my apartment for me? If they thought I was dead, would I go home to strangers living in my home? What about my job? My boss was making do with too few reporters as it was. Would I be unemployed soon?

I swallowed a dry laugh.

This wasn't the grandeur I'd once imagined.

While I'd been writing the Federov story, I'd imagined how my life would change after its publication. I'd pictured myself getting award nominations and personal accolades from the justice department. I'd seen promotions and pay increases at the paper. I had dreamed of being a modern-day heroine.

Anton Federov had checked my ego.

Never had I imagined that things could have gone so terribly wrong.

"What now?" Beau asked.

"Huh?"

His eyebrows furrowed. "You were fine a minute ago and then the smile fell right off your face. What's rattling around in your head now?"

"I was just thinking about all the stuff I left behind." I confessed my worries and he sympathized, but unfortunately, where he'd offered a solution to my other concerns, there wasn't much either of us could come up with this time around. Nevertheless, it helped to talk it out.

Beau was a skilled listener, and even though I'd only known him for a week, I trusted him to dole out honest advice. He had my full respect. I couldn't think of the last time I'd dated a man as admirable as he was.

He could have pressed it earlier this week, taken advantage of my vulnerabilities and attraction for him. Most of my ex-boyfriends or ex-lovers would have, and god knows, I wouldn't have put up a fight had he dragged me to his sleeping bag. But that just wasn't Beau Holt's style.

I liked that. A lot.

"Thanks, Beau."

"Anytime." He bumped me with his enormous shoulder. I was sure he only intended me to sidestep a bit, but the jolt sent me flying. If not for his quick reflexes, my ass would have landed in the grass and dirt.

"Fuck. Sorry," he said, standing me up. "Did I hurt you?"

I shook my head and giggled. The sting in my ribs was nothing to make him feel bad about. "Let me guess. You don't know your own strength?"

He laughed too. "Something like that."

My breath hitched a bit at the wide smile softening his face. Our eyes locked, but before it lasted too long, I broke away and started walking again. Why did he have to be so hot? Being trapped here with a mullet man or booger eater would have been so much easier. Well . . . maybe not easier, but certainly less tempting.

Beau and I crossed the remaining distance to the edge of the meadow and eased back into the shadow of the trees. I instantly missed the sunshine and challenged myself to come out on a more regular basis. Maybe I'd even offer to help Beau with his projects. With the awkwardness from the last seven days gone, I could embrace his company instead of avoiding it. After all, soon I'd be alone. I needed to soak up his company while I still had it.

"What do you feel like for dinner?" I asked as we approached the outpost.

"Let's take a drive first. Go ahead and hop in, I'll be right back." Beau called for Boone and the dog came sprinting over.

A drive sounded like a nice way to pass the rest of the afternoon and it wasn't like my e-books were going anywhere. I had enjoyed my walk through the meadow and wouldn't mind seeing more of the area. At night, the wilderness still scared the crap out of me, but during the day, the mountains and trees were kind of majestic.

Beau and Boone got in the truck and the dog settled right into my side. He, much like the rustic scenery, was growing on me.

I rode quietly as Beau drove us through the trees. We weren't on a road and I said a silent prayer that he would be able to find his way back to the outpost. When he pointed the truck up a narrow and extremely steep hill, I gasped and gripped my door handle while my heart jumped into my throat. The truck was inverted at such a steep angle it was akin to a rollercoaster riding up that first terrifying incline before the inevitable plunge.

Please, truck, don't roll over. I really wanted to live to my thirty-fifth birthday.

It took a few minutes after we crested the ridge for my racing heart to settle. Beau parked, and once my panic had subsided, I took a look at the incredible view. From up here, I could see forever.

"Wow. I feel like I'm in Middle Earth." The tall, snow-capped mountains in the distance stood like giants above the open, gold plains in between.

"I wouldn't have taken you for a *Lord of the Rings* fan," Beau said. "Movies or books?"

"As a rule, books, but those movies were incredible so they are an exception."

Beau hummed in agreement before pulling out his cell phone. "Here." He held it out. "There's probably only one bar or two but go crazy. Use my profile and cyber stalk your family. You can check the news to see what's up with the Federovs."

I sat frozen for a second until his words registered. He'd brought me up here because there was cell service. Taking the phone, I beamed. "Thank you."

I tapped the Facebook app but stopped before typing my mom's name into the search bar. I looked up at Beau, tears pooling in my eyes. "What if the Federovs got to them?" I could barely choke out the words.

His eyes softened and he reached out a hand, placing it on the side of my neck. "They're okay. Jess would have found us if something bad had happened."

"You think?"

"I know." His thumb rubbed the underside of my jaw

and I couldn't help but lean my weight further into his soothing grip.

"Okay." I blinked away my tears. Then, diving right in, I Facebook-stalked my family.

My parents, brothers and entire extended family had been posting regular pleas, begging for information on my whereabouts. Their words were laced so heavily with concern that I couldn't stop the tears from running down my cheeks. The video my dad had posted was heartbreaking. His skin was splotchy from crying and he looked wrecked with worry.

I felt unbearably guilty for making them suffer but at the same time incredibly relieved, because even worried, they were all safe and unharmed.

"Well?" Beau asked.

I held out the phone for him to see the post I'd opened. "I'm the contemporary girl on the milk carton."

"That's quite the hairdo." We both chuckled at his joke. I was grateful for his humor to help me get my emotions under control.

"I was going through a big-hair phase." Clearly, I needed to get some more recent photographs to my parents. The one they seemed to be circulating the most was from my college graduation. I'd had a huge bump teased into the top of my head.

Looking out across the beautiful distance, I made a silent promise. I would build a stronger relationship with my family. Once I was free to leave my Montana hideout, I was going to be a better daughter and sister.

Turning back to the phone, I started digging into recent news articles from my paper. Immense relief flowed through my veins when I read that the Federovs had been arrested and the FBI was conducting a major investigation into their ties to the Russian mafia. I let out an audible sigh, relieved my hard work had not been in vain.

An hour later, I was in a better mental state than I'd been in since Seattle.

"Thank you," I told Beau. "So much." I wouldn't ever be able to explain how much this hour connected to the real world had meant.

"No problem." His easy smile made my heart beat double time.

Curses. My attraction for Beau wasn't fading, not in the slightest. The new-guy flutters were morphing into all-consuming desire. My heart would fall for this sweet and thoughtful man. It was inevitable. And it would be the forever kind of fall. A disastrous descent that would splatter my heart on the pavement and leave no possible hope for repair.

Because a future with Beau was impossible.

We're from two different worlds.

His words rang in my ears and sounded even worse than they had a week ago.

I turned back to his phone as a dull ache settled into my heart. When this ordeal was over, I'd go back to my life and Beau would stay here in his. The sooner I accepted that fate the better.

"One more minute?" I asked.

"Take as long as you need."

My fingers worked automatically, typing in a name for one last Facebook search. Again, I was met with my picture, this one much more recent, having been taken just four weeks ago. But unlike the photos my family had posted, in this picture I was not alone.

Anton was standing at my side, an arm thrown around my shoulders. The smile on my face would look genuine to all those that didn't know me well. Anton's handsome face was split wide, laughing at the photographer, his brother Ivan.

The photo was unsettling but it was the caption that sent ice prickling down my spine.

Please help me find my beautiful girlfriend, Sabrina. We're desperate to bring her back home.

CHAPTER FIVE

SABRINA

I couldn't breathe. Pain radiated in hot, sharp pulses from my ribs throughout my entire body. My fingernails clawed at the carpet as I tried to roll into the fetal position but my hips were pinned. Anton loomed above me, his legs straddling my hips and trapping me on the floor.

"You're fucking dead," he sneered. "I'll make you pay for playing me. Did you think I wouldn't find out that you're a reporter? That you've been digging around my office at night?"

"Anton—" But before I could plead for my life, his fist connected with my already-throbbing cheek. My vision turned white. My mouth hung open but the pain was too much for me to even scream.

"You're nothing but a whore. I'll show you how I treat whores."

"No!" The word screamed in my head but nothing came out of my mouth. Anton's hand had clamped around my *throat again, rendering me mute and panicked for air. Things started to blur, his face, the ceiling above him, the couch at my side. But just before the world faded to black, he let me go. My lungs burned as I gulped for air. My voice started to work again and I let out a raspy plea for help.*

He stopped my scream with a sharp backhand to my jaw before standing to unbuckle his belt.

Two strong hands shook me awake. "Sabrina, wake up."

My eyes snapped open. Beau loomed above me, his eyes full of concern. I pushed up off my cot and swiped sticky hair off my forehead. My heart was pounding and my chest heaved with panicked breaths.

Another nightmare.

I'd been having them all week, ever since the afternoon I'd looked up Anton's social-media accounts and seen my picture with its phony caption. Any time I tried to sleep, I fell back into the same dream.

"Sorry," I panted, breathing deeply to slow my racing heart.

"Don't be sorry. Same nightmare?"

I nodded.

After my third night of waking up shouting and drenched with sweat, Beau had refused to let me brush it off as just a bad dream. He'd sat with me on my cot and demanded I spill.

And spill I had. He'd gotten it all, more than I'd confessed even to Felicity. It wasn't that I'd purposefully kept pieces from her, but I remembered more now than when I'd first arrived in Montana. The nightmares brought it all back in vivid detail. Every hit. Every slap. Every one of Anton's words. Beau heard it all.

When I'd told him about Anton's plan to rape me, he'd

gotten so mad that he'd had to go outside in the dark and chop wood until well after sunrise.

"I think I'm going to take a shower." It was still dark but sleep after my nightmare was impossible.

"Okay." Beau stood first and helped me to my feet.

I shuffled to the bathroom and cranked up the water to scalding. When it turned cold, I stepped out and tossed on a fresh pair of pajama shorts and a thin camisole. I wouldn't be going back to bed but at least it was comfortable.

My arms felt heavy as I combed out my hair. Exhaustion had settled into my bones and I was basically a zombie, too scared to drift off, so I'd been forcing myself to stay awake. The instant coffee that should have lasted Beau and I a month was now almost gone.

With my hair hanging damp down my back, I stepped out of the bathroom on tiptoe, hoping that Beau had been able to go back to sleep. My feet froze at what had happened to the living area while I'd been in the shower. My sleeping bag was no longer on my cot but instead spread out full on the floor. Beau's had been unzipped and then reconnected to mine, making one large bed.

"What's going on?"

Beau held out a hand. "Come here."

I took a hesitant step and laid my hand in his. Beau was only wearing a pair of dark gray boxer briefs and a T-shirt, his normal bedtime attire, but his expression said this wasn't about sex. His eyes were full of worry and there wasn't a flicker of lust in sight.

He led me to the bed and kneeled down, tugging me to the floor. Then settling on his back, he patted the spot next to him.

"Beau, I'm not going to be able to sleep."

"Well, you're going to try. You're dead on your feet, and if you don't get some rest, you're going to wear yourself too thin."

I shook my head. "I don't want to." Anton's voice was still in my ears. Another nightmare would be too much for me to cope with tonight.

"Trust me. Please?" he asked. "I've got you."

His words melted my resolve and I slid into the warm pocket. One of his arms curled under my neck as the other twisted me into his chest. With my face tucked into his shoulder and my arms pinned between us, I was securely locked in his embrace.

"Try to relax," he whispered into my hair.

"Okay." It took me a few moments, but soon the tension in my muscles melted away. The fretting thoughts vanished and an epiphany sparked to life.

No man would ever hold me this well.

I was made to be wrapped in these arms.

A woman could tell a lot by the way a man holds her. She could tell if he had the strength to endure the rougher moments. If he had a mighty yet kind heart. If he could make her feel safe and cherished.

Beau's embrace said all that and more.

He knew I was having a tough time, but instead of picking me up and taking the burden, he was just giving me the support to beat it back myself. He was propping me up. I didn't need or want a man to fight my battles for me, even if they were against the demons in my mind. I wanted a man who would hold my hand, squeezing it every now and again so I knew I wasn't alone as I waged my own war. I wanted a man who would push me to keep battling because he knew I'd eventually win.

Being held in Beau's strong arms was exactly what I had needed. This time, when Anton crept into my sleep and the nightmare began, I wouldn't be alone as I fought to push him away.

I doubted I'd ever find such a perfect embrace again.

"Sleep," Beau whispered into my hair.

And, for the first time in a week, I did just that.

———

I'D BEEN SLEEPING in Beau's embrace for the past six nights and not once had Anton revisited my dreams. Just like this morning, I woke peacefully to warm arms wrapped around my back and Beau's heartbeat vibrating against my cheek.

"Good morning," he rumbled to the top of my head.

I rolled away and stretched in the sleeping bag bed. "Morning."

Boone's toenails clicked on the floor and I slapped my hands over my face before his wet nose could touch my mouth.

"Boone, get out of here," Beau said.

"He's okay." I giggled and sat up, reaching out to rub Boone's floppy ears. I was holding fast to my stance that I wasn't a pet person, but as with most rules, there were some exceptions. Boone was mine. His fur was soft and he didn't shed that much. He was affectionate, and much like his master, he was a calming presence in my mixed-up world.

"I'm going to shower." Beau stood from the floor and walked away as I continued to pet Boone.

Since it would be a crime not to take a moment and appreciate his sexy, rounded butt clad only in his underwear,

I snuck a peek before he disappeared into the bathroom. A trail of shivers ran down my back before I stood and started rolling up the bed.

Our bed.

Beau and I were absolutely playing house.

We'd work together outside during the day before returning to the outpost to cook dinner in the tiny kitchen. After eating, we'd spend our evenings in front of the fire, playing gin rummy or cribbage. Then he'd set up our bed and tuck me into his chest, and we'd both fall asleep, unmoving until morning.

Like newlyweds, we were spending as much time with one another as we could, but without the sex. That was still a no-go area.

Had my attraction for Beau faded? Not in the slightest and it was a bit unnerving. I'd never been in this situation before. The longest I'd ever felt attracted to a man had been two weeks. This week marked three at the outpost, and I was still burning hotter than ever.

I knew Beau was still feeling it too. There was a reason he always took the first shower, that being the mammoth appendage poking me in the hip every morning.

Damn these circumstances.

In a different setting, a different time, Beau would be perfect lover material. I *liked* him. I couldn't remember the last time I liked a guy this much. His steady personality was tugging at my heart strings, his dry sense of humor matched my own and his playful teasing had me smiling more often than not. My body crackled when it was near his and I had no doubts that sex with him would knock my socks off.

If only I had met him before Anton and my story. If only

he weren't so attached to Montana. If only I weren't so attached to the city.

If only Beau weren't going back to his life in Prescott today.

"Are you going to miss me, Boone?"

He wagged his tail and turned to the door.

I guess not.

"I'm done." Beau emerged from the bathroom, towel drying his hair. My mouth watered at the sight of him barefoot in jeans and a simple black T-shirt.

I stepped past him, our arms brushing, and quickly shut the bathroom door so he wouldn't see my blushing cheeks.

Damn those crackles.

It was probably good he was leaving. The longer he stayed, the more likely we'd be to slip up and give into this chemistry, and I needed Beau as a friend more than a lover right now.

When I came out of the bathroom twenty minutes later, all the good flutters in my belly had been replaced with the bad. Beau was kneeling next to his duffel bag, packing up to leave for town. His shoes were no longer laid out next to mine and he'd already taken out the empty cooler we'd been using as a dining room table.

"Do you have laundry you'd like me to take?" he asked.

I nodded and went to my bag sitting next to his. "I'm not sure how much to send. When do you think you'll be back?"

Say tomorrow.

"A week."

My shoulders fell. The last time I'd felt this much anxiety about an upcoming week had been after high school when I'd left Florida to drive across the country to Seattle.

"Hey." His hand gently rubbed my back. "You'll be fine."

"Sure." My outward confidence betrayed my inner feelings but I didn't want Beau to know how much I was dreading this week. Not only would my nightmares likely return but I was also bound to get miserably bored again. If Beau knew that I was freaking out, he wouldn't leave.

And he needed to leave.

He needed to go back to his life and his responsibilities. I'd taken up enough of his time, and besides that, I was desperate for more coffee. I was running low on food. I wanted clothes that had been cleaned in a washing machine, not the bathroom sink.

And we needed to put some space between us. I needed some time to remind myself that a friendship with Beau was as much of a relationship as we'd ever have. Maybe by the time he came back, I wouldn't find him so devastatingly handsome.

Now you're just kidding yourself.

"Do you want me to bring you back anything special?" he asked, taking my laundry and stuffing it in his duffel.

"Hmm." I tapped my chin. "A couch would be nice. Maybe a big screen and some chick flicks. I'd love a coffee machine too."

He laughed and I couldn't help but smile back.

Ever since our walk in the meadow, I'd made it my goal to do something to make him laugh every day. Beau had an amazing sense of humor, and he laughed often, but it sounded even better when I was the catalyst. The sound of his laughter was a balm to my broken spirit.

I was going to really miss hearing that laugh every day.

"Will you check in with Felicity?" I asked after he had loaded up the truck.

"Yep. Boone," he called and the dog came bounding inside. "Stay."

"Are you sure?" I asked. "I'll be fine if you want to take him back home with you."

"I'm sure." He reached out and ran his thumb across my jaw. "He'll be okay here. And so will you."

I wish I were as sure.

"We'll be great," I lied, willing my voice not to crack as I said good-bye.

He pulled on his sunglasses and a hunter-green baseball hat before striding out the door. I stood in the doorway, Boone at my feet, and waved as his truck backed away from the outpost and disappeared down the two-lane road.

His tires crunched on the small rocks in the dirt road. The sound of my crumbling spirits sounded much the same.

"Just you and me, Boone," I said as Beau's truck disappeared from my sight. "Alone. Are you going to cook me those fancy scrambled eggs? Or teach me how to play poker? Or make me feel like I haven't ruined my entire life?"

No, he wasn't. The only person in the world that could do those things was driving away. I was alone in this silent forest. I was a hopeless city girl stranded in the middle of the mountains with nothing but my regrets.

I let out a strangled cry when the sound of Beau's diesel engine no longer hummed against the trees in the distance. That pained sound preceded a flood of tears and uncontrollable, gut-wrenching sobs. For the first time since Anton's attack, I let myself cry. Really cry. Face-twisting, snot-smearing, ugly-wailing cry.

When the pain in my ribs was too much to bear standing, I crossed the room and curled up on my cot. Now that Beau was gone, I realized that he'd been the one keeping the gray fog of depression away. With him here, I had convinced myself that the aftershocks of my story had been worth it.

The truth was that I had been reckless. I had been blinded by the allure of heroics.

But I wasn't a hero.

I was a fool.

————

"WHAT. THE. FUCK."

Splendid. My imagination was now conjuring up Beau's voice. Depression had turned into delusion.

"Sabrina."

Couldn't I have conjured up a happy Beau?

Boone barked and abandoned the spot by my cot where he'd been keeping me company for the past four days. He'd been jumpy and excited for the last few minutes so I'd covered my head with a pillow and ignored him. I guess he was getting sick of me just lying around. *Whatever*. It wasn't like he couldn't come and go as he pleased. The door was cracked open so I wouldn't have to get out of bed during the day. What was he barking about?

I pulled the corners of the pillow tighter and shoved my nose into my sleeping bag mattress. The dog could pester me all he wanted. I wasn't getting up until after dark and that was only to close the door so no other creatures would come in for a visit.

Another bark and I'd just about had it. What was wrong with this dog? Couldn't he leave me to my wallowing in peace?

"Sabrina." And Beau's voice wouldn't leave me alone

either. No more barking. No more angry voices. I needed quiet so I could relish in my misery.

I tugged the pillow down further but it was yanked from my hands. I gasped and turned, only to see two beefy legs planted next to my cot. My eyes traveled up the denim thighs, the narrow hips, the flat stomach and wide chest to the scowl waiting at the top.

Well, at least I hadn't gone totally fucking bonkers.

"What. The. Fuck," Beau repeated.

"Huh?"

"You heard me. What the fuck? I see you haven't bothered to change since I left and I'm guessing from all these wrappers on the floor that you haven't eaten much either. What is going on? You're a wreck."

"Nice," I deadpanned. "Just what a woman wants to hear. Now give me back my pillow." I tried to swipe it out of his hands but he held it up too high for me to reach. "Argh! What are you even doing here? I still have three days until I have to fake happy." I got up on my knees and went for the pillow again but he tossed it across the room.

"What's going on?" His tone had completely shifted from hard and terse to soft and concerned.

My body sagged. "I'm bummed out, okay? I've got a lot going on in my head and I just needed to wallow for a while. There's nothing you can do but just let me be."

He considered my words for a minute. *"Bullshit."*

"What?" My spine snapped straight. "You don't get to say bulls—"

His arms banded around my back and he hauled me off the cot.

Hell no. I did not like to be hauled around, not even for sex.

"Put me down!" I shrieked into his face.

"No."

I started squirming and kicking but he was too strong. "Beau, I mean it. Put me down."

His response was a growl and a tighter grip. He carried me into the bathroom and turned on the shower.

"What are you doing?" I yelled.

"You need to wallow? Do that in here." He set me down, fully clothed, under the cold spray.

"It's cold!" I screamed but he ignored me, closing the shower curtain, stomping out of the bathroom and slamming the bathroom door behind him.

"I cannot believe he did that." With gritted teeth, I stripped off my drenched clothes as the water started to warm up. I took out my frustration on my hair and skin, scrubbing and lathering with vengeance.

I was in the middle of my second shampoo when the bathroom door clicked open and then closed again. When I stepped out of the shower, clean laundry and a hair dryer were sitting on the counter.

Curses. It was going to be really tough to stay mad when he'd brought me the one beauty tool I coveted more than any other.

I got dressed, dried my hair, and by the time I emerged from the steamy bathroom, my temper had fizzled. Four days had been much too long without a shower and I was glad Beau had forced me to get up. Something I would never admit out loud, obviously, but I would apologize for yelling at him.

"Hey. Sorry I was a bi—" I stopped short when I saw what he was doing in the kitchen. "You brought me a coffee machine?"

He shrugged. "A couch was too big."

And with that, all residual anger vanished. "I'm sorry for yelling at you."

He grinned. "Don't worry about it. Sorry for throwing you in the shower."

"I needed one." So much for keeping that tidbit to myself.

"So, are you done pouting?"

"What? I wasn't pouting," I said defensively. "Sometimes I just get sad and it takes a while to work itself out."

"You were pouting, Sabrina. Just like that first week we were here and you were avoiding me."

"I think I'm more qualified to evaluate my mental state than you are, Beau."

"Oh, I'm plenty qualified. I told you already, I've got a damn accurate read on you. You were moping around. I'm not saying you haven't been through some shit, but last week you were perfectly content. I leave and you go back to pouting."

"I have gone through some 'shit,'" I snapped. "So let me deal with it in whatever way I need. If that means 'moping around,' then that's what I'm going to do."

"Stop with the air quotes and calm the hell down."

My blood pressure skyrocketed again, but before I could open my mouth to kick his ass back to Prescott, he picked me up and set me on the kitchen counter.

"I've had quite enough of your manhandling." My pointed finger didn't faze him a bit.

He just pulled it down and trapped it on the counter under his big mitt. "Do you think Maisy wasn't depressed after all that shit went down with Coby's dad?" His question stunned me into silence. "She went through a really difficult period and we all took care to respect the way she needed to come to grips with it all. She needed to be handled gently. You don't."

That hurt. My situation wasn't nearly as difficult as Maisy's must have been but that didn't mean I wasn't reeling from all of the sudden changes to my life.

He noticed the pained expression on my face and stepped closer, moving right into my space and stroking down the sides of my arms. "You've got grit. I've seen it. I'm not making light of what you've got going on. You've had a difficult month and I understand that. But sometimes even the toughest people need a kick in the ass to snap themselves into a better place."

I searched his eyes for any hint of exaggeration but they were pure and honest. His faith in me was humbling. "You're giving me too much credit."

"You're not giving yourself enough."

"Okay. I'm done pouting now," I whispered.

He chuckled and moved his hands to my face, leaning in to brush his soft, full, pink lips against my forehead.

Oh, boy. I was so smitten with this man.

"How long do you get to stay?" I hoped the change of topic would help me resist the urge to lean into Beau's space and test those lips against my own.

"Just until tomorrow. Things are a wreck at work so I need to get back but I didn't want you to wait a whole week for supplies."

"I'm glad to have you back. I'll help you unload the truck."

He stared at me for a long moment, still sharing my space. "We're good?"

I nodded. "We're good."

He squeezed my arms one last time before turning to leave. He'd been back for no more than an hour and I felt like a new woman. He had done the right thing, giving me that figurative kick in the ass. No one had ever done that for me before.

My parents would cater to my bad moods, fussing and fawning over me until I snapped myself out of the funk. Even Felicity had tended to indulge my sad days when we'd been roommates. She'd bring me chocolate and paint my nails until I was ready to get out of bed and go to class or work.

Beau did have a good read on me. Maybe better than I had on myself.

"Beau?" I called from the counter before he could step outside. "Thanks. Most people tend to avoid me when I get blue."

"You're welcome. Does it happen a lot?"

"Not so much anymore." I took a deep breath, summoning the strength to tell him something that I had only confessed to a few people. "I went through a tough time after Janessa committed suicide. She was my best friend in high school."

That got his attention. "What?"

"She died when we were sixteen."

"Shit. I'm sorry." He came back inside and stood beside me, his hip brushing my knee.

"Me too." I gave him a sad smile. "My parents and brothers didn't really know how to deal with me back then. I was sad and angry most of the time, lashing out at them and my teachers when I wasn't curled up in bed crying. They finally took me to a therapist so I had someone impartial to talk to."

My therapist had helped me through the darkest time in my young life. She'd given me permission to grieve and feel sad, but she'd also taught me that life goes on and I had to put a time limit on wallowing.

"It wasn't until after college that I realized there wasn't anything I could have done for Janessa. But the sad times, they still happen. When they do, I revert back to some of those old habits. I let the sad run its course, then put it in the past."

"Fuck me." He rubbed a hand over his beard. "I didn't know. I shouldn't have—"

"No, trust me. You did the right thing."

"Really? Then why do I feel like such a prick right now?"

I smiled. "Don't feel bad. Wallowing wasn't helping me. I've been using a coping mechanism that was appropriate for a sixteen-year-old girl, not a thirty-four-year-old woman. You were right. I was moping around and feeling sorry for myself. It was time to get up. Please don't feel bad. I'm just telling you all this because . . . well, I felt safe telling you."

He threw an arm around my shoulders. "You can tell me anything."

Of that, I had no doubt.

CHAPTER SIX

SABRINA

"You brought me a TV too?" I screamed in delight when I saw the small box in the back seat of Beau's truck.

"Don't get too excited," he said. "It's pretty fucking old. I picked it up at the pawn shop and the clerk said the built-in DVD player might not work."

"I appreciate it anyway."

There were few men as thoughtful as Beau. He made me realize the men I had chosen to date were nothing but a group of pompous jerks and narcissists. Men more interested in their bank account balance and social status than me. Those men liked me because I was arm candy. Beau actually listened when we were talking. He cared what I had to say.

I'd bet millions that Beau was a world-class boyfriend. He didn't give a lick about his hairstyle or fashion sense. His Hanes T-shirts and ten-dollar haircuts suited him just fine. The ladies of Prescott were probably falling all over themselves for his attention.

I was lucky to have it, even for a brief time, and when I got back to Seattle, I was upping my standards.

"What's in here?" I asked, lifting a huge black backpack off the truck's floor and slugging it over my shoulder. He'd already brought me everything from my wish list, except the couch.

"It's from Felicity. There's a letter from her in the glove box too."

My smile grew to kilowatt levels as I scrambled to the front of the truck, desperate for any connection to my friend. Ripping open the envelope, I took in her beautiful, swirly handwriting. It was the same script I used to see on our shared bathroom mirror when she'd leave me little messages before tests or job interviews.

Miss you.
You're probably going crazy so I've thought of a solution.
Write me a story.
xoxo

I smiled, tucked the note in my pocket and hustled inside, excited to see what was in my backpack. When I pulled out a sleek gray laptop, I laughed at her trickery.

Felicity loved romance novels and had begged me more times than I could count to write one of my own. I had always brushed it off, being too busy with the newspaper and advancing my career to even consider moonlighting in fiction. But now that I had nothing but time, I had no excuse not to try something I had secretly always wanted to do.

My friend knew me all too well.

I went back to the bag and fished out a bag of my favorite dark chocolates, a manicure kit and some feminine products.

I laughed again, grateful that she'd thought to refill my tampons so I wouldn't have to add them to Beau's grocery list, though I doubted he would have cared. He was the type of man who would bring his woman tampons without comment or complaint.

"Yes!" I cheered when I retrieved my last item.

Felicity had sent me a pair of jeans from my favorite designer. I hugged them to my chest and pressed my face into the soft denim. I'd missed jeans. My wardrobe of leggings, yoga pants, T-shirts, athletic zip-ups and hoodies was comfortable but slouchy. I rushed to the bathroom and quickly swapped out pants. The structured seams and thick material felt glorious against my skin.

"Good stuff?" Beau asked, bringing in a cooler as I emerged in my new attire. His eyes lingered on my legs for a brief moment before he got to work stocking up the fridge.

"Yeah," I said. "I miss my Felicity though. Is she doing okay?"

I hadn't seen her in a month. April had come and gone and now it was May. I was in that weird limbo of time where it seemed like I'd been here forever and yet no time at all.

"She's good. Keeping Silas on his toes."

"I bet he likes it."

Beau chuckled. "I know he does."

I was grateful that my friend had found her happily ever after. Felicity was so hard on herself, taking the blame for things that were outside of her control. I was overjoyed that Silas had helped her see just how special she was. To see what I had always seen. Behind her prickly exterior was a heart of gold.

I put away my new belongings, sending good thoughts

into the universe for my beautiful, caring and feisty friend before going back outside.

Beau and I spent the next hour unloading supplies and setting up my new entertainment unit, that being a box with the, luckily, working television on top. When Beau handed me a pile of movies, I scanned the titles and stared at him in disbelief. I had asked for chick flicks but what he'd brought were even better. Cheesy action films and unrated comedies. I didn't believe in soul mates but Beau was starting to make me rethink that position.

Since I couldn't thank him with a kiss, I did the next best thing. I gave him the tightest hug I could muster with my scrawny arms. "Thank you, Goliath."

He didn't hesitate in wrapping me up, my cheek squishing even further into his rock-solid chest. "You're welcome, Shortcake."

I leaned back so I could look at his face. "Shortcake?"

"Seems only fair that you have a nickname too."

I shook my head. "But I'm not short. And cake? I'm the farthest thing from sweet."

One of his arms unwound from behind me so his hand could cup my jaw. With his thumb stroking my cheek and his fingers threaded into my hair, he whispered, "You're sweet, and to me, you'll always be short."

My knees buckled. They actually *buckled* and he hadn't even kissed me. Heaven help me if he ever did. I'd probably faint and miss all the good stuff.

"Easy," he said, taking my weight and lifting me back up. "Are you okay?" His sexy, low voice made my knees wobble again.

"Uh-huh," I breathed. When his brows furrowed, I

cleared my throat and spoke with more confidence. "I'm okay."

"Are you sure? Do you need to sit?"

I shook my head, not wanting his arms to go anywhere. "Just a little light-headed."

The heat from his chest was radiating against my breasts and my heart started pumping double time. When Beau and I were close like this, my body's reaction was completely out of my control. I wanted him with a wildness I'd never felt before.

The throbbing between my legs wasn't just a dull twinge, it was a fierce and desperate ache. It took every ounce of willpower not to unwind my hands from his waist and move them to the button on his jeans.

I doubted he'd push me away but I didn't want to put him in the uncomfortable position to make that choice. He had been clear. *We are just friends. Repeat. We are just friends.*

"Sabrina?" Beau's concerned voice snapped me out of my sexual haze.

Needing some distance before I did something to embarrass myself, I pushed out of his hold and took a step back. "I'm better now. Maybe I'm just hungry or need some air."

He grinned. "That happens when you spend four days living off nothing but granola bars."

"Ha, ha," I said dryly. "Do you, uh, want to go for a walk before dinner?"

Having spent the last four days inside, I was craving some sunshine and fresh air. That and I needed to cool off. That hug had turned me really hot, really fast. Too bad it was one-sided. Beau was still staring at me like I might faint.

"Okay," he drawled. "If you think you can handle it."

"I'm sure."

He nodded and walked around me to the door, calling for Boone as he stepped outside.

I was relieved that my low-blood-sugar lie had worked and he hadn't seemed to notice that my reaction had been purely sexual. I didn't need another one of his reminders that we would always be platonic. My own affirmations were harsh enough.

Beau was way too good for me. He deserved a wholesome woman. The minute I'd started to date Anton, wholesome had gone out the window.

As I walked outside, I reminded myself again and again that Beau and I were from two different worlds, wincing with the familiar twist in my stomach. But by the time we stepped out of the trees and into the open meadow, my disappointment had been pushed to the back of my mind—not forgotten, but no longer center stage.

Beau and I wandered across the empty field, taking in the warm sunlight and slight breeze. Our pace was much slower than the last time we'd come out together. The green grasses, now thick and lush, had surged to new heights these last few weeks of spring and I had to bring my knees up high just to wade through it all.

I kept thinking about Beau's words from earlier today. *You can tell me anything.* The only person I really confided in was Felicity, but Beau shared her confidence and strength. He wasn't letting me shut him out. So by the midpoint of our walk, I had decided to take him up on that offer and tell him what I'd been considering recently.

"So, while I was resting these last few days, I did some thinking."

"Resting?" He looked at me skeptically, like he expected

whatever I had concocted during my four-day wallow session to be pure insanity.

"Resting," I insisted. "Let's move on, shall we?"

He smirked. "Continue."

"I've been thinking about returning home and going to the FBI."

His feet ground to a halt. "What?"

"It might be for the best. I'm in way over my head here and there's only so much hiding out I can do. Eventually, I have to return to civilization."

"You really hate it here that much?"

"No! Not at all." Surprisingly, that was the truth.

Sometime in the last month, I had grown to like my little outpost home, especially when Beau was around. But he couldn't stay with me forever and, at some point, I'd have to face the dangers waiting for me in Seattle.

The corners of his mouth curled up. "I'm glad to hear it. So why would you want to leave?"

"I don't want to be a burden." It was cathartic to say that out loud.

I had grown accustomed to relying on no one and standing on my own two feet. My successes had come from *my* hard work. My failures from *my* shortcomings. My independence was a huge part of my self-worth. Now that it was gone? I was struggling to find myself.

And I hated being at the mercy of another person.

My aversion to dependence was probably the reason why I'd never had a successful long-term relationship. When it was just me, I wouldn't have to worry that someone else would let me down. Janessa had let me down when she'd killed herself, and besides Felicity, I hadn't let someone else in that fully ever since. Except Beau.

He was sneaking past my weakened defenses. My reliance on him was pushing some of those personal limits I'd come to rely on to keep from getting hurt and maybe that was a sign I needed to leave.

"You're not a burden, Sabrina."

"I need you for everything. That is the definition of a burden."

"No, the definition of a burden is a heavy load. Nothing about this feels heavy to me. I've told you before, I don't mind. You know how much I love it up here. And spending time with you is fun. Well, when you shower."

I smiled at his tease. "Eventually, you're going to want to get back to your life."

"Forget about me. What about you? What happens when you go to the FBI?"

I shrugged. "I'm not sure. Witness protection maybe?"

"Witness protection? You'd have to say good-bye to your friends and family. You wouldn't even get to be *you* anymore. That's the life you want?"

"Honestly? I'm not sure I have any other choice."

My throat tightened at the thought of never seeing my family again. Never getting to hug my mom or standing on my tiptoes to kiss my dad's cheek. And I'd have to say good-bye to Felicity. I wouldn't get to be a part of her wedding or meet the babies she and Silas would someday create.

In my time at the outpost, I'd come to see things more clearly. Panic and stubbornness had disguised it earlier, but my choices were limited.

Eventually, I'd say good-bye to Beau and this mountain valley. Sabrina MacKenzie would be no more.

My life would end, whether the Federovs killed me or not.

"Just . . . chill out, little dude," Beau declared. His easy tone was such a departure from the dark thoughts in my head it shocked me, and the words "chill" and "dude" sounded hilariously out of place coming from Beau's serious face.

" 'Chill out, little dude'? A phrase I never would have expected you to say."

"It's Maisy," he grumbled. "She says it to Coby all the time and I guess it rubbed off. Anyway. What I mean is, *relax*. You've only been here for a month. Give it more time. In a few more months, the Federovs might be locked up for good and you can go back to being Sabrina MacKenzie, superhero reporter."

I grinned and sighed. "Okay."

He was right. It was too soon to know how this would all shake out.

We resumed our walk, silently strolling further into the meadow. My head started churning again, this time thinking about my career. Beau had called me a superhero reporter. Was that who I still was? Could I even be a reporter anymore?

Even if my boss had had to give away my job, I had no doubt that I would be able to find a new one. But did I even want that life anymore? My twenty-two-year-old self would be aghast that I was considering giving up a career I had worked so hard to attain.

I missed that young woman. I longed to be her again. She was a fledgling, idealistic journalist fresh out of college, excited at what her future had in store. She had such a bright outlook on life. She was untainted by the harsh realities of just how far a reporter could fall when tempted by that unattainable story.

Could I ever get back to where she was?

No.

Too many lines had been crossed. Too many of my principles had been compromised. Over the years, I'd lied to get information from sources. I'd manipulated confessions from witnesses who had wanted to remain quiet. But using sex and seduction to get the Federov story had been my final fall from grace.

That wasn't the type of journalist I'd set out to become. I'd learned the hard way that undercover work like that didn't sit well with my conscience.

No, my dreams of being a reporter were over.

My career had been my sole focus for so long, did I even know how to dream anymore?

"What are your dreams, Beau?"

He was so put-together, so confident. Not in a cocky way, just sure of himself and the path he was on. If he still had dreams to achieve, maybe I wouldn't feel so far behind. I wouldn't feel like I had just crossed the finish line only to learn the race I was supposed to be running had just begun and my competitors were already halfway around the track.

"Dreams?" he asked, surprised by my seemingly random question.

"Yeah, your dreams. Do you have everything you want in life?"

He pulled in a deep breath before answering, his chest swelling to twice its gigantic size. "I don't know if I've ever had dreams."

Was it wrong that his sad statement made me feel better? Maybe I didn't need dreams either.

"I'm not really a dreamer," he said. "I set goals and work hard to achieve them."

Goals. I liked that. The word itself seemed less daunting. Goals were reached methodically. Goals were within one's control. If you missed a goal, your soul wouldn't be crushed and your hopes wouldn't be shattered. You'd just reset your priorities, make a new plan and trudge onward. Heartache and disappointment were not part of the equation.

Forget dreams. Beau's goals sounded like just the thing for me.

"Tell me more about your goals."

"I wouldn't say they're anything out of the ordinary. They're probably fairly similar to most peoples'. I've got the only job I've ever wanted. After twelve years, I still like going to work every day. I have a good relationship with my family, and the time we spend together is fun. I love my town and do my best to support my community. My biggest goal is not fucking that up."

He bent to pick up a long stem of grass, twirling it between his fingers. "But you asked, do I have everything I want in life? No, not yet. I would like a family someday. A wife. Kids of my own. I want to make memories with them like the ones I have from my childhood. Take them to all those places my dad took me."

"I'm intrigued."

He smiled. "It wasn't anything fancy. My parents didn't have a ton of extra cash for five people to fly all over the world so we mostly just traveled around Montana. We camped and fished in the summer. Went skiing in the winter. My dad bought a ski boat when I started high school so, from that summer on, we went waterskiing as much as we could."

His childhood vacations sounded simple and pure. The exact opposite of any family trip I could remember.

"My parents only believed in *enlightening* travel experiences," I told him. "My entire life, I can't remember a single trip we took that was just for fun. You'd think that since we lived in Florida, they would have at least taken us to Disney World, but I've never been."

"Child abuse." He grinned, tucking the piece of grass he'd been twirling into the hair behind my ear. "I'll make you a deal, Shortcake. When the mafia isn't a threat, you're not considering WITSEC and life goes back to normal, I'll meet you in Disney World and take you on the vacation six-year-old Sabrina never had."

I smiled. "You've got a deal, Goliath."

"Good. Now, tell me. What exactly are 'enlightening' travel experiences?"

I laughed and told him all about the trips I had taken in my youth.

He listened to me talk about the month we had spent in Europe, bouncing from country to country. How we had all contracted bed bugs in one of our last stops and brought them back home.

He laughed when I told him that my parents had taken us to China and gotten sick one night when they'd insisted on eating duck heads and deep-fried scorpions from a street vendor.

He smiled when I told him about the beach cottage my parents had rented one winter on the Oregon coast. My parents had purposefully reserved it during the worse possible season so we would learn to appreciate the warm weather of Florida. My brothers had obviously learned the intended lesson since they hadn't strayed much from home but, much to my mom's chagrin, I had found the rain mixed with the salty air comforting. That trip had inspired me to choose Seattle when I was browsing colleges.

"It was eye-opening to see different cultures and environments," I said, "and it wasn't that the trips were horrible. My parents paid a lot for them, so I don't want to sound ungrateful. But when my friends came home from their summer breaks with stories about amusement parks and beach expeditions, I was so jealous. Teenage me didn't appreciate my experiences like I do now."

"So, you just needed time. Does that mean one day you'll appreciate *this* enlightening travel experience?"

I laughed. "Yes, I'm sure I will. What would you say your most educational trip has been?"

"Probably my senior class trip to Washington D.C. It was the first and only trip I've ever taken to the East Coast. It was my first real trip period. Before then, I'd never been on an airplane. Hell, I'd rarely ever stayed in a hotel room before that. The museums and monuments were awesome but the whole travel adventure itself was what I remember the most."

"Have you traveled much since?" I asked.

"Nah. I went to Denver with some buddies for a concert in college. Vegas for a party weekend. Michael's the traveler in our family. He takes a vacation at least once a year to someplace exotic. Maisy probably would too if it weren't for Coby. I'm content to stay here where I belong."

Where he belonged.

Where I didn't.

Why did that idea bother me so much? It was the truth.

I had no desire to live in rural Montana. I'd go crazy in Prescott. I needed fast-paced streets and faceless crowds. I needed to live in a county where there were more people than cows. I was a city girl.

Even if I liked the clear night skies of the mountains. Even if I liked the quiet evenings blessedly free of traffic noise. Even if I liked the longer days because I wasn't wasting time waiting for a late bus. I was a city girl.

So why wouldn't the knot in my stomach go away?

It had to be this crazy fucking situation, right?

Right.

Having my life turned upside down was unearthing all of these new doubts.

Being around Beau wasn't helping.

This pull I had toward him was magnetic, the strongest I'd ever felt toward another person. In the deepest, darkest recesses of my mind, I pictured a relationship with him. I pictured a *life* with him.

Impossible pictures.

Beau needed a woman who would be his camping co-captain. Who would trail along behind him on an outdoor adventure as he taught their children about wildlife and navigating forest trails. A woman who would love his sleepy town and going to the small-town high school's football games each Friday night.

He needed a woman who didn't get ecstatic at the sight of a hair dryer and designer jeans.

So why, when I knew all these things, were they so hard to accept?

Because I liked him that much.

It probably wasn't helping that he was giving me mixed signals. He was so damn affectionate. Was this how he was with his other female friends? The hair touching. The hand-holding. The hugs. He'd gone to high school with Felicity; I wished I could ask her.

But since I couldn't, I resigned myself to putting some distance between us.

Somehow, I had to kill these silly feelings. These silly dreams.

I was done dreaming.

My goal was to survive this experience and go home, without a broken heart.

As we walked back to the outpost, I made sure to let Boone run between our feet so my shoulder couldn't brush against Beau's arm. I cooked him dinner, insisting that he hang out in the living area so I had full control of the kitchen and wouldn't risk bumping against him. And while we watched a movie together, I curled up on my cot while he sat on the log chair, three feet away.

I had done well all evening, establishing distance, but when I emerged from the bathroom, wearing pajamas and my long hair tied in a sleek ponytail, I couldn't resist climbing into the bed Beau had laid out on the floor and sleeping in his strong arms.

BEAU

"Unka Bo!"

"Hey, buddy." I bent low to catch Coby as he launched his small body at my legs. With one quick toss, he was flying in the air, nearly skimming the ceiling. I'd missed his little laugh and squeal so much, I did it again.

"Good thing we've got tall ceilings in here," Maisy said.

The lobby of her motel wasn't a big space but it was nice and inviting. I had helped Maisy remodel it and her adjoining office when she'd bought the motel from the previous owners. Maisy had great style but a small budget, and I'd spent more weekends than I could count helping her fix it up so she could save some cash.

Propping Coby on my side, I reached out to give Maisy a one-arm hug. "Thanks for having me over for dinner."

"Anytime. We've missed you."

"I've missed you guys too."

"I'm glad we'll finally have a chance to catch up."

Maisy wanted the full scoop on Sabrina and how things had gone at the outpost this last month. There had been so much activity since I'd come home after those first three weeks I hadn't had the time to catch her up.

Instead, I'd been putting out fires.

Work was a disaster. When I wasn't at the outpost, I was in the office, picking up dropped balls and getting projects back on track from my three-week disappearance. I'd only taken one break and that was to have dinner at my parents' house.

Mom and Dad had wanted to know all about my fake search and rescue case so I'd spent the meal evading questions. Luckily, Maisy had been there too and she'd helped distract them with stories about motel guests.

"Do you need to finish anything?" I asked, glancing around the lobby. "I can hang with Coby for a while if you need to stay down here."

She shook her head. "I'll just put a sign up for people to call if they need anything."

Most of the year, Maisy was a one-woman show at the motel. During the summer tourist season, when things were at their busiest, she'd hire a part-time housekeeper to help clean and do the laundry, but even then, she worked from sunup to sundown.

I was proud of my sister for making this a successful business. Her hard work had built a great life for her and Coby.

While Maisy locked the door, cleared off the front desk and shut off the light in her office, I tickled and teased Coby. Then we went up the stairwell that led to her small loft apartment above the motel's lobby.

"Pway Wegos," Coby said, pulling me to his room the second we crossed into his home.

I looked over my shoulder at Maisy, who was smiling and waving us out of her way. "I'll call you when dinner is ready."

"Thanks." I had spent so little time with Coby the last month I couldn't believe how much he'd changed. He was right in the middle of the transition from toddler to little boy. Maisy had cut his hair recently and he looked more grown-up than ever.

Playing Legos with him was exactly what I'd needed to let go of some of the stress. After playtime and an awesome meal, Maisy gave Coby a bath and I tucked him into bed. Then Maisy and I settled on opposite sides of her couch to talk.

"So, how is Sabrina doing?"

"She's okay. The beginning was rough but I think she's getting settled." Rough was an understatement. When I'd seen the pained and terrified look in Sabrina's eyes that first night, I'd almost loaded her back up in the truck and brought her home with me.

"Have all of her injuries healed okay?"

I nodded. "Her ribs are still tender but everything else is

fine." Sabrina's face was back to normal. Her full lips and perfectly shaped nose were no longer covered in welts and gashes. She was as beautiful a woman as I'd ever seen.

Maisy grinned and mischief flickered in her eyes. "And you two got along okay?"

"Maze, stop."

"What?" she said, feigning innocence.

"No matchmaking. Save it for your single friends or Michael."

"I'm not matchmaking, but I'm not blind. That woman totally liked you and you're no good at hiding a crush from me, big brother."

Damn it. There was no point in pretending she wasn't right. "I like her," I admitted. "She's smart and funny. We have a good time together. I just don't see us having a future. The second she's free to return to the city, she'll be gone in a flash and never look back."

"You don't know that."

"I know it. Trust me, Maze. She doesn't have a country bone in her body."

"People change, Beau."

"Not that much." I couldn't get my hopes up with this one. Sabrina was everything I'd ever wanted in a woman but fitting her into my lifestyle was the definition of square peg, round hole.

"You could move with her."

I scoffed. "Me in the city? I'd hate it."

Besides that, who else could do my job? Or be around to help Maisy with her motel remodeling projects? Or be a father figure to Coby? That kid needed me in Prescott. A lot of people needed me in Prescott. Which meant when Sabrina went back to Seattle, I'd be left behind.

"Well," Maisy said, "I don't think you should count her out yet. She might end up liking it here if you two got together."

I shook my head. "I'll do whatever I can to keep her safe, but our relationship is going to stay platonic." Anything more would be asking for trouble.

I'd already gone too far.

Sleeping with Sabrina in my arms had been a huge fucking mistake. It was too easy to picture her there for good. It was the best sleep I'd ever had. When I'd left the outpost three nights ago, I'd known it was time to pull back. I was getting way too fucking attached.

My life was here in Prescott and Sabrina's was in Seattle. This was temporary.

Which meant it was time to put some distance between me and the outpost.

No more staying the night. No more cuddling and sleeping together. No more kidding myself that she'd learn to love it here.

Because she'd never stay.

CHAPTER SEVEN

SABRINA

My eyes were closed but I knew Beau was moving in. The heat from his full lips intensified as they came closer and closer. My heart pounded louder with every passing second that his lips hovered above mine but didn't touch.

I fought to keep my eyes closed, but eventually, I gave into the temptation and opened them. Beau's gaze was waiting to lock with mine. His eyes were a hurricane of gray and blue clouds, darkening with every one of his heavy pants. The erection against my hip was swelling, hard and thick. I lifted my hips up further, wanting my body touching its entire length.

His tongue darted out and touched his lip, causing a wave of heat to pool between my legs. I desperately wanted to be the one to wet that soft, pink bottom lip. I slowly lifted my head, inching my face closer to his, but then he was gone.

Beau's head jerked back a foot, recoiling from me like a

spring. His arm yanked from underneath my neck. The hand that had lifted up my camisole to splay across my ribs was now held high in the air like he'd touched a hot plate. The desire in his eyes had vanished, replaced by disgust. The top lip I had been longing to feel against my own was now curled up on one side.

He didn't have to explain. I knew exactly why he had retreated.

Beau Holt did not get involved with whores like me.

I pressed my face further into my pillow and groaned. That dream was getting old. Really fucking old.

I'd been having the same one off and on for the last couple of weeks. It was almost guaranteed that I'd have it after writing a sex scene in my novel, and since yesterday I'd written a doozy, it came as no shock that Beau had found my sleep. If only I had the ability to change that ending and feel his lips move against mine. Even if it were all in my head, I'd take it. I was beyond sexually frustrated—another side effect of writing sex scenes.

Beau's presence always left me charged, so the fact that he'd been scarce lately should have cooled me off. But here I was, desperate for some relief.

It had been over a month since Beau had spent the night at the outpost. Not since the day he had forced me into the shower and out of my funk. The same night we had crossed some invisible emotional boundary, causing him to pull back and put some distance between us.

After I had crawled into his arms that last night, we'd talked in hushed voices, laughing and teasing one another. Minus the actual sex, it had been the most perfect postcoital cuddle of my entire life. It had been intimate and raw. Real and honest. The threads connecting our hearts had felt stronger, like industrial chains rather than loosely woven fibers.

The next morning, I had woken up alone, something I hadn't done since I'd started sleeping with Beau on the floor. He had avoided my eyes and left not long after breakfast.

Since then, he had only come up for brief, once-a-week day trips. He'd leave Prescott in the morning, arriving at the outpost before lunch. We'd share a quiet but polite meal before unpacking whatever supplies he'd brought, then he'd say good-bye, leaving to make the three-hour journey back to town so he could get home before dinner.

The distance was a good thing—my new mantra.

Yes, it had dinged my pride to feel that rejection from Beau but it really had been good for me.

During the first month at the outpost, I had let myself get swept up in all that Beau goodness. His strength. His gentle nature. His calming essence. I had convinced myself that I'd be fine at the outpost as long as he was by my side.

But he'd left and I had found a new determination to make this work on my own. I'd prove to myself that I could stay in this place alone. That I could be content here. I'd take back some of the independence I had lost when I'd been forced to hide in the woods.

Those were my goals.

My plan for achieving them was simple.

Write a book.

Now, a month later, it was almost done.

Forcing my face out of the pillow, I sat on the edge of my cot, swinging the sleep from my legs as I stretched my arms to the ceiling. Boone crawled out from beneath me and rested his chin on my thigh for a good-morning scratch.

"Last chapter today, buddy," I said. "Let's get after it."

Quickly showering and blow-drying my hair, I threw on my freshly hand-washed jeans and a simple white T-shirt. The June weather was cool in the morning, but by mid-afternoon, the outpost would be quite warm and I would drag my chair outside to write in the shade of the trees.

I made myself coffee, savoring its bitter warmth, and settled into the log chair.

My writing chair.

I was already rehearsing my speech to beg Beau to let me take it home to Seattle.

Opening my laptop, I scrolled to the bottom of my novel and started hammering away at the keyboard. My heroine's ending was perfectly scripted in my mind. Today, she and her hero were finally getting their happily ever after.

Four hours later, I stared at my screen, unblinking.

I'd done it. I'd written a novel.

It was undeniably surreal. Remarkable, really. Pride swelled in my chest as tears of joy flooded my eyes.

I *loved* my story.

The manuscript needed editing and a thorough proofread, but the story itself was a solid first draft. My characters weren't perfect, they were real. Fitting one another into their lives took work. They struggled on their journey, dealing with personal battles not easy to fight alone, but they learned how to trust in each other.

I loved *my* story.

I had loved *writing* my story.

Giving myself to it completely, I had let this process consume me in a freeing way. There were no rules to my writing. I could dictate everything and anything I wanted for my characters.

There wasn't a fact-checker questioning everything I had

done. My boss wasn't pressuring me to beat a deadline. The newspaper executives weren't requiring me to spin the story a certain way. It had been, by far, the most enlightening and rewarding writing experience I'd had since college.

Even if I only sold ten copies, I didn't care. Writing this novel had been better therapy than paying a trained professional ever could have been.

The main character was the flawed version of myself, struggling to overcome poor decisions. Her biggest regret was mine, having traded her morals to advance her career. Yet the hero loved her anyway. He cherished her imperfections.

Fiction was remarkable. I could give her the man I'd never find, a man that didn't exist in the real world. Because no decent, honorable, kind man would want anything to do with me.

Anton had called me a whore the night he'd nearly beaten me to death.

It was true.

I'd slept my way to a story.

Had I screwed him to get evidence to stop his criminal empire? Yes.

Had I had sex with him because I'd known it would advance my career? Unfortunately, the answer to that question was also yes.

I'd slept with Anton—a man I loathed—for months because I'd wanted to become the next Diane Sawyer or Barbara Walters.

I doubted I'd ever forgive myself, but writing my book had helped.

It had given me a chance to write the ending *I* wanted.

My heroine had moved past her former transgressions.

She had found a new life where she could feel good about herself.

Maybe someday I'd find a piece of her happy ending for myself.

Regardless, the writing had given me an outlet. Not only had writing been therapeutic, it had given me a purpose. I was working toward something, not just sitting idle. I was finding the driven, ambitious woman that had been missing since I'd arrived at the outpost.

I was finding me again.

A tear rolled down my cheek and dropped on my shirt. I didn't try to blink it away, I just let it, and the ones that followed, fall.

They weren't sad.

They were full of hope.

I smiled, bringing a hand over my mouth to laugh.

I wrote a book.

Closing the lid on my laptop, I set it aside and stood. The room was too small for how big I felt so I rushed outside. By the time I hit the tree line into the meadow, I was running with Boone nipping playfully at my heels.

I bounced and twirled into the open sunlight, the scent of pine needles and green grass filling my nose, the smell intoxicating and wonderful. It was light and clean, sweet and full of promise.

"Woo-hoo!" I yelled into the open air, tipping my head back to the sky as I twirled with my arms out at my sides. Boone barked and jumped at my feet. "I wrote a book!" I laughed and shouted again.

Spinning and dancing, I let my smile shine. I was going full-on *Sound of Music*, "The hills are alive." Julie Andrews had nothing on the pure joy I felt for the first time in . . . far too long.

And then it hit me.

An idea for novel number two.

I smiled, yelled for Boone and dashed back to the outpost.

The words on my first book were barely dry, metaphorically speaking, but I didn't care.

Hours later, I had crafted chapter one of my second novel and it felt *amazing*.

I wasn't a reporter anymore. I was an author.

And I wasn't ever looking back.

———

I STOWED my laptop and rushed to the door when the noise of an approaching vehicle sounded outside.

Just like I always did, I cracked the door and peered through the small opening to make sure it was Beau. It hadn't been a week yet since his last visit so my heart was pounding faster than normal. When his truck, Green Colossus, came into view, I relaxed and let out the breath I'd been holding.

I had no idea what I'd do if someone other than Beau came to the outpost. Probably freak the fuck out, then hide in the bathroom.

Beau parked and got out of his truck, rounding the hood my way. I sucked in a couple short breaths as my heart skipped a beat. The sight of him affected me every damn time just like the first.

"Hey, Goliath."

"Hey." He didn't smile. He didn't call me Shortcake. He

just came right into my space and steered me by the elbow back inside.

Something wasn't right.

"What's wrong?" My hands started trembling as panic set in. Was it my family? Or Felicity? Had the Federovs gotten to someone I loved?

He let my elbow go and looked me up and down. When he'd determined I was fine, he started rubbing his bearded jaw.

"Beau?" My voice cracked. Nothing good was going to come from his mouth.

"Ivan Federov showed in Prescott today."

My heart dropped to my stomach and the blood drained from my face. Beau reached out and caught my hand, steadying me.

Why was Anton's brother in Prescott? Shouldn't he be confined to the city? And if Ivan had come to Montana, did that mean Anton was in Florida?

"Come here," Beau said, leading me to the log chair to sit. He crouched down in front of me and took my hand. "Everyone is fine. Take a breath."

I nodded and sucked in some air. My hands were still shaking but the oxygen stopped my head from spinning.

"Better?" he asked.

"Yeah. What happened?"

"Ivan showed at the motel this morning. He asked Maisy for a room and chatted with her a bit. He gave her a fake ID and some bullshit story about being a private investigator hired by your family to track you down. Then he showed her your picture and asked if you had come by."

Damn my story. Not only had I endangered my friends and family but I had pulled Beau's family into this mix too.

His sister, with an adorable little boy, was conversing with criminals.

"You're sure it was Ivan and not Anton? They look a lot alike." Ivan was more relaxed than his brother and, as far as I knew, less violent. I didn't want Anton anywhere near Prescott.

"I'm sure. We've all been keeping an eye on the papers and their pictures. It was Ivan."

I let out a relieved sigh. "Okay. Then what?"

"Obviously, Maisy lied and said she'd never seen you before," Beau continued. "Ivan bought it, and after he went to his room, Maisy called me."

"You're sure that Ivan believed her?"

He nodded. "I'm sure. I was in the office when he came back in for an extra towel. The fucker was flirting with my sister and she played right along. He didn't suspect a thing."

"Good. What about Felicity?"

"She's fine. When Maisy called, I was with Silas and Jess eating breakfast at the café. I went to the motel and both of them went straight to Felicity's office."

"Did Ivan talk to her?"

"Yeah," he said. "He went down there after leaving the motel. Jess told me Felicity put on quite the show. Cried and everything as she begged Ivan to do everything he could to find you. How upset she's been since you went missing. She even thanked him for helping with the search."

Beau grinned and I couldn't help but do the same. The mental image of Felicity Cleary putting on an Oscar-winning performance to a fake private investigator was too much. I was almost sorry I missed it.

"Is he still in Prescott?" I asked.

"Yeah. Jess is keeping tabs on him. Ivan's been going all

over Prescott flashing your picture around. Silas is glued to Felicity's side. Dad and Michael are camping out with Maisy until he leaves the motel. I came here, just in case."

I was so glad that Beau had forced me to come to the outpost that first night and that I hadn't stayed in town and risked being seen. Ivan wouldn't learn a thing from this trip to Montana.

"How was Ivan allowed to leave Seattle?" The FBI should have been watching him. The articles I had read last month said he'd been arrested with his father and Anton. If they were out on bail, the judge would have ordered them to stay in the city.

"My guess is no one knows he's here," Beau said. "When I was at the motel, the vehicle he came in had Washington plates. He probably snuck out of town and drove over last night."

"He's taking a big risk if he's breaking bond. Why wouldn't they have just sent one of their goons? Why Ivan?"

He shook his head. "I don't know. If I had to guess? I'd say the Federovs are scrambling. Maybe they don't have anyone they can trust right now. Maybe their 'goons' are being watched too. Plus, Ivan is convincing. He's got charisma. Maybe they thought he'd have an easier time getting information from people around here."

A cold shiver crept up my back. "I hate that he's in Prescott."

These two months, I had fooled myself into thinking that running away had been the right decision. So much time had passed, I'd started to think that I was safe and that my loved ones were out of harm's way. Foolish hope. If any harm came to my friends or family, I would never forgive myself.

"I never should have run. I should have stayed in Seattle."

"What?"

My eyes met his as my mind raced through worst-case scenarios. "What if something bad happens? If I had just stayed in Seattle, then Ivan wouldn't be in Prescott. What if Anton is going to my family?"

"If you had stayed in Seattle, you'd probably be dead. Your parents would be planning your funeral, and the Federovs would be walking free. Let's just be glad you're here and hope Anton hasn't found a way to Florida."

I slumped in the chair. "I hate that I'm stuck here. That I'm in the dark with no information. I feel helpless."

"Come on." Beau held out a hand and pulled me up. "Let's take a drive up the ridge. You can check on your family. Read the news."

I nodded. "Okay."

"Just hang tough, Shortcake. This is going to end well. I promise." Beau's words held such conviction, I almost believed them.

We quickly made the terrifying trip up the ridge so I could use Beau's phone to research the case against the Federovs and check in on my family via social media. Unfortunately, the news articles weren't all that forthcoming, and as of late, the FBI hadn't made any revealing statements. All any article said was that the case was pending trial.

Thankfully, my family's posts were much more comforting.

"Well? Do you think your family got your letter?" Beau asked.

I smiled and nodded. "I'm sure of it. Look." I held the

phone out for him to see my brother's latest post. "He put one asterisk at the bottom."

The letter I'd sent to my parents earlier this spring had been fairly vague. I'd told them that I was okay, safe in hiding, and that I'd periodically check in on social media to make sure they were okay. I had instructed them to keep posting their pleas but I'd also asked that they include a code of asterisks so I knew they were okay. One asterisk for safe. Two if there had been any sign of the Federovs in Florida. Three if something bad had happened.

"That was a good idea to have them use the code," Beau said.

"Thanks. It was your good idea to send the letter in the first place."

"It's going to work out." This time his words were easier to believe.

When I was done checking in on my family, I looked up at Beau. "Can I watch the video again?"

He smiled and nodded.

I turned back to the phone, sure this video would put a smile on my face.

On Beau's last visit to the outpost, he'd brought me this video. I think I must have watched it fifty times that day and nearly cried each time.

Tapping play, I smiled as Main Street Prescott filled the small screen. The sound of an airplane buzzing through the air preceded a white plane zooming over town and streaming a sky banner.

Silas had asked Felicity to marry him on that banner. Beau had been there, and luckily for me since he stood so much taller than the average person, he had been able to capture not only the plane's proposal but also my friend's reaction. Felicity had rushed into Silas's arms to say yes.

Even though I hadn't been there, I hadn't missed it. Beau had seen to that.

"I'm sorry you weren't able to be there," Beau said after I watched the video twice.

I nodded. "Me too, but I'm glad Silas didn't wait for me."

Silas had sent a note along with Beau on one of his visits, telling me his plan to propose and asking if he should wait for me to be there. I'd told him no, not wanting to delay something that would make Felicity blissfully happy. I had already inconvenienced them enough. I didn't want their lives to be on hold because of me.

"Will you take another letter to Felicity?" I asked even though I knew the answer. Beau had become my own personal courier.

"You bet."

With a heavy heart, I was going to write Felicity and tell her to plan her wedding without me. I didn't want her to delay her special day on my account. Not with how uncertain things were. Missing her wedding would be brutal but I couldn't risk going. If the Federovs were smart, which they were, they'd likely be watching my best friend's wedding to see if I made an appearance.

With my phone tasks complete, Beau drove us down the opposite side of the ridge. The descent was far less treacherous than the journey up, though it took twice as long. By the time we got back to the outpost, it was early evening and I figured he'd be setting off for Prescott.

"Do you want any dinner before you go?" I asked.

"I'm staying tonight."

"Oh, okay." A swell of nervous energy bubbled up in my

chest. Beau hadn't stayed in over a month, and the last time, we'd had that amazing connection. The one that had caused him to pull away. Was tonight going to be miserably awkward? Or would we fall back into that place where we had been?

I hoped for the latter as I opened the truck door.

Before I could hop down, Beau declared, "Before it gets dark, we're going to do some shooting."

I froze. "What was that?" I had no desire to be anywhere near a gun. I hoped he meant shooting slingshots.

"Shooting. You know, with a gun."

"Yeah, that's not going to happen." I hated guns. It was one of the reasons why I had pushed so hard to take down the Federovs, and after what had happened to my high-school friend Janessa, I had every right.

"It is." Beau got out of the truck, completely ignoring me, and shut his truck door.

"Hey!" I jumped out after him and rounded the hood. "You don't get to dictate what I do."

He kept ignoring me as he opened the back door and pulled out a small, black handgun from under the driver's seat followed by a box of ammunition that had been resting on the floor.

"Let's go," he called, walking toward the meadow with Boone happily bouncing along at his feet.

"No." I fisted my hands and marched into the outpost.

Who did he think he was? He didn't get to summon me. To force me to do something I didn't want to do. He'd have to drag me into that meadow.

I paced the outpost, waiting for him to come in on my heels. Sure enough, he marched right inside too. His foot-steps pounded in the dirt as he came back toward the outpost, and my heart started thundering as I prepared for the face-off.

"I said, let's go." He wasn't yelling, but he wasn't happy. "I want you to have plenty of time to practice before it gets dark."

"I'm not going to learn how to use a gun." So. There.

"Why?" His patience was fading.

" 'Why?' Because I don't want to! I hate guns. And I really hate being ordered around. That doesn't work for me."

"Look, I understand you're scared," he said more calmly. "Most people are until they know how to use a gun correctly but it will be perfectly safe."

"That's not my reason." Though guns did scare the crap out of me. "I just don't want to use one. Okay?"

"Why?" he repeated, cocking his head to the side, sounding less irritated and more curious.

"I don't want to get into my reasons so I'd appreciate it if you'd just respect my decision. No guns."

"Fine." His face got a cocky smirk. "So how exactly do you plan on defending yourself if you get an unwelcome visitor and I'm not here?"

Damn it. I'd had the same question myself earlier today and hadn't had time to figure out a better answer than shutting myself in the bathroom. "I'll, uh, run away." That would work, right?

"And what if that unwelcome visitor is faster than you?"

"I'm really fast."

"Sure you are." His chest started to shake but he held in his laughter.

"I don't know, okay? I have no idea what I'd do. Hide behind Boone, I guess, and hope he licks the person to death.

Or maybe I'll hide in the biffy. No person in their right mind would go anywhere near that outhouse."

At my declaration, he gave up trying to keep it in and his laughter echoed off the walls. I glared at him, my fists clenching even tighter as he bent over, belly-laughing to the floor. Finally, he got it under control and stood tall, shaking his head as he smiled.

"No guns," he said. "I won't make you use one. And I wouldn't want you to get anywhere near the biffy again so I'll bring you a can of bear spray next week."

"Thank you." The tension in my arms disappeared and I relaxed my hands.

"You're welcome," he said. "Will you at least come outside and watch while I shoot a couple rounds?"

I didn't especially want to but since he'd given on his end, I could give a little on mine. "Fine."

For the next hour, Beau patiently showed me how to use a handgun. He taught me to load it, where the safety was and how to squeeze the trigger to fire. Though my hands never touched the black metal, I did feel more comfortable around the weapon by the time we walked back to the outpost for dinner.

And for the rest of the night, I couldn't shake the feeling that I would one day be grateful for his lesson.

CHAPTER EIGHT

BEAU

"Mom, I'm sorry. I can't go to your party this year." I'd told her the same thing five times over the phone but she'd stopped by my office this morning to ask again.

"Please?" She summoned a sad and pleading look that tugged at my heart.

Fuck. She was pulling out all the stops. It was nearly impossible for me to say no to Marissa Holt's big doe eyes. Mom had used this look for as long as I could remember, almost always getting her way.

I'd seen it before every family reunion, when she'd guilt me into manning the barbeque and cooking for fifty people. Once, that look had convinced me to volunteer for the dunk tank at her church's annual fundraiser. The worst had been when she'd guilted me into a dinner with Annie Stevens— first date from hell.

But I wasn't giving in this time. "No."

My holiday plans were, for once, something I really

wanted to do. Not that I minded Mom's annual Fourth of July party, but it was more for her than me. This year, I was being selfish for my holiday. I was taking an extra day and spending it at the outpost.

"Annie Stevens is going to be there."

Now I had another reason to stay away from the party. "Mom, I've told you a hundred times. Annie Stevens is a very nice girl but she's not my type."

"Because she's too pretty? Too sweet?"

Too obsessed? On our one and only date, she'd brought with her a binder full of newspaper clippings that mentioned my name. I think Mom liked her because she had the matching binder. While I loved that my mom was so proud of me, Annie's fascination bordered too close to stalking.

"I'm sorry. I know this party means a lot to you but I can't make it." I reached out and pulled her in for a hug. "Besides, you won't even miss me." Last year, I'd left after an hour and she hadn't even noticed.

"Fine," she sighed. "I miss the days that you kids all came to my parties. Michael can't come now that he's running the firework show. Maisy has plans with friends. And now you seem to always be camping these days. Maybe I should change it from an evening barbeque to a lunchtime party."

"Good idea, but even still, I can't make it. How about when I come back from the mountains, I take you out for a special lunch at the café to make it up to you? Just you and me."

She hugged me tighter. "I'm ordering pie. With ice cream."

I smiled and let her go. "Deal."

"All right." She collected her purse off my desk. "I'll let you get back to work. Enjoy your weekend."

"You too." I waved to her as she made her way out of my office and toward the front desk. She'd probably spend the next hour gossiping with Rose, my office manager.

I ran a hand over my beard and went back to my desk. If I spent the next three hours completely focused, I'd get through the stack of papers on my desk, clear my email inbox and be out of town on time. I was finally catching up from all my time away from work but it hadn't been easy. Now that things were back on track, I'd actually be able to relax during my long weekend at the outpost.

My long weekend with Sabrina.

This would be my first time staying the night in a month. I'd stayed strong with my decision to keep boundaries with Sabrina but I felt my resolve slipping. The last time I'd stayed—the night I'd gone to the outpost to warn her about Ivan—I'd slept on the floor alone. This time, I didn't know if I'd be able to do the same.

Sabrina MacKenzie was completely under my skin.

Every time I drove away from her at the outpost, I fought the urge to turn back.

I wanted her. Every piece.

Maybe Maisy had been right and Sabrina could find a way to like it here after all. I was going to start doing whatever I could to make her fall in love with Montana.

If she did? I'd be one lucky man.

If she didn't? Well, I'd still be lucky. I was coming to realize that even if I only had Sabrina for a short time, anything with her was better than nothing.

———

SABRINA

"Here." Beau tossed me a plastic sack.

It had been a month since Ivan Federov had left Prescott with no clue about my whereabouts. Since that visit, Beau had gone back to his day-only trips to check on me and deliver supplies. But this weekend, he was spending the holiday with me, and from the playful gleam in his eyes, he had plans.

"What's this?" I asked.

"A swimming suit." He chuckled at my sideways glance. "Don't worry, I didn't pick it out. Felicity bought it."

"And we're going swimming? Where?" The only water nearby was the small creek that ran along the far edge of the meadow.

"We're going on a hike." He tossed me another sack. This one had a shoe box inside.

"I'm confused. Why would I need a swimming suit to hike?"

"I've got a cool place to show you. Just trust me. Get changed and we'll head out."

"Okay." I went to the bathroom and put on the simple two-piece black bikini Felicity had sent. Thankfully, it wasn't skimpy triangles held together by dental floss but instead a halter top with a wide strap and hipster briefs that would cover ninety percent of my butt cheeks.

The new tennis shoes were a simple charcoal gray. They looked cute with my plain white tank and frayed denim shorts. Maybe our hike wouldn't be entirely through the trees and my pasty skin could get some sun.

Dressed and ready to go, I came out of the bathroom and nearly tripped at the sight of Beau in something other than jeans and boots. He had changed into khaki cargo shorts and navy tennis shoes. In his white T-shirt and mirrored sunglasses, he looked more like an island tourist than a mountain man.

My eyes were immediately glued to Beau's muscled calves. When had a man's calf muscles become sexy? Beau's were huge, at least twice the size of mine, and perfectly sculpted. His skin had a dusting of hair that stopped mid-calf. I loved that Beau did not believe in waxing. Did they even do waxing in Montana?

"All set?" he asked, snapping me out of my daze.

I smiled and nodded, not daring to speak because the words would certainly come out squeaky. Sometimes I felt like an awkward teenage girl around Beau. I stuttered my sentences, I had no idea what to do with my hands, and my face always burned a shade too pink.

This crush was seriously damaging my mojo.

I followed him outside and climbed in Green Colossus. Beau's scent filled my nose and I dragged in a huge breath. The natural forest smell was lovely but it paled in comparison to Beau.

After a few minutes of scratching Boone's ears while Beau drove, my curiosity got the better of me. "So where are we going?"

"There is a waterfall a couple miles away. The hike up is steep but short."

"Sounds good." I had been seriously slacking on my exercise since arriving at the outpost. I had been taking daily walks in the meadow but they weren't nearly as rigorous as the spinning and Pure Barre classes I had taken in the city. A hike sounded like a refreshing activity and a good way to burn a few extra calories.

Beau drove us down the two-lane road until he stopped at the base of a hill. Separating the truck from the incline was a creek gently flowing through the trees. It wasn't wide, maybe four feet across. We both climbed out of the truck and walked to the water's edge. He stepped over the creek with one large stride. I had to take a running leap to clear the opposite bank.

"Up we go."

I nodded and let Beau start off first with Boone at his side.

The trail he followed wasn't much more than a footpath and I was forced to walk behind him for the first half of our hike. But as we approached the top of the steep hill, our path leveled and I joined him at his side.

"Are you doing okay?" he asked.

"Yeah." I was breathless but smiling. My lungs and legs were burning but it felt great to work up a sweat.

"The rest is pretty easy." Beau wasn't straining a bit. To him, this was probably like a stroll through the mall, not that I could imagine him ever setting foot inside a mall.

We walked easily for a while. I did my best to keep my footing even as I watched birds fly above us through the trees. "I'm going to miss seeing fireworks on Independence Day but at least we get to see some beautiful things today."

"I'd take this over fireworks any day of the week."

"Does Prescott have a big firework show?" I asked.

"They do all right for a small town. Now that Michael is the fire chief, he'll be supervising it this year. I'm just hoping they don't have a wreck. The guy in charge of buying the fireworks has a tendency to go a little crazy."

"You're not missing anything on my account, are you?"

He was so dedicated to his family, I worried he'd regret missing his younger brother's big night.

"Nope. I'm glad to be away from the madness. Michael will be fine. He doesn't need me hovering over his shoulder."

"What about a hot date? Are you missing watching the fireworks with someone special?" I couldn't help asking. The words slipped out so quickly, I didn't have a chance to think them through.

Did he have a girlfriend? We'd been around each other for months now, but maybe he'd found someone. Maybe that was the reason for the distance and boundaries he'd put between us.

"Come again?" Beau looked down at me with furrowed brows.

"You're not missing a date, are you? Because I'm fine here on my own if you need to get back."

He grinned and shook his head. "I'm exactly where I want to be. The only date I have is with you, the steaks I brought for dinner, the bottle of Crown Royal for dessert and the cribbage board."

My wide smile stretched my lips to their fullest. "Okay."

"Though I am going to miss seeing Coby watch the fireworks. Well, if he can stay up that late. Maisy thinks he'll fall asleep before they start."

"I hope he makes it."

"Me too." Beau smiled down at me and I saw mine flashing back through his mirrored shades. It wasn't the first time I had thought how lucky Coby Holt was to have such an incredible uncle. Beau's own children would be blessed with a wonderful dad.

"You said you wanted kids. How many do you think you and the future Mrs. Holt will have?"

Beau chuckled. "There's the reporter. I haven't seen her in a while."

"She's been taking some time off to write a couple of books. Now answer the question before she's forced to get pushy."

"Pushy? I don't believe it. I bet most people tell you whatever you want to know."

"For the most part."

I was lucky; interviewing others had always come easy. I tended to build a quick rapport with my interview subjects, and the question-and-answer dynamic would develop naturally and without force.

Until Beau. He seemed to like making me work for my answers.

"Are you going to answer my question?" I nudged his elbow with mine.

"How many kids will I have? I don't know. I guess I'd like at least two. What about you? Do you want kids?"

Another thing about questioning Beau was that he made me answer my own questions. I tried to remember that and pick my topics carefully.

"My career has been front and center for as long as I can remember. Kids weren't a part of that plan and the guys I've dated were so far from good father material that I wasn't ever tempted to deviate from my career path."

"And if you found the right man?" Beau asked.

"Two kids would be nice." My answer surprised me a bit. Up until that moment, I hadn't thought about children in detail, but all of a sudden, the mental image of two little boys chasing one another in a park popped into my head.

I was not going to let myself analyze the fact that my

imaginary sons were remarkably similar to the man at my side.

Time to deflect questions away from me.

"Have you ever been close to finding the right woman?"

"Not really. I dated a girl all through college but we broke up right after graduation. Neither of us wanted to take the next step."

"Why?"

He shrugged. "We were better friends than lovers. Things between us were always easy but the spark wasn't there."

I had only ever had a physical spark with the men I'd dated, never wanting anything but casual sex. None of them had ever been the kind of men I'd want as a friend.

But like many other aspects of my life, things were changing. I was ready for the relationship. The give and take. The passionate kisses and the lazy cuddles. Writing my novel had taught me that too. I was envious of the love my fictional heroine had found.

Beau and I walked in silence for the rest of the short hike until he steered us around one last clump of trees and the forest opened up. Damp rocks replaced dry dirt under my feet. Fresh mist floated in the air, clearing my nose of the forest's musky aroma. The dull rush of the waterfall filled my ears, drowning out the quiet lull of the swaying trees.

"Wow," I whispered.

The waterfall in front of us was breathtaking. It wasn't all that tall or wide but it had such an intricate fall pattern it was mesmerizing. The water bounced from rock to rock as it traveled sideways nearly twenty feet until it finally dropped into a round pool.

The pond itself was completely clear, giving me a

perfect view of the smooth black and gray rocks under the water's glassy surface. Like an infinity pool, the water slipped over the pond's far edge to travel down a rocky path where it eventually formed the small creek that descended the hill we had just climbed.

"How did you find this place?" I asked Beau. "It's incredible."

"Just by luck. I was up here hiking a couple of years ago and stumbled upon it."

"Amazing find." The place was nothing short of magical.

Boone abandoned his post by Beau's legs to climb across the rocks and drink from the pond. Beau held out his hand and mine immediately fell into his palm. He helped me across the slick rocks to a larger one that made a platform at the edge of the pool.

"Want to go for a swim?" he asked.

"Uh, isn't it a little cold?" The spray from the waterfall was far from lukewarm.

Beau shrugged. "It's not that bad once you get used to it."

"You first."

He grinned and handed me his sunglasses. His eyes sparkled beautifully in the bright sunlight before he reached behind his head and yanked off his T-shirt. Squished together on the platform, my face was inches away from Beau's naked chest.

My knees started to sway and I willed myself not to fall fully clothed into the water. Shirtless Beau was incredible. Not one muscle wasn't defined on his arms and chest. His pecs were covered in just the right amount of dark chest hair. The skin on his stomach was smooth across his—two, four, six, eight!—rippled abs.

And he had a happy trail.

Hot damn.

I desperately wanted to grab on to his chiseled hipbones while my tongue found exactly where that trail ended.

Thankfully, before I could start drooling, Beau dropped his T-shirt on my head. By the sound of his chuckle, he had definitely caught my visual perusal of his chest.

Curses.

I pulled his shirt off my face just in time to see him drop the cargo shorts and reveal his black swimming trunks. They hung low on his waist, revealing two dimples at the base of his sculpted back.

Without a backward glance, he waded into the water. My suspicions about the temperature were confirmed when he sucked in a sharp, hissing breath, but by the time he made it across the pond and to the far rock wall, he seemed to have acclimated to the cold. The water only came up to his waist but he sank down low and let the waterfall run over his face.

I toed off my shoes and sat, letting my feet and calves lazily float in the cool water. Closing my eyes and tipping my head to the sky, I let the sunshine heat my face.

"This is so wonderful," I told the air.

When my own words hit my ears, I sat up straight as my eyes flew open wide.

Wonderful? I'd just said that spending an afternoon in nature was wonderful? What was happening to me? Old Sabrina would never have enjoyed this. There were bugs out here. And dirt. The water was crystal clear but certainly there were microscopic bacteria swimming between my toes. Old Sabrina would have found this akin to torture. Her only acceptable outdoor excursions required a sandy beach and a cabana boy.

But the Montana wilderness really was wonderful. At

some point during my three months at the outpost, new Sabrina had started to appreciate the woods.

I laughed to myself and went back to lounging, enjoying my new appreciation for this beautiful part of the world.

"Are you coming in or not?" Beau asked.

"Not. I like my rock."

"Okay." He dipped his body back down into the water.

"That's it? No pressure?" I was braced and ready to defend my choice but Beau just kept swimming.

He shook his head. "No pressure. Not today."

I gave him a wary glance, but he just kept lazing around in the water, floating back and forth from one edge to the other. The chill from the water must have only been temporary because he looked relaxed and comfortable.

Evil genius. Now I wanted to get in the water.

"Fine. You win."

He chuckled. "I didn't say anything."

"Exactly." I pushed myself up to standing and unbuttoned my shorts, sliding them off my legs. Then I went for my tank, whipping it over my head and tossing it on the rock.

Beau's eyes raked up my bare legs. As his gaze rose, a rush of heat followed, my skin warming from the heat in his eyes. I wasn't worried about the cold water anymore—not in the slightest. I needed to get in that water and cool off before I did something crazy like untie my top and let it join the pile of clothes.

I tore my eyes away from Beau's and sat back down, putting my legs in first. *One. Two. Three.* I pushed off the rock and into the water, sinking all the way to my shoulders. "Oh my god," I gasped. "That is cold."

I breathed through the chill and took a few breaths before looking over to Beau.

He was rubbing his wet hands over his face. When he brought them down, his eyes were still hooded with lust. "Good?" His voice was hoarse.

I nodded. "Good."

"I'm going to . . ." He trailed off and swam to the waterfall, letting the water run over his hair and face.

Thanks for the suit, Felicity. I smiled to myself, glad I wasn't the only person affected by the other in this pool.

Swimming for a few minutes, I made my way around the pool but avoided the waterfall so I wouldn't get my hair wet. Though the water wasn't frigid, it was cool and I decided to get out and let the sun warm me back up.

I hoisted myself up on the rock and was just brushing off the extra water drops when Beau left the waterfall and swam to the edge of the pool. "Boone!"

The dog approached hesitantly—knowing what I didn't —that Beau was going to pull him into the water for a bath. As quickly as Boone could swim free, he hauled his dripping body out of the water and did his doggy shake.

"Gah!" I yelled, holding up my hands to shield my face. The yell was a mistake. A couple of droplets landed in my mouth. "Yuck." I swallowed and fought back a gag.

"Sorry," Beau said, wading closer to the rock platform. "Get out of here, Boone."

I wiped my face and rinsed my hands in the pool, laughing at the irony of the situation. "I was just reflecting earlier on how nice it was out here, despite my previous aversion to nature. Then I get dog bathwater in my mouth and realize I'm not as close to nature as I thought."

Looking up from the pond, I expected to see Beau smiling at my joke. Instead he was studying my face in complete seriousness.

"What?" I asked.

"Is that true?"

"What? That I don't like dog bathwater in my mouth? Of course, who would?"

"No." He shook his head. "That you like it here."

"Oh. Well, yeah."

All the muscles in his face relaxed except for the corner of his mouth that turned up. "Good. That didn't take as long as I thought it would."

"Huh?"

"Nothing, Shortcake." He chuckled and sank backward into the water. "I'm just glad you approve."

Who wouldn't approve of this waterfall or that water? Maybe he meant something else. Before I could ask him to clarify, he took a deep breath, then sank under the water. Beneath the surface, I could see him inching closer.

I was about to move up onto my knees when he rose up out of the water and sent a streaming burst of water out of his mouth and into my face. I did my best to block the stream but I got soaked.

"Lovely," I deadpanned once the onslaught had stopped and water was dripping down off my nose and chin.

"Better than dog bathwater, though."

I didn't acknowledge the truth of that comment as I stood and dried off my face. "Don't you think you'd better get out of there before you turn into an icicle?"

He grinned and pulled himself up on the rock. Beau tugged on his tennis shoes and wadded up his dry shirt and cargo shorts rather than put them on.

Once I had my clothes and shoes back on too, we set off back down the trail. Maybe one day I'd get the chance to visit this place again. I could take a vacation back in

Montana when my ordeal with the Federovs was all over. Until then, I'd find a way to work that waterfall setting into a future novel. My memory of that magical place wouldn't just live on in my own head but through the written word that others could cherish too.

I smiled, thinking that place might be just the right spot for my current novel's heroine to get frisky with her hero.

"Are you going to tell me what's making you smile?" Beau asked.

Definitely not in detail. "I was just thinking about a scene for my book."

"How's the writing going?"

"Good." I smiled. "Great, actually. I'm working on my second novel. The first one is done and pretty special, if I do say so myself."

"Impressive. What's it about?"

"Well, since I know you will never read it, I guess I can tell you."

"Hey, I might read it."

"Goliath, let me assure you, it is not your type of book."

"No pictures?" he asked, making me laugh. "Come on." He nudged my shoulder. "Tell me what's it about."

"Me," I answered honestly. "It's a lot about me and this experience."

"An autobiography?"

I shook my head. "No, it's fiction but I based the main character's struggles on mine. She gets thrown into an unknown environment, she's cut off from the people she loves, and she's trying to work through some of the bad decisions she's made."

"What kind of bad decisions?"

I took a deep breath before explaining. To divulge my

main character's shame was to share my own, and I was dreading the inevitable disgust on his face and disappointment in his eyes.

"My character is a famous actress. She earned her fame by using others as she climbed. Then she took a proposition to sleep with a director for an Oscar-winning role. In the book, she's trying to come to terms with those bad decisions and wondering if her career was worth feeling like a whore."

Beau didn't say anything and I kept my eyes glued to the path as we walked. The farther we went, the more I regretted telling him about my book. Waves of anger and disappointment rolled off his bare shoulders.

Had I made the wrong assumption? Hadn't he realized I'd slept with Anton? Beau was smart, so surely he'd read between the lines when I'd told him that I'd been faking a relationship, right?

When he stopped walking, I stopped too, holding my breath as I braced for his response. Turning to me, he slid his sunglasses onto his hair. His eyes were narrowed and his eyebrows were furrowed together.

"You feel like a whore?"

I nodded. "Most days."

The concern in his eyes vanished in a flash, fury taking its place. Without a word, he turned and stormed down the path. His long legs took him away from me so quickly I had to jog to keep up.

Tears welled in my eyes but I blinked furiously to keep them from falling. My heart didn't just hurt, my entire body ached. I wasn't sure what to make of Beau's reaction, but the more distance he put between us, the more I wanted to curl into a ball and cry.

Up ahead, the trail took a sharp curve and Beau disappeared from my sight. Panic set in at the idea of being lost in the woods alone and I started jogging again, rushing to catch him before I lost the trail.

Right as I was rounding the curve, Beau's bare chest appeared and I crashed into him. My feet tripped over themselves and I would have fallen if not for his large hands gripping my arms.

"I thought you left." I dropped my eyes to the ground to avoid his angry face.

"Sorry. I just needed a second to cool off and get my head back on."

I nodded and waved him off. "Sure."

So much for opening up. Why had he gotten so angry? Was my honesty really that upsetting? Our otherwise lovely afternoon was ruined. My feet were steady now and I tried to step away but Beau's grip remained firm.

"Sabrina, look at me," he said gently.

"Can we just go?" I asked our shoes.

"Hey." He let me go and cupped my chin, tipping my eyes to his. "We need to talk about this."

The last thing I wanted was to dive into this subject any further. Apparently, I had already said too much. "It's fine," I lied, avoiding eye contact.

"It's not. Calling yourself that word is not fine."

I jerked and my eyes whipped back to his. "What would you call me then?"

"Brave. Selfless."

I scoffed. "How can you say that?"

"Because the truth feels right. The lies hurt. And hearing you call yourself a whore felt like someone had kicked me in the gut."

I stared at Beau, dumbfounded, tears pooling again.

"Don't ever talk about yourself like that again. Ever." He reached up and pulled the lock of hair I had been twirling from my fingers. "You did something no one else had been able to do. Putting a stop to those gun shipments saved lives. You sacrificed yourself for the good of others even though you took a major hit. Literally. Don't forget the destination as you analyze the journey."

"But Beau, that wasn't the only reason. I wanted to get ahead. I wanted to make a name for myself."

"I don't believe that was your only reason." His hands framed my face. "People do things for a lot of complicated reasons. Think about it: if you were just in it for the glory and the fame, you wouldn't have become an investigative reporter. If you really wanted to use your looks to get ahead, you'd be in Hollywood, interviewing celebrities or some shit like that. You wouldn't be taking stories that could get you killed."

"But—"

"No." His hands left my face and settled on my shoulders. "No. Did you take the story to get guns off the streets?"

"Yes, but—"

"Then that's it." He cut me off again. "Leave it there. You did what you had to do to get evidence. Do you think there aren't cops that go undercover and have to do the things you did?"

"I'm sure there are."

"Damn straight, there are. Would you call them whores?"

"No! Of course not."

His eyes gentled as his point was made. "Then there you go."

There you go.

My shoulders relaxed, the sting in my nose starting to fade. "Okay," I whispered.

I hadn't realized how much I needed someone other than myself to tell me that I'd made the right choice. That it hadn't just been about the fame, but the guns too. That in the end, the good outweighed the bad. Much like my writing, Beau's words had been healing.

Good people don't just see the good in others, they see it in themselves too.

My dad's voice popped into my head. He used to say that to me whenever I was down on myself. He wasn't here to help me through this but I was sure he'd approve of Beau taking his place.

"You're a good person, Beau Holt."

"So are you, Sabrina MacKenzie." He reached out and grabbed my hand. "Come on. Let's go home." With Beau leading me down the path, we made the careful descent back to the truck.

On the drive back to the outpost, I realized that Beau had captured another piece of my heart today. Little by little, he was taking them all.

I just hoped that when I left, he'd give them all back.

CHAPTER NINE

SABRINA

"Looks like we're going to get a sky show after all," Beau said, staring out the kitchen window.

"What do you mean?"

"There's a thunderstorm rolling in."

I squeezed in next to Beau to look outside. Between the trees, the sky was darkening to an ominous gray, and the wind was whipping the tops of the evergreens.

"Cool! I love thunderstorms. Seattle rarely gets them but back home in Florida they happened all the time. Lightning fascinates me."

"You probably won't see much from inside."

I shrugged. "That's okay. It's still cool."

He sighed. "I hope it doesn't hit town until after the fireworks show."

I smiled, knowing he didn't want his little brother's big night to be ruined by the weather. "Me neither."

"Tomorrow we'll have to take a walk in the meadow," he said. "It'll smell pretty fucking awesome after a good rain."

"Sounds great." I went back to the dishes in the sink. While I washed, Beau dried and put them away, our movements so in sync, we were like a couple that had done this together for years.

We had come back from the waterfall and spent some time apart. I'd written while Beau had cut up a fallen tree and chopped it for firewood. Even though it was summer, I'd been lighting a fire at night to ward off the chill. I rarely used the electric baseboard heaters now that I knew how to build a fire. Only once had I made the mistake of smoking up the outpost because I hadn't set the vent correctly. Luckily, Beau hadn't been here when that had happened so my embarrassment—and smoky home—had only been shared with Boone.

By the time Beau had come inside from chopping wood, my somber mood from earlier had disappeared. I'd volunteered to cook our steaks and make a salad, then we'd eaten at our makeshift cooler table on the floor, chatting about nothing serious, before we'd gotten up to do the dishes.

"Want to play a game?" Beau asked, putting away the last plate and pulling out two glasses.

"Sure. Cribbage?"

"Or gin."

"Cribbage. You always beat me at gin."

He chuckled while filling up our glasses with the whiskey he'd brought earlier. Grabbing a couple cubes from the freezer's plastic ice trays, he plopped them into the glasses and handed one over.

I took a small sip, wincing as the burn spread down my throat and into my belly.

"Not a fan?" Beau asked.

"Whiskey is Felicity's thing, not mine. If there isn't red wine, I default to top-shelf tequila."

"Good to know. Next time."

I smiled, hoping there would be a next time and that the rekindled closeness between us wouldn't vanish when he got back to town. I had missed him being at the outpost these last couple of months. Not just because I was lonely but because I'd often found myself wanting to tell him something or ask him a question.

Without a doubt, I would miss Beau a great deal when I went back home to Seattle.

An hour and two glasses of whiskey later, I was tipsy and had gotten my ass kicked at cribbage.

"I give up." I threw my cards on the deck. My slightly inebriated state made me happy and curious along with really bad at simple math. "Let's play a new game. For the rest of the night, we can ask each other anything we want and the other person has to answer."

"Isn't that what we always do?" he asked. "You badger me with personal questions until I finally give in."

I giggled. "Yes, but this time I won't have to badger you."

"I'm game but we each get a pass at one question."

"Agreed."

Beau stood from the floor and put the cribbage board away, then quickly started a fire before going to the kitchen to refill his drink.

When he tipped the bottle at me, I shook my head. "I think I'll switch to water."

I'd had enough to drink, and if I kept going, there was a real chance my already-too-thin verbal filter would disintegrate like wet toilet paper. The last thing I needed was to go blurting how much I wanted Beau to satisfy the three-month-long craving I had for him.

Beau came back into the main room and settled against the wall on the opposite side from my log chair where I was now sitting. His long legs ate up the short distance between us. With his bare feet aimed my way, I got a good look at just how big they were.

"What size shoe do you wear?" He gave me a strange look but before he could comment, I said, "Remember. We agreed no badgering."

He grinned. "Thirteen." *Big. Oh, boy.*

I smiled. "See, that wasn't so hard, was it? Now it's your turn."

"Most embarrassing moment from when you were a kid."

"Probably when Janessa and I tried drinking for the first time. We got smashed on cinnamon schnapps and I puked all over myself and the boy I had a crush on. He never talked to me again. Even after all these years, I still can't stomach the taste of artificial cinnamon."

"No Big Red gum?"

I made a sour face and he laughed.

"My turn." I shifted on the chair as the wind outside the outpost started howling. "What's the scariest thing to ever happen to you?"

Beau leaned his head back against the wall and spoke to the ceiling. The tortured look on his face made me want to take back my question.

"A couple of years ago, Jess, one of his deputies and me were up in the woods searching for a meth house. We found it, but before we could check it out, an old propane tank exploded. It was some sort of trap. Milo, the deputy, got third-degree burns. Jess got thrown into a fallen tree and a branch punctured his side. Lucky for me, I was far enough away that it just knocked me down but they both almost died that day."

"God. I'm so sorry." My hand went to my chest. The pain in his voice was palpable.

He lifted his head off the wall. "We got lucky. Both of them survived. But Gigi, Jess's wife, was at the hospital when I brought them in. She's a nurse. The scariest moment of my life was when I was sitting with her, waiting for a doctor to come out and tell us if Jess was going to live. I knew if he didn't make it, I'd see her heart break."

I sat silent and stunned. Beau wouldn't meet my eyes. He just kept staring at the ceiling as he relived the memory.

Me and my damn questions. I hadn't thought that question through. It had just come flying out of my mouth and now I'd dredged up that awful pain for him to relive.

"I don't know what to say," I whispered. "I'm sorry. I think we'd better quit this game."

He shook his head and looked back down. "Don't be sorry, Sabrina. I'll tell you anything you want to know. Maybe just make the next question a little lighter."

"I can do that. Your turn?"

"You go again."

I smiled, thinking of a topic sure to cheer him up. "Okay, I've got one. Who's your favorite sibling?"

"Michael." He grinned but then pointed his index finger at me in warning. "But if you ever tell Maisy, I'm taking you over my knee."

"I'll take it to my grave." I held up three fingers in the scout's salute. "Why Michael? I would have bet good money that you'd say Maisy."

He shrugged. "I love my sister, don't get me wrong. But

Michael and I have always been tight. He used to be my shadow growing up. A lot of guys I knew would have hated their little brother tailing them around but it never bothered me. He was my little buddy."

"What's the age difference between you guys?" Beau had graduated with Felicity so I knew we were both thirty-four.

"Maisy is six years younger than me. Michael is nine. Mom had some health problems after I was born so they waited awhile to have more kids."

We talked about his parents and siblings until he started asking me about mine. Then the conversation veered to even lighter topics. I learned that we both hated folding socks more than any other household chore, including toilet scrubbing. We both had a deep love for chocolate and his aversion to strawberry yogurt was as strong as mine was to blueberry.

After a couple of hours, I had completely forgotten this was a game. The back and forth was so easy and comfortable it felt like the best date I'd ever had.

The buzz from my whiskey had faded and I decided to have a little more before bed. I went to the kitchen to refill my glass and did the same for Beau, but just as I was walking back to deliver his drink, a bright flash filled the room, immediately followed by a deafening crack of thunder.

My whole body jolted and whiskey sloshed in our tall cups. Had they been any fuller, I would have gotten an alcohol shower. I started to relax but lightning flashed again and a boom rattled my bones.

"You okay?" Beau asked, sitting up off the wall.

I shook my head. "I like to watch thunderstorms, not be in the middle of one. That felt way too close." At any moment, lightning was bound to strike a tree and it would fall onto the outpost.

He chuckled and patted the floor next to him. "Come and sit. We're completely safe inside."

I hustled to the floor and settled in close with my knees pulled into my chest. When another flash and crack split the air, Beau's arm came around my shoulders and he tucked me tighter into his side. On his other side was a freaked-out Boone.

We all sat quietly, listening to the wind and rain beat against the outpost's walls and roof. When the thunder and lightning finally blew over, my body relaxed and I started to breathe deeply again.

The thunderstorm left a steady rain in its wake and the drops dinged and drizzled loudly against the tin roof. The noise was comforting, louder than a rainy day in Seattle, but so blissfully familiar that I melted further into Beau's side.

"I missed the rain," I whispered. "It feels like home."

Beau's frame deflated and he pushed out a pained breath. I couldn't even begin to guess why.

"What?" I asked.

"Nothing," he muttered.

"You have to tell me. Game rules."

"Then I'll take my pass."

My spirits fell. "Okay."

What did that mean? Why wouldn't he tell me what was wrong? The questions begged to be asked but I respected his decision to pass and let them be. Still, I didn't understand how my love of the rain could possibly be upsetting.

"Hey." He squeezed my shoulder and gave me a small smile. "I'm fine. Let's keep playing. Ask me a different question."

"Okay." I thought for a few moments before asking, "If you could travel anywhere in the world, where would you go?"

"Disney World," he answered immediately.

I smiled, glad he was teasing me to lighten the mood. "No, seriously. Where would you go?"

"Disney World," he repeated.

My smile dropped. "Why?" He had promised to take me there when the Federovs were no longer a threat. Was it because he wanted to see me again? Would he miss me too after I was gone?

"Because that means you're safe from the Federovs," he said, "and this whole mess will be over."

Right. He didn't want to see me again. He wanted to be done with this mess.

The hope I'd felt seconds ago vanished. When I was gone, Beau would go back to his normal life and forget all about the headache that I'd caused him this summer.

"I think we'd better take Disney World off the table," I said. "Once this *mess* is over, I'm sure you'll be glad to be free of me. I don't want you to feel obligated to meet me at a kid's resort just because we were joking around."

I picked up my glass to take a drink, but before the plastic rim hit my lips, Beau grabbed it out of my hand. With a loud clink, he set it on the floor.

"What just happened?" he asked.

"I'm letting you off the hook."

"No, you're taking away something I was looking forward to. Why?"

My eyes found his. "You're looking forward to it?"

"Yes. Of course." His face was so gentle and soft, I realized I'd made the wrong assumption when he'd called this a mess.

My head fell against his chest and I snaked an arm around his waist. "Me too."

We both sat quietly, enjoying the sound of the rain and Boone snoring softly on the floor. I didn't move my arm, and as time went on, I rested further against Beau. My knees fell from their upright position to drape across his big thigh while my head burrowed further into his shoulder.

Eventually, his cheek hit the top of my head and his breathing slowed. But before either one of us fell asleep, I had to ask one more question.

"Beau?"

"Hmm."

"Why did you stop spending the night?" I whispered.

"You know why," he whispered back.

I did. We had gotten too close. The intimacy of sleeping together was far too tempting. Had he not put that distance between us, we would have wound up doing much more than cuddling.

Yet here we were again, curled into one another. Though we both knew separation was for the best, neither one of us could resist the pull. My body fit into Beau's side like a missing puzzle piece. He filled my heart like his waterfall filled its pool—until it was overflowing.

"Will you promise me something, Beau?"

"Sure."

"Before I leave, will you kiss me? Just once?"

"Sabrina, we—"

"I know," I interrupted him. "Two different worlds, I remember. One day I'll go back to my life and you'll be here with yours. But I'll always wonder what it would have been like."

He lifted his cheek from my head and reached for my chin, tipping it back. "That's not what I was going to say."

"It isn't?"

"We would never stop at just a kiss."

I smiled. "Would that be so bad?"

"Woman, it would be fucking incredible."

My smile got wider. I had no doubt that he was right. A rush of heat went straight to my core and the intensity between my legs skyrocketed so quickly I wondered if Beau could feel my throbbing through the floorboards.

"But . . ." *No!* He lifted his hand up and lightly stroked my cheek. "You're not ready."

"Ready for what?"

"For me."

What did that mean? I was more than ready for Beau and had been for months. Was it my appearance? I normally did myself up a bit more if I knew I was going to have sex and tonight I definitely wasn't looking my best.

My hair was in a messy knot on top of my head. My roots were showing and I needed some highlights and a trim like no one's business. My nails hadn't gone this long without a manicure since high school. But beauty-regimen issues aside, I was still a pretty woman that was practically lying on his lap and definitely willing to have sex.

What was he waiting for? My pride wouldn't let me ask.

I stayed quiet, hoping he would explain further, but after a few brutal minutes, I realized that I'd just been rejected. Again.

It was time to regain our usual distance.

"It's probably for the best," I said. "We've both been

drinking and it's been an emotional day." I patted Beau's flat stomach and peeled myself away from his side. "We'd better call it a night."

"Hey—" Beau started.

"It's fine. I'm just tired," I lied.

Before he could stop me, I hustled into the bathroom and closed the door. The cold water I splashed on my face did little to relieve the hot flush of embarrassment.

After finishing my nightly routine, I came back out to the main room, relieved that Beau had kept our beds separate. He was on the floor. I was on my cot. Without delay, I got into my bed.

"Sabrina—"

"Good night, Beau," I said, turning my back to him and facing the wall. The talking portion of our evening was over.

Beau sighed. "Night, Shortcake."

Maybe in my dreams, I'd get a kiss because I had no idea what it would take to get one for real.

———

"MORNING."

I gave Beau a small smile and a wide berth but didn't respond. Instead, my eyes stayed firmly locked on the coffee machine as I maneuvered around him to the counter.

"Sabrina."

I ignored that too. My embarrassment from last night hadn't faded a bit.

"Hey, can you look at me?" he asked. When I didn't move, he did his jungle growl.

I turned from my coffee cup and leaned back against the counter, crossing my arms over my chest.

"Look, we need to talk about last night," he said.

"We don't. Let's forget it."

"I had fun last night. I'm not going to forget about it."

Fun? Rejecting me when I'd asked him to kiss me had been fun? Telling me I wasn't ready for sex with him, whatever the hell that meant, had been fun?

Embarrassment morphed to utter mortification and then to blood-boiling anger. Heat rose from my chest and up my throat, but before I breathed fire, I clenched my teeth together so hard my molars hurt.

"I pissed you off," he guessed.

Opening my mouth still wasn't safe so I widened my eyes and nodded vigorously.

"Would you mind telling me how?"

Men! Did they always need women to spell things out? Fine. I'd make his mistake perfectly clear. His innocent expression was doing nothing to save him.

With one hand firmly planted on my hip and the other holding up three fingers, I let my temper rip. "Number one. When a beautiful woman asks you to kiss her, unless you're married, have a girlfriend or have a damn good reason not to, do the right thing and kiss her. Number two. If you don't kiss her, it is not an appropriate excuse to tell her that it's because sex between you would be incredible. That makes it worse! And number three. When you completely embarrass a woman, the last thing you should say was that it was fun!"

I added a fourth finger, not exactly sure what it would entail, but he stopped my rant by stepping into my space and hoisting me up on the counter.

"Beau, I hate to be hauled around," I said through clenched teeth.

"Quiet and listen. It's my turn." He said it loudly enough

that I shut my mouth. Somewhere during my rant his innocent expression had hardened in frustration. "I told you that
if I kissed you, we wouldn't stop there. There was no way I
was fucking you the same day you told me that you considered yourself a whore. That's my damn good reason for not
kissing you last night."

My teeth stopped grinding together and my spine
relaxed. That *was* a good reason. *Damn.*

"I didn't mean to embarrass you," he said. "I'm not sure
what kind of assholes you're used to spending time around
but I don't get off on hurting a woman's feelings or embarrassing her."

My embarrassment came back but this time at my own
hand. Beau was one of the good guys and I had just gone off
the deep end and assumed the worse.

"Okay," I said, holding up my hands. "I'm sorry." I had
no desire to fight and I was woman enough to know I'd just
been beaten in that argument.

Beau jerked back an inch, staring at me with wary eyes.
"That's it?"

I nodded. "You've won your case."

"This was too easy. It feels like a trap." His eyes
narrowed. "Is this going to come back and bite me in the
ass?"

I grinned. "No. Once my bruised ego heals, this will be
all but forgotten." Though it might take a day or two. Beau's
refusal to kiss me had been quite the blow.

"I didn't mean to bruise your ego."

"Then what did you mean when you said I wasn't
ready?" It had been bothering me all night and morning.
These cryptic messages he had been giving me were making
me crazy.

"That you're not ready. When you are, you'll be the first to know."

My head fell and I spoke to my knees. "I don't know what that means."

"I know. You just have to trust me." His thumb hooked under my chin and lifted it up. "Christ," he muttered. "Don't look at me like that."

"Like what?"

"Like your heart hurts. It's killing me."

"I'm fine." I reached up and put my hand on his shoulder, giving it a reassuring squeeze. The heat from his skin flowed through my hand to my elbow. When my grip lingered, he inched closer, stepping between my legs spread wide on the counter where he had me trapped.

The angry fire in his eyes was gone, replaced with a dark heat. Without thinking about my movements, my hand traveled from his shoulder to his heart. Under my fingers, its thundering pace matched my own.

"Beau." His name came out in a breathless plea.

"Fuck it," he growled.

"Huh?"

His soft, full lips came crashing down on mine. His tongue thrust inside at the same time he erased the remaining inches separating us. I unpinned my arm from his chest to throw it over his shoulder while the other went immediately to his hair.

With one roll of his hips, the hardness behind his jeans rubbed against my center. Even through my own jeans, I could feel how much he wanted me. One of my legs wound around his hips, putting my pulsing core right against his cock again. My moan spurred Beau's tongue to ravage and his teeth to nip.

Kissing Beau was all-consuming. It was brazen, yet tender. The most beautiful words in the world couldn't describe how his lips turned me to liquid in his arms. We each poured all of the sexual frustration and desire from the last few months into this kiss, neither of us breaking apart even to breathe.

His palms spanned my ribs as his fingers balled up the loose material of my T-shirt. When they found bare skin, I lost any shred of control and tugged harder on Beau's hair, urging him to give me more.

Instead, he ripped his lips away from mine when Boone's barking echoed off the walls. The quick change made my head spin so fast I had to grip the counter's edge to keep from falling off.

"Fuck," Beau cursed.

"What?" I panted.

"Someone's coming. Stay here."

Without another word, he grabbed the gun from on top of the fridge and walked outside. Standing by his truck, he waited for the approaching vehicle to appear on the road to the outpost. When a red truck emerged from behind the trees, Beau shook his head and jogged back inside.

"Who is it?" I asked.

"Michael. Stay inside."

What was Beau's brother doing here? I didn't get the chance to ask. Beau put the gun away and ran back outside just in time to greet our two visitors.

Hidden behind the door and peeking out through its crack, I could see both men shake hands with Beau. I knew Michael right away because of his resemblance to his older brother. Michael's large frame wasn't as muscular as Beau's and he was missing the beard but they shared the same angular shoulders, straight nose and square jaw.

The other man was a few inches shorter than the Holt brothers but he had an incredible physique. His short brown beard matched the color of his shaggy hair, and when he gave Beau a playful smile, it was clear that the men were good friends.

When all three turned toward the outpost, I flew away from the door, scrambling backward to stand in the center of the room and attempt to look like I hadn't been spying on them.

Beau entered first and didn't waste any time with introductions. "Sabrina, this is my brother, Michael." After shaking Michael's hand, Beau continued. "And this is Nick Slater."

"Nice to meet you both."

"Sabrina's out here studying our pine beetle problem," Beau lied. "She's over here from Washington."

I nodded and smiled, playing along with Beau's story. I could ask him later what the hell a pine beetle was.

"These guys are here because the storm last night caused a fire about five miles up the mountain," Beau said.

"Sorry, Sabrina," Nick said, "but you're about to get invaded. There's a forest fire crew on their way here."

CHAPTER TEN

SABRINA

"When are your volunteers getting here?" Beau asked his brother.

Michael shook his head. "It's not my team. We just came here to give you a heads-up. Dylan's bringing his hotshot crew over from Bozeman."

"Fuck," Beau clipped.

Michael winced. "Sorry. I know you don't like the guy."

"He's a hothead and he's going to get someone killed one of these days," Beau grumbled and ran a hand over his beard.

"It wasn't our call," Nick said. "The wind is working against us and the Prescott FD volunteers is too small for this one."

I tried to keep up with the conversation while remaining quiet, but it was difficult with my mind stuck on the fact that an unknown number of people would soon be descending on my super-secret hideout.

This was not good. My armpits were sweating and my hands clammy.

"Did we get a flyover to see how many acres we're talking about?" Beau asked Michael.

"Yeah. It's about twenty acres right now but you know that terrain up there is dense. That monster's going to spread fast. We need a retardant drop because a foot crew alone isn't going to keep it contained. Sorry, Beau, but we had to call Dylan. We couldn't get ahold of you."

Beau sighed and rubbed his beard. "It was the right call."

Michael's tense frame relaxed at his brother's approval.

"How far behind you is Dylan?" Beau asked.

"An hour probably," Michael said. "Figured you'd want to oversee this one. Since you were here, we decided it was as good a place as any for base camp. We told him to just meet us here."

"Right." Beau's jaw was clamped so tight I worried the throbbing vein on his forehead was going to burst. "Did you bring my gear?"

Gear? Gear for what? I thought Beau ran the forest service office and did search and rescue. Did he put out fires too?

I swallowed my questions because as a fake pine-beetle scientist, I should probably know what they were talking about.

"Yeah, we brought your gear." Michael nodded. "It's in the truck."

"Okay." Beau pushed out a loud breath. "Let's get it unloaded."

While the men went back outside, I paced and brainstormed getaway options. Staying at the outpost wasn't going to work. What if someone recognized me? The world was a much smaller place these days thanks to social media. I had no idea how far the news of my disappearance had traveled but it could have very well spread from Seattle to Montana. I couldn't afford to be recognized.

And besides that, I couldn't pretend I was studying some weird forest bug. Just saying the word "beetle" sent chills down my spine. People would see through that lie in a second.

Deciding my best course of action was to be prepared, I started packing my bag. If I needed to get out of here quickly, I didn't want to leave anything behind, especially my laptop.

I was so stuck in my head, thinking about where on earth I could disappear to, I didn't hear Beau approach.

"What are you doing?" he asked from the doorway.

I jumped, clutched my heart and then resumed my packing. "Warn a girl, will you? I'm packing." I shoved a shirt in my bag, then peered around Beau to see if Michael or Nick were close by.

"They're in the meadow seeing if they can spot the smoke from here."

"Oh." I relaxed and went back to my bag. Beau's footsteps came closer but I kept working. One second I was folding up a pair of leggings and the next they were yanked out of my hands.

"Sit down," he ordered. "Let's talk this out."

He sat on my cot and I obeyed, plopping down next to him.

"Fuck." He started rubbing his jaw as my hand nervously twirled some hair. "What are the fucking chances? We never use this place. I can't remember the last time there was a fire on this side of the ridge. The one year when I don't want anyone up here and now it's going to be crawling with people."

The odds were not in my favor. This was the longest string of bad luck I could ever remember.

"And what a fucking time for me to take a vacation," Beau said. "If I had been in town, I could have steered everyone somewhere else. We need a fucking telephone out here. It's going to cost a fortune but I'm having one put in all the outposts in my jurisdiction. They should be able to run a line by the power poles."

Beau was rambling, something I'd never seen him do, and his fretting was doing nothing to ease my worries. With every word, I just felt guiltier for putting him in this position to begin with.

Part of me wished he had been in town too, but at the same time, yesterday had been wonderful. That waterfall hike had soothed so many of my troubles. And our kiss this morning? I couldn't regret that. Still, I just kept adding to Beau's stress level.

"Sorry," I said. "This is my fault."

"It's not your fault. Shit happens. Murphy's Law, I guess."

"I could go back to town," I suggested. "Maybe hide out at the ranch with Felicity and Silas."

"Not an option. I wouldn't put it past Ivan to come back. Right now, I don't want you anywhere near town."

I smiled at his protectiveness and fell into his side. He threw an arm around my shoulders and pulled me closer.

"Why didn't you tell Michael and Nick who I was?" I asked.

"The fewer people who know about your situation, the better. I trust them both but let's not drag them into our trouble if we don't have to. If we have to tell them, we can, but for now, let's go with the fake story."

"What if someone on the crew recognizes me? Or talks about me when they get back to town?"

He sighed. "I don't know what else to do. We're going to have to take a chance and go with the fake story. Fingers crossed people buy it."

"There's no way I can pull it off, Beau. Why did you have to make my pretend job about bugs? I hate bugs. I don't even know what a pine beetle looks like."

He chuckled. "Sorry, it was the first thing that came to me. Just do your best to be vague and avoid the subject completely. Stick close to me and we'll keep people off that topic. With any luck, the crew will get the fire contained in a day or two and everyone will clear out."

"I have a bad feeling about all this."

He sighed again. "Me too."

We sat quietly for a few minutes. As the trees rustled outside, my mind swam through all of the things that could happen in the next hour. Would someone on the firefighting crew recognize me? If I did need to escape the outpost, where would I go? I had come to feel safe and secure here.

I *liked* it here.

"Come on." Beau unwrapped me and stood. "Let's go outside."

He didn't hold my hand as we walked, which didn't surprise me. We needed to have a long conversation about that kiss and how quickly things between us had escalated, but now wasn't the time. Right now, he was Beau Holt, mountain-man hero. I was Sabrina MacKenzie, beetle lover. *Yuck.*

As we emerged from the trees and into the meadow, I

161

noticed a change in the air. The normal bright-blue sky had a filmy overlay and the fresh smell was now tainted with smoke. My eyes immediately started burning. From the meadow, I couldn't see a plume of smoke but there was enough of it in the air to determine the direction from which it came.

"So, how did the fireworks show go?" Beau asked Michael.

Michael blushed but just said, "Good."

"It was awesome," Nick said, patting Michael's back. "Best year yet."

"Congrats. What kind of stuff did you light up?"

The men started talking about the fireworks as I stared at them dumbly. How was this fire business not driving them crazy? It was driving me crazy! How could they be so calm? Of course, they were all used to this and none of them were on the lam from a dangerous criminal family. I had a few more problems on my mind. But still, fireworks? Couldn't that conversation wait until later?

"Have you ever been around a fire crew before, Sabrina?" Nick asked, pulling me from my thoughts.

"No." I shook my head. "I'm, uh, new to this line of work." I wasn't sure if that was the right answer or not but I didn't dare lie and risk being asked a specific question. I had no idea how a forest fire was managed.

"Some of the guys on their way here are a little rough around the edges," Nick warned. "The hotshots are adrenaline junkies."

"Good to know." I had never heard of a hotshot crew before so when I looked up to Beau, he grinned before I even had to ask my question.

"Hotshots are special firefighters for forest fires. They get trained differently than Michael's volunteer firefighters in town. The hotshots program is harder and they get pushed to the max physically. We send them into some rugged country and they've got to be able to hike at a fairly fast clip."

"The fires themselves are different too," Michael added.

"How so?" My curiosity was running rampant and I wanted to know more, but I also wanted to keep the conversation off of me and my "job" here at the outpost.

"They can be a lot more dangerous," Beau said. "A forest fire is always changing directions. There aren't walls to keep it in and the wind plays a huge role in how fast it grows. The firefighters get up close and personal with a burn. If they aren't paying attention, a fire can overtake them in an instant."

"That sounds . . . terrifying." Why any person would want to be around a wildfire was beyond me, adrenaline junkie or not.

"Hopefully, this one won't be too hard to manage," Beau added. "I'll know when I get a closer look."

"How exactly are you going to get a closer look? You're not going up there, are you?" I asked him, ignoring the smirk Nick threw Michael.

"Maybe. The fire is in my jurisdiction so I might go up to make sure the crew doesn't get lost. I was a hotshot for years so I know the drill. We'll see what happens when they get here." I did not like Beau's answer. He reached out and squeezed my shoulder. "This is an easy one. It's small and the crew should be able to get it under wraps pretty quickly."

Well then why did he need to go and help? I didn't ask. I knew the answer. Beau always helped. It wasn't in his makeup to stand by the wayside.

"What will they do?" I asked him. If he was going up

there, I wanted to know exactly what he'd be doing. Not that it would keep me from worrying.

"The crew's job is containment," he said. "For a fire like this, we'll send a plane or a helicopter up to drop a load of retardant around the border. Then the crew will hike up and start digging trenches, lighting backfires and putting out spot fires before they grow. Anything we can do to keep it from moving down the mountain."

"Yeah, like toward me."

All the men chuckled but I was serious. I had no desire to be anywhere near a fire and this one was already too close.

Question and answer time was cut short when the sound of vehicles echoed off the trees. Our huddle quickly disbanded as we all walked briskly across the meadow, anxious to greet the approaching crew.

Three oddly shaped trucks squeezed themselves into the open space by the outpost. The front of each sea-foam-green vehicle was shaped like a large truck, but instead of a bed behind the cab, there was a large rectangular box fitted with small windows. They reminded me of beefed-up armored cars, but instead of cash in the back, they were carrying people.

Beau hadn't been kidding about the physical requirements. Every man that jumped out from the backs of the trucks looked like he could take first place in an Ironman race. I was suddenly conscious of my lack of muscle tone. Everywhere I looked there were ripped biceps, washboard abs and buns of steel.

"Holt!" the driver of one of the trucks called.

Beau stepped away from my side to shake the man's hand. "Dylan. How are you?" Beau's tone was as distant and unfriendly as I'd ever heard.

"First fire of the season. We're pumped!" Dylan clapped his hands together and rubbed them back and forth. The grin on his face was borderline crazy. "Isn't that right, boys?"

The crowd around the outpost hollered and cheered. Nick had called these guys adrenaline junkies but that may have been an understatement.

"Holt, are you coming up with us?" one of the younger men called.

"Yeah! We could use your help."

Cheers filled the air as the men begged Beau to go.

He wasn't going up, was he? It was dangerous and he wasn't part of this firefighting crew. Didn't they already have Dylan as a leader?

As the cheers got louder and louder, Beau's shoulders fell. He held up his hands to quiet the crowd and said, "We'll see."

That meant he was going.

And while the hotshots were excited and anxious to get going, Beau's posture deflated a bit. He'd just added another heavy load to his already burdened shoulders. He didn't want to go up to fight the fire, but he would. He would because everyone had asked for his help.

Everyone except Dylan.

"We got this, Holt," Dylan snapped. "You can stay."

Beau's face hardened. "Like I said, we'll see. Show me your plan."

Dylan marched back to a truck and Beau followed. Spreading out a map on its hood, they hashed out a plan as the twenty-man crew unpacked supplies.

And with everyone busy, I slunk further away from the group. On top of worrying that one of these men would

165

recognize me, now I was worried that Beau would go with them up the mountain.

Nick must have sensed my unease because he backed away too. "Your boy is one of the best there is. If he goes up with Dylan's crew, they'll all be coming back."

"He's, um, not my 'boy,' " I corrected, though his statement did loosen the knot in my stomach a bit.

"Right," Nick said dryly. "Next you're going to tell me that you two weren't going at it right as we pulled up."

Curses.

Nick chuckled. "If I were going for a man, Beau would be my number one. Good thing for you, I'm married." He nudged my shoulder and I realized there was no use pretending he hadn't caught me.

I grinned. "Good thing for me."

"Seriously, though, Beau is one of the best. When it comes to navigating the woods, there's no one better in this part of Montana. The search and rescue team he's built in Jamison County is legendary. He gets pulled all over the state to help with tough cases. If he goes up with Dylan, everyone will come back safe."

I believed him. "Thanks, Nick."

"You're welcome." He bent low to speak quietly. "When things settle down, maybe you can tell me what you're really doing up here."

Caught again. "Okay," I whispered. Nick hadn't bought our fake story but I hoped that everyone else would be easier to convince. I didn't need a bunch of strangers trying to figure out my real identify.

"Suit up!" Dylan called out to his men. "We're going to hike up from here. The trail will be longer but it's an easier first mile."

A rumble of agreement sounded before bags were opened and the men began donning special clothing and boots with practiced ease. From the trucks, one man unloaded a variety of pickaxes and hand shovels. Beau folded up the map he'd been reviewing with Dylan before both men came my way.

"Sabrina," Beau said, "this is Dylan Prosser. He's the lead off the Big Sky Hotshots."

I held out my hand and greeted Dylan, but before Beau could explain who I was, Michael called him and Nick over to his truck, leaving me alone with Dylan, who still hadn't let go of my hand.

"What's a sexy gal like you doing up here?" Dylan asked with a smug grin.

"Working." I wiggled my fingers free and tucked my hand in my back pocket.

I kept my answer short and vague. This guy's cocky arrogance was seeping from his pores. I'd dealt with enough of his kind to know that the less you said, the better. He'd take even the slightest bit of kindness as a green light to hit on me relentlessly.

In college, Felicity and I had deemed men like him a Creepy Carl.

Dylan didn't get my hint and stepped too close into my personal space. "Working? Maybe later you can tell me what you like to do for fun."

I didn't have to tell him to back off. One of his crew members came over and interrupted his advance. "Would you mind if I filled my CamelBak with fresh water?" the man asked.

"Not at all." I smiled at the welcome escape and stepped around Dylan, giving him a wide berth as I went inside the outpost. I sensed his eyes on my ass the entire time.

The man that I had led inside wasn't the only visitor to my temporary home. Soon a line formed at the sink as the entire crew filled canteens and water packs. I slunk back into the corner and listened to their banter, grateful for an excuse to stay inside and away from Dylan.

Most of the hotshots were young men, I guessed in their twenties, and though a few of them had that roughness Nick had warned me about, for the most part they all behaved like gentlemen in my presence. Though, with as tightly as I was hugging the wall, I think most of them didn't even notice I was there.

"Holt said he was coming with us," a guy at the sink said to the man behind him.

"Maybe he can keep Dylan in line," another man muttered.

"Holt outranks Dylan and has more experience," a man third-deep in line said.

"Well, if Dylan keeps pushing the limits, I'm transferring teams," the guy at the sink announced. "Holt isn't going to be around all season."

"Dylan needs to pull his head out."

A couple of men nodded. "Fuck, yeah. I'm done taking stupid risks."

From the sounds of the team's dissension, Beau wasn't the only one who thought Dylan was reckless. Adrenaline junkies maybe, but these guys knew they were being pushed to the extreme. And though I didn't care for the idea of Beau out fighting forest fires, I was glad that he'd be going along to make sure this young group made it back safely.

"Sabrina." Beau was hovering in the doorway. I followed

him outside and around the corner of the outpost where no one could hear us.

"You're going up," I said, knowing his answer. He nodded. "Be careful, Goliath."

"I will, Shortcake."

"How long do you think it will take?"

"It's hard to say. If things go our way, a day or two. If they don't, then it'll be longer."

"Okay." I'd be back to pacing until he was back safely. I doubted even writing would keep my anxiety at bay.

"Listen, Michael's going to stay here just in case. I didn't tell him anything. I just said that with the fire so close, I didn't want you here alone."

"Okay. But I'm not going to be able to lie to him this whole time, Beau. Nick already knows something is off."

"Do what you think is best. I trust my brother to keep quiet. But—"

"I get it. You're protecting your little brother."

He nodded.

"I won't lie to him but I'll do my best to keep us off the subject of me." Though I had no idea how that was going to work. We'd be sharing close quarters for the next day or two at a minimum. The story of Sabrina MacKenzie was bound to come up.

"We need to talk about what happened in the kitchen," Beau said softly. "Are you okay?"

He was worried about my feelings at a time like this? Beau Holt was one of a kind. "Don't worry about me. Go. Save the forest. We can talk later."

"You're good with that?"

I smiled. "I'm good." I had a lot of questions about our kiss and what had suddenly caused Beau to change his mind but they could all wait. He needed to focus on getting himself and these young men back without harm.

"The gun is on the fridge," he reminded me. "I know you won't use it but Michael will."

"Okay."

He pulled me into his chest for a tight but brief hug before kissing the top of my hair and letting me go. As he finished gearing up, I stood with Nick and Michael, watching as the hotshots strapped on their heavy packs and tools. Then, like a line of ants, they started up into the mountains with Beau leading the way. The second he disappeared from my sight, a lead weight settled in my stomach.

"Beau's fought a lot of fires, Sabrina," Michael said. "He was a hotshot in college and then a team leader for a few years. He'd still be running a crew if he had the time."

"Thanks." I gave him a weak smile and bent down to rub Boone's ears. This dog had given me more comfort in the last three months than I could have ever imagined.

"Well, I'd better get back to town," Nick said. "Everyone's going to want an update. I'll park your truck at the station," he told Michael. "You're good to go back with Beau?"

"Yep," Michael said.

"It was nice to meet you," I said, standing up from Boone to shake Nick's hand.

"You too. When you get done working here with your beetles," he smirked at the way my shoulders shivered, "make Beau bring you to town. My wife, Emmy, and I will have you two over for dinner."

"Thank you." I waved good-bye.

Dinner with Beau's friends would never be an option. In all likelihood, I'd never see Nick again or meet his wife,

Emmy. It was a harsh reminder that Beau and I didn't have a future and that the kiss we'd shared this morning was courting nothing but trouble.

Something we would need to talk about later once the forest around my outpost wasn't on fire.

———————

TWO DAYS LATER, Michael and I were walking through the meadow alone.

Though I was still anxious for Beau's return, Michael had been a godsend these last couple of days. When I'd start to get worried, he'd assure me everything would be fine. When I'd start to panic that the smoke in the air wasn't clearing, he'd distract me with a new topic.

But best of all, he hadn't pried into my reasons for being at the outpost. He had asked me once and I'd told him that my situation was complicated. With one nod, he'd dropped the subject and hadn't brought it up again. Instead, we'd spent the majority of the last couple of days talking about him.

Michael Holt, much like his older brother, was an incredibly good man and he wanted nothing more than to make Beau proud.

"You really think I shouldn't worry?" he asked.

I laughed. "Yes, for the hundredth time. You have nothing to worry about. Beau is not going to care that you want to get a dog just like Boone."

"Mom and Dad are always telling stories about how I was Beau's shadow. I don't want him to think that I'm still that little kid, copying everything he does. I just really like his dog."

I could relate to that. If I ever got a pet, it would have to be Boone's long-lost twin. "Michael," I said, "trust me when I say that he will be flattered."

"You think?"

"I know."

He sighed. "He's my hero. Some guys look up to pro athletes. I've always looked up to my dad and Beau."

I swallowed an *aww* and patted his arm. "That's sweet. Buy the dog. Beau will see it as a compliment."

"Okay," he said. "I'm gonna do it."

"Now on to a more important topic, what are you going to name it?" I asked.

Michael smiled and started rattling off both male and female dog names. None were as great as Boone but I kept that opinion to myself. We were in the middle of a debate between Zoey and Sadie when a loud, thumping noise rang in the distance.

Michael immediately stopped talking and grabbed my elbow, turning me around and pulling me to the far edge of the meadow opposite the outpost. His long legs were moving so quickly, I had to run to keep up.

"What's wrong?" I asked when he slowed.

"Chopper." His arm reached up and pointed to the source of the noise, a helicopter coming right toward us. With every passing second, it grew bigger and louder in the sky. When it reached the airspace above us, the pounding of its blades reverberated against my chest.

My hair whipped around my face as the enormous machine hovered in the center of the meadow. The tall grasses flattened to the ground in a near perfect circle as it set down, and though the blades were starting to slow, the engine noise was still deafening.

"I'll be right back!" Michael yelled.

I nodded and covered my ears as he jogged the distance to the bright red helicopter. Ducking low when he reached the blades, he went to the passenger door, pulling it open and revealing the words Fire & Rescue painted on the side. Michael talked to the pilot for a few minutes, and when their conversation was finished, he waved, ducked again and ran back to me.

My heart was hammering in my chest, hoping that this unexpected visit was not to deliver bad news. When Michael grinned, my entire body sagged in relief.

"The fire is under control," he said. "They're on their way back."

CHAPTER ELEVEN

SABRINA

The firefighters in my meadow were having a bonfire.

"Don't you think it's just a little ironic?" I asked Beau.

He chuckled as he towel dried his wet hair. "Not really."

I turned from Beau standing in the middle of the room to Michael sitting in the log chair next to me on my cot. "You agree with me, don't you?"

I didn't get the reinforcement I'd been looking for. Michael just shrugged and smiled at his brother.

"Why am I the only one in this room that thinks a fire, *today* of all days, is ludicrous?"

"They're just celebrating," Beau said. "A lot of crews have traditions like this. The Big Sky Hotshots always camp out and party after their first fire of the year."

"I don't understand you Montana men. If I was covered in black soot and smelled like a burnt match, the only thing I'd want would be two consecutive showers, a gallon of soap and an actual bed. Having a campfire party would be the last thing on my mind."

"These guys don't give a shit about soap and most like sleeping under the stars," Beau said.

"Don't get me wrong. I don't begrudge them the chance to relax and celebrate a job well done. I can't imagine the stress and demands of their job but I'm just surprised they aren't making the quick trip home to party there."

Beau gave me a gentle smile. "It'll be fine."

He knew I was worried about these men hanging at the outpost longer than necessary. There was still a chance one of them could recognize me and question my presence. Though if they hadn't suspected anything by now, I was likely in the clear. Even if they did start asking too many questions, the amount of alcohol they were consuming would probably make it difficult to remember in the morning anyway.

Another irony, the crew hadn't bothered packing tents but had found plenty of room for alcohol. I decided not to bring that one up to the Holt brothers, knowing I wouldn't get any sympathy on that topic either.

"You guys want to go out there for a while?" Michael asked, standing from his chair.

"Sure," Beau answered for us both.

What? He wanted me to mingle at a bonfire while I was supposed to be in hiding?

While Michael rummaged around the kitchen, Beau tossed his towel aside and came to me on the cot. With one good tug, he pulled me up and into his space.

"Um, what are you thinking?" I hissed. "Don't you think it would be best if I stayed in here? You know, in *hiding*?"

"Yeah, I do. But I also think it will be kind of suspicious

if you stay inside. Trust me, they'll ask more questions about you if you stay inside than if you're out there with them."

"I'll hide in plain sight."

"Exactly."

"Okay," I sighed. "Just no talking about pine beetles."

He chuckled. "Deal. Did everything go okay with Michael?"

I smiled. "He's great. I had fun getting to know him."

"No problems?"

"None."

Beau and I hadn't had a chance to debrief from the last two days. After the helicopter had landed, Michael and I had stuck close to the outpost, waiting for the team to make the hike back down. The pilot had stayed, needing to discuss something with Beau, and shared some details about how fighting the fire had gone.

The wind, which had started out working against the crew, had settled that first night and the team had been able to dig a good perimeter trench and start backfires. With a series of strategically placed air drops of water and fire retardant, the blaze had been tamed and was no longer at risk of spreading. The crew was free to return, job well done.

The team had emerged from the forest early this evening, dirty and happy to shed their heavy packs. Beau's face had been nearly black, the skin around his eyes and cheeks the same color as his beard, but when he'd flashed me a bright, white smile, I'd almost cried with joy.

Whatever my future held, I'd never forget that smile. It had taken my breath away.

Beau hadn't wasted any time debriefing the team and talking to the helicopter pilot. The entire time, Dylan had stood away from the crowd, doling out angry glares to anyone who dared make eye contact. Clearly, something had happened up on the mountain but I hadn't had a chance to ask what.

After the debrief, the team relocated their gear and vehicles to the meadow for their party and the pilot flew his helicopter home. Beau had gone straight into the shower to clean up so now that he was fresh and crisp, I could finally ask what had happened.

"What's going on with Dylan?"

His jaw clenched tight as he shook his head. "He's a fucking fool. He wanted to take the team up a ridge that would have trapped us against a cliff. We got into it and I overruled him. He's pissed but I don't give a fuck. I'm reporting him as soon as I get back to town."

"That guy's a douchebag," Michael called from the kitchen. "Hey, can I have some of this Crown?"

"Go ahead," Beau and I said in unison, smiling at his brother.

Michael's playful nature was such a contrast from Beau's seriousness. Beau took on so much with those broad shoulders. I liked that he had someone to give him some lightness.

"You guys ready?" Michael asked, the whiskey tucked securely under his arm

"Ready," Beau said.

All I wanted was to snuggle up with Beau and let him curl me into his arms, but with Michael sharing the outpost's floor space, that wasn't going to be an option until his next visit. That was, if Beau didn't deem our kiss a mistake and stop spending the night again.

The three of us strolled outside and I took care to appreciate the beautiful scenery. The late evening sun was setting behind the mountains as we emerged into the meadow. With the sky above us darkening to navy and the horizon glowing gold, it felt like the heavens were smiling good night.

In the center of the meadow, the bonfire was burning tall. The crew had built a ring of stones in the circle where the helicopter had landed. The grasses were still plastered to the earth, making a smooth surface for the party's gathering point. Branches and small logs from the forest were piled in small clumps between groups of visiting men.

Men who were substantially cleaner than they had been earlier. How had that happened? Their faces were fresh and most had wet hair. Their protective outer layers, which had been covered in soot and filth, had been stripped away to mostly clean T-shirts and utility pants.

"Where did they clean—never mind." In the creek at the far end of the meadow, I saw a young brunette man washing himself in the cold water. "Shouldn't we tell them they can use the shower at the outpost?" I asked Beau. "That is what it's there for."

He shook his head. "I offered but they didn't want to intrude on your space."

"I don't mind."

"Don't worry about it, Shortcake. They're fine." He threw his arm around my shoulders for a sideways hug. My arm slid behind his waist and rested perfectly against his lower back. Walking with him in this position, like an actual couple, was too nice not to smile about.

We joined the party and I reluctantly let Beau go so he could shake hands with the crew. Most of the young men looked up at him with reverence. Michael wasn't the only one with stars in his eyes.

"Would you like a drink, ma'am?" A man with shaggy red hair offered me his bottle of gin. I recognized him from the line of men that had been in the outpost filling their canteens in the kitchen sink.

"No, thank you." Glancing around the bonfire, I realized I wouldn't be drinking tonight. No one had glasses and I didn't see a single bottle label that I recognized.

While Beau and Michael visited, I stood between them and people-watched. A couple guys had already laid out their beds on the grass and another was in the process of doing the same. From the bottom of his pack, the man unrolled a green mat, then dug around the inside of the bag to pull out a wool plaid blanket. With a proud smile, he patted his resting place, then stood to join the others.

It was impressive how little these men needed to be comfortable.

I looked to my feet and smiled to myself.

It was impressive how little *I* needed to be comfortable. Three months ago, I'd likened my time at the outpost to pure torture. Now, I'd be making some changes when I eventually got home.

My life in Seattle would be simpler, better, if I downsized a bit. My closet needed to be cleaned out and clothes sent to charity. I would do a better job of cooking for myself rather than constantly eating out. I might even consider finding a smaller, less extravagant apartment.

"Holt!" My attention snapped back to the party when a man summoned Beau over to his group.

"Be right back," Beau told me and Michael.

With his brother out of earshot, Michael asked, "So what happened with Dylan? Beau just gave us the high level."

The three men in our group shared knowing glances. The redhead stood between two black men that I'd learned were cousins. I'd already forgotten their names so I'd silently granted them all nicknames. Red, for the ginger. Tall Cousin and Short Cousin, for obvious reasons.

"It was bad," Tall Cousin said. "Dylan took a swing at Beau."

"Fuck," Michael hissed at the same time my mouth fell open.

"Yeah. The fucking dickhead was lucky your brother has extreme self-control. If it'd been me, I would have leveled Dylan," Short Cousin added.

My eyes scanned the crowd, searching for Dylan, but he was nowhere to be seen. Michael and the guys changed subjects but the back of my neck prickled. Even though I couldn't see him, I felt Dylan's creepy stare. I turned around, squinting through the dim evening light, until I caught him in the distance near the tree line.

"Oh, no," I muttered. My turn had sent the wrong message. Dylan pushed off the tree he'd been leaning against and started walking my way. A half-empty bottle of some dark liquor dangled from one of his hands.

Dylan's swaying steps crossed the distance between us surprisingly fast. The closer he got, the closer I inched to Michael. Where was Beau? He'd disappeared a few minutes ago behind one of the hotshot trucks.

"Hey, Sabrina," Dylan slurred as he stepped next to my side.

"Hi," I muttered, leaning back when he bent too close to my face and I got a whiff of his drunk breath.

"Dylan, back off," Michael warned.

I was practically hanging off Michael's hip now. I couldn't explain it, Dylan hadn't done anything other than just talk to me and invade my personal bubble but something was off. Maybe it was woman's intuition but I knew Dylan wasn't just a Creepy Carl. His interest in me went well beyond an ill-placed crush.

Dylan grumbled at Michael's order but took a step away, then tipped the bottle to his mouth. Bubbles burst inside the glass as the alcohol was sucked into Dylan's already drunk body. "Back off? She wants me, guys." Dylan wiped a dribble of liquid from his chin. "You know how it is. She's just playing hard to get."

"The fuck she is," Michael said, pulling me farther behind him.

"You'll see, Holt. You'll all see." His strange threat sent an icy wave of chills down my spine. The men in our circle all stared at Dylan in disgust until, finally, Red broke away and pushed Dylan toward one of the rigs.

I stared, unable to look away, as Red set up Dylan's bedroll, then forcefully shoved Dylan's ass onto his blanket. A slew of curse words were volleyed back and forth until Red threw his hands in the air and left Dylan to stew alone, slurping down more of his almost-empty bottle of booze.

"That guy's going to get his ass handed to him one of these days," Michael said. "He's just lucky Beau wasn't here."

"Hmm," I hummed my agreement, though I had a feeling it was *because* Beau hadn't been here that Dylan had approached in the first place.

"Talk about a mood killer," Michael said.

"Let's get something to eat," Tall Cousin said. "I'm starving."

I followed all of them over to one of the vehicles where Short Cousin rifled through a box filled with silver packets. Ripping one open, he held it out to me first. "Ice cream?"

"What?" I stepped closer and saw the inside was filled

with freeze-dried ice cream. "This is what you guys are eating?"

He shrugged. "MREs aren't so bad."

I broke off a piece of the cardboard-white square and sniffed it before popping it into my mouth. "That is not good. Not at all," I said, swallowing my bite. "Come on, Michael, let's raid my stash and bring these guys some decent snacks."

An hour later, most of the alcohol had been consumed, my food tubs had been decimated, and we were all having an awesome time.

Beau had returned to my side not long after Michael and I had brought out the food. I'd let out a huge sigh of relief when I'd looked over at Dylan's cot and seen that he had finally passed out.

With Dylan no longer staring at me, I was finally able to relax and enjoy my first campfire party. As the lingering sunbeams vanished and stars appeared, we all settled around the fire for an evening spent telling stories.

Me, the Holts and the hotshots.

"Having fun?" Beau asked softly as Short Cousin told the group a joke.

I was perched on one of my food tubs while he was sitting on the ground at my side. I looked down at him and smiled. "Yeah. I am."

"Hey, Holt. Tell us about your first fire."

It wasn't the first request the young men had asked of Beau. He'd told just as many stories tonight as he'd listened to. Everyone around the fire, including me, wanted to soak up as much Beau as they could before morning.

"It was a small fire," Beau answered. "Kind of like this one. I had just finished training and was the new guy on my crew."

Beau continued to tell the men about his experience on that first fire and the others he fought during his first summer as a hotshot. With every story, I felt closer and closer to him. Learning about his past cemented what I'd always known: Beau was as steady as a mountain in a storm. Nothing seemed to scare him.

I couldn't imagine him young and wide-eyed, like the men in our campfire circle. I bet his parents would attest to Beau always being an old soul. A part of me longed for the chance to meet them and learn about his childhood. To see his baby pictures. To see him relaxed and enjoying time with his family.

A sad and hopeless feeling settled into my heart. Our time together was fleeting. I needed to make a choice: push Beau away and spare my heart any further agony, or take as much of him as I could until our time was up. If that kiss we'd shared was any indication, the closer we got physically, the harder it would be to eventually leave.

The weight of that looming decision drained all of my energy reserves, and my eyelids started to droop. I yawned and patted Beau's shoulder. "I think I'm going to go to bed."

"Oh, uh, okay," he said, pushing up off the ground.

"That's okay. You stay. These guys would hate me forever if I deprived them of hero-worship time."

He chuckled. "Okay. Michael and I will be in after we finish our drinks. Here, take a flashlight."

I smiled and said my good nights to the men. Before I set off across the meadow, I took one last glance at Dylan, still passed out by the truck. Sleeping, he didn't look nearly as menacing as he had earlier.

Was I being overly paranoid? Dylan was very drunk and maybe I'd imagined the worst. I frowned, mentally cursing

Anton Federov. Other than the nightmares, I hadn't really experienced much post-traumatic stress from Anton's attack. I had thought I'd come through fairly unscathed, but now I was realizing he hadn't just done a number on my body with his beating. Apparently, he'd also given me a slew of trust issues when it came to strange men.

Shaking off those ugly thoughts, I made my way back to the outpost. The warmth of my little home chased away the chill I'd gotten after leaving the fire, and grabbing some sleep shorts and a T-shirt from my bag, I went right to the bathroom to get ready for bed.

I was in the middle of brushing and braiding my hair when I heard the door open and footsteps cross the living room. Hurrying, I tugged out the braid and tied my hair in a topknot. Beau must have left Michael at the fire and I was hoping we'd have a few minutes to talk about our kiss the other day.

"Decided to come back after all?" I asked, stepping out of the bathroom. My feet froze. It wasn't Beau, but Dylan, in my living room. "Uh, hi. What are you doing here?"

Now that we were inside and in better light, I could see how bloodshot and unfocused his eyes were. Dylan wasn't drunk. He was hammered. It was a wonder he could even stand.

"Just wanted some better company," he slurred. "Fucking sick of hearing Beau tell the guys how fucking great he is."

I had made a mistake in thinking Dylan had been passed out this whole time. Had he been waiting for this chance to follow me back? Surely someone must have seen him leave the campsite, right? My heart was racing but I fought to appear calm.

My eyes darted to the door, willing Beau or Michael to walk through it. Dylan's body swayed back and forth as he stood in silence and watched me. What was he doing here? The worry I'd felt earlier about his mental health was back in full force.

"Do you want some water?" I abandoned my spot by the bathroom door and walked sideways along the far wall. If the bathroom had a lock, I would have barricaded myself inside, but as it didn't, my gut was telling me to get as close to the front door as possible.

"Where you goin'?" Dylan took one step closer and I stopped mid-step.

"I'm just getting you some water. You look thirsty," I lied. He looked crazy.

"You know what I'm tired of?"

I shook my head.

"I'm tired of everyone always talking about fucking Beau Holt. The trainers. My boss. My own fucking crew! Be more like Beau. Do what Beau would do. Play it safe like Beau. Fuck safe. And fuck Beau!"

I flinched as he threw a hand out to the side while he yelled. The stumbling, bumbling drunk in front of me morphed into a raging lunatic. His movements, which had been sloppy seconds ago, were now oddly controlled as his anger boiled to the surface.

"Calm down," I said, holding up my hands and inching closer to the kitchen.

"Fuck calm!" he roared and I flinched again.

"Dylan, just take a breath. Let me get you some water. We can sit and talk this out."

When I took another step, he came at me with one long stride. "Talk. You don't want to talk. You want to get over

185

here and gimme a kiss. I saw the way you were eyeing me earlier. Wouldn't Beau just love that? Walk in on me kissin' his girl."

My whole body started trembling. This was too familiar, too terrifying. I'd lived through this with Anton and survived. I had fought to keep Anton out of my dreams. I wasn't going through this again with Dylan.

I just had to make it out the door. It was time to act fast.

With one huge step, I faked a lunge to the bathroom. Dylan bought my false move and dived for me. I was banking on the fact that he was drunk and his reflexes slow. While his momentum carried him one way, I jumped back the opposite way.

I made it one step before Dylan yelled and flung his long body backward. His boots slid on the wooden floor and he lost his footing, but as he fell, his arm swung wildly at my bare feet. His arm hit my ankle, causing me to stumble.

With a loud thud, my body crashed into the floor. The impact sent a shooting pain through my hip but I ignored it and scrambled onto my hands and knees, clawing with desperation toward the kitchen as Dylan awkwardly struggled to stand.

Dylan cussed and yelled again but the two fast steps I'd taken put me out of his reach. I exploded out the door and immediately started screaming Beau's name. Pine needles and small rocks dug into the soles of my feet as I sprinted through the night. As my eyes adjusted to the darkness, I held my arms in front of me, hoping not to collide with a tree on my way to the meadow.

"Sabrina!" I heard Beau's yell right before Boone barked and collided with my shins.

I lost my balance, but before I fell, Beau's mammoth arms were wrapped around my shoulders.

"It's Dylan," I gasped, pointing back to the outpost. I gulped a huge breath, trying to settle my heart. It was beating so hard it actually hurt inside my chest.

"What's Dylan?" Beau asked.

"He came after me," I panted.

Beau's frame locked tight. "Michael!" he bellowed, though his brother was already at his side shining a flashlight at our feet. "Stay with Sabrina."

"Calm down, Beau," Michael said. Behind him were nineteen hotshot bodies. I couldn't make out faces but their outlines were illuminated by the fire in the distance.

"Stay with Sabrina," Beau repeated through clenched teeth. His chest expanded in an angry breath before his arms around me loosened and were replaced by his brother's.

I pushed out of Michael's embrace and started walking after Beau. The adrenaline was leaving my system and my teeth began to chatter loudly. "Michael, stop him." Beau was furious and Dylan didn't stand a chance. His self-control wouldn't hold this time, and as much as I would like Beau to beat the crap out of that asshole, the last thing we needed was attention from the police.

I walked faster, my bare feet limiting my speed, but Michael clapped a hand on my shoulder. "Wait." With one swift move, Michael picked me up, looping his arm around my back and one under my knees. "Come on, guys." He called behind him as he jogged after Beau with me in his arms. A couple of the guys ran ahead of us and latched on to Beau's arms just as Dylan came stumbling out the door.

"What?" Dylan slurred. "I was just gonna kiss her."

Beau jerked his arms free and stepped right up to Dylan.

The punch he threw was so fast and hard, all I saw was a flash of skin before the resounding crack of Dylan's jaw split the air.

"Fuck," Michael muttered.

The hotshots were all hovering around Beau, though they didn't need to worry. He was already backing off a very unconscious Dylan.

Beau spun around and his eyes searched me out. He took two long strides and lifted me out of Michael's arms. My head fell into his neck as he walked inside without haste. Gently, he set me down on my cot and tucked my sleeping bag around my shoulders and bare legs. My teeth were still chattering and my muscles had started to shake from the mixture of cold and fear.

"Are you all right?" he asked

I nodded. "He just scared me. My hip hurts a little from where he tripped me and I fell, but I'm okay."

Beau blew out a long breath and hung his head. "I'm so fucking sorry." His eyes found mine. "I should have come inside with you."

I gave him a small smile. "It's not your fault and I'm fine."

"What happened?" he asked.

I recounted Dylan's visit quickly so the men outside wouldn't hear. The stress in Beau's shoulders eased when he learned that nothing serious had happened.

"We can't make a big deal out of this, Beau," I said quietly.

"He should get his ass thrown in jail."

"I agree but then my name would be on a police report. I'd rather have Dylan walking free than the Federovs knowing I'm in Montana." Besides, I had a feeling that

Dylan's sore jaw would be a nice reminder of his indiscretion. That was, if he even remembered what had happened.

Beau shook his head and thought about it for a minute before sighing. "Fine."

"Beau?" Michael called from the doorway. "What should we do? One of the guys went to get the sat phone from the trucks. Do you want me to have Jess come up?"

"No," Beau and I said in unison.

Michael gave us a sideways glance but shrugged and turned to the men crowded at his back. "No cops," he told the crew. "Let's wake Douchebag up and make sure he's alive."

The audience at my door dispersed and the men shuffled around outside. Boone jogged in and came right to my side. Michael came in soon after and declared he was going to hang with the guys for the rest of the night and just camp outside.

"Are you still cold?" Beau asked after Michael left with a couple extra blankets.

I nodded and burrowed further under my sleeping bag.

"Come here." He held out a hand and helped me off my cot. Then with practiced ease, he set up our sleeping-bag bed on the floor. Tucked into his arms, it only took ten minutes for the chill that had seeped into my bones to finally disappear.

The scare from earlier was still fresh but I said a silent prayer of thanks that it hadn't turned out worse. As it was, I'd be able to brush it off after a few days.

I sent up another grateful message to whichever angel had sent Beau Holt into my life. Because though tonight's circumstances had been extreme, I was undeniably happy to be back in his arms.

CHAPTER TWELVE

SABRINA

Early the next morning, the hotshot crew was in a subdued mood. As the first ray of sun lit the sky, they all roused from their simple beds and started packing up camp. Beau and I woke early too, anxious to see our visitors—one individual in particular—gone.

As his crew cleaned up the fire pit, loaded bags and repacked their vehicles, Dylan sat in the passenger seat of one truck with his head tipped back and his eyes closed. One entire side of his face was red and swollen from where Beau had clobbered him. I tried but couldn't summon a single ounce of sympathy for the asshole. Dylan had deserved that hit and the pain he'd be feeling for the next few days.

When the crew was loaded and ready to leave, Beau, Michael and I stood in a row, saying good-bye to the team. Michael promised to visit the guys that lived in Bozeman after forest fire season was over. Beau praised each and every one of the men for the hard work they'd put forward on this fire. And I plastered on a smile, doing my best to ease the worry etched on the men's faces as they apologized on Dylan's behalf.

As the crew's trucks disappeared down the rough road, a mountain of tension went with them.

"How did the rest of the party go?" Beau asked Michael.

"Quiet. We pretty much all stared at the fire, then fell asleep."

"Sorry," I said. "I had a bad feeling about Dylan and shouldn't have left the party alone."

"Don't apologize," Beau said. "We all thought he was passed out. I wish I'd hit that fucker harder."

"Down, boy," I teased, touching his arm so his fists would unclench. He grumbled but relaxed.

Beau was right. I didn't need to apologize. The fault was Dylan's, but regardless, next time I would be more careful.

Wait, next time?

I hoped that was just a mental blip because I didn't think I had it in me to fight off another Anton or Dylan. As promised, Beau had brought me my bear spray but I had no desire to learn how to use it. Hell, I hadn't even considered using the spray last night. Instead I'd run into the dark woods, barefoot.

God, Sabrina. You're worse than those stupid horror movie girls.

I pressed my lips together to keep my laughter inside. "I need more coffee," I told the guys, turning to walk inside. I didn't want to explain a sudden fit of giggles.

"So how are the supplies?" Beau asked, joining me in the kitchen a few minutes later.

I took a quick inventory of the cupboards and fridge. My

food tubs had been mostly cleaned out last night at the party but I still had enough to last a while.

"I've got enough for at least a week by myself."

"Okay. I need to get Michael back to town and check in at the office. I want to get my formal complaint in to Dylan's boss as soon as possible. I really hate leaving you after all that shit last night but—"

"Go, I'm fine."

"What if you have a nightmare or—"

"Beau, I'm fine. You need to report Dylan. I don't want something bad to happen to those guys because you were too worried to leave me here alone. I've got Boone and a novel to write. Really, go. I'm fine."

And I was. Being with him last night, sleeping safely in his arms, had done wonders to reassure me that I was safe in the outpost. I wasn't going to let Dylan take this place from me.

Beau dropped his head and sighed. "I'm sorry, Shortcake. If I could, I'd send Michael back and hang with you for the week."

"I know you would."

He reached out and cupped my jaw, stroking my cheek with his thumb. "We need to talk."

"We do but it can wait."

As much as I'd like to hash things out and talk about our kiss, a week to myself might be best. I needed the peace and quiet of my little forest house to reflect on just how much my heart could take.

"Okay." He dropped his hand. "You know I wouldn't leave if I didn't think you were safe."

I smiled. "I know, I'm safe. No one knows I'm here. I've got my bear spray and Boone. The outhouse is my backup."

He grinned. "I'll be back as soon as I can. Do you want anything in particular from town?"

"Hmm. A pint or five of Ben & Jerry's wouldn't go uneaten."

He chuckled. "Ice cream. Anything else?"

"Nope. Just don't worry about me and rush. Take the time to do what you need to do."

"You're the toughest woman I've ever met, Sabrina MacKenzie." He grabbed the hair I'd been twirling out of my fingers. "But I think I'll always worry about you."

Just like I'd always worry about him when we were apart.

———

THE NEXT WEEK dragged on until finally Friday came and Beau was back at the outpost.

Back, and torturing me.

"Again," he ordered.

"It's not going to work. You're too big!"

"I'm not too big. Try again."

I huffed and assumed my stance. With one swift move, Beau lunged for me, his arms reaching right for my throat.

I sidestepped and grabbed for his extended wrist and forearm like he'd shown me, locking his elbow straight. Then I brought my knee up hard to his groin, only pulling power at the last second so I wouldn't damage his man parts. I did the takedown he'd taught me, leveraging his forward momentum and his locked arm to get him on the ground with his shoulder at an odd and painful angle in the air while I twisted his wrist in a direction it wasn't meant to go.

"Can you get out?" I asked. He tried to roll but I pushed harder on his wrist.

"No. I'm stuck. Now you kick me in the gut with all your might. If you've got the right angle, you can always do another shot to the groin. A hard stomp on the lower back would work too. The goal is to inflict pain fast and hard so you can let go and run like hell."

"Okay." I nodded, releasing his wrist.

Beau jumped to his feet and brushed the dirt off the front of his gray T-shirt and jeans. "See? I told you that you could do it. Even though your attacker might be bigger, use what you've got to your advantage. You're quick on your feet. Use the weaker joints to inflict pain. And remember, big bodies fall hard when they miss their target. You did awesome."

I smiled as my chest swelled with pride. "Thanks."

Beau had come to the outpost for the weekend and our first activity was this self-defense class. He insisted that after Dylan's attack, I needed to be better prepared for the future. We'd been at it for hours and I'd only learned three techniques, but I had successfully completed each one. This last had been the most difficult, but with continued practice, I hoped to get more comfortable with the movements.

"Where'd you learn all this?" I asked as we each took a drink from our water bottles.

"I've got a black belt in karate."

"Really? That's awesome. I'm tempted to change your nickname from Goliath to Badass Beau."

He chuckled. "Let's not get crazy."

"How long have you been doing karate? Tell me everything." I had never met a black belt before. My gym in Seattle had a self-defense class taught by some police officers who were trained in the martial arts but I'd never made the time to sign up.

"I actually started in college. I got into it my freshman year and worked my way up to a black belt right before I graduated. I fell out of it after moving back home since there wasn't anyone in Prescott who taught."

"But you picked it back up?"

"Yeah. After Maisy got kidnapped and attacked, she asked me to teach her some basics and I started doing it again. Mostly, I practice in my garage but once every couple of months I try and get over to a dojo in Bozeman."

"That's amazing. Do you wear the white pajamas?"

He laughed. "It's called a gi. And yes. I wear a gi when I visit the dojo."

"Have you ever thought about starting up your own dojo in Prescott? You're an awesome teacher."

He shrugged. "I could probably build up a nice school, teaching one or two nights a week, but I just don't have the time. Maybe someday when I have kids."

"Well, I appreciate the lesson. Now if anyone tries to attack me, which seems to be happening much too frequently lately, I can take them out." I did a series of exaggerated karate chops in the air with a shrieking, "Hiyah!"

Beau laughed and shook his head. "Shortcake, you are one of a kind."

I smiled. "I'm taking that as a compliment."

"You should." He reached out and freed a lock of my ponytail that had gotten stuck in my ear.

My eyes locked with his as the mood shifted from playful to heavy. I inhaled but it hitched in my chest. Was he going to kiss me again? *Please, please kiss me again.* It seemed like so long ago that we'd kissed in the kitchen. It had only been a little over a week, but with the forest fire, the incident with Dylan and then him being gone in town, it felt like forever.

We hadn't talked about our first kiss yet, but for the life of me, I couldn't remember why we even needed the discussion. With Beau's eyes staring right into my soul, I didn't have one worry about where we were headed.

I'd follow him anywhere on earth.

Beau's chin tipped down another notch as we closed the small gap between us. My hand lifted up to his chest, but before I could touch him, he caught my hand and pulled it down to our sides. Linking his fingers with mine, he took a step back. My hopes of another kiss evaporated as he pulled me away from the outpost and into the sunny meadow.

"We should probably talk about that kiss," he said.

I frowned. "Okay."

"I'm sorry, Sabrina."

Sorry? Fabulous, he regretted it. Well, I didn't and I wasn't going to apologize. "I'm not," I clipped.

"Hey." He tugged on my hand. "That's not what I mean."

"Then can you please explain?" I was tired of trying to interpret Beau. Sometimes I thought we were on the same page, but other times, it was like we were on different sides of the library.

"I'm sorry if I've been sending you mixed messages. I had every intention of waiting for you to be ready but you looked so sad that morning. All I wanted was to take that away. I don't want to be the guy that hurts you, Sabrina."

Here he was with that "ready" crap again. During the last week, I'd replayed our conversations on loop and had come to the conclusion that he'd been talking about my ordeal with Anton. That he thought I wasn't ready for a new man because I was still emotionally and physically fragile from Anton's abuse.

"When you say I'm not ready, do you mean that I'm not ready to be hurt again? You think you'll hurt me?"

He nodded.

"Why?"

"You know why."

I really didn't. Beau was the kindest, sweetest and most thoughtful man I'd ever met. He'd move mountains to keep me safe. How could he think he'd hurt me?

Two different worlds. Beau's words popped in my head and my shoulders fell as it dawned on me. He was country. I was city.

I closed my eyes and took a deep breath as the realization cleared away my confusion. All along, I had known it would hurt when I eventually left Beau. He had been giving me time so that I could decide if I wanted to go through that pain or not.

Beau Holt was *such* a good man.

And if he was willing, there was no way I was going to keep up a barrier between us. I was an expert at self-preservation, but pushing Beau away to spare my feelings just wasn't an option. He was already a part of my heart. If it was going to get shredded when I left, I was going to take as much Beau as I could get until then.

"I don't know what's going to happen in one month or two, Beau. I don't really even know what's going to happen tomorrow, but I do know that you'd never intentionally hurt me."

"This thing between us isn't small."

"No, but it's not going away."

"Are you sure you want to sign up for something that could end in disaster?"

"Are you?"

He nodded. "I'm not going to lie and say I don't want you. We both know I do. But I'm going into this with eyes wide open."

"Me too. I don't want to always wonder 'what if.' "

He studied me for a moment before sighing. "Okay."

My heart filled with joy and my smile stretched wide. "The sex will probably be horrible anyway," I teased.

He laughed and stepped into my space. With one burst of strength, he picked me up and crushed me against his chest. My legs wrapped around his hips as he bounced me up further so we were nose to nose.

I closed my eyes, waiting for him to kiss me, but his soft lips just barely skimmed mine as he asked, "Should we find out?"

I nodded, breathing, "Yes."

Beau's lips spread into a grin before he spun us around and walked back toward the outpost. As soon as his feet were on the right course, his mouth claimed mine. *Damn, he could kiss.* Everything about him took control. Not just his mouth, but his entire body. One of his arms banded even more tightly around my rear while the other came to the back of my hair. His hand was so large, he had complete control over my head.

With one gentle twist, he slanted my face and thrust his tongue between my lips again. I opened for him immediately so our tongues could tangle. My arms and legs squeezed tighter and my hands dug into his back, clinging to him with every ounce of strength as he walked. I didn't need to keep a grip, he'd never drop me, but I clutched at his shoulders anyway.

I'd told him on numerous occasions that I didn't like to be hauled around but Beau could carry me like this any day of the week. How he managed not to trip on the uneven ground or run us into a tree was amazing given how fast he was moving. It seemed like we had just started our kiss when he broke away, fumbling with the door of his truck.

"What are you doing?" I panted.

"Condoms." He didn't set me down as he reached into the truck and rifled through the console. It was a good thing he had some stashed away or I would have forced him to drive back to town to buy a box. My birth control shot had run out weeks ago, and now that we'd finally agreed to sex, I was not going to sleep tonight without it.

As soon as he had condoms in hand, his mouth came back to me, this time working its way from the corner of my lips, across my jaw and down my neck. My head lulled to the side as Beau's soft lips traveled. The tickling of his beard sent shivers all the way down to my belly.

"Hurry," I moaned, tipping my hips up to grind even further into his body.

Beau wasted no time carrying me inside. He crossed the threshold and slammed the door closed with a kick, leaving Boone outside. In the middle off the room, he carefully set me down so he could whip the sleeping bag off my cot and fan it out on the floor.

I swallowed hard, trying to keep my feet steady, but the room was spinning. Beau's kiss had the power to make me nearly faint. Whatever was coming next might kill me, but at the moment, I couldn't think of a better way to die.

"Sabrina." Beau's sexy, deep rumble filled the room as he held out a hand. The instant my fingers brushed his palm, he tugged me into his hard chest and wrapped me up in his arms.

Between us, I dropped both hands to the hem of his shirt, sliding my fingertips under the cotton to trace the dips of his muscled stomach up to his pecs. I lifted his T-shirt as my fingers explored, and when I finally reached his collarbone, Beau reached behind his neck to jerk the shirt off and sent it flying behind my back.

My eyes dropped from his face to his chest and as my fingers continued to explore, I leaned in and pressed a kiss against one of Beau's nipples before doing the same to the other. Each time my tongue darted out and found his skin, he sucked in a sharp breath. The erection behind his jeans jutted firmly against my stomach and got harder with every lick.

I alternated between his nipples, enjoying the brush of his chest hair against my lips, until Beau grabbed both my hands, stopping them from reaching for his belt buckle.

"My turn." The tank top I'd been wearing disappeared to the floor and my bra wasn't far behind. Beau dropped to his knees on the sleeping bag and wrapped his arms around my hips, pulling me into his space. He was so tall that, even kneeling, I didn't stand much taller than him on the floor. His lips found my ribs as his hands slid up to my breasts, cupping them completely as his thumb and middle finger rolled my nipples into hard pebbles.

"Goliath, you're making me dizzy."

He chuckled but kept worshiping my skin.

My head fell to one side as I closed my eyes, savoring the feel of Beau's kisses and tugs. When his mouth started moving up, I looked down only to realize he wasn't moving, I was sinking. My knees were slowly giving out as I descended to Beau's lap.

When I straddled him at last, Beau's mouth replaced his fingers on one of my breasts. The ache between my legs became desperate as he sucked and flicked my nipple with his tongue.

"Beau." My soft plea filled the room.

"Lie down," he ordered.

Once I was laid out on our sleeping-bag bed, Beau's fingers started kneading my thighs. His strong fingers pushed hard into my denim-covered legs and ass, squeezing, then releasing until every muscle awakened. It was the most erotic massage I'd ever had. My hips were still resting on Beau's thighs so I lifted them up, urging him to go after the button on my jeans.

With a quick flick, the button was undone and the zipper pulled down, revealing my pink lace panties. Carefully, Beau slid the jeans off my hips and ass, down one leg, then the other. His rushed movements from earlier were now slow and deliberate. My panties, which he could have shredded with minimal force, were carefully eased down inch by inch until he looped them off each foot and I was lying bare.

"Fuck, Sabrina." The color of Beau's eyes as he took in my naked body was breathtaking. The light, stormy blue-gray was gone and in its place was a ring of deep slate.

Holding his eyes, I pushed up on one elbow and reached for his jeans but he gently swatted my hand away. He stood to unbutton them himself so I lay back, content to watch. Off came his boots and socks, then his jeans. His familiar boxer briefs were tented at the front and my eyes widened as I finally got a glimpse of what was underneath the cotton.

Beau's cock was enormous, just like I had suspected for a

man of his size. With one hand at its root, Beau started stroking. My breath hitched at the beautiful sight of him thick and rock-hard, just for me.

Quickly, he put on a condom, then knelt between my open thighs, coming down on top of me and resting his weight on a forearm. As his chest hair rubbed against my nipples, I arched up, wanting to feel his skin against mine as he pushed inside.

"I'm big, angel," he said, gripping his cock and rubbing it in my wetness. "Tell me if I hurt you."

I nodded and gulped, willing myself to stay relaxed, but Beau didn't thrust inside like I had expected. Instead, he kissed me again. All of my worries about his size disappeared as he kissed me lazily, his tongue working magic to clear my mind. The only thing I felt was burning desire and a throbbing, desperate ache.

Of course, he knew that. He knew his lips were magical, that they held the power to erase any thought that might flitter through my mind. All that was left was burning desire.

"Beau, please," I breathed.

He broke away and hovered above me, then inch by inch, he pressed inside. His hips rocked back and forth until he was buried as deeply as I could take him. My inner muscles burned and protested as they stretched, but soon the pain was gone and I sighed, ready for Beau to move.

"Eyes on me, Sabrina," he whispered. His strokes started slow, his body hovering over mine as he stared into my eyes. His sheer size alone had me trembling and on edge. But as I built closer and closer to my release, Beau's restraint lessened. With a power unmatched by any man in my past, his hips hammered deep, proving what I had once suspected.

Beau could fuck a girl into oblivion.

His cock hit just the right spot over and over, and before I could warn him I was coming, the most intense and blinding orgasm of my life exploded, ripping through every muscle of my body.

"Fuck," Beau groaned as I clenched around him, pulsing and squeezing his cock. "Fuck, you are beautiful."

The white spots in my vision finally cleared and I opened my eyes to watch Beau as he kept thrusting. My hands traced up and down his chest, then snaked around his sides and drifted toward his ass. When my fingers dug into the hard muscle, the cords in his neck tightened and his arms started shaking. Then with a loud groan and hiss, Beau's eyes snapped shut as he found his own release.

He managed not to crush me as he relaxed, giving me his weight for a brief second before twisting us both so I was lying limp on his chest. My head rested in the crook of his neck as we both returned from the stars.

"Definitely not horrible," I panted.

He chuckled, then framed my face with his hands, lifting it up to give me a quick kiss. "We better go again just to be sure."

My laughter was interrupted by another spectacular Beau kiss.

Then we double-checked that the sex wasn't horrible.

CHAPTER THIRTEEN

BEAU

In the month that had passed since Sabrina and I had started having sex, I'd learned one thing for certain.

I was fucked.

For every minute we spent together, I wanted ten more. And the sex? Fuck me. We connected on every level that existed.

So, yeah. *I. Was. Fucked.*

I didn't want her for right now. I wanted her for always.

I wanted what I'd never have.

"She's leaving," I reminded myself, something I did about a hundred times a day.

"Who? Sabrina?" Michael said, sliding into my booth at the café.

Shit. "Uh, yeah." He had left for the bathroom but there must have been a line. Now that he'd overheard a comment intended for my ears only, there would be no avoiding the Sabrina subject.

"You should get her a job here," Michael said. "She's awesome and then you two can keep dating."

Dating. Did walks in the meadow and dinners on the outpost floor count as dates? I'd never taken her to a nice dinner or a movie. Hell, I'd never taken her out in public. Were we dating? Regardless of the label, it was the best time I'd ever had with a woman, which made the fact that we had an expiration date really fucking depressing.

"I don't think that's going to happen," I told Michael. "She's from the city and I don't think Montana is where she wants to live."

"Have you asked her?"

"No." Why would I ask a question when I already knew the answer?

"You should." He unrolled his silverware from the white napkin, oblivious to the pain in my chest. Michael had completely taken to Sabrina after his visit to the outpost during the forest fire and I wasn't surprised he was pushing for her to stay. He had this look in his eyes every time he talked about her that said *please make her my sister-in-law.*

We needed to be done talking about Sabrina. Things were better at the outpost when I was with her. Back in Prescott, that's when the reality of our situation really sank in and left me feeling miserable.

Talking about it wasn't therapeutic. It just made things worse.

"So how's everything at the station going?" I asked, changing the subject.

"Good. Busy." Michael spent the next thirty minutes giving me an update on his job. When our lunches arrived, we ate quietly and I let my thoughts wander back to Sabrina.

She's leaving.

She's made for bigger and better things than a simple life with me.

She doesn't belong in Montana.

Now there was a total lie. Sabrina had professed her hatred of nature and all things outdoors, but she'd taken to it better than most women who had grown up in this area. She couldn't hide her love for the outpost. She was the happiest when we were strolling through her grassy meadow. And she'd looked like she was made to sit on the rocks when we'd hiked up to the waterfall.

She belonged.

Maybe if I could keep her in Montana long enough, she'd see that for herself.

———

SABRINA

The days were flying by.

It was the middle of August and summer was nearly over. I had been at the outpost for over four months and was as happy and relaxed as I had been in my entire adult life.

My enjoyment from writing, the peaceful environment and my budding relationship with Beau had created the perfect balance of contentment and excitement.

Beau and I had fallen into our best routine yet. He worked in Prescott during the week while I was writing, then he'd spend the weekends with me at the outpost, where we were basically having sex like rock stars. The few times we'd forced ourselves apart, Beau had guided me on short hikes or made me practice my self-defense.

The only thing I needed to be happier was an air conditioner to battle the late-afternoon heat in the outpost.

It was a good thing that neither Beau nor Boone minded if I was dressed in as little as possible. My wardrobe these days consisted of thin tank tops, cutoff denim shorts and black rubber flip-flops.

Even though I would have preferred a Sunday afternoon spent naked with Beau, the outpost was so stuffy this afternoon that we'd forced ourselves outside for a walk in the meadow before he had to leave for the week.

"The weekends go too fast," I said. "It feels like you just got here."

He reached out to grab my hand, threading his fingers with mine. "Yeah. And next weekend I'm not going to get here until Saturday morning."

"Oh." My shoulders slumped. "Okay."

After spending an entire week apart and without any contact, I lived for Friday nights when Beau would arrive. I never even attempted writing on Fridays because I couldn't sit still. Instead, I cleaned and listened for the sound of his approaching truck, running to the door at the slightest noise.

When he did show up, I usually attacked him the second his foot stepped out of his truck. This last Friday, we hadn't even bothered going inside before ripping each other's clothes off. Instead, he'd fucked me right up against the side of his truck.

Delaying my Beau time was not a welcome surprise. Who knew how many nights together we had left? Yesterday, he had driven me up on the ridge to check the news. The case against the Federovs was progressing more quickly than I had imagined and the papers had speculated they'd be sentenced before winter.

If we only had a couple months left, selfishly, I wanted all of his Friday nights.

"What's happening Friday?" I asked.

"I got a call from a friend from college. She's coming through town and wanted to have dinner to catch up."

"She?" I was completely jealous and didn't even try and sound cool. Beau and I hadn't really discussed exclusivity, and until now, I didn't think we needed to. Who was I going to meet in hiding? But it hadn't occurred to me that he might be dating other women because he just didn't seem the type to play the field.

He squeezed my hand and grinned. "Relax. She's just an old friend. Her best friend was my girlfriend so we spent a lot of time together in college."

I pouted. "Okay."

"Call me a barbarian but I like you looking all jealous."

"There's no use lying or pretending that I'm not. I hate that this *woman* gets one of my nights."

"Imagine how I feel. I'm jealous of my own damn dog because he gets to see you every day."

I smiled. "Does that mean you're smitten with me, Goliath?"

He shrugged. "You're just okay."

"Yeah. You're just okay too."

He looked down at me with a wide, white smile that made my heart jump. Smitten wasn't the right word to describe how I felt about Beau but the real word terrified me too much to even consider.

Beau's smile vanished and his head whipped back to the trees.

"What?" I followed his eyes but didn't see anything.

He held a finger up to his lips. He listened again, then

208

turned, tugging me along at his side. "Come on." He kept his strides short so I didn't have to jog but I hustled anyway. The clench of his jaw and tight shoulders couldn't mean good things.

The sound of an approaching vehicle filled the air as we got close to the tree line. That Beau had heard it earlier was remarkable.

Standing in front of me, Beau was my shield as we waited for the vehicle to arrive. My hands rested on his lower back, clinging to his T-shirt, and though I was scared, I reminded myself that Beau was here and the only visitors that had ever come to the outpost had nothing to do with my situation. This could easily be Michael coming to tell Beau about another forest fire.

When a black truck emerged from the trees and pulled into the clearing, Beau's entire frame relaxed. I peeked around him and saw Silas. My eyes darted to the passenger seat, hoping to see Felicity too but Silas was alone.

Silas parked and got out, then came right to us, shaking Beau's hand. "Hey, man. Hi, Sabrina."

"Hi. Is everything okay with Felicity?" I didn't care how many mafia goons were after me, if my friend was in trouble, I was going back to Prescott.

"She's fine. Well, she's not fine. She's stressed about the wedding, but other than that, she's all good." His face softened as he talked about his fiancée.

"Then what's going on?" Beau asked.

Silas shook his head and frowned. "We had a visitor in town today."

"Oh, no," I said at the same time Beau cursed. "Was it Ivan?"

"No. It was a guy from the FBI. He showed at the sheriff's station and spent the better part of the morning talking to Jess. He suspects you're either in Montana, or were. He said he got a letter from you a while back postmarked from Wyoming. Sounds like he's trying to trace your footsteps and guessed you'd come here."

I nodded. "It must be Henry Dalton. We got word to him months ago that I was alive. He's the FBI agent I sent all of my evidence against the Federovs to before my flight from Seattle."

"Well, he's been fairly insistent he talk to Felicity but Jess is stalling him. We could all lie, play it off and tell him you were here but left. Or we could arrange for you to meet him in a safe spot. It's your call."

It wasn't all that surprising that Henry had tracked me down. We'd been friends in Seattle and he knew how close I was to Felicity. It made sense he'd come looking in her hometown. What concerned me most was why he'd come calling now. I'd disappeared months ago.

"Why is he here now? Do you think something happened with the case?" I looked between Silas and Beau for an answer.

"I didn't talk to him," Silas said. "All I know is that Jess spent the better part of his day checking this guy out and then keeping him occupied at the station so I could come up here and talk to you."

Without any information as to why Henry was here, I didn't have much of a choice. Something had to be wrong if Henry had come looking for me now and I had to know why he was in Montana.

"How would this meeting work?" I asked.

"We'll pick a spot in the country," Silas said. "Jess will bring Henry and I'll bring you."

"Okay." My fingers found a lock of my hair. "Let's arrange the meeting."

"I'm coming." Beau's tone was final.

Silas nodded. "I didn't expect you'd sit this one out."

A nervous knot settled in my stomach, making it hard for me to take a full breath.

"All right," Silas said. "Let's go. Once we hit cell service, I'll call Jess and tell him where to meet us."

We wasted no time getting in Silas's truck and driving down the road. I was grateful for Boone being in the back seat with me so I could keep my hands busy by petting his head.

Beau turned around from the front, reaching over the console to set his hand on my knee. "It's going to be fine."

I nodded. "I just want to find out why he's here. Do you think he's here to tell me I can come home?"

"I don't know, Shortcake." His thumb drew gentle circles on my skin even as he turned back to the front.

We rode in silence for most of the trip, bumping along the slow track. My mind was spinning, and no matter how many deep, calming breaths I inhaled, nothing was easing the nervous sickness in my stomach. Finally, I'd had enough of the quiet and started peppering Silas with questions about the wedding.

"Did the seamstress finish Felicity's dress?" I asked. "Her last letter said she was worried it might not be ready in time."

Silas nodded. "Yeah. She got it yesterday."

Silas and Felicity were getting married in less than two weeks. Felicity had been keeping me apprised of the wedding details with letters she sent with Beau each week, so even though I couldn't be there in person, I was still a part of planning her special day.

"Good. And Rowen is all set to be the flower girl?"

He chuckled. "She's ready. Gigi's brought her over twice now because Roe insisted on practicing with Felicity. I guess having Jess pretend to be the bride and practicing at the farmhouse wasn't good enough."

I smiled, wishing I could have seen that. I'd never met Jess's wife, Gigi, or their daughter, Rowen, but from everything Felicity had told me about her niece, nothing about Silas's story surprised me.

Silas looked back at me through the rearview mirror. "She misses you like crazy, Sabrina. If you said the word, she'd postpone the wedding in a heartbeat so you could be there. I'd be fine with it too."

I gave him a sad smile. "There will be no postponing. You two have waited long enough."

For months, Felicity's letters had offered to postpone but my replies had always been final. My drama was not going to get in the way of their wedding.

"Take lots of pictures, make sure someone videos the ceremony, and freeze me a slice of wedding cake. That's all I want. I refuse to have anything this happy be delayed on my account. Refuse."

Silas chuckled. "Lis has one hell of a stubborn streak, but damn, Sabrina, I think you might have her beat. I'd pay good money to watch you two go head-to-head and see who comes out on top."

"My money is on Sabrina," Beau said.

I smiled, grateful for the easy banter.

We chatted more about the wedding, then Silas and Beau visited about things in Prescott while I sat quietly in the back. When we emerged from the forest and into the prairie, Silas called Jess and arranged for a meeting place outside of town while I swiped Beau's phone to quickly check on my family's social-media posts.

"Thirty minutes," Silas said after he hung up with Jess.

Too anxious to speak, I just nodded and turned to my window. The late afternoon sun was bright on the tall grasses swaying in the breeze. I had been so confined to my forest and meadow, being in the open was unsettling. Out here, I was an easy target, not protected by the mountain walls of my valley.

I had only been gone three hours but I already missed the outpost.

It was hard to believe four months had passed since I'd made this trip. In a lot of ways, it felt as if I were stepping back in time. I was climbing out of the wardrobe from Narnia, rejoining the real world as if no time at all had passed since I'd entered a different realm.

Taking a deep breath, I willed my knees to stop shaking. I hoped that whatever Henry had to say wouldn't take too long so the drive back wouldn't be in the dark. Silas and Beau still had to get back to Prescott tonight.

I hadn't appreciated just how much driving Beau had been doing to visit me. The thought of him coming back and forth was nearly as endearing as all the wonderful things he'd told me these last four months.

"There's Jess," Silas said exactly thirty minutes later, pulling off the side of a gravel road behind the sheriff's huge, bronze truck.

I swallowed the lump in my throat, took a deep breath and pushed my door open with shaking hands. Beau led the way to Jess's truck, and I followed on his heels, not wanting him out of my reach.

"Jess," Beau said, planting his hands on his hips, effectively hiding me behind his massive frame.

Jess jerked his head to Henry. "This is Henry Dalton with the FBI. He's here to talk with Sabrina."

Beau stood taller, not letting me sidestep him. I was sure that behind his mirrored sunglasses, he was glaring at Henry, but because he kept leaning to block my side steps, I couldn't get around him to see his face. His uber-protectiveness would have been funny if not for my jumping nerves. Finally, Beau dropped his arms and reached back to pull me right into the middle of the men's circle.

I gave Henry an awkward wave and a small smile. "Hi, Henry."

He frowned. "Sabrina."

I'd always thought Henry was tall, standing an inch or two over six feet, but in this group, he was the shortest other than me. His wavy brown hair was perfectly styled, per usual, but his normal boyish grin was gone. Agent Dalton was not happy with me in the slightest.

"Well, thank god you're not dead," he said. "You know, you could have just told me where you were. It would have saved me from having to track you down."

"Sorry," I muttered. "Secrecy has kind of been my thing lately."

"No shit?" he deadpanned.

"How about instead of giving her a hard time, you tell us what you're doing here?" Beau asked.

Henry glared over my head at Beau, then tipped his brown eyes back to me. "I'm here to take you into witness protection."

"What?" My mouth fell open. "Why?"

"Probably because you decided to investigate a family

with known Russian mafia ties without so much as a phone call to let me know about your ridiculous plan. Fuck, Sabrina. They could have killed you!"

At Henry's outburst, Beau's heat hit my back and Jess and Silas both stepped closer to my side.

"It's okay," I said, holding up my hands to try and calm everyone down. "He deserves the chance to yell. We've known each other for a long time, and he's right, I should have called him."

"Yeah," Henry muttered. "You should have."

"Back to the point. Why do I need to go into witness protection?"

"The rumor is that Russians from the mother country are getting involved in the Federov case. I've got a CIA contact on the inside who sent word that some of the higher-ups are taking a personal interest in this one."

My heart dropped into my stomach as Silas and Jess both muttered, "Fuck." Beau wrapped an arm around my chest, holding me tight.

How could I have been so stupid? My happy life at the outpost had been a dream. A delay in the inevitable. I didn't stand a chance against the Russian mafia.

"What did your guy on the inside say exactly? Is there a hit out for her?" Jess asked.

"No, not yet. It's strange, but right now, they're just looking at the evidence in the case. Doesn't matter. With them in the mix, I don't want to risk it. She has to come in."

"Why?" Beau asked. "Just because the case is getting more attention, that doesn't mean they're necessarily looking for her. She doesn't need to come in and risk a fuck-up on your part. You could have come here months ago when she sent you that letter but you didn't and she's been perfectly safe."

Henry snarled. "We don't fuck up WITSEC. And I didn't come here, because I've got eyes on the Federovs and every one of their known associates. If you add the Russians into the mix, I don't have enough manpower to make sure the focus stays in Seattle. You haven't had any visitors here yet, but trust me, you won't like it if they come."

"Trust me when I say you don't have as much control over Seattle as you'd like to think," Beau shot back. "Unless you'd like to tell me that you knew Ivan Federov came to Prescott in June."

None of us missed the flash of surprise on Henry's face. My confidence in witness protection was falling by the second because either Henry had an agent falling asleep on the job or someone on his team was playing both sides.

"She stays here," Beau declared.

"I agree," Silas added.

Jess nodded. "Me too."

"I found her, eventually someone else will too," Henry said. "Is that what you really want, Sabrina? Just waiting for someone to hunt you down?"

I shook my head. Henry was right. I wasn't safe. I had been able to ignore that reality at the outpost. Hidden away in the mountains, I had lost touch with how much my life was at risk. But now, here in the open, the fears I'd had in April came back in full force.

I didn't want to leave. I didn't want to be in witness protection, but what other choice did I have?

"Okay, Henry," I sighed. "I'll go."

Beau's arm clenched tight. "No."

I twisted my neck to look up to his face. "No?"

216

"It's too soon, Shortcake. Don't leave yet. Give it a couple more months at least." His soft plea melted my heart.

I turned back to Henry. "Do I have to decide today? What's the harm in me staying hidden here for a little while longer? We could wait and see how the trial shakes out. Maybe your source with the Russians can give you a better idea of what they want and if they're even interested in me at all."

"Sabrina, this is stupid." Henry's jaw clenched tight and he threw an arm out to the open prairie. "I can't protect you out here."

"You don't need to," Beau said. "We've got her."

Henry and Beau went into another stare down but I didn't let it go on long.

"Henry, please?" I begged, drawing his focus. "I'm not ready to say good-bye to Sabrina MacKenzie yet. If that's what needs to happen, fine. But let's just make absolutely sure first. Please?"

"We've known each other for years," he said. "I don't want to say good-bye to Sabrina MacKenzie either, but I'd much rather know you were alive living as someone new rather than a murder waiting to be investigated. Witness protection is the answer."

"I promise I'll go willingly if that is what needs to happen. But not yet."

"I can't agree to this," he clipped.

"Please?" I whispered.

His suit-clad chest expanded before he blew out a loud huff. "Fine. It's your choice."

"Thank you." I rushed out of Beau's embrace and gave Henry a hug. "Thank you."

He hugged me back, his designer cologne filling my nose.

"You know, I was the one who came to your apartment the morning after you disappeared. I got that file you sent and then the call that there had been a disturbance at your house. I swear, Sabrina, I thought I'd find you dead."

"I'm glad you didn't."

He sighed. "Me too."

I squeezed him tighter before stepping away. Once upon a time, I'd had a crush on Henry Dalton. He was handsome and smart, and when he smiled, he had an adorable dimple in one cheek. But even his pretty brown eyes couldn't conjure the butterflies I used to feel for him.

Those little flutters all belonged to Beau now.

"Would you do me a favor when you get back to Seattle?"

He nodded. "Name it."

"Will you check in on my family? I'd like to make sure they're all okay."

"They are," he said. "We've had an agent watching them since you went missing. Everyone's fine."

Checking social media was one thing but hearing from someone I trusted that my parents and brothers were fine was an immense relief. "Thank you."

"I need to be able to call you."

"Okay," I said at the same time Beau declared, "No."

"Why not?" I asked, turning around. "Don't you think it would be good to know what's happening?"

"Any message he needs to send can go through Jess. You're going to disappear again."

Henry let out a dry laugh. "You know I could find her. Obviously, she's been with you. How long do you think it will take me to figure out who the fuck you are and where she could be staying?"

Beau's hands fisted and a couple of knuckles cracked. "I'm thinking you're going to leave here and not draw any unnecessary attention to why you've been on *vacation* in Montana. That would include asking a bunch of questions about me and my relationship with Sabrina. You wouldn't want anyone to follow your tracks, now would you?"

Henry's jaw ticked as he gave Beau a short nod before looking to me. "I hope you know what you're doing with this guy."

I wasn't sure if he meant my relationship with Beau or that I was trusting Beau with my safety. Regardless, my response was the same. "Yes, we know what we're doing."

Henry turned to Jess. "You can get word to Sabrina if we need to in a hurry?"

"Yeah." Jess nodded.

"Okay. Take care of yourself," Henry told me.

"I will. You too."

He pulled a pair of Ray-Bans from his suit pocket and slid them over his eyes. Then without another word, he walked back to Jess's truck.

"Let's go," Silas said.

Without delay, I got back in Silas's truck, leaning down to give Boone a short hug. Silas and Beau loaded up and we roared away, Jess's truck leaving a dust stream in its wake as it went the opposite direction.

"I don't trust that guy," Beau said.

Silas chuckled. "That's just because he wants what you have."

Beau mumbled something under his breath but I couldn't hear him. I was too busy replaying Silas's jest.

Did Henry have feelings for me? I'd always thought my

crush on him was one-sided. No wonder Beau and Henry had both been puffing up their chests.

Men.

They might have an issue with one another but I was content to let a group of large, strapping men act as my protectors.

Because if the Russian mafia was after me too, I would need all of the protection I could get.

CHAPTER FOURTEEN

SABRINA

The drive to the outpost the second time was just as nerve-racking as it had been the first.

Different but no less stressful.

On my first journey into the woods, I'd been nervous about where I was going, scared of the forest creatures and uncomfortable next to Beau's dog. Now, those worries were long gone but new concerns had sprouted in their place. The outlook for my future was just as bleak as it had been in April.

I hadn't gone with Henry to witness protection but was I just postponing the inevitable? Would I ever get my life back? As my body jostled around on the bumpy road, I sat silently wondering if it was pointless for me to wish for anything other than to simply stay alive.

Silas and Beau stayed mostly quiet too on the drive back. It wasn't until we were an hour into the wilderness that either of the men spoke. Even then, their conversation was limited.

"We should have driven part of the way so you didn't have to take us all the way back to the outpost. You'll be lucky to get home by ten," Beau told Silas.

"I don't mind. Felicity has wedding stuff with Gigi tonight anyway."

A stab of jealousy zinged through my side. Felicity wasn't having attendants because I couldn't be a part of their wedding but it still hurt that I was missing everything.

Maybe I needed to get used to this. Was her wedding just a preview of my eventual reality? Would I be trapped in a new identity in a faraway town, forced to watch silently through Facebook posts and Instagram photos how my family and friends were living?

I didn't want that life. I didn't want to start over. I didn't want to lose the people that I loved.

A tear dripped down my cheek and I swiped it away, not wanting Beau or Silas to know I was crying. It was selfish to feel sorry for myself. The only person to blame for these circumstances was me. Had I not written the Federov story, I would be safe in Seattle, having my bridesmaid dress fitted and packing for a vacation to Montana to be in Felicity's wedding.

On the whole, my story had triggered more positive outcomes than bad, but it had come at great personal cost. The worst of it was, had I known this was how it would all turn out, I don't know if I would have written the article. Would I have let the gun smuggling continue? Would I have let the Federovs keep ruining lives?

No. Even though it might have destroyed my life, I still would have written the story.

For Janessa.

By the time we pulled up to the outpost, it was nearly seven. I didn't feel much like eating but my stomach was growling for dinner.

"Do you guys want something to eat before you head back to town?" I asked.

"I'd take a sandwich for the road," Silas said.

"Sure thing." I hopped out of the truck and hustled inside. By the time the guys joined me, I was in the middle of slapping together four peanut butter and jelly sandwiches. I wrapped up two in a paper towel for Silas and gave him my last bag of chips with a bottled water.

"Thanks," he said.

I smiled. "You're welcome. Can you give something to Felicity for me?"

He nodded. "You bet."

Then I rushed into his arms, hugging his waist as tightly as I could. His hand patted my back but I didn't let go until my nose was no longer stinging with the threat of tears.

When I stepped away, I forced a smile. "There, give her that hug. Tell her I miss her, I love her and that she'll be the most beautiful bride in history."

He reached out and squeezed my shoulder. "You'll see her again, Sabrina."

"I really hope so." My voice cracked but I didn't let it stop me from saying what I needed to say. "But if I don't, promise me you'll make her happy. Give her cute little blond babies and spoil her rotten at Christmas. Take her on a vacation once a year so she can get a tan. She deserves to be happy, Silas."

"I promise," he said softly. "I'll make her the happiest woman alive."

"Thank you," I whispered as my eyes flooded.

Beau stepped up and curled me into his side. With his free hand, he shook Silas's, then pulled me tighter as Silas walked outside and drove away.

"It's going to be all right." Beau held me tight as I lost control of my tears. My shoulders shook violently as I kept trying to tamp down the loud sobs. I couldn't cry long because Beau needed to get home, but when he was safely on the road, I'd let my emotions loose. I could hold it in for just a little while longer.

"I'm good," I hiccuped and stepped away. "Let me get your sandwiches so you can go."

He reached out and pulled me back into his arms. "I'm staying tonight."

"You don't have to." There wasn't any conviction in my words. I wanted him to stay and hold me all night long.

"I'm staying," he repeated.

I lifted my chin so he could bend down and lightly brush his lips to mine. He lingered a bit but broke apart when my stomach growled again.

"We'd better eat." I demolished one peanut butter and jelly in record time while Beau ate the other.

"How are you feeling?" Beau asked as I made him another sandwich.

I shrugged. "Sad. I'm starting to lose hope that I'll ever get to go home again."

"Would that really be so bad?"

I set down my butter knife. "What?"

"If you couldn't go back, would that really be so bad?"

I spun around from the counter, angry at him for making light of the situation. The stress of the day made me snap. "How could you even ask that? Of course it would be bad. I want my life back." I'd be making some changes to my former lifestyle but at least I'd still be me.

"You want your Seattle life back?" he asked.

"Yes." I was baffled by his question. "What other life do I have?"

Beau's jaw clenched tight and the vein on his forehead bulged. "Seriously?"

Gah! Why the hell was he angry? I was the one who had the right to be upset. It wasn't his life, his identity on the line here. His temper had spiked for no reason except that I wanted to go home. This was ridiculous. *He* was being ridiculous.

"Yes, seriously. I want to go home. I want to live my life. I want to be free to make my own choices." I didn't know what witness protection entailed but my freedom and independence would most likely be limited.

Beau shook his head. "You're hell-bent on going home and picking up right where you left off?"

"Yes!" How was this a shock? Witness protection would be any sane person's last resort.

"You wouldn't even consider living somewhere else?"

"No." My mouth hung open as I gaped at him. I wouldn't even get to pick my new home. The FBI would do that for me. Of course I wouldn't want that. Was he crazy?

"Huh," he scoffed. "I guess I shouldn't be surprised." I stared at him wordlessly as he marched over to the fridge and yanked out a water, slamming the door closed so hard the condiments in the door's shelves went crashing.

I crossed my arms over my chest. "I can't believe you're mad at me."

"And I can't believe I'm falling for a girl who is so stubborn, she won't even consider that the life she wants to return to so badly is complete shit." Without looking back, he grabbed his keys off the counter and stormed outside.

"At least that life is of my own making!" I yelled at his back.

Beau didn't respond other than to slam his truck door shut and gun the engine when it roared to life. Tires spun and dirt flew as he drove away at reckless speed.

"Don't drive crazy! You'll hit a tree!" I shouted, not that he could hear me.

No sooner had his taillights disappeared than I saw them coming back, full speed in reverse. Beau left the truck running and his door open as he strode my way. "I need my bag."

I marched inside first, grabbing his backpack from the floor and throwing it at him. He caught it and slung it over his shoulder, not sparing me another second before turning around.

He might have been done with our fight but I wasn't. I didn't even know why we were fighting, but since I didn't have the luxury of running away, I kept shouting before he could disappear again, "If you wanted me to go into witness protection so badly, what was all that about with Henry today? Why didn't you just let him take me?"

His feet ground to a halt on the wooden floor. "What?"

"If you think my current life is 'complete shit,' then why didn't you just let me leave today? Henry would have erased that life you deem so bad and I'd have an entirely new existence."

Beau turned around, the hard scowl on his face replaced with confusion. "What are you talking about?"

I threw my hands in the air. "What are *you* talking about? You asked me how I was feeling and I told you I was sad that I couldn't go home. Then you got angry because I don't want to give up my entire life, my family and my friends just to start over as a figment of the FBI's imagination. Even if my life is crap, Beau, it's better than witness protection. But if you think otherwise, why didn't you send me with Henry?"

His bag slid off his shoulder and both hands came up to rub his face as he sighed, "Fuck. I'm sorry."

Okay, now I was confused. "Sorry for what?"

"I didn't know you were talking about witness protection."

"You didn't?" I replayed our argument. If he didn't think I was talking about witness protection, then why had he gotten so angry? "You need to keep explaining."

He sighed and waved me over. "You need to come over here."

I frowned and shook my head. "You come here."

"Meet in the middle?"

I took one step and waited for him to do the same. One foot at a time, we only stopped when my bare toes were up against his tennis shoes.

"Why do you always do that?" I whispered when his hand lifted and pulled away the lock of hair I'd been twirling.

"Because you have nothing to be worried about."

Beau knew me well. I wished I had a better handle on him so maybe I wouldn't have to ask so many questions. "Why did you get mad?"

"Let's just say, I was upset that you didn't have an open mind."

"Huh?"

"No more questions." He smiled and bent down to press

227

a kiss to my forehead. Then another to my nose. Then another on my lips. "Don't move."

I wanted to ask more questions but he vanished from my space and jogged outside, turning off his truck and shutting the door. Then he was back, this time rushing into my space and slamming his lips onto mine. I opened immediately, letting him take control and explore my mouth with that magical tongue.

Kisses now. Questions later.

His fingers roamed feverishly, running up my spine and through my hair, then working down my front, squeezing my breasts roughly through my tank top and bra. He may have been dominating our kiss but my hands were probing as frantically as his were.

I pressed hard into his back but my fingers were no match for the defined, toned muscles that ran from his shoulders to his hips. My palms skimmed lower, sliding under the waistband of his jeans. When my hands were molded perfectly to his sculpted ass, I gave him one tight squeeze, pulling his hips further into my space so I could feel his growing erection against my belly.

He groaned into my mouth, the vibration sending a whole new wave of heat to my center. Needing more, I slipped my hands out of his jeans and brought them between us, working the button on Beau's jeans and carefully undoing the zipper.

One hand dove inside his boxers and gripped his hard cock tight. My strokes were short, but Beau ripped his lips off mine with a loud hiss.

"Turn around," he ordered.

I immediately obeyed. Beau always preferred for our eyes to be locked during sex and had never taken me from behind. The idea of his powerful hips slamming into me while I was on my hands and knees? So hot I shivered and my pussy clenched.

The sound of rustling clothes filled the room as Beau stripped down, tossing his shirt and jeans into a pile by our feet. Then his hands came to my shirt, jerking it over my head, while I worked down my shorts and panties. With a flick on the clasp, he undid my bra so I could toss it to the floor.

"Down on all fours, angel," he whispered to the soft skin under my ear.

I shivered and dropped, closing my eyes and savoring the sound of him calling me "angel" in that gravelly voice.

The front of Beau's thighs rested against the back of mine as he joined me on the floor. Glancing over my shoulder, I saw him rip open a condom packet with his teeth then drop his eyes as he rolled it on. His gaze came to mine and with a sexy smirk, he guided that hard cock right to my entrance, rubbing it against my clit a couple of times before pressing it against my opening.

I was so primed and ready, he eased inside without any resistance. Moaning, I closed my eyes and savored the stretch of my body around his thickness. I ached for him to let go of his restraint.

Over the last month, I'd developed a theory about sex with Beau. When he was inside me, he could read my mind. I rarely had to beg and even then, my pleas were more automatic responses to whatever he was already doing.

Unleashed, Beau started pounding into me hard and fast, giving me exactly what I needed. His cock thrust deep and with every slap of his skin to my ass, he hit a spot inside my body that made me gasp and tremble.

"Sabrina," he groaned. "You feel so good." His hands came to my hips, digging into my soft curves as he lifted me up just an inch to find that angle that sent me from needy to desperate.

Thrust after thrust, he pulled me back onto his cock as his hips powered forward. I opened my mouth to say harder but I couldn't speak. My orgasm was right there, building and building until all I could do was feel it explode. "Beau," I cried out as it hit and rushed over me in waves so intense my arms gave out and I had to rest my elbows on the floor.

"Fuck," Beau hissed as my inner walls clenched around him, pulsing as I came longer and harder than ever before.

He didn't give me a chance to recover from my first orgasm. Just as I was starting to breathe again, one of his hands slipped around my stomach and found my clit. With the perfect combination of speed and pressure, his middle finger sent another orgasm ripping through my body. This one was shorter but even harder than the last.

Completely limp and wrung out, I rested my head on my hands as Beau continued to pound with force, reaching for his own release. Just in time to see him come, I opened my eyes and looked over my shoulder. His beautiful chest was covered in a sheen of glistening sweat and his eyes squeezed shut as he moaned my name.

That sexy man was all mine. For today, tomorrow and however long we had, he was mine.

Beau's eyes opened and we locked gazes. With those dark ocean blues, he silently claimed me too.

Without breaking our connection, he reached down and lifted me up against his chest, wrapping one arm around my breasts as the other kept my hips pinned so I was resting on his softening cock.

I tipped up my chin to give him my mouth for a kiss entirely gentle and sweet. His beard tickled my chin as our lips worshipped one another. When he broke away, his arms hugged me tight for a moment before letting go and helping me stand. I instantly missed him as we slid apart.

Brushing the hair away from my face, I caught my breath while Beau went to take care of the condom. When he rejoined me in the living room, I fell into his arms, giving him most of my weight.

"Hmm. I could sleep here."

He chuckled. "Don't go passing out on me yet."

"Did you have plans?" I grinned.

"I've always wanted to know if we could both fit in the shower."

I laughed and shook my head. "No way. It's too small."

"There's only one way to find out."

An hour later, the bathroom floor was covered with water that had escaped the curtain, all my toiletries had been knocked down off their shelf and I was sated from another amazing orgasm.

As long as Beau had me pinned against the wall with my legs wrapped around his waist, we could both fit in the shower.

———

"I'M glad you forgot your bag, Goliath."

His fingers were tracing circles on my lower back. "Me too."

After our shower, he had set up our bed on the floor and we'd curled in for an early bedtime so Beau could get up before five and make the trip back to Prescott in the morning.

Normally, we both slept on our sides facing one another, but tonight, Beau was on his back and I was draped across his chest. I wasn't sure why he liked the other position better but this was my new favorite. My toes were running up and down his muscled calves and my ear was pressed right against his heartbeat.

"Let's play our question game," I said.

He hummed his agreement.

"You're falling for me?" I asked his chest. Even though he'd said it during our argument, I hadn't missed it.

"I think you know the answer to that one, Shortcake." His lips pressed into the top of my hair.

I was falling for him too.

"My turn," he said. "Would you ever consider moving away from Seattle?"

I had asked myself that same question for the last month. The idea of being with Beau in Prescott was so tempting, but on the other hand, I knew myself well enough to know that I would suffocate in a place so small. The last thing I wanted was to resent him for trapping me in Montana.

"I don't know," I said. "There might be some things to change so I'm happier but I miss Seattle. Would you ever live in the city?"

He sighed. "I can't leave Prescott. I need to be here for family. Especially Coby. And I can't see myself being happy in a place like Seattle. No space. So many people. I think it would slowly choke me to death."

I hated his answer but at least it was honest.

Our argument from the kitchen earlier now made sense. When he'd asked if not going back to Seattle would be so bad, he'd been asking if I'd consider a life in Prescott.

"Where does that leave us?" I asked.

"The same place we've always been. Here together for as long as we have."

"Okay." My throat started to close but I held off tears. If I didn't get to keep Beau for a lifetime, I wanted to fill the time we did have with only happy moments.

When my emotions were under control, I propped my chin up on his chest so I could memorize the way Beau's face looked tonight. His eyes were light in the darkening room. The crease between his eyebrows was relaxed and disappearing. His hair needed a trim but his beard was shorter than it had been when we'd first met.

"What do you look like without your beard?" I asked.

He grinned. "Younger. More like Michael."

"When was the last time you shaved?"

"I shave my neck every day for work but I haven't been without the beard in ages. Eight years, I think. Why?"

"Just curious, I guess. I doubt I'll ever get the chance to meet your mom so she can show me your baby book and high-school yearbook pictures."

Why did that realization hurt? I was infatuated with Beau's beard, but right now, I wanted nothing more than to see him without it. To have that glimpse of him as a younger man. To run my hands across his smooth skin and learn every angle of his strong jaw.

Just once.

"I'll make an agreement with you, Shortcake. I'll shave my beard if you promise me you'll never cut your hair short."

"Really?"

"Really. I love your long hair." His hand abandoned my skin to tug at the ends of my hair resting on our bed. It had grown two or three inches since I'd been at the outpost and now hung to my waist.

"But don't men usually love their beards?"

He grinned. "Yeah, I love my beard, but I think I'm getting the better end of the bargain. Besides, give it two weeks, and I'll have it grown back."

I smiled. "I'm in."

"Good. Now let me up and go find me your razor."

"What? Tonight?" I asked, pushing off his chest.

"I like to lock in my agreements before people have a chance to change the terms."

My smile got wider as I stood and went to my bag, pulling on some panties and pajamas. Beau wandered into the kitchen and I heard him rattling around while I went to the bathroom and found my razor and shaving cream.

"This will have to work since I don't have my trimmer." Beau held up a pocketknife and sharpening steel that he'd brought into the bathroom. He assumed his place at the sink and I sat on the toilet seat to watch in utter fascination.

"You're really going to do this?" I knew how attached men got to their facial hair. At any moment, I expected him to back out.

He nodded. "I think you're underestimating how much I love your hair."

I smiled as my heart swelled.

After sharpening the knife, slowly and with extreme care, Beau began dragging the blade across his jaw. Small hairs fell into the sink as he scraped off the longer hairs on his face. Next, he wet his patchy scruff and lathered on a thick layer of my Gillette pink shaving cream. Then with my yellow Venus razor, he worked his way across his face, erasing the beard and leaving behind a new Beau.

After washing off the remnants of the shaving cream, he

inspected himself in the mirror before patting his face dry with a towel and turning to me.

Standing stark naked in all his glory, Beau had gotten rid of something he'd had for eight years just to satisfy my curious nature and make me happy.

"Well?"

My eyes welled and I lost sight of him in the blur.

I was in love with him.

I knew I'd fallen before, but I hadn't admitted it to myself. But sitting in this tiny bathroom, I couldn't deny it any longer. I was hopelessly in love with Beau Holt.

"That bad?" he asked.

I shook my head and wiped my eyes dry. "Not bad at all."

Beau was undeniably the sexiest man alive, with or without the beard. Clean-shaven, his jaw was just as strong and now I could see that his chin was perfect for the shape of his face. He did look younger but he was still my Beau.

"Which do you like better?" he asked, turning back to the mirror.

I stood from my seat and walked to him at the sink. "I need to do some research before I can answer."

My hands found his jaw, gently rubbing the smooth skin before pulling his face down to mine. I kissed his mouth first but then trailed my lips across the lines of his jaw, up one side and down the other. The fresh scent of my shaving cream somehow blended with his rich woodsy smell into an intoxicating mixture, and by the time I made it back to his lips, I was dizzy.

After one last kiss, I leaned back and found his eyes. "I can't decide. I like you with or without the beard."

His sexy smirk set my pulse to racing. "That's not good

enough, Shortcake. I think you just haven't done enough research."

"Oh, yeah?" I breathed.

He nabbed my hand and pulled me through the door to our bed. Then he spent the next hour making sure I researched just exactly how his smooth skin felt against every inch of my body.

Just as we were drifting off to sleep, I whispered, "Goliath?"

"Hmm."

"Grow back the beard."

He pulled me closer and kissed the top of my hair. "Your wish, Shortcake."

CHAPTER FIFTEEN

BEAU

"Hey, Dad."

"Hi, there," he said, holding out his hand as the Monday Night Football pregame show blared in the background.

I took a seat in the recliner opposite his after we shook.

"Beau?" Mom called from the kitchen, shouting so she could be heard over the blaring TV. "Do you want a beer?"

"Me too!" Dad yelled before I could answer.

"I'll go get them." I stood and made my way to the beer fridge in the garage. Mom lived to wait on us, it was one of many things she did to show just how much she cared, but I tried to serve myself when I was here. Mom had enough to do in the kitchen on nights like this. Making a meal to feed her husband's oversized belly and her two enormous sons was no small task.

"Here you go," I said, handing Dad his Budweiser before opening my Bud Light.

"Michael called," Mom said, coming into the living room. "He's going to be late." She bent down to kiss Dad's cheek, then went back to the kitchen.

"What's new?" Dad asked me, muting the commercials on the television.

"Nothing new. Just more of the same. Busy." I'd been working as hard as I could during the week so I could take off as soon as possible Friday afternoons. For the first time in my life, I was living for my weekends. I was living for my time with Sabrina. Because of her, I was starting to live my own life.

"You sure have been spending a lot of time in the mountains this year." Dad chuckled. "Reminds me of your grandpa. When I was a kid, he'd drag us all out camping as soon as the snow started to melt and keep taking us up until the first snow stuck."

I smiled. "That was Grandpa." Though, I was sure he hadn't been disappearing into the mountains to meet up with the woman he'd stashed there.

"Well, now that the weather's changing, it will be nice to have you around more on the weekends."

"Yeah," I muttered as he turned the volume back up.

The weather had been on my mind a lot this week. Seasons were changing and having Sabrina at the outpost alone during the winter just wasn't an option. The snow in those mountain valleys came early and stayed deep. Since there was no way in hell I'd let her go into witness protection, I really only had one choice.

It was time to bring her into my home.

And once she was settled there, I was going to ask her to stay. For good.

SABRINA

August passed and with it the hot weather.

It was the middle of September and the mountain hills had already gotten a light snow. My new weekday routine now included pulling on thick socks and lighting a fire before starting my coffee. On the weekends, Beau was in charge of making the outpost toasty warm. Even though the little building had electric baseboard heat, it just couldn't stand up to a nice fire.

"What do you want to do today?" I asked, burrowed into our sleeping bag while Beau was at the wood stove.

"Let's go for a hike."

I smiled. "Sounds perfect."

The leaves of the deciduous trees had started to turn. Their neon yellow and warm amber leaves shone brightly against the deep green of the fir trees, and the hills surrounding my outpost valley were as beautiful as they'd ever been.

Beau and I didn't rush outside. We spent the first part of the morning inside, waiting for the chill to burn off before setting out through the meadow and up a familiar trail. The hike was easy but long, and after an hour, we'd risen high enough in the mountains that small clumps of snow dotted the forest floor around us.

"We need to talk." Beau stopped in a small clearing and sat down on a dry rock, patting the space at his side for me to join him.

I gave him a sideways glance. "Are you breaking up with

me? Is it the sex? I'm too much for you to keep up with, aren't I?"

He chuckled and shook his head. "Sit down."

I frowned but sat. Our seat was small so Beau threw an arm around my back to pin me to his side.

"In case you didn't know, when a man starts a conversation with 'we need to talk,' a woman automatically assumes the worst."

The crease between his eyebrows got deeper. "I'm honestly not sure how you're going to take this."

"Okay, you're not making me feel better."

He bent down and gave me a soft kiss. "Better?"

I nodded. I was always better when he kissed me.

"I think we need to make some changes."

"Uh, what kind of changes, exactly?"

He pushed out a loud breath, then blurted, "I think it's time for you to leave the outpost."

It was a good thing he had a grip on me or I would have swayed off our rock and found my ass in the dirt.

This is where he'd brought me to be safe and "off the grid." Did he want me to go into witness protection? It had only been a month since Henry Dalton's visit. Had he already given up hope?

"Why would you want me to leave?"

His arm pulled me tighter. "I'm worried about you. Hunting season is just getting started and this whole area is public land, so anyone could stumble on you out here alone."

"Can't I just lie and say I'm one of your employees studying those tree beetle things?"

"It's not just the risk of hunters I'm worried about. Winter is coming soon. We're a lot higher up here than we are in town. You'll have three or four times the snow as we do in the valley. I don't want to chance you getting stranded up here alone."

I didn't have a solution to that problem. Truth be told, I despised the snow and ice. It rarely snowed in Seattle, and when it did, I called in sick to work and refused to leave my apartment.

"If the snow gets too deep," he said, "the only way I'll be able to get to you is by snowmobile. Too much could go wrong."

I shook my head and squeezed my eyes shut. This wasn't happening. This wasn't the end. I needed more time. I'd been holding out hope since Henry's visit that he'd find a way to lock up the Federovs and the Russians would lose interest in anything related to me.

But hope was foolish, just like dreams. I'd had a gnawing feeling since my meeting with Henry that things were about to get worse.

Today was the bad day I'd been dreading.

"So what's the plan?" I asked my feet. "Go back to town and contact Henry?"

Beau's arm jerked. "What? You're not going back with that guy."

My head whipped up so I could see his face. "I'm not?"

His hand came to my cheek. "The only person who hates the idea of you in witness protection more than you is me."

My whole body sagged in relief.

"I've got a plan. You're going to come home with me."

"Home?" I couldn't hide the excitement in my voice. "Is that safe?"

"It can be, but I'll warn you, it won't be fun. You'll have less freedom than you do here. You'll be confined inside the entire time and I don't think we should tell anyone you're in town."

"Not even Felicity?"

He shook his head. "People will notice if my friend's wife starts to visit all the time."

I frowned. "Yeah, that would look bad."

Standing from the rock, I started pacing. It wasn't ideal, but if staying at the outpost was dangerous, I didn't want to take an unnecessary risk. I'd reached my lifetime quota of those already. So house arrest was my only option.

"Okay, let's do it."

He stood and smiled. "Look on the bright side. I'll get to see you every day."

I smiled back. "Definitely a pro. What else do you have for me?"

"You'll have complete control over the TV remote when I'm at work. Weekends are reserved for football, but if there isn't a game on, it can be ladies' choice."

"We're going to have a problem with that, Goliath. Me and sports? Oil and water. Tequila and good decisions. Cell phones and toilet water."

Beau leaned back and let out a roaring laugh, yanking me into his side for a tight hug. I started laughing too, staring up at his jaw now covered with his new beard. It felt so good to just let my laughter loose. I couldn't remember the last time I'd laughed so hard my sides ached and I had to force myself to stop so the stitches would go away.

When our combined noise was no longer echoing off the trees, Beau leaned down for another chaste kiss.

"You've got a talent for making me smile, Sabrina."

My cheeks flushed. "Same to you, Beau."

"Come on." He bent and kissed my forehead. "Let's get back."

My outpost adventure was coming to an end. If anyone had asked me five and a half months ago if I'd be sad to leave, I would have called them crazy. Beau was right; staying here alone in the winter wasn't safe, but I wasn't quite ready to say good-bye yet.

"Beau?" I called after we'd hiked halfway back.

He paused on the trail and looked over his shoulder.

"Can I have one more week at the outpost?"

"Sure." He smiled and turned to keep walking.

I smiled too, knowing that I was going to make the most of the time I had left.

––––––––

MY LAST WEEK at the outpost had been spent writing.

I'd set aside the novel I'd been working on to start something new. This book wasn't going to be a romance like the others I'd written, and though it was fictional, the story had a strong resemblance to my last five and a half months in Montana.

I'd taken my time with the beginning on this one, carefully crafting the novel's cabin setting. If I never had the chance to come back to the outpost, I wanted a written memory. I didn't want to risk forgetting what it smelled like or how the soft yellow lights created the perfect evening glow. I didn't want to forget the seventies kitchen and my closet bathroom.

And now I never would.

Safely saved on my laptop, I had the words that would bring me back here whenever I needed the escape.

"Sabrina," Beau called from outside.

"Be right there!" I zipped the backpack carrying my computer and my letters from Felicity and set it on the floor next to the duffel bag already packed with my clothes. Then I headed outside, glancing around the nearly empty room as I walked.

My cot, the TV and my food tubs were all loaded into Beau's truck. I still needed to pack up the contents of the refrigerator into a cooler and my personal belongings needed to be hauled outside, but other than that, the outpost looked more like it had the night I'd arrived than the home it had been a day ago.

"What's up?" I asked Beau.

"I'm going to shut off the water pump on the well. Do you need to use the bathroom one last time?"

"Yes!" I yelled, running back inside. I may have learned to love my outpost but there was no way in hell I was setting foot back in the *biffy* again. One experience in an outhouse had been one too many.

I finished my packing and cleaned out the fridge, then did a final sweep of the floor while Beau loaded the last items into the truck.

"Do you want to take one last walk with me?" he asked.

"Yeah." I took his outstretched hand and followed his lead into the meadow. I'd added it to my new novel's setting too, but not because I was worried I'd forget. Just like I'd never forget the first time Beau and I'd had sex or how he'd looked in the bathroom after shaving his beard, this meadow was permanently etched into my memory. No, I'd included it in my book because I wanted to share it with others.

If I ever got the chance to share my books.

"Are you doing okay?" he asked as we strolled.

"I'm sad."

The three-letter word didn't really describe how I was feeling but it was the best I could come up with. This little building was where I'd found myself again. Where I'd found a new path. Where I'd found love. Saying good-bye to the place that had nurtured it all wasn't just *sad*.

"It doesn't have to be forever. Anytime you want to come back, I'll bring you."

I hoped I'd get the chance.

"Thank you, Beau." I squeezed his hand. "I don't know if I've ever told you that. Thank you for everything. For bringing me up here. For keeping me safe. I'll always be grateful for the time I had here."

"You're welcome, Sabrina." He squeezed my hand right back.

We let Boone run and play in the open field as we wandered slowly through the wilting grasses. As the sun started to descend, we made our way back to the outpost to say one last good-bye.

Standing in the middle of the open room, my eyes wandered over the bare walls and the empty floors. They lingered on the place where Beau and I had set up our bed, the same place where he'd made love to me last night. When my gaze hit the log chair, I smiled, thinking about all of the hours I'd spent writing in that seat.

As much as I wanted to take that chair with me, it needed to stay.

"Ready to go?" Beau asked, wrapping his arms around me from behind.

I leaned back into him, resting against his heart and gripping his forearms under my chin. "Not really, but we'd better go anyway."

Beau kissed the top of my hair before letting me go. Then, hand in hand, we walked outside, locking up the door before climbing in his truck.

As he pulled away, I lost control of my tears and they dripped down my cheeks. Boone snuggled into my side as I sniffled, resting his cute face on my lap to give me the only comfort he knew how. Beau reached out and laced his fingers with mine, holding them tight but staying quiet so I could have my moment to grieve the loss of my home.

Just as abruptly as it had started, it was over.

I watched my outpost disappear into the trees through blurry eyes and a side-view mirror. I left a part of my heart at the outpost today.

And if it hurt this much to say good-bye to a building, I'd never be able to say good-bye to Beau. If I weren't in danger —if life could go back to normal—I'd uproot everything and fit my life to his just to avoid the pain of leaving his side.

All he had to do was ask me to stay.

———

IT TOOK ALMOST the entire three-hour drive back to Prescott for my mood to improve, but my spirits finally lifted once I focused on all the positives of this new chapter in my Montana escape.

I would get to see Beau every single day. We'd sleep together every single night. We'd wake up together every single morning. So what if I was confined to the walls of his home like a recluse? At least he'd be inside with me.

The sun was slowly setting by the time we pulled off the gravel road and onto the highway that led to Prescott. A few miles later, we crossed the bridge into town and slowed as we passed through downtown. The sky was a beautiful peach color and cast a soft glow on the town.

"Everything is so well-kept." The last time I'd driven through Prescott had been during the middle of the night and I hadn't been able to see inside the tiny shop windows or into the restaurants that filled the short road. "There's more here than I would have thought for a small town. Why is that?"

"Bozeman is the closest city and it's over an hour away, so Prescott has to serve as the hub for the whole county. We've got more commerce than you might find in other small towns, and in general, people here like to shop local when they can and support one another."

"That makes sense."

"We get a lot of business from tourists driving through to Yellowstone National Park too. Most owners have found that if they keep things up and give it a certain Western feel, the tourists are more willing to stop and spend money."

They had that right. I could already see myself buying things I didn't really need. That was, if I was ever allowed to leave the house and roam free.

I soaked it all in until Beau turned and maneuvered down some side streets. I'd been to his house before, the night I'd arrived in Montana, but it had been so dark that I hadn't been able to see the neighborhood well. Now that it was light and my mind wasn't distracted, I could really take it all in.

The houses closest to Main Street were older and small. Short yards crowded the homes together on each block. The further we drove, the more the yards started to widen, and though the houses weren't brand new, they were nicer and larger.

Soon Boone perked up and started whining in excitement as Beau turned down a street full of nice bungalows. Most looked to have been remodeled from their original form, with freshened exteriors, additions and garages built onto their spacious lots. The neighborhood itself had to be at least fifty years old given the height and width of the beautiful trees that lined the streets and shaded the yards.

Beau turned into a long, narrow driveway next to a beautiful shale-gray home with pale-cream trim, gleaming bay windows and an adorable covered porch filled with tan wicker furniture.

"This is your house? I remembered it differently."

He chuckled. "Yeah. What did you remember?"

"Not this. For some reason, I had it in my head that your house screamed 'bachelor.' " Instead, his home said "take off your shoes before you come inside."

The exterior landscaping was immaculate, highlighting the brown brick sidewalk that trailed up from the street to four matching steps leading to the sunken front door. The porch itself was deep and wide, running along half of the front but also along the side of the house toward Beau's attached garage, which was set off the back of the house.

Boone dove out of the truck door the second I had it open only to disappear through a doggy door out the back of the garage. I grabbed a bag from the back seat, then followed Beau up three cement steps and through the interior door to his house.

"Let's do the tour and then we can unload." He lifted my bag off my shoulder and set it on his white washing machine while I inspected the laundry room and pantry where we'd come in.

The floor tiles were a rich terra cotta and the walls a blue so deep it was nearly black. The white farmhouse sink in the corner and the hickory cabinets offset the dark walls flawlessly.

"I only take credit for the carpentry," Beau said as I followed him into an enormous kitchen. "Maisy is obsessed with home-decorating shows so she gets credit for the decorating and paint."

"Now I really can't wait to see her motel." If her rooms were anything like Beau's house, her motel would rival some of the most stylish in Seattle.

The kitchen and living room were all part of a huge open main floor, only separated by a massive butcher-block island and iron-backed stools. The espresso leather couches and the pale stone fireplace in the living area were the perfect accents to the light hardwood floors.

The best part was that the television wasn't too big or stacked on top of the mantel. Instead, it was tucked away in a beautiful set of built-in cabinets opposite the picture window that looked into the front yard.

Beau went through the rest of the tour quickly, showing me his office, the guest bedroom and a bathroom on the main floor. Next, he took me to the cool basement that had clearly not been part of Maisy's scope of work.

"Here's the bachelor I was looking for."

He chuckled and turned on the florescent lights. At one end of the long, wide man cave was a home gym. At the other end was a massive sectional aimed at an entertainment unit the size of which I'd never seen before. In it was the enormous TV that I'd expected upstairs.

I shivered as the cold from the cement floors bled through my socks. I peeked inside a storage room full of an extra refrigerator and a chest freezer before following Beau back to the main floor.

"Upstairs is my bedroom and another spare," Beau said, going back to the garage to unload.

"Wow. I wouldn't have guessed this place was so big from the outside."

"This block was the ritzy part of Prescott back in the day. Now all the new construction is done along the river or up in the mountains but I wanted one of these older places. I like that they have character and history. So I bought it and have been slowly making updates."

"Have you done much work?" I asked, carrying a plastic tub into the laundry room.

"Quite a bit. I tore out a wall upstairs to expand the master bedroom and bathroom. That was my biggest project. Everything else has been mostly cosmetic. New floors. New paint and trim. Better finishes. The people that owned it before me did the hard part by putting on the extension where the kitchen is now."

"Well, it is not going to be hard for me to stay here, I can tell you that."

He chuckled, setting down the cooler and taking the tub from my hands. "Good. Why don't you raid the fridge for dinner and I'll finish unloading?"

I nodded, standing on my tiptoes so he could give me a soft kiss before going back to the garage. Boone appeared and settled into his doggy bed by the back-patio doors while I made us a late dinner of grilled cheese sandwiches and tomato soup.

I had gotten so used to cooking with only an electric stovetop at the outpost that I felt spoiled with Beau's top-of-the-line gas range and dual convection oven. If all I had to do was hang out inside every day, I was going to get creative with our menu.

No more trail mix, jerky and granola bars for me. I'd had enough of those to last a lifetime.

Beau and I ate at the island, then I tossed in a load of laundry while he loaded the dishwasher. Another positive: no more hand-washing my clothes. I was back in the land of modern-day appliances.

"Do you want to take a shower before bed?" he asked.

"I'd love one." I was sticky and still smelled like wood fire. I hadn't minded at the outpost, but here, I was feeling grimy and I wanted clean hair.

I followed Beau up the stairs that ran along the far side of the house. At the top of the landing, a picture collage lined the hallway to the bedrooms. Maisy must have made this too because they were in gray-matted black frames. The photos themselves were all black and whites except one in the center.

"Are these your parents?" I asked, pointing to the color picture.

"Yeah. That was taken my senior year in high school. Dad's beer belly is twice as big now but Mom looks exactly the same."

The photo was your typical family picture. The Holts were at a park, surrounded by green grass and tall trees. Beau stood nearly as tall as his dad while Michael was still a boy at his mother's side. Maisy stood proudly in the middle with her little hands linked with her parents.

"What are their names?"

"Marissa and Brock."

"All Ms and Bs," I said, still inspecting the photo.

Beau was nearly a carbon copy of his dad. They had the

same large build and square face. Michael resembled Brock too, except as a child, his features hadn't been quite as angular. Maisy, on the other hand, looked nothing like her father because she was the exact replica of Marissa with the same doe eyes and white-blond hair.

"And this is Coby?" Next to the color picture was a black and white of Beau with a little boy resting on his shoulders.

"Yeah. He likes to ride up there so we can pretend he's a giant."

I smiled at the softness in Beau's face as he looked at his nephew's picture. Beau would make a wonderful father, of that I had no doubt. "How old is Coby?"

"He just turned two."

We turned away from the pictures and passed by the spare room before entering Beau's master suite. The walls had been painted a dark gray offset by the house's white trim and doors. In the center of the room was Beau's gigantic bed with a simple dove-gray quilt and white pillows. The light wood furniture was simple but rustic enough that the room didn't feel too feminine.

"That's a beautiful pic—" I gasped and clapped a hand over my mouth.

Above Beau's bed was a large black-and-white panoramic canvas of the meadow by the outpost.

Somehow, Beau had gotten that canvas made for me this last week. There had been a dead tree in the tree line where he'd taken the photo. He'd cut down that tree right after we'd taken our hike and he'd told me it was time to leave the outpost. The canvas didn't have that tree.

"Beau, I . . . thank you."

"You're welcome." His hands came to my shoulders and

he bent to kiss my hair. Then he steered me into the bathroom. "Make yourself at home."

Between the dual sinks, he'd already set out my bag of toiletries and my duffel. One of the vanity drawers had been cleaned out and left open.

By the time I dried off from my long and steamy shower, I was dead on my feet. I slipped on some pajamas and tied up my wet hair, emerging from the bathroom to find that Beau had showered too and was already in bed.

"I need to switch the laundry. Be right back."

"It's done, angel. Come to bed."

My feet changed course and I wasted no time scooting into bed next to Beau.

I moaned as I sank into the soft, thick mattress. Beau's sheets were cool and smooth against my bare legs. His quilt and the down comforter underneath were just the right weight to guarantee I'd sleep like the dead.

"I missed beds. I might spend all day in here tomorrow."

He chuckled and reached out, sliding me into his side. "I could get on board with that. I haven't lazed a Sunday away in ages."

"Then it's a plan." I yawned. "Good night, Goliath."

"Night, Shortcake."

His arms pulled me closer, and even though I was in an unfamiliar place, I was home.

CHAPTER SIXTEEN

SABRINA

"Holy fuck," Beau panted.

The room was spinning, there was a lock of hair in my mouth and my heart was pounding like I'd just run a mile being chased by a bear.

It. Was. Awesome.

"I love this bed," I sighed once I could breathe again.

I was going to be a happy and thoroughly satisfied woman by the end of our lazy Sunday in bed. Beau and I'd had sex twice already this morning and it was only nine.

"I need food." Beau sat up on the edge of the bed, reaching back to tickle my naked side.

I giggled, swatting his hand away as his phone started buzzing on the nightstand again. It had rung three times earlier, but since I'd been riding him hard at the time, he'd ignored it.

Rolling onto my side and propping up on an elbow, I

stared greedily at Beau's naked backside as he walked into the bathroom with his phone pressed to his ear. *Oh, boy.*

"Yeah, I'm home," Beau said to whoever was on the phone. "Okay. See you in a few."

I shot up in a panic. Was someone coming over here? Did that mean I needed to hide out? I definitely needed to get dressed.

Beau came out of the bathroom and I flew past him, frantically digging in my bag to get some panties.

"Jess is on his way over," he said

"Okay." I nodded but kept digging for a bra. "I'll get dressed and just stay up here. Or should I go downstairs? Shit, I need my laundry."

"Calm down." Beau chuckled and hugged me from behind, trapping my flailing arms. "We can let him know you're here."

"Are you sure?" I used the mirror to find his eyes. "I thought I was on secret lockdown here."

"I think it's safe to tell the sheriff, don't you?"

"Yeah." My shoulders relaxed away from my ears. "But I still need my laundry."

Beau kissed my hair and let me go. "I'll go get it."

I did my business in the bathroom while Beau dressed in the walk-in closet and hauled up my basket of clean clothes.

"There's a couple of drawers free in the closet," he said. "Take as much space as you need."

"Thanks." I blew him a kiss and finished getting dressed.

By the time I came downstairs, Beau was opening the door for Jess. The sheriff's eyes snapped to me and he frowned at Beau. "I see we've got some catching up to do."

"Yep. Come on in." Beau led Jess to the kitchen and held

out a hand for me to join them. "Sabrina came back with me yesterday. I don't want her up in the mountains alone when the snow hits so she's going to lay low here. Other than me and you, I don't think we need to broadcast her new location."

"Agreed." Jess leaned his forearms on the counter.

"Coffee?" Beau asked.

"Sure. Listen, sorry to barge in, but we've got a problem. Couple of kids went hunting up by Wade Lake yesterday and didn't come back. Parents called it into the station this morning, requesting you personally go find them."

"Shit," Beau muttered and glanced at me by the coffee pot. "So much for a day off."

"Sorry," Jess said. "My guess is that the boys got something big and by the time they packed it out, it was dark. We'll probably drive up there and find them sleeping in their car but there's a chance they got turned around."

"Who are they?"

"Levi and Chase Brooks."

Beau shook his head. "Ah, now I get it."

"Get what?" I asked.

"Levi and Chase Brooks's mom is in my mom's quilting club." Beau pulled his phone from his pocket and waved it in the air. "Mom was the one calling me earlier when we were busy."

"Oh." I blushed and looked to my coffee cup.

Jess tried to hide it, but I caught his grin. He knew exactly what we'd been doing during those missed calls.

"This is a pretty small search and rescue case for you, hotshot," Jess said. "But if you don't go up there, all of those women in your mom's quilting club are going to be calling me all damn day. My guess is they'll be banging down your door too."

I didn't want to miss out on my lazy day with Beau but I really didn't want his mom or her friends coming to his house.

"I'll go up." Beau ran a hand over his beard. "Let's not call in the whole search and rescue team unless we need to though. I'll see if I can track them down first."

"Want some company?" Jess asked. "I bet Silas would come up with us."

"Sure, that would be great. Let me eat some breakfast and call Mom back, then I'll get my gear."

"I'll call the guys," Jess said, going into the living room.

I went to the fridge for the eggs. "And I'll make breakfast before you go."

"Sorry, Shortcake."

I smiled. "Don't be."

I *loved* that Beau was part of the hero squad. I just wished he had more time to do what he really wanted to do. He was always rushing to someone's rescue, mine included. What did Beau want from his life?

But since now wasn't the time for that question, I hustled to cook him breakfast.

Twenty minutes later, Jess had left to pick up Silas, I was doing the dishes and Beau was changed and ready to go, pulling a baseball cap over his hair.

"Have you seen my compass?" he asked.

"Your what?"

"My compass. Silver." He made a two-inch circle with his hand. "About this big."

"Oh, I thought that was a pocket watch."

I'd seen it at the outpost before but had never opened it. Beau had always left it in the middle of the counter with his keys and the contents of his jeans pockets. This morning, I'd set it aside with his truck keys so it wouldn't be in the way of my cooking.

"Here you go," I said, handing it over. "It's lovely."

The antique silver faces on both the front and back had been tooled with intricate swirls and feathers around the word HOLT. It reminded me of an oversized locket but without the chain.

"This was my grandpa's. He gave it to me when I was a kid since he knew how much I loved camping and hiking. He taught me how to use it and promised that if I kept it close, I'd never get lost."

"That's amazing." What a wonderful story. *Holt's Compass.* The words popped into my head and I instantly loved it as a title for my new book.

Beau swiped his thumb across the compass's face, then dropped it in his jeans pocket. "Grandpa died five years ago but I like carrying this piece of him around."

"Sorry."

"It's okay." He gave me a sad smile. "Anyway, I better get going."

"Good luck."

He bent and kissed my cheek. "Be back soon. Come on, Boone."

When the garage door closed behind Beau and Boone, I stood in the quiet kitchen and looked around, unsure what to do with myself. I could write another chapter in my new book or watch TV. It was strange not to have Boone around and his absence was making me twitchy. At the outpost, I'd spend a good part of my day talking to him.

"Is it crazy to talk to a dog?" I asked myself. "No, but it is crazy to talk to a kitchen."

Thinking about the kitchen sent me snooping, and when

I came across the cleaning supplies under the sink, I decided that mopping and dusting was the perfect Sunday activity to keep myself occupied until Beau came back with Boone. The place was fairly clean already, but since I couldn't do household errands like going to the grocery store, I figured cleaning and cooking could be my contribution.

So I dove right in, starting with the kitchen floors.

I was on my hands and knees scrubbing the tile between the fridge and the island when I heard the front door lock click open.

Someone was here. *Oh, shit.* I crouched lower and froze, listening for voices. It wasn't Beau, he would have come through the garage. Was it his mom? Whoever it was definitely had a key. How would I explain to her what I was doing in Beau's house? Maybe I could say I was a cleaning lady.

The door swung open and I started to panic. Escape wasn't an option and I couldn't just pop up from behind the counter now, pretending to be Beau's housekeeper. I'd scare the visitor half to death.

Maybe it was Michael. *Please be Michael.*

"Come on, buddy," a woman's voice called outside.

Curses! Not Michael.

"Let's see if we can find your me-me," she said.

"Where do you think he left it?" another woman's voice called from outside.

I knew that voice.

I'd lived with that voice for years.

Felicity.

Little feet pounded across the wood floors and the door clicked shut. This had to be Maisy and Coby with Felicity in tow.

People I really wanted to see but couldn't. People who would be at risk if they knew I was staying in Beau's house. People who were just on the other side of the island from where I was hiding.

Maybe they'll leave. Maybe they'll get what they came for and then slip out. If I stayed right here, hidden, they might not even know I was in the house.

"All right, buddy, where did you leave your me-me?" Maisy asked Coby as the front door closed.

"Boone bed," his little voice answered.

"Okay, let's check his bed."

No! The dog's bed was between me and the laundry room. I started to inch backward, hoping I could slink around the far side of the island and hide until they'd gone by. I was almost to the corner when my hand slipped on the wet tile and went crashing into the water bucket. Suds and water splashed everywhere and the bucket clanked, causing me to wince and my visitors to gasp.

"Oh my god," Maisy cried. "What was that?"

"Who's there?" Felicity demanded.

Damn. Damn. Damn. So much for hiding out.

"Sorry," I squeaked, then slowly stood from behind the counter to reveal myself. I gave them an awkward wave when I cleared the counter. "It's just me."

"Sabrina?" Felicity gasped. "What? You're here? When — How—" She rushed around the couch in the living room. I met her on the other side of the island, and without hesitation, she pulled me into her arms.

"Hi." I hugged her back.

"Hi." She squeezed tighter. "Are you okay?"

I nodded. "Yeah. I'm good."

She let me go and did a thorough inspection of my face,

her fingers brushing over the gash that had healed into just a small pink scar.

"See? I'm okay."

"I've been so worried. And I missed you."

"I missed you too." I smiled at my friend and then turned to Maisy with another wave. "Hey. Sorry to scare you."

The shock on Maisy's face had disappeared and she finally let go of the death grip she had on Coby's hand. "It's okay. I'm just glad it's you."

"What are you doing here?" Felicity asked.

"Well, I'm supposed to be here hiding out. But so far you guys and Jess have discovered me and I've been here for less than twelve hours."

"But why? Why aren't you at the outpost?"

Before I could answer Felicity's question, Coby yelled, "Me-me!"

Abandoning Maisy's side, he ran to Boone's bed and pulled out a small blue blanket from underneath.

"Oh, thank god we found it," Maisy sighed. "He had a complete meltdown last night when we couldn't find that blanket and then wouldn't sleep in his own bed. There is no such thing as sleeping when a two-year-old's foot is in your side. I'm exhausted."

"Then I'm glad you found it."

"Great, we've got the blanket," Felicity huffed. "Now tell me, what is going on?"

"Coby, no!" Maisy shouted before I could answer. We all whirled around to see Coby dragging his "me-me" through the water I'd spilled on the floor.

"Shoot!" I rushed to grab a towel, mopping up my puddle before Coby got soaking wet. "Sorry." I picked up my bucket and sponge, then wrung out the sopping towel in the sink.

"It's no problem," Maisy said, pulling Coby away from the water. "He's just obsessed with water puddles. It's our fault for barging in. Honestly, I thought Beau would be gone again this weekend."

"We just got here last night."

"I'm going to ask this again and hope this time I get an answer." Felicity's voice was getting louder. "Why are you here? Why would you leave the outpost? Is it really safe for you to be in town? Did something happen? Can I get some answers here please *before I completely panic?*"

"I'm fine, so calm down. Nothing happened. Beau just didn't think the outpost was a great spot for me with winter coming."

"Oh," she breathed and the tension in her shoulders vanished. "Okay, good thinking."

"Mama! Chaca milk." Coby tugged on Maisy's purse.

She reached in and handed him a sippy cup of chocolate milk, then set her bag on the counter. "Give me one minute. I want to hear this story. Let me get Coby set up with a cartoon and then we can talk."

Maisy led Coby to the living room and Felicity started drumming her fingers on the island.

"Do you want some coffee?"

"Yes." I turned to get her a mug but she stopped me. "No. Never mind."

"Um, okay." My friend had never once turned down coffee. "Are you feeling all right?" Her face was a little pale. I would have chalked that up to the shock of seeing me but surprise didn't explain the dark circles and bags under her eyes.

"Not really." Felicity shook her head. "And I can't have coffee right now."

"Because . . ." I searched her face for an answer.

She gave me wider eyes.

"Is that supposed to mean something? Because I've kind of been trapped in the middle of nowhere for a while now and I'm out of the loop."

Felicity frowned and leaned in closer to whisper. "I can't have coffee and I feel like shit because I'm pregnant."

"What!" I shouted then clapped a hand over my mouth.

"Shh," she hissed and looked over her shoulder at Maisy and Coby in the living room. "We're not telling people yet."

I dropped my hand and smiled. "But you told me?"

"You're an exception. I blame it on the shock of seeing you pop up behind Beau's counter."

I smiled wider and wrapped my arms around her waist. "I'm happy for you, lady."

"I'm happy for me too."

We broke apart and I couldn't help but grin. "Are you excited?"

"Yeah. A little scared too but I think that's to be expected."

"You have nothing to worry about. You'll be a wonderful mother."

"Thanks." She smiled. "I hope you're still here when he or she is born."

"If not, I'll be back to visit and spoil that baby rotten." I had new motivation to stay out of witness protection. I wanted to see Felicity's baby at least once.

"Okay. He's settled for a little while." Maisy came back into the kitchen. "So? How are you? Beau said all of your injuries healed okay?"

I nodded. "I'm all better. My ribs took the longest to heal but I'm back to a hundred percent."

She patted my hand. "Good."

Maisy moved through the kitchen with ease, filling a coffee cup for herself and getting a small bowl of goldfish crackers to deliver to Coby, who was sprawled on his uncle's couch. He'd traded his wet blanket for one of Beau's throws and curled up with a stuffed animal he'd found in the ottoman. Probably something he'd stashed during one of his countless visits to Beau's house.

"Okay. He's set." Maisy came back and pulled out a stool from beneath the island. Felicity settled into the other stool and both stared at me, waiting for an explanation.

I grabbed my own coffee and leaned a hip against the island to start explaining. "So, like I said, Beau didn't want me at the outpost this winter."

"I get that," Felicity said, "but when you showed up months ago, everyone said town was out. Is it really safe to come back?"

Beau's idea that I could just lay low had made sense earlier, but with Maisy and Felicity now aware of my presence, I was starting to think this move was just courting trouble. How many other family members had keys to Beau's house? Would his neighbors start to wonder why his lights were on all day if he was at work? Would someone see me through the windows?

As much as I wanted to stay with Beau, was this really safe?

"I thought it would be okay, but now I'm not so sure."

"I don't know where else you'd go," Maisy said. "Beau's right, the mountains in the winter would be dangerous. This will just have to work until spring."

"Or until things with the Federovs get wrapped up. Have you heard anything from the FBI?" Felicity asked.

"FBI?" Maisy asked. "Have they been in contact?"

I nodded. "The agent I sent my evidence to tracked me down. I met with him about a month ago."

"What did he want?" she asked.

"He wanted me to go into witness protection but we convinced him to let me stay at the outpost until we knew more about what was happening with the case."

"Ah, gotcha." Maisy nodded. "Did he tell you anything? Did he give you a timeline for how long it would take to put them away?"

I shook my head. "Not really. And since the case isn't new anymore, there hasn't been much in the headlines lately. I'm pretty much in the dark."

I wasn't sure if it was better or worse to have internet access every day. At the outpost, it had been easier to push my worries about the Federovs aside because I had no way of tracking the FBI's case. But now, I found myself refreshing *The Seattle Time's* website every thirty minutes.

"No news is probably good news," Felicity said.

"I hope so."

"Well, Maisy's right. There's nothing we can do about this now. You're here so at least we can catch up today. Tell us everything. I want to know what happened at the outpost."

Maisy smiled into her coffee mug. "And I'd like to know what is going on with you and my brother."

"What?" Felicity's eyes snapped to mine. "You and Beau?"

I blushed and looked to my coffee. "Yeah. Me and Beau."

"For how long?"

"A couple months."

"All right. Then hurry up and give us the outpost recap first. Then get to the good stuff."

I smiled and laughed with my friend. We spent the next thirty minutes talking through everything that had happened at the outpost. I told them all about my journey into writing. About Dylan and the hotshot crew. And about my meeting with Henry Dalton.

"I'm so glad you didn't go into witness protection," Maisy said.

"Me too." Though, I still thought staying in Montana was just delaying the inevitable. Regardless, I was glad he hadn't come back to collect me. That had to be a sign that things with the Federovs were progressing, right?

"Wait a minute." Felicity frowned and counted out a couple of fingers. "Were you and Beau together when Silas came up to the outpost and brought you down to meet with Henry?"

I nodded. "Yeah."

She threw her hands in the air. "And he didn't tell me anything! Silas is in trouble." She pointed at my nose. "And so are you. This is all information you should have been sending in your letters."

I winced and scrunched up my face. "Sorry?" My letters had been so focused on wedding details, I'd left out the details of my budding relationship.

"You're forgiven, but only if you give us all the details now. What's going on with you two?"

Felicity and Maisy both leaned further into the island, anxious for me to share the juicy gossip.

I shrugged. "We're temporary, I guess. I don't know how else to describe it. Our circumstances are completely insane, but no matter what, I'm really glad I've gotten the chance to know him. We'll just have to see what develops."

"Would you ever consider staying?" Felicity asked.

Beau and I had only ever talked about parting ways eventually, but what if we didn't have to? I wanted to keep seeing him and I think he wanted that too. Excitement at the possibility bubbled up in my chest.

"Yes. If it was safe, I'd stay."

"Yay!" Maisy cheered at the same time I said, "But."

Her hands came down from above her head. "Uh-oh."

"You don't want to get your hopes up." Felicity voiced my fears.

I nodded. "I'm still in trouble. I don't know if I'll ever get to have a normal life. If I'll ever be free. I'd love to stay here with Beau, but not if I'm in danger. There's a very real chance I'll be going into witness protection and never get to see him again."

"That sucks," Maisy muttered.

I rounded the island and took a seat on the last stool. "Yeah. It sucks. But Beau and I have always gone into this with clear expectations. We're enjoying the time we have, for as long as it lasts. Let's do the same. Tell me everything about the wedding."

"The wedding? No. I want to hear more about you and Beau."

"Please?" I begged. "There isn't much more to tell and I really want to hear about the wedding. Just because you know I'm here doesn't mean I'm going to get to see you often. So let's use this afternoon as a chance to catch up because I don't know if it's going to happen again."

She sighed and nodded. "Okay."

"I've got lots of pictures on my phone." Maisy jumped up from her stool to dig through her purse.

"Good. Beau took lots of pictures and videos, but I want to see more. He didn't get a lot of the behind-the-scenes stuff."

And I wanted to hear everything straight from Felicity's mouth. If I could see her face light up as she described her dress or how the cake tasted, then maybe I wouldn't feel so sad about missing my best friend's wedding day. The Federov story had taken that away from me too. And though I was sad, I wasn't sorry. Beau had helped me see that everything I'd done—all I'd lost and would miss out on—had been worth it to take them down.

So for the next hour, I swiped through hundreds of wedding pictures and listened to countless stories about Felicity and Silas's day. There was something magical about being surrounded by these women, listening to them recount every detail of the wedding, because after that hour, I didn't feel like I'd missed the wedding entirely after all.

Coby got bored with his cartoons not long after that and Maisy decided it best to take him home. So I hugged her good-bye and ruffled Coby's hair before they went outside to get buckled into the car.

"Thanks for showing me pictures," I told Felicity as I walked her to the door.

"We could have pushed the wedding back, you know."

"I know, but I didn't want that. It could be years until my drama blows over, if ever."

"Don't say things like that," she chided. "This could all work out."

"You're right." I pulled her into my arms. "It could."

Or it couldn't.

I didn't voice that last bit. I'd let my friend keep hoping that this would all turn out for the best.

And maybe she'd be right.

"Take care of yourself, okay? And that baby."

She squeezed me once more, then let me go. "Promise. You take care too."

"Love you, lady."

"Love you too." With a sad wave, she walked out the door, closing it behind her so I wouldn't be seen standing by the window.

As I watched Felicity get into the passenger seat and Maisy pull away from the curb, Beau's truck appeared and pulled into the driveway.

I heard the garage door roll open and I walked back to the kitchen to greet him as he came inside.

The smile on my face fell when the door opened.

Beau was home, and he was not happy.

CHAPTER SEVENTEEN

SABRINA

"Hey. What's wrong? Didn't you find the kids?" I asked.

"Yeah, I found them," he clipped, brushing past me to toss his keys on the island. When he spun around, he planted his hands on his hips. "Was that Felicity I saw leaving with Maisy and Coby?"

"Um, yeah." Where was he going with this? And why was he mad?

"So when I told you that we weren't going to tell anyone you were here, did that not sink in? Exactly how long did you wait after I left before getting ahold of Felicity? Five minutes? Ten?"

"Beau, they—"

"And you pulled my sister and nephew into this too? For Christ's sake, Sabrina." He yanked off his cap and threw it on the island with his keys. "You're supposed to be in hiding. It's dangerous for people to know you're here. I brought you back from the outpost to keep you safe, not for you to have a social life."

I fisted my hands on my hips to mirror his stance. "Now wait a second. I didn't invite them over here. I was cleaning and they just showed up. What was I supposed to do?"

"How about hide? I can't protect you if people know where you are!"

"I was standing right there!" I shouted, pointing to the spot where I'd been scrubbing. "And don't get mad at me, you weren't here. You were busy running off to rescue someone else and leaving me behind."

The words came out without thought, but before I could take them back, Beau's anger spiked.

"That's right. I'm always doing something for someone else. Excuse me for fucking helping other people. Do you think I like it? Always on the run, doing things for others while my life gets put on hold? But what else should I say, Sabrina? You've got all the answers, tell me. I guess the next time two kids get lost or a woman comes to Montana in the middle of the night and needs a place to hide out, I should just say, 'Sorry, I'm fucking busy.' Is that how I can get out of the hassle of everyone else's shit?"

I'd walked right into an argument I couldn't win. I didn't have any answers to his questions. But I did know that it really hurt to be called a hassle. "You're right. You're trying to help everyone else out. I guess if you told people no, maybe those of us that are such a fucking *hassle* would have to figure it out ourselves." I stormed past Beau, rushing upstairs as anger and guilt settled heavy on my back.

Beau had likely saved my life. He'd taken me on as a burden, and any time I'd apologized for inconveniencing his life, he'd sworn it had been fine.

I didn't know where I'd be without Beau's help. I had needed him. Not just to keep me safe, but just . . . for me. I still needed him. Just like his mom. His sister. His nephew.

The line of people that needed Beau was stacked deep and I wasn't at the front.

I was halfway up the stairs when the doorbell rang, but I didn't stop moving.

I went upstairs and sank onto the end of the bed, burying my face in my hands.

If the chaos of my life ever settled, Beau wouldn't want me to stay. I'd been kidding myself to think a life in Montana could be my future, that Beau and I might make a relationship out of this thing between us.

The truth was, I didn't belong in Montana. I didn't belong with Beau.

We'd always been temporary and he'd been nothing but up front about expectations. Anything else had just been my imagination running wild. My romance novels must have made me delusional, because clearly, I'd been reading *much* more into Beau's words and actions than he had intended.

And fuck, did that hurt.

When the one man you wanted more than any other thought you were a hassle, it hurt.

His footsteps sounded in the hallway and I looked up, waiting for his body to fill the doorframe. When he appeared, the scowl on his face had just gotten harder.

"You have a visitor."

I stood up. "Me?"

He nodded.

"Who?"

"Your FBI friend."

"What? Henry's here?"

"See for yourself." He spun around and walked down the hallway.

I rushed across the room, following Beau downstairs. Henry Dalton stood in the living room, wearing his signature black suit and white shirt.

Another visit from the FBI could not mean good things.

My heart was pounding as I darted around Beau and into the living room, firing off questions as they popped into my head. "Why are you back, Henry? Is everything okay with my family? Did something happen with the Federovs? Do they know where I am?"

"Hello, Sabrina." Henry chuckled. "Your family is fine. How about we sit and go through those questions one by one?"

"Sure." I swung out a hand, inviting him to sit on the couch. I took the chair directly across from him and sat on my nervous hands.

Beau came to my side but he didn't sit. He just crossed his arms over his chest and planted his legs wide as he glared down at Henry.

"How are you?" Henry asked me, ignoring the waves of anger pulsing from Beau and how I was shaking with nerves.

"Um, fine." Something was different about this visit. Unlike last time, Henry wasn't tense. Instead, he was relaxed, almost carefree as he tossed a hand over the back of the couch and swung a foot up on his knee.

"What's going on?" I asked.

"Nice place," Henry said, looking around the house and not answering my question.

Beau growled, his jaw clenched even tighter.

I reached up and touched his elbow. "Would you please sit down? You're making me even more nervous."

For a second I thought he was going to remain standing, but he finally sank onto the arm of my chair with an angry huff.

Henry was still inspecting Beau's house.

"Henry," I snapped, getting his attention. "Why are you here?"

"I'm here to bring you home, MacKenzie."

My stomach dropped. "Did something happen?"

Henry nodded and looked to Beau. "Your hiding spot wasn't as secure as you thought. We caught some social-media traffic yesterday about a woman hiding up in the mountains of Montana. Blond hair. Green eyes. Sound familiar?"

My eyes closed as my shoulders fell. "It had to be the hotshots. Who did the post come from?"

"Do you know someone named Dylan Prosser?" Henry asked.

Dylan. "That. Asshole!" My fingernails dug into my palms as I clenched my fists.

Beau had gotten Dylan fired from his hotshot crew, and rather than take that opportunity to grow the fuck up, he'd ratted me out.

"I'll take that as a yes?"

"Yeah, we know Prosser," Beau growled. His hands were fisted even tighter than mine. "What happened?"

"He's taken a lot of interest in Sabrina. From what we can tell, he's spent the better part of two months trying to figure out who you are. He must have finally stumbled onto Anton's social-media feeds, because yesterday, we caught a comment that he had information about your whereabouts. For a price, of course."

Which meant I'd been found. My time was up.

"So that's it?" I asked. "Now you take me into witness protection and I become some random Jane Doe?"

Henry grinned and shook his head. "I'm not here with only bad news, MacKenzie. I've got some good too. You have to come home but you get to stay *you*."

"She doesn't have to go into witness protection?" Beau asked, his arm wrapping around my shoulders and pulling me toward his hip.

Henry shook his head. "She doesn't need to. She's safe to come back to Seattle as Sabrina MacKenzie."

"You're kidding." My mouth fell open. "Really?"

Henry nodded. "Really."

"Why? How?" Even though I'd been hoping this would come true, I'd never really expected it to happen. A part of me had come to terms with the fact that eventually I'd be disappearing from my own life and saying good-bye to my loved ones. "What about the Federovs? I don't understand how this is possible."

"Your article saved your ass," Henry declared.

What was he talking about? My article had put me in this position. "What do you mean?"

"Remember I told you the inside guy with the Russians said they were poking around the case?"

"Of course I remember. That was less than two months ago. Tell me something new." My patience was running out.

Henry smiled, completely unaffected by my sharp tone. "Well, it turns out they weren't interested in you at all, just your article."

"That doesn't make any sense."

"The numbers you included were what drew the Russians' interest."

I thought back to the story and exactly what I had

included. At Anton's, I'd found a copy of a ledger documenting the gun shipments and another documenting sales. High-res photos had been sent to Henry along with the evidence my source and I had gained from Federov Shipping. But the only thing my article had included were estimates on gun imports over the last ten years and some income estimates for Viktor Federov and his sons.

"Why would the Russians care about how many guns were being imported?" I asked. "Wouldn't they already know that?"

"Imports weren't the issue. Sales were."

"The Federovs were skimming," Beau said, voicing my thoughts.

Henry nodded. "Yep."

"And the Russians are only just now noticing?" I asked. "Because of my article? That seems suspicious."

"I thought so too," Henry said, "but my inside source says it's solid intel. The Federovs have been careful, taking just enough to inflate their take but not enough to draw suspicion from their Russian counterparts. Compound small draws over thousands of shipments, though, and they got themselves a nice pay bump. Your article put a spotlight on their operation, so the Russians started running numbers."

It didn't surprise me that Anton and his family had gotten greedy. Viktor, Anton's father, had always seemed fairly levelheaded—for a criminal—but Anton and Ivan were reckless and arrogant.

"Okay. So the Russians aren't a threat, but what about the Federovs? They'll still be after me, right? How is it safe to go back to Seattle?"

"The Federovs aren't going to be around much longer,"

Henry said. "They're marked by the Russians. I give them a week in prison, two tops."

"They aren't in prison yet, Henry," I said. "Their trial and any appeals could take months or years."

He shook his head. "The U.S. Attorney's office has the Federovs dead to rights and the grand jury will indict fast. No way a judge will grant them bail, so they'll have to plea-bargain or prepare for their trial from prison—if they live that long. Six months, a year at most, and they're gone."

"And until then?" I asked. An ongoing trial did not guarantee my safety, nor did having the Federovs sitting in a jail cell. "It's not just Viktor, Ivan and Anton I'm worried about. What about their goons?"

"Word is out that the Russians aren't backing the Federovs," Henry explained. "All of their former employees, your 'goons,' are in the wind or have found new criminal undertakings. The Federovs are drowning and no one is stupid enough to tie a rope to their ship."

"She could still be in danger. What are you going to do to keep her safe?" Beau asked.

Henry leaned forward and dropped his elbows to his knees. "She'll have round-the-clock protection from some of my best agents. I'll see to it myself. And if anything changes with the Federovs, if by some miracle they get out on bail, we'll go the WITSEC route. We'll have to play it as it comes. But one thing is for sure, she can't stay here."

No, I couldn't. Not with Dylan Prosser broadcasting my whereabouts and my connection to Beau. I wouldn't bring more stress into his life or risk putting his family in harm's way.

I wouldn't keep being a hassle.

"Look," Henry said, "if I didn't think you'd be secure, I

wouldn't have come here again. But like I told your sheriff when I called him earlier to track you down, things are a lot different than they were six weeks ago."

That was an understatement. Six weeks ago I was at the outpost, happier than I'd been in a decade.

"You promise I'll be safe?" I asked Henry.

He nodded. "I'll have three or four men on you at all times. Your apartment will be monitored with someone stationed outside the door. And when I'm not needed at the office or in the courtroom, I'll be by your side the whole time."

I looked up to Beau. "What do you think?"

"She'll be safe?" Beau asked Henry.

"On my life, she'll be safe," Henry said.

Beau's eyes dropped to mine. "Then you should go home. If I can't keep you safe here, you have to go."

I knew that's what he'd say. I knew he'd send me away. I knew it was the smartest choice.

But knowing didn't make it easier to hear.

"You're right." I nodded and stood from my chair, ignoring the sharp sting in my nose. "This is probably for the best." I looked to Henry. "I'll, um . . . just go and pack."

I dropped my eyes as they flooded and rushed to the stairs. With my back to the living room, I slapped a hand over my mouth to muffle my cries as I ran up the steps. I let a few tears fall, but by the time I hit the closet, I had blinked more away.

Frantically, I started shoving clothes into my duffel bag. All the time I'd spent unpacking this morning had been wasted effort. My neatly folded clothes hadn't been a part of Beau's closet for even one day.

With my drawers clean and my hangers swinging empty,

I stood and stared unfocused at the closet wall. I'd never be in this closet again. Or Beau's room. Or his bed. I turned and took a long look at his bed, wishing we could go back to this morning when we'd been planning a lazy Sunday together.

I wished we could go back to a time when I had hope that we'd make it through this together.

Foolish hope.

An emotional break was coming but I managed to hold it back as I knelt and zipped up my bag. When I came out of the closet, Beau was sitting on the edge of the bed.

"You got everything?"

I nodded. "Yeah."

We stared at each other for a few long moments until Beau broke the silence.

"I didn't mean what I said earlier, Sabrina. You're not a hassle."

"I know," I lied. "We were just mad and talking crazy. And hey," I shrugged, "this all worked out for the best. Now we don't need to worry about too many people finding out I'm here. It will be good for you to go back to a normal routine and for me to go back to the city. I've really missed it."

That lie was so convincing, I almost believed it myself.

"I'm ready to go home." That part was almost true. I'd been in Montana for almost six months, and the constant emotional ups and downs had drained me completely. "I want to get back to my apartment and my life. To my job."

Beau's eyes narrowed. "Your job? I thought you were going to quit and write books."

"Oh, I don't know. I like writing but journalism is in my blood. Besides, once the Federovs are gone, I'll have an easier time getting stories." What was I saying? I didn't really want to go back into journalism. I wanted to pursue writing novels. But telling Beau I was going to retreat into my old life made the sting of leaving go away. Or maybe I was trying to come across as unaffected. Whatever it was, I'd say anything to make the pain fade.

Except nothing worked. Every word just made my heart twist harder.

"Well," Beau stood, "then I guess it's good you're going back to the city."

"Yep. Time for this city girl to go back where she belongs."

"I'll wait for you downstairs."

I watched him go, then ran to the bathroom, shoving my things into my bag. I zipped it closed one last time, then carried it downstairs. The lump in my throat doubled in size when I saw Henry waiting by the door, ready to whisk me away.

Beau was leaning against the fireplace, staring at the floor, Boone at his side.

"Can you give us a minute?" I asked Henry.

"Sure." He nodded and took my bag outside.

I took a deep breath and crossed the living room. He looked up and locked eyes with mine, and I took a moment to memorize the stormy blue I would miss every minute of every day for the rest of my life. I couldn't manage to choke out a good-bye so instead I whispered, "Thank you. For everything you've done for me. Thank you."

"You're welcome." The pain in his voice brought on a fresh wave of tears.

"Beau, I . . ."

I don't want to go. I want to see you again. I want more time.

280

None of those words found their way out. Instead, I lost control of my emotions and started crying at the same time Beau yanked me into his chest, wrapping me up tight as he pressed his cheek to my hair.

I cried for the future we'd never have. The happiness I'd never find without him. The pieces of my heart I was leaving here.

"Please, be careful, Sabrina."

I nodded but kept crying.

"I'm sorry I couldn't keep you safe here longer."

Me too.

"I'll miss you," he whispered.

Then tell me not to go. Tell me there is somewhere else to keep me safe. Tell me you'll come with me to Seattle.

Tell me anything.

I kept those words inside too. Saying them out loud when we only had minutes left wouldn't solve anything. It would just make this harder, so I just whispered, "I'll miss you too."

We held on to one another for a few more minutes, my tears soaking his shirt as our arms clung to the last few moments we had together.

When the door clicked open, I knew our time was up.

"Sabrina," Henry said, poking his head inside. "We'll need to leave soon or we'll miss the last flight out."

I let Beau go and stepped away. "All right."

"One more minute," Beau told him. When Henry closed the door, Beau pulled me back into his arms.

"If you ever need anything else, you call me, okay?"

"Okay."

This was it. This was our good-bye.

And I *hated* it. I wanted to kiss him. To make love to him one last time. To spend one more night in his arms.

But I wouldn't get that good-bye.

We didn't have time.

We only had this one last hug that crumbled my already-shattered heart.

When Boone nudged between our legs, I dropped to the floor and wrapped my arms around his neck, the sobs coming uncontrollably as I said good-bye to Beau's dog.

As I said good-bye to *my* dog.

"I love you," I whispered to Boone, hoping that Beau would know I was talking to him too.

Then I stood and quickly moved through the rest of the house, grabbing my laptop from the kitchen and shoving it in my backpack from the laundry room.

With everything loaded, I walked straight to the door, turning back for one last look at Beau.

Every bit the mountain man I'd met six months ago, he was standing tall in the middle of the room, his arms crossed over his broad chest. His beard was thicker now than it had been back then but his hair was shorter, having just been trimmed at the barber earlier in the week. And even though his face was full of sadness, he was still utterly breathtaking.

"Good-bye, Goliath."

"Bye, Shortcake."

One minute later, Henry was driving us to Bozeman to catch the last flight to Seattle.

"You'll be home before midnight," Henry said as we breezed through security with a flick of his badge. True to his word, he had me standing outside my apartment door at eleven forty-nine.

I greeted the three agents standing guard, then let Henry lead me inside.

The chair that had been knocked over during Anton's attack had been righted and the apartment cleaned. The broken lock had been replaced and a shiny new key was on my kitchen counter. Next to the key was my phone and purse, right where I'd left them in April.

Just as abruptly as it had started, my time in Montana, my time with Beau, was over.

CHAPTER EIGHTEEN

SABRINA

even months later . . .

"Thank you," Bryce Ryan said for the fifth time, shaking my hand after our interview.

"You're welcome." Though her interview questions had been slightly predictable, at least she had been sincere, unlike a few of the journalists I'd met with these last two weeks.

"I'd love to meet for a drink sometime. Do you have any plans this evening?"

I glanced at my watch. Five o'clock on the nose. I considered brushing her off, going home and taking a long hot bath before ordering a pizza and eating the entire pie alone, but I'd made myself a promise to make new friends. In all the months I'd been back in Seattle, I hadn't made any progress, so even though I was exhausted, I was going to accept.

"No plans." I smiled. "I'd love to meet for a drink.

There's a great wine bar around the corner. How does that sound?"

"Perfect! I'll leave you to collect your things and then I'll meet you out front. Fifteen minutes?"

I nodded and wasted no time getting my purse from the dressing room and going outside, sighing with relief the moment I left the studio. The fresh summer air blew across my face as I tipped my head to the sky and let the sunshine warm my skin.

Today had been my last interview on this whirlwind press tour.

My publicist had insisted on the tour, following the announcement that I'd won the Pulitzer Prize for investigative journalism. She had wanted me to take interviews for a month but I'd refused. We'd compromised on two brutal weeks down and up the West Coast, bouncing from airport to hotel to Uber car.

Not only was the travel grueling but the interviews had been miserable. My heart wasn't in anything these days, certainly not talking about my article or my future. Those two topics were equally depressing.

But now I was done and I could retreat to the quiet comfort of my apartment to lie low. Having a drink with Bryce tonight was probably going to be my one and only social activity for at least a month.

"Sabrina." I dropped my chin and smiled at Henry as he walked my way. "You know you should really wait to go outside until I can go with you." He was trying to look stern but his dimple betrayed him.

"Sorry, I needed the air. Besides, I was out of your sight for maybe five seconds."

Henry was my only bodyguard today, though there was

another agent stationed permanently outside my apartment door. When I'd first come back to Seattle, I'd had three agents hovering over me constantly, but as the months went by and the Federovs paid me no attention, we all relaxed a bit.

Now, most days I only had one or two escorts. Henry was busy with other cases so he hadn't been around much the last few months, but he had made the time to personally accompany me on my press tour.

He was about as sick of these interviews as I was, judging by the frown he'd been wearing the last three days.

"Ready to go home?" he asked, sliding on his sunglasses.

"I'm actually going to meet Bryce for a drink." I peered around him and waved to Bryce coming through the studio's doors. "Is that okay?"

"Of course. I'll hang back and let you two talk. Afterward, we can get some dinner and celebrate the end of this fucking press tour."

"Sounds good to me. Maybe we can just order in and relax." After a glass of wine or two, I'd probably be walking like a zombie the three blocks to my apartment building.

Bryce joined us on the sidewalk and I quickly did the introductions before we all walked across the block to the wine bar, our heels clicking on the sidewalk as Henry followed closely behind.

"Congratulations again on your award," Bryce said after we'd settled into our seats at a cocktail table and each ordered the happy-hour red. Henry had taken a post closer to the door to give us some privacy.

"Thank you. Honestly? I'm still in shock that I won." Now that there weren't cameras pointed at us, talking with Bryce was much more appealing.

"Why's that? Your story was amazing."

"Off the record?"

She nodded. "Of course. This is just drinks with a friend."

"Thank you." I smiled. "I'm shocked because some would say I crossed an ethical line by getting personally involved with Anton Federov. But I did what I had to do to shut them down and I was glad the Pulitzer committee saw that too."

My commitment to the investigation and protecting my source was probably what had drawn the committee toward me in the first place.

"I think what you did took guts." Bryce flicked her wrist toward Henry. "You were able to shut down an international arms dealer when the local police and FBI couldn't. I'm glad the awards committee selected you, because you deserve it. And personally, I don't think what you did was immoral or unethical. I think it was courageous."

Beau had said basically the same thing. Did he know I'd won an award? If so, I liked to think he'd be proud.

"I appreciate that." I smiled as our waiter delivered our wine. "Anyway, since we've spent all afternoon talking about me, tell me about yourself. Are you from Seattle?"

She took a sip, then shook her head. "No, I grew up in Montana, then moved here after college to get a job with a TV station."

"Montana?" My spine straightened. "Where at?"

"Bozeman. Have you been?"

I shook my head. "Just once but it was dark so I didn't see much other than the airport."

"It's an awesome town and I miss it. Between you and me, I've been considering moving back."

"Is there a TV station there you could work for?"

She shrugged. "Probably, but if I went back, I'd give up TV. After I moved out here, my parents relocated to a smaller town called Clifton Forge. My dad runs the newspaper and has been begging me to come home and take it over so he can retire. TV is wearing me out and the paper business is tempting. I'm tired of producers telling me what to wear, how to cut my hair and that I need to go on a diet."

I laughed. "I thought about going the TV route for about five minutes in college. It's got the glamour but I shadowed a woman at Channel 4 and hated the hours."

"Tell me about it. It's taken me ten years to get out of morning TV. I can finally stay up later than seven o'clock at night and sleep past three o'clock in the morning."

I laughed again and took a drink of my wine. This was nice. She was nice. The FBI agents that had been guarding me were great but they all were men. It was refreshing to have some girl time.

"So why were you in Montana?" Bryce asked.

My good mood fell a bit and my eyes dropped to my glass. "It's a long story."

Even though it had only been seven months since I'd left, it felt like years had gone by. Winter had passed and spring was turning into summer. A year ago, I was alone at the outpost. Now, I was back to my fancy life in the bustling city, constantly with other people, and had never been so lonely.

"I'd love to hear that story if you've got time," Bryce said.

Her pretty brown eyes were so kind and inviting that I found myself spilling the entire story of my time in Montana.

It was cathartic. It was the first time I'd shared my whole experience and talked about all that had happened with Beau. Not even Felicity knew the whole story. I'd shared bits and pieces with her during our regular phone calls but we were both so excited about her baby's upcoming arrival that our calls tended to be dominated by nursery décor discussions and rants about gender-neutral greens.

Bryce listened intently, and talking to her was just what I'd needed. Keeping everything bottled inside and constantly wearing a stoic face was part of why I was so tired. One hour talking with her had given me more energy than a full night's sleep.

"Have you talked to Beau since you've been back?" she asked.

I shook my head. "No, I don't even have his phone number. I could get it from Felicity but neither of us ever brings him up. She knows it's a sad subject and I can't bring myself to ask how he's doing." I wanted him to be happy but I was terrified he'd found someone new. For now, I was clinging to ignorance as I kept trying to put the pieces of my heart back together.

Bryce shook her head and worried her bottom lip between her teeth. "I'm so sorry things didn't work out between you two."

You and me both. I reached out and patted her hand, grateful for her sympathy. "It's done now and probably for the best." I'd been repeating that mantra every day since I'd left Prescott. Time would heal my heart, or at least dull the pain.

I hope.

The waiter came over and Bryce and I ordered another glass of wine, the interruption a good segue to a different subject.

"Have you done much writing since you've been back?"

"No," I sighed. "I polished the three books I wrote at the

outpost and had those published but I haven't written anything new." Between the insanity of being back and my complete lack of motivation, I had all but abandoned the novel I had started my last week at the outpost. My computer hadn't been opened in a month because I just couldn't bring myself to write.

"I'm scared of my laptop," I admitted. "I feel like when my fingers hit the keyboard, it will rip open fresh wounds."

"Maybe you just need time. Will you go back to the newspaper?"

Bryce had asked me the same question during our interview earlier but I'd dodged it with a vague answer.

I felt guilty for quitting a job in which I'd won a prestigious award. I felt guilty quitting a job so many would covet. I felt guilty for quitting a job that had once been my life's aspiration. But my heart wasn't in journalism anymore, and I couldn't stay just to appease the guilt.

So this time, I answered Bryce's question with the truth. "No. That chapter of my life is over. Effective this morning, I am no longer Sabrina MacKenzie, investigative reporter for *The Seattle Times*."

My boss had been begging me to return to work, offering me promotions and pay raises, but this morning I had emailed him my official resignation. He'd hired someone to replace me months ago, but when I'd come back to Seattle, he had been so overjoyed that he'd pulled every string he could to put me on paid sabbatical.

I was extremely grateful for his loyalty but I wasn't the reporter he needed on staff. Not anymore.

"I can see why you'd need a change," Bryce said.

"You might be the only one. Well, you and my parents. They are thrilled with my decision to change careers." When

I'd called to tell them the news this morning, my dad had cheered and my mom had started crying. They were thrilled I was quitting the job that had put my life in danger.

The six months I'd spent in hiding had been horrible for my parents. My dad had gotten another ulcer and my mom had worn a path in their new carpet from pacing. After I'd gotten back to the city and arranged for my life to be turned back on, I'd spent three weeks in Florida, then gone back again for the holidays. It had been the best time I'd spent with my family in decades and we'd found a new closeness.

My brothers both texted me daily and I talked to my parents at least four times a week. They were planning on visiting Seattle this summer and I had already booked a vacation to go home in the fall.

Our new-formed bond was the one amazing thing to come out of this entire Federov disaster. That and my brief time with Beau. Even though I was in pain, I'd never regret being with him.

Bryce and I chatted for a little while longer about her job and some of the interviews she'd done lately. Then, after we'd finished our drinks, we exchanged phone numbers. Selfishly, I hoped she'd stay in Seattle and not move home to Montana. She'd be a great friend.

"Whether you stay with television or move to Clifton Forge's paper, you will be incredibly successful." I shook her hand good-bye. "You are one easy person to talk to, Bryce Ryan."

She blushed and her face broke into a wide, white smile. "Coming from you, that's the best compliment I may have ever gotten."

I waved as she pushed through the door and disappeared into the crowd on the sidewalk.

"Ready?" I asked Henry.

"You bet." He smiled and led me outside, escorting me home.

Henry was the reason I even had a home. While I'd been in Montana, he had arranged for my bills to be paused and my rent to be paid. He'd gone above the normal call of duty and I'd always be grateful.

"Did you have a nice time?" he asked.

"I did. It was nice to make a new friend."

"Good."

"Speaking of friends, I was thinking of going back to Prescott after Felicity's baby is born. Any objections?"

He shook his head. "Do you know when?"

"She isn't due until the end of the month and I want to give her a chance to settle in before I invade. So maybe the end of June?"

"Okay. I'll try and go with you, but if I can't, I'll make sure you're covered."

"Do you think I'll even need an agent with me by then?" The Federovs were scheduled to be sentenced next week, and by the time June rolled around, there might not be any danger left to worry about.

"I'd rather plan to go with you, just in case."

"Okay."

Maybe if Henry came with me, he'd act as a buffer between me and Beau. I was certain our reunion would be awkward—if I even saw him. I assumed that if I were in Montana he'd want to see me, but what if he didn't? A wave of nervous energy rushed to my stomach.

"Do you still want dinner?" Henry asked.

"Sure." I wasn't hungry anymore, but if I didn't get something in my system, I'd have a wicked wine hangover in the morning. I wasn't drunk but two glasses were just enough to punish me the next day.

"How about we get you home and I'll go pick up a pizza?"

"Perfect."

We walked the rest of the way to my apartment building in silence. Normally, I'd spend a few minutes visiting with my doorman but my feet hurt so badly that I only said a quick hello and went straight to the elevator, pushing the button for the fifth floor.

The doors opened with a ding and Henry grumbled something under his breath before stepping into the hallway.

"Mitchell." Henry's angry snap sent the young agent's head flying up and his hands fumbling his phone into his jacket pocket.

"Agent Dalton." Mitchell stood from his brown metal folding chair, nervously smoothing out his wrinkled suit.

"Haven't we discussed cell-phone usage when you're on duty?" Henry asked.

Mitchell nodded frantically. "Sorry, it was my girlfriend. She's pregnant and I just—"

"Don't let it happen again. Remember why you're here."

"Sure. No problem, Agent Dalton."

"And shouldn't you be down by the stairwell?"

"Shit. I mean, right! Sorry, Ms. MacKenzie."

I nodded and fought a smile.

Mitchell fumbled to fold up the chair. "I just wanted to sit down."

"Then take the chair down there." Henry pointed down the hall.

"Right, right." Mitchell picked up his chair and rushed down the hallway toward the emergency exit sign.

The only way to get to my apartment was from either the elevator or the back stairs. To get on the elevator, you had to pass my doorman and have a key. To come up the stairs, all you needed was a key card. Though the stairwell door was under video surveillance, Henry had deemed it the weakest point in the building, so I'd had a guard by my door for seven months.

"He's terrified of you," I whispered as we followed Agent Mitchell, who walked at warp speed ahead of us.

Henry sighed. "He's not even supposed to be here but I was short on options. We had a break in another case and I needed my full team to wrap it up. So I had to pull him from desk duty. He's been on probation since he was too busy on that fucking phone to pay attention during surveillance."

Could Agent Mitchell be the reason why Ivan Federov had been able to visit Montana last summer? Or had he dropped the ball on some other surveillance assignment? I didn't ask; instead, I frowned when I realized I'd been burdening Henry and taking his focus these last two weeks.

"Henry, if you had another big case, why did you insist on going on my press tour? I would have been fine with another agent."

"I wanted to go with you." He took the keys from my hand and unlocked my door. "Come on, let's get you inside."

I followed him inside my apartment, still feeling guilty. "I'm so sorry. I should have stayed in Prescott longer." At least there, I wouldn't have kept FBI agents from solving other crimes.

"No, it was time for you to get out of there. I'm really glad you're back." He stepped into my space and looked down at me with soft eyes. His chest was just inches away from mine and I didn't breathe for fear they would touch.

What was he doing? Was he making a move on me?

My heart started to race but not with excitement or attraction. This was panic. I wasn't ready for someone new. As it was, I was barely hanging on to the pieces of my shattered heart. I couldn't fathom any other man taking Beau's place. Not now. Maybe not ever.

When Henry's face started to descend toward mine, I unfroze and stepped back, bumping against the small table by my door. "Henry, I . . ."

His entire frame deflated and his eyes dropped to his feet. "It's okay."

Fuck. I had been so consumed with my own emotions I hadn't been paying attention to Henry's. How had I missed this? "I am so, *so* sorry."

He looked up and gave me a sad smile. "It's my fault. You seemed more like your old self today. Going out for drinks with a friend. Planning a trip back to Montana. I thought maybe you were moving on."

I shook my head but didn't speak. There wasn't anything to say.

"Can we forget this happened?" he asked.

"Okay."

"I'll get that pizza." He turned and opened the door. "Do you want me to pick you up more wine?"

"No, thank you. I have some."

His smile was forced. "Be back soon. Lock this behind me."

I nodded and closed the door, sagging against its surface as I turned the lock.

When my heart rate returned to noncritical levels, I kicked off my white shoes and let the cool marble tile soothe my aching soles.

Damn it. No matter how much we both pretended like that moment hadn't happened, things between Henry and me were bound to get awkward. Maybe he'd have his other agents take over Sabrina duty for a while, and after some space, we'd get back to our easy friendship.

I hoped so. While Henry would never be a love interest, I still wanted him as a friend.

Forcing my feet to move, I walked further into my apartment. My cleaning crew had been in today and there was a light citrus scent in the air. Though I was still considering downsizing, I did love this space.

The walls were a soft gray, just a shade lighter than the white trim. Other than the tiled entryway, the rest of the apartment had espresso hardwood floors. I had decorated with light and muted tones to offset the dark walnut doors and cabinets.

The hall that extended from the entryway split the place in half. On the right were my office and a wide, sunken living room. On the left were my master suite and the kitchen. The U-shaped kitchen was at the back of the apartment, separated from the living room by a tall island and barstools.

Tossing my purse onto a couch, I yawned and turned to the kitchen.

My heart jumped into my throat and I gasped. A nightmare stood across from me.

Anton.

He was leaning against the stove on the other side of the island, a hand tucked casually in a pocket. He stood in just the right spot, hidden by the hallway that led to my bedroom, so that the only way to see him was by being completely inside the apartment. Since I had been looking out the floor-to-ceiling living-room windows when I'd walked in, I'd been oblivious to his presence.

"Hello, Sabrina." His voice sent chills down my spine.

I took one step toward the door but stopped when he snapped straight and held out a gun. "Ah, ah, ah. Don't go running away from me again. We've got some things to talk about, kitten."

I shuddered at his pet name. He'd called me that for months, usually when we were in bed and I was faking an orgasm.

He pushed off the stove and walked to the side of the island, casually propping himself against its edge and setting the gun on its granite top. He was dressed in black slacks and a gray button-down shirt. His ink-black hair was styled perfectly, giving him the deceptive appearance of a normal, handsome man, but his cunning black eyes betrayed him.

"Aren't you going to say hello?" It wasn't a request.

I cringed. "Hello, Anton."

I wanted to scream, to run for my life, but it wouldn't get me anywhere. Even if I shouted for Agent Mitchell, Anton would shoot me before I could be rescued. My feet stayed firmly on the floor as fear coursed through my veins. There would be no flight, and I wouldn't survive a fight.

But at least I wouldn't be going alone.

"They'll kill you, Anton. The second the FBI comes through that door, you're dead."

He took a step away from the counter and spat, "Bitch, I'm already dead because of you."

I shuffled backward but had nowhere to go. Only a miracle would save me now, and since I'd already had one of those where Anton was concerned, I didn't think I'd be granted another.

My death would wreck my parents and brothers. Felicity would be destroyed. And Beau? He'd think he'd failed me.

A numbness settled into my skin. Maybe it was from fear. Maybe it was from sheer hopelessness.

"What do you want, Anton? To take your revenge on me, then go out guns blazing?" My cool voice shocked Anton and he eyed me suspiciously.

"Something like that."

I stood firm in my spot as I braced for his approach. Just because I didn't expect to survive a fight didn't mean I wasn't going to try. My bear spray was tucked away in my purse, too far away to grab, but Beau had given me another weapon.

Me.

I was no match for Anton's size and strength, and he'd likely overpower me, but I'd use every self-defense move Beau had taught me and fight to my death. All I wanted was to inflict just a little pain on this fucking asshole before he killed me.

That momentary numbness was going away. Burning rage was bringing me back to life.

My spine straightened and my eyes challenged Anton to do his worst. Maybe this confidence was stupid. Maybe he'd go for the gun and I wouldn't get the chance to fight back. But I was betting on Anton's ego winning out. He had underestimated me once. Maybe I'd get lucky and he'd do it again.

He wasn't just here to shoot me quickly and spit on my dead body. He could have done that already. No, he was here to do what he'd started last year but hadn't gotten to finish.

Beat me, rape me, then choke the life out of me.

Anton stood taller, trying to intimidate me, but I didn't

cower. Instead I held his eyes in silence, daring him to make his move.

I was ready when he lunged for me, his hands reaching right for my throat. Just like Beau had taught me, I side-stepped and thrust a knee into his groin.

He grunted and doubled over as I tried to get a lock on his elbow but my hands were too slippery with sweat. When I tried to bend back his wrist, I lost my grip and he squirmed free. The shock of my attack quickly wore off and Anton turned, preparing to lunge for me again.

I took my opening and kicked out hard at his knee, not doing any damage, but the force of the blow was enough to make it bend, and Anton dropped to the floor.

With Anton down, I had a split second of freedom to scramble for his gun on the counter. The second my palm hit the cool black metal, Anton's fist reached out and grabbed my hair.

As he jerked me backward, Beau's words echoed in my mind.

Safety. Hammer. Trigger.

I twisted in Anton's grip, pain radiating through my scalp.

Bang.

CHAPTER NINETEEN

SABRINA

Twenty. *Twenty-one. Twenty-two.*
Blink.

I was sitting in a living room chair that I had turned backward toward my windows. With my legs tucked under my rear, I stared into the dark city, counting how many seconds I could go without blinking.

I'd done my best to become invisible, and over the last six hours, most of the people in my apartment had forgotten I was sitting here. Behind me, a team of investigators was talking in hushed voices while others snapped countless pictures of the crime scene. An hour ago, the coroner had zippered Anton's body in a bag and loaded it onto a squeaky cart that would wheel him to the morgue.

Through it all, my eyes stayed glued to the windows. Even though I was trying to block out conversation, my ears were still active and I listened to a couple of newcomers get an update.

"Are we taking her down to the station?"

"No. Agent Dalton says she stays here."

"Has she been questioned?"

"I don't know. I only got here a couple of hours ago."

One man pushed out a loud breath. "That's a lot of blood."

"No shit. Bullet straight to the heart at close range. That fucker was dead before he hit the floor."

A chill crept down my spine.

I killed a person today.

I had taken a life.

One tear slid down my cheek but I quickly swiped it away. I couldn't cry. I wouldn't cry. Not yet.

Somehow, I had managed to keep it together as I stood over Anton's lifeless body with a gun in my hand. When Agent Mitchell had broken through my door, his gun drawn for an already neutralized threat, somehow I hadn't panicked. And somehow, I hadn't cracked when agents had photographed my white clothes streaked with blood before leaving me in my bathroom to strip them off into a plastic evidence bag.

Somehow, I was keeping it together. And I would keep keeping it together.

My breakdown would have to wait because Henry still had to take my official statement. He'd gotten a high-level recap earlier but then had to leave, promising to come back soon to go through everything again in detail.

Ignoring the men behind me, I went back to counting and staring until the mood in the room tensed.

"Have you finished processing the scene?" Henry demanded behind me.

"Uh, not yet."

"Finish," he ordered. "Now." Shoes scuffled as people scurried. Henry came and crouched next to my chair, patting one of my knees. "How are you doing?"

I shrugged and unglued my eyes from the windows to look at his face. His forehead was creased with worry and his eyes were pleading for forgiveness.

"I'm so sorry, Sabrina."

I shook my head. "It's not your fault." I didn't blame Henry for any of this. If he had come inside and not gone out for pizza, Anton would have shot him. I was glad he hadn't been here.

"It is my fault."

I didn't have the energy to convince him otherwise so I turned back to the window.

He sighed. "I've got to talk to a few people and then I'll be back to get your official statement."

"Okay."

"Sorry, it's going to take a while longer tonight."

"It's fine." At least he'd arranged for me to stay here instead of taking me to a police station for questioning.

He patted my knee again and stood while I went back to staring. The sound of more clicking cameras filled the room, and I closed my eyes, resting my head against the back of the chair. A headache was coming on strong.

I stayed quiet, listening to the activity behind me and trying to rest my eyes while I lost all track of time.

A commotion in the outside hallway caught my attention but I kept my eyes closed.

"You can't go in there. Sir! Stop! This is a crime scene! You can't—"

"What's going on out here?" Henry said, intervening.

"Where is she?"

My eyes flew open. I knew that deep voice.

I held my breath and waited, listening as heavy footsteps grew louder. When Beau knelt down in front of me, a sob escaped my throat. His big hands slid around my waist and he pulled me out of the chair, right into his lap on the floor. My arms clutched his shoulders and I buried my face in his neck, inhaling the smell that I had missed so much.

Now I could cry.

"I killed him," I whispered, another sob working free.

"I know. Give it to me, angel."

And I did.

Once the seal was broken, my tears flowed unrestrained. The breakdown I'd been holding back came rushing forward like an avalanche. I cried, hard, giving Beau all of my pain from tonight. Giving him all the heartbreak and anguish I'd felt these last seven months.

When my loud cries became muffled whimpers and sniffles, I unburied my face and looked into his beautiful eyes. He was a miracle. The one and only person who could pull me from this nightmare had appeared like my savior.

"How did you know?"

He jerked his chin behind me toward the door. "Henry called Felicity. Felicity called me."

"And you came right here?"

He nodded. "I drove like hell to Bozeman and caught the last flight out."

"How did you know where I was?"

"I didn't but figured this was as good a place as any to start looking. I knew someone here could point me in the right direction."

My head fell back into the crook of his neck. "Thank you."

"I'll always come if you need me, Sabrina. Never doubt that," he whispered into my hair as his arms banded around me tighter.

Henry cleared his throat at our side and I reluctantly let go of Beau to stand. "I'm ready to take your statement."

I nodded. "Okay. Here? Or do I have to go somewhere else?"

"We'll do it here. Have a seat."

Beau's hand on the small of my back steered me to the couch. He sat first then pulled me down to his side, securing me firmly to his torso with an arm around my shoulders. I laced my fingers with his free hand and took a deep breath.

"Ready." I nodded to Henry, who sat across from us.

Henry placed a small tape recorder on my coffee table. He spoke first, verbalizing the date, time and my name, then looked up to me. "Sabrina. Would you please walk me through the events that occurred around six o'clock this evening?"

My fingers gripped Beau's tighter as I took one more fortifying breath and launched into the details of the attack. By the time I was done, the crease between Beau's eyebrows was as deep and worried as I'd ever seen it.

Henry asked me a few more questions and then shut off the recorder. "Thanks, that's all I need. I'm sorry we made you wait so long to finish this up. It's been a busy night." He raked a hand through his hair. "You should know, Viktor and Ivan Federov were murdered."

I gasped at the same time Beau's arm jerked. "What? What happened?"

"I can't tell you much. We'll release a statement tomorrow, but they were both killed in a riot at the prison this evening."

"Russian hit?" Beau asked quietly.

Henry just nodded.

Anton had planned his escape the same day the Russians had planned their hit. His escape might have been thwarted if there hadn't been that prison riot. The Russians would have killed him, not me. The coincidence was just . . . so fucking unfair.

"So that's it?" I asked. "They're all gone?"

"Yeah. They're all gone." Henry's sad eyes were full of guilt. "I have a specialized cleaning crew coming in tomorrow, so you'll have to stay out until Sunday. We'll put you up in a hotel."

"Okay." I started to stand but Beau kept me on the couch.

"We're not done, Dalton." Beau's voice was quiet but angry. "You said she'd be safe."

"And I fucked up. I won't make any excuses. I fucked up and I'll always be sorry. I should have put her in WITSEC." Henry's eyes left Beau's and came to mine. "I'm sorry, Sabrina. This never should have happened. What can I do?"

Killing Anton had been my only choice but maybe if I had more of the facts, it would help me make sense of all that had happened tonight. "I'd like to know how Anton got in here."

"Okay." Henry looked up at an agent with a camera, hovering by the door. "Are you all done?"

"Yes, sir. Is there anything else you'd like us to finish?"

"No. I'll escort Ms. MacKenzie to her hotel when we're done talking. Get everything back to the office and put a rush on processing. I want her to be able to come back by Sunday morning at the latest."

"Yes, sir."

He waited until everyone had left and the door clicked shut to resume talking.

"This has to stay between us until the official report is released."

I nodded.

"Anton wasn't with his father or brother, because he was in the infirmary. He faked appendicitis and bribed a corrections officer to smuggle him out of the prison with a change of clothes and a weapon. With the Russian hit causing a big stir, none of us even knew he was gone until it was too late."

"So he had been planning this for a while?" I asked. "He was never going to let me go, was he?"

Henry shook his head and looked to his feet. "I should have known."

"And I shouldn't have let you leave Montana," Beau said, pressing a kiss to my temple. "I should have found another place for you to hide."

"There's no use looking back. It's over now." I leaned further into Beau's side. I had no idea what that kiss meant or where we went from here, but I didn't care. I was going to lean on him until I could stand on my own. Then we'd deal with the rest.

"How did Anton get in here?" I asked.

Henry's face hardened. "He came in through the stairwell entrance. We've got him on video coming in with another tenant. He must have known your cleaning crew's schedule because he slipped in while they were leaving. He probably pretended to be an agent."

"But Agent Mitchell . . ." I didn't need to finish my sentence. Agent Mitchell had been by the elevator on his phone. "Huh," I scoffed. "That folding chair and phone probably saved his life."

"Maybe," Henry said. "Or else he was bribed too. I'll be finding out and he'll either get fired or go to prison himself."

We all sat quietly for a few moments. I was out of questions about Anton and hoped never to mutter his name again.

"What now?" Beau asked, breaking the silence.

"You're free to go," Henry told us. "Though I'd like to keep an agent with you for a few more weeks."

"Is that really necessary?" There were much more important things for the FBI than babysitting me.

"Please?" Henry said. "Let me keep someone with you if nothing more than to appease my own worries. I'd like to give our Russian visitors the chance to return home and I'd also like to confirm with our inside man that they don't have any interest in returning."

"Fine," I muttered.

Beau shifted and stood, bringing me with him off the couch. "Let's get out of here."

"All right. I'll just pack a few things."

Henry stood and reached out to touch my shoulder before I could walk away. "Sabrina, I'm sorry. I'll never forgive myself for letting you down."

I gave him a small smile. "I don't know if anyone could have stopped Anton. You didn't let me down, Henry. I wish none of this had happened but . . . it's done now."

Beau's arm found my shoulders again. "Come on."

He guided me out of the living room but my feet paused before we could make it to the hallway leading to my bedroom. I took one last look at the black pool of blood where Anton's body had been. It was drying around the edges and I was grateful that someone else would be scrubbing it away. Still, I doubted I'd ever let my feet step in that space again. I'd always see blood, even after it had been washed away.

"I touched a gun today," I muttered.

"What?" Beau asked.

"I touched a gun today," I repeated, my eyes locked on the blood pool.

Eighteen years ago, I had vowed never to touch a gun. Not after I'd found Janessa's silver pistol, the one she'd used to kill herself. The gun she'd bought out of the trunk of some gangster's car. The gun I had found lying next to her lifeless feet.

She'd been sick so I'd ditched study hall to visit her at home. I'd found her in bed, not sick, but dead, her beautiful turquoise quilt covered in blood and brain matter because she'd put that gun in her mouth and pulled the trigger.

Once the nightmare of that scene had subsided, I'd promised myself I'd never touch a gun. Never.

Shooting Anton had been my only option, but the realization that I'd broken my vow— something I'd held tight to for so long—broke the last hold I had on my control.

My legs gave out and I would have crumbled to the floor if not for Beau's strong arms wrapping me up and cradling me into his chest. There in the safety of his embrace, I lost it. Completely.

"I've got you."

Don't ever let me go. The words didn't come out, only more wails and heart-wrenching screams.

Beau said something to Henry but I couldn't hear him over my own noise. We were moving but I couldn't get a handle on myself to stop crying and open my eyes. My stomach dipped when we went down the elevator and my body jostled as we got into a car. My screams stopped but the

308

wrenching sobs continued until we made it to a hotel and Beau locked us safely into our room.

Gently laying me on the bed, his arms only left me for a moment to shut off the light. Then I was curled tightly into his chest, where the darkness took over and I fell asleep.

———

I WOKE up to the sun shining through the hotel room windows.

My eyes were puffy and swollen. My throat was on fire. My entire body ached. But because I was waking up in Beau's arms, I felt better than I would have ever imagined possible the morning after being nearly murdered and taking another person's life.

"Hi, Goliath," I whispered into his chest.

"Hi, Shortcake." He brushed the hair off my cheek. "How are you feeling today?"

"Better. I'm sorry about last night."

"Don't ever be sorry."

I don't know what I would have done if he hadn't been there. "Thank you."

"You're welcome. What do you want to do today?" he asked.

"You're staying?" *Say yes. Say yes.*

"Of course I'm staying."

I smiled and snuggled closer. "Good."

"So, what do you think? Movies and room service?"

A day spent lying around with Beau sounded wonderful but I didn't want to stay in the hotel room and dwell. I'd have plenty of time to analyze everything that had happened when Beau left and I was back on my own again.

"What if we explored Seattle a bit? I could show you all the tourist stops. I don't want to sit around and mope all day."

He leaned back to study my face. "Really?"

"Is that bad?" I had no idea how to act right now. It wasn't like I was happy and carefree. I just didn't want to keep replaying the events of last night on an endless loop. I needed the distraction of the outdoors and crowds.

"No, it's not bad." Beau rolled me onto my back, hovering over me. "You can't feel guilty about what happened last night. It was you or him. You did what you had to do."

The truth in his eyes spread to my heart, knitting together a couple of the broken pieces. I had so much I wanted to say, but instead, I brushed my lips against his.

Beau kissed me back, gentle and sweet, breaking us apart before it could get heated, but the kiss didn't erase any of the concern in his eyes. "I'm worried about you."

"I'll be okay," I reassured us both. "Let's get through today, then go from there."

"All right. Then show me your city."

We spent the entire day playing tourist. I took him up the Space Needle and on the Seattle Great Wheel. We spent hours strolling through Pike Place Market and along the piers. Then I took him to my favorite seafood restaurant, where we caught up on the last seven months and ate way too much.

It was by far the best day I'd ever had in Seattle, all because I'd been with Beau.

"I had fun today," I told him as we ambled back to the hotel. "That's kind of weird, huh?"

"Not weird." His thumb caressed the back of my hand. "I had fun too. How are you doing?"

We hadn't talked at all about Anton the entire day, or last night's ordeal. I didn't need to. Just walking around, holding Beau's hand had helped me put it all into perspective. I had done what I'd had to do. What anyone else would have done. I didn't like it, but I wasn't going to blame myself. I was going to do my best to move on.

"I'm okay," I said. "I'm sure there will be bad days ahead but getting through today, the distractions, they really helped."

"Good." His free hand reached out and tipped up the brim of my baseball hat. He'd been doing that all day, grinning each time. "My hat looks better on you than it does on me."

"I beg to differ." He looked sexy as hell in his old hat but he'd given it to me to wear today because I hadn't had any sunglasses. Henry had packed me a few things while I'd been sobbing in Beau's arms last night but he'd stuck to the bare essentials.

"I like your hair," Beau said. "It looks good lighter."

"Thanks. My stylist nearly fainted at my first appointment after coming back. She was distraught at my split ends and wanted to cut off six inches but I told her all she could do was a trim because I'd made a deal never to cut my hair."

He smiled. "Damn straight."

I looked to the side and saw our reflection in a store window. Even in the dim evening light, I could see huge bags under my eyes. "Ugh," I groaned.

"What?"

"It's a good thing I've got this hat on. I look horrible. I probably scared the children at the Space Needle today."

311

"Hey," Beau said, bumping my shoulder with his arm. "Don't be talking about my Shortcake like that. She's always beautiful. Even after being forced to use an outhouse."

I laughed. "I don't know what was worse. Hovering over that hole or knowing that you could hear me pee."

He laughed too and let go of my hand to toss his arm around my shoulders. I leaned into his side and wrapped my arms around his waist.

"I missed you, Beau."

He kissed my hat-covered head. "You too."

By the time we got back to the hotel, I was wiped out. Beau opened the glass doors and let me inside first, waving to the agent that had been following us all day.

The man Henry had assigned to us wasn't anyone I recognized but I could tell he had experience. He had been so discreet that I'd forgotten he was even with us. The only time I'd noticed he was close was when he'd silently communicated something with Beau.

My phone rang at the same time Beau flipped the lock closed in our room. It had been ringing nonstop all day so Beau and I had made a game of guessing who the caller was each time. Without looking at the screen, I said, "I'm guessing Felicity."

He shook his head. "Dalton."

I flipped the screen up. Beau was the winner. Again. "Hi," I answered. I should have guessed the call was from Henry. His agent had probably reported we were no longer on the loose.

"Are you back at the hotel for the night?" He sounded exhausted.

"Yes."

"Good. Your apartment is clean and you can go home

tomorrow. You've got new locks since Mitchell busted in the old ones. Your doorman has your new keys."

"Okay. Thank you for taking care of that."

"No problem. How are you?"

I looked at Beau, sitting on the edge of the bed kicking off his shoes. His soft smile was aimed my way. "I'm okay. Good night, Henry."

"Good night, Sabrina."

I tossed my phone on the bed next to Beau. "Henry says I can go home tomorrow. Will you go with me?"

"Try to keep me away."

I smiled and plopped down next to him. I wasn't sure how it would feel going back to my apartment. That place was starting to have more bad memories than good.

"One day at a time," Beau said, reading my thoughts.

One day at a time.

———

TAKING A DEEP BREATH, I turned the key in the lock. Bleach and air freshener assaulted my nose as the door swung open to reveal the bright afternoon sun beaming through my living room windows. Beau's hand rested on the small of my back. He stayed glued to my side with each step into my apartment.

I had told him at lunch that I wanted to rip off the Band-Aid. To waltz right into my apartment and walk directly to the spot where I had killed Anton. There wasn't much waltzing with my heavy footsteps but they took me right to the spot.

On my left was a bouquet of flowers someone had left on the island. It rested in the exact place where Anton's gun had been. On the right, someone had turned my staring chair around so it no longer faced the windows. And at my feet was a clean and polished floor. All traces of Anton had been erased.

Once I blocked him from my memories, he'd be gone forever.

"Okay?" Beau asked.

"Would it be strange to say yes?" I'd thought it would be scary and emotional to come back in here but it just felt like . . . nothing. I looked up into Beau's eyes. "I think I let it all out the other night."

His hand cupped my jaw. "I think you did too."

I wished there had been another way but it didn't change the facts. Anton was gone and he wouldn't be coming after me again.

For the first time in over a year, I was truly safe to live my life.

I was free of Anton.

And Beau could be free of me. Of my hassle.

A decision cemented itself firmly in my head. It was going to destroy me, but I had to send Beau home.

Beau would always be rescuing someone or something; it just wouldn't be me anymore. I had to release him from my burdens. All I had to give him for his troubles was my heart but he would have it all until the day I died.

I stepped into his space and wrapped my arms around his waist, resting my ear against his heart. I couldn't say what I needed to say if I was looking into his eyes.

He'd see right through my lies.

"I'll never be able to thank you enough for everything you've done for me, and I can't tell you how much it meant that you came here the other night and stayed with me yesterday. I don't know what I would have done without you, but I can't keep interrupting your life. You should go home. I'll be okay."

I would be miserable, but if he knew the truth, he'd stay. And the longer we stayed together, the harder it would be on both of us in the end.

His arms came to my shoulders and pushed me back. "Say that again? You want me to go?"

No. "I want you to be free."

His face softened. "Sabrina, I—"

"Please," I whispered, my voice cracking. "I can't, Beau. I can't drag this out. It will hurt too much and nothing has changed. I belong here. You belong there."

His shoulders fell and his hands dropped to his sides. "That's what you want?"

"Yes."

It was the worst lie I'd ever told.

He stared at me for a few moments but I kept my eyes locked firmly to his chest. Finally, he whispered, "Okay."

"Will you do something for me before you go? One last thing?"

"Your wish, Shortcake."

This hurt. *God, this fucking hurt.*

I swallowed the lump in my throat and locked my eyes with his. "I hated how everything ended in Prescott. This time, I want a real good-bye."

Beau didn't need any explanation. His mouth crashed down on mine, urgent and hungry, as we both poured our hearts into the kiss. He wasted no time, hoisting me up and carrying me to my bedroom, where he laid me down gently on the bed and stripped off my clothes. When he'd done the same with his, he came down on top of me, careful not to crush me under his heavy weight.

He started kissing my neck, traveling slowly to my breasts but stopped abruptly and pulled away.

"Fuck," he hissed.

"What?"

"I don't have a condom."

"I'm back on birth control. There hasn't been anyone since you." I braced, hoping that he could say the same.

"Me either."

What a relief.

"Are you sure?" he asked.

I nodded. "I want you, Beau. Just you."

When he slid inside without anything between us, a single tear escaped my eye. This moment deserved a tear.

It deserved all the tears.

Beau and I stayed in bed together for the rest of the afternoon and into the evening. We lay cuddled together, mostly in silence. One or the both of us would drift off, then wake to reach for the other and make love, again and again. Finally, night fell and I slipped into a deep sleep with Beau's arms wrapped around me like ropes.

When I woke the next morning, cold and untethered, I didn't need to reach out to know that he was gone.

———

BEAU

Staring out an airport window, I mindlessly watched a ground crew prepare for the day. It was only four thirty in the morning and I'd be waking Michael up with my phone call but I touched his name anyway.

"Hey." Michael's voice was rough with sleep. "Is everything okay? How's Sabrina doing?"

"She's fine," I said. "Listen, I'm at the airport and should be home early afternoon. I'm going to swing by and pick up Boone from your place and then head out into the mountains for a couple days."

"What? I thought you were staying for a week or two."

"Things changed."

"Oh, okay."

I knew he'd be disappointed. Michael was worse than Maisy when it came to Sabrina. He asked daily when I'd be bringing her back, whereas Maisy limited her nosiness to once a week.

Months ago, I had spilled Sabrina's whole story to Michael over a bottle of Crown. The moment she left Prescott, I'd turned into a grouchy and miserable son of a bitch. Michael had been the family nominee to intervene.

"Are you sure you shouldn't stay longer?" he asked. "She might surprise you if you asked her to come back."

"I can't force her into a life she doesn't want, Michael." She didn't want that life—my life—even if she wanted me.

He sighed. "But you love her."

With everything I had.

"Let's talk about this later, okay? See you in a bit." I hung up and walked farther down the row of windows, taking a chair in a secluded corner near my gate. The second I got home, I was leaving again. I needed some time alone in the mountains to think clearly and make a plan.

I couldn't force Sabrina into my life in Montana, but I could fit myself into her life here.

It meant I needed a plan to unload a lot of responsibility. It meant I would be choosing myself over everything and everyone else in my life.

Sabrina thought yesterday was our good-bye.

It wasn't. I'd prove to her that she was more important than anything else. My job. My family. My mountains.

I'd say good-bye to it all, just so I could say hello to her every morning for the rest of my life.

CHAPTER TWENTY

SABRINA

The end.

Tears were streaming down my face as I typed.

For the last three weeks, the book that I'd started at the outpost, *Holt's Compass*, had been my life. After Beau had left, I'd sequestered myself in my office and done nothing but write. Occasionally I'd shower, but mostly I sat in front of my computer, leaving only to answer the door for takeout deliveries.

And today, it was done. Finally.

The portion that I'd written at the outpost had been reworked and now it was my most powerful romance to date. I loved the hero. I was the heroine. And the elements of their love story were flawless.

None of my college papers or newspaper articles had ever given me this sense of satisfaction. This was my masterpiece.

I was proud of the story I'd written but my favorite part wasn't the fiction. It was the dedication.

I'd given this story to Beau.

He'd probably never read the words I'd written for him but it gave me a great deal of peace to know they were there.

Wiping the tears off my damp cheeks, I closed my eyes and tipped my head to the ceiling. *I miss you. I hope you have a nice day.* Every time I thought of Beau, I closed my eyes and sent him good thoughts. And since I thought of him about a hundred times a day, I did this a lot.

"Morning."

I opened my eyes and spun my chair around to see my dad leaning against the doorframe. "Hi, Dad. Did you sleep okay?"

He nodded, the lines in his forehead deepening. "I did, but it doesn't look like you did."

I stood from my chair and crossed the room, hugging him at the waist. "I slept okay. I just got up early so I could finish my book. It's always a little emotional at the end."

He hugged me tighter. "Congratulations, Sabrina. I'm so proud of you."

"Thanks, Dad." I smiled against his navy polo then stepped away, reaching up to knot my messy hair. "So what's the plan for today? Is there anything you guys would like to do?"

"Oh, I don't know. Whatever you and your mom want to do is fine with me. Let's decide over breakfast. Though, between you and me, I'd rather not spend the entire day shopping."

"Your secret is safe with me. I'll hop in the shower and then we can head out. There's a coffee shop around the corner that has the best pastries."

"Chocolate croissants?"

"The best you'll ever have."

Dad and I shared the same weakness for breakfast pastries so I grinned when he rubbed his hands together.

"Morning, dear," Mom called. She waved at me and Dad but was making a beeline for the coffee pot.

"Morning, Mom." I followed her into the kitchen and gave her a quick hug before disappearing into my bathroom.

My parents had just gotten to Seattle last night, their first visit out since that horrible night with Anton. They had been distraught over everything that had happened and had wanted to come up immediately to check on me, but I had assured them I was fine and asked for a little time alone to process everything. Only after I'd spilled everything about Beau and told them that he had been here to help me through the rough patch did they agree to wait a few weeks.

But when I'd picked them up at the airport last night, I'd realized that three weeks had been too long. While I had needed time alone, they had needed to see for themselves that I was okay. With just one hug, a few of my mom's gray hairs had turned back to their normal blond and my dad had lost fifteen worry lines from his forehead.

Spending a week with them would be healing. For all of us.

"Ready!" I called, coming out of my bedroom, wearing cuffed jeans and a simple black blouse. "After breakfast, we should visit the market before it gets too crowded." I strapped on my black gladiator sandals.

"Sounds lovely!" Mom always wore dresses and heels, but since she'd traded her normal shoes for flats this morning, I'd taken it as a hint that she wanted to do some exploring. I just hoped my sandals would hold up for the inevitable miles she would put us through today. My dad never wore anything other than golf polos, chinos and sneakers, so no matter what we decided to do, he'd be comfortable.

We set out for coffee and pastries, then wandered toward the market. Sipping my vanilla chai, I followed my parents through Pike Place. While Mom was busy buying fresh fish and produce for dinner, Dad was struggling to pick out a bouquet of flowers from the plethora of available options.

"These?" he mouthed, pointing to an enormous bundle of green buds and deep purple peonies.

I smiled and gave him a thumbs-up. While he handed a wad of cash to the merchant, I glanced over my shoulder, expecting to see an FBI agent close by. I'd been doing that all morning out of habit even though Henry had finally deemed it safe for me to be on my own. It had been a week but I still found it strange to come out of my apartment door and not see someone in my hallway.

Mom called me over to a vegetable stand and pulled me from my thoughts. I helped her pick out the rest of our dinner menu and then we strolled back to my apartment with food bags and flowers in hand.

"We've got some news," Mom said as we walked. "Kameron's girlfriend is pregnant."

"Really?" I did a little skip. "I'm going to be an aunt?"

Dad smiled. "Yep. And we're finally getting some grandbabies."

"I'm so excited! I can't believe he didn't tell me. I talked to him two days ago."

Mom laughed. "He said I could tell you as long as I promised to take a picture of your smile."

My smile got bigger as she pulled out her phone and snapped a quick photo, immediately texting it to my brother.

"That's not all," Dad said. "Kellan and his girlfriend are having a baby too. And they're getting married."

"What?" I laughed. "You're kidding."

Mom's beaming smile got wider and she started laughing again. "Those boys. You'd think at some point they'd stop doing everything together, but I swear, they're just as in sync now as they were when they were little boys."

"At least it makes birthday and Christmas shopping easy." Whatever I bought one brother, I bought the other.

Dad laughed at my joke. "True."

When I was younger, I'd been jealous of Kameron and Kellan. They weren't just brothers, they were best friends. They had done their best to include me, but as the younger sister, I had been destined to be the third wheel.

And now they were both building families of their own.

I was glad they could give my parents grandchildren to love and spoil, because without Beau, I didn't see myself having kids.

I briefly closed my eyes and sent him more good thoughts. *I hope you can do something fun for yourself today. I miss you. Tell Boone I miss him too.*

I ignored a sting of sadness and turned back to my parents.

"Are you okay, dear?" Mom asked, touching my hand.

I forced a wide smile. "I'm great! Really happy for Kameron and Kellan."

"You'll have to come home when the babies are born," Dad said.

"I'll be there. I wish I didn't live so far away, but I guess I'll be earning lots of frequent flyer miles." I may not become a mother but I could be one amazing aunt. At the outpost, I had vowed to become a better daughter and sister. Today, I was vowing to be a loving and present auntie, even from a distance.

Dad threw his arm around my shoulders. "You can always move home."

Move to Florida? I hadn't even considered that as an option.

It would be wonderful to be closer to my family. I didn't have a job in Seattle tying me down anymore. And though I hadn't let Anton's death taint my home, I also wouldn't be heartbroken to leave my apartment behind. Could moving home be my next step?

"I'll think about it, Dad."

"Good." He pulled me tighter into his tall frame and kept me latched to his side all the way back to my apartment. We unloaded the groceries and then set out to do some sight-seeing and shopping. By the time we made it back home in the late afternoon, I was dead on my feet.

"I need to get back to the gym." I plopped down onto my living room couch. "I am out of shape." Spending three weeks writing in my office chair hadn't done my physical endurance any favors.

"You relax and I'll get started on an early dinner," Mom said. "I'll get you a glass of wine too."

Dad and I visited in the living room while I sipped a light chardonnay and Mom bustled around in the kitchen.

"How's Felicity doing?" Dad asked.

I smiled. "Good. She's due any day now."

"And they're having a girl?"

I nodded just as the doorbell rang. I started to stand but Dad beat me to standing. "You sit, I'll get it."

I had no idea who could be visiting. My doorman normally called with outside visitors so I figured it was one of my neighbors or someone at the wrong door. When two pairs of footsteps came back down the hall, I sat up straighter.

"Henry?"

"Hi." He waved to me and then my mom. "Sorry to intrude. I'll come back a different day."

"No, it's fine. Please, come in." Standing from the couch, I introduced him to Mom and Dad.

"Stay for dinner?" Mom asked him.

Henry looked to me for an invitation and I nodded. "Stay, please."

The week after Beau had left, Henry had checked in on me twice but I hadn't seen him since. I had been so consumed with writing and he'd been busy with work that we'd resorted to the occasional text, but even then, our exchanges had been brief. It would be nice to catch up with him tonight and Mom was cooking a feast.

"Would you like wine?" Dad asked him.

"Sure. Thanks."

Dad brought Henry a glass and refilled my own, then joined us in the living room.

"It seems like I haven't seen you in ages," I said. "I'm glad you stopped by."

"I was in the area and thought I'd make sure you hadn't been sucked into your computer."

Dad laughed. "We got here just in the nick of time."

"No teasing!" Mom yelled from the kitchen, coming to my defense. "I haven't had anything good to read for weeks and I'm desperate for her next book."

"Thanks, Mom," I said, giving Dad and Henry my "so there" look.

Henry smiled and turned to my dad. "So how long are you visiting Seattle?"

I sank further into my chair and listened to Dad and Henry chat while Mom's kitchen noises echoed in the background.

It was strange to see Henry so relaxed, off duty with a wine glass and not wearing his signature black suit. He looked so different, so casual, in jeans and an untucked white linen shirt. He was handsome in his suit but this look fit him better. It went with his dimple.

"Dinner!" Mom announced and we all retreated to the kitchen. Ever since that horrible night with Anton, I couldn't bring myself to sit at the kitchen island, so with my plate loaded, I came back to the living room and sat on the floor by the coffee table.

I smiled to myself, thinking of how many nights I'd spent at the outpost in a similar position, using a cooler instead of a coffee table. Beau was so big that in order to be comfortable, he always had to have the cooler between his open legs.

My eyes closed as I tipped back my head. *Whatever you're eating, I hope you have a nice dinner tonight.*

My parents and Henry joined me in the living room and we all ate Mom's delicious meal. I volunteered to clean up but Dad insisted I relax and talk with Henry while he and Mom did the dishes.

"How are you?" Henry asked.

"I'm doing okay. There have been a couple of bad nights here and there, but for the most part, I'm good. Writing has helped keep my mind off things."

He pushed out a slow breath. "I'm glad. I know I've said it a million times but I'm truly sorry."

"It's over now, Henry. You're not to blame. How have you been?"

"Busy. Really busy."

"Those darn criminals. Don't they ever take vacations?"

He grinned. "The next case I pick up, I'll be sure to find a bad guy with regularly scheduled holidays."

I tapped my temple. "Now you're thinking."

My ringing phone interrupted our conversation. Felicity's name flashed on the screen, requesting to FaceTime. My heart started to race as I bounced in my seat, waiting for the video feed to load.

Either she was stuck in a chair and was calling to bitch because she couldn't get up, or she was in the hospital with my self-proclaimed niece.

Silas's face appeared on the screen and my heart jumped. His smile was so wide, his happiness radiated through the phone. "Hey there," he said. "We've got someone we'd like you to meet."

Tears filled my eyes as he aimed the camera at Felicity in her hospital bed and a precious bundle in her arms.

"She's so beautiful," I whispered. The baby was swaddled in a white muslin blanket and her hair was covered with a pale-pink cap as she slept peacefully in her mother's arms.

"I think so too." Felicity smiled and turned her eyes to her daughter, touching the tip of Victoria's tiny nose.

"I can't wait to hold her," I said. "How are you doing?"

Felicity looked back to the camera and sighed. "I'm tired. She came pretty quickly and I'm worn out."

"She did awesome," Silas said in the background.

"Of course she did. Is everyone healthy?"

She nodded. "We're all perfect."

"Oh, good. I wish I were there to give you both a hug."

"Me too," Felicity said. "Come and visit us soon?"

"Very soon." When Victoria squeaked, I took it as my

cue to say good-bye. "I'll let you go. Thanks for calling me. Will you send me pictures?"

Felicity nodded and smiled. "Prepare to be flooded. I've taken about a hundred in the last three hours. Once we get home and settled, I'll call you."

"Okay. Congratulations. I'm so happy for you."

"Thanks. It's been a day I'll never forget." The joy on her face was something *I'd* never forget.

Silas joined the shot and kissed Felicity's cheek.

"Congratulations to you too, Daddy. You guys take care." I waved and smiled, then ended the call. When I turned back to the living room, I was met with more smiling faces.

"That's so exciting!" Mom said. "I hope Kameron or Kellan has a sweet baby girl."

My phone started to ding as the flood of promised pictures started coming through.

"Let's see those baby pictures," Dad said.

I immediately went for my phone, not needing any encouragement to thumb through pictures. With me in the middle of the couch, Henry on one side and Mom and Dad on the other, I started swiping and saving pictures.

"Oh, she's beautiful," Mom said, "and Felicity looks amazing. You'd never guess she just had a baby."

I smiled. "If I didn't love her so much, I'd hate her for being so photogenic. It's not fair."

Henry scoffed. "Says the woman who had my entire team begging to be put on Sabrina duty."

I blushed and swiped through more photos, pointing out the people that I knew and guessing at those I didn't. When I got to the last picture, my smile fell and my fingers froze.

Felicity had sent me a picture of Beau and Victoria.

Beau was standing, smiling down at the baby, as his

massive arms cradled her tight. His hair was longer underneath his baseball cap, its ends curling up at his neck. The skin at his forearms and cheeks was tanner than when he'd been here weeks ago. He looked so perfect with that baby I could hardly breathe. His expression was so soft and loving, it was hard to believe that little girl wasn't his own.

"Who's that?" Dad asked.

I forced my eyes away from the picture and swallowed the lump in my throat. "That's Beau."

"Oh." Mom gave me a sad smile and patted my hand. "I'll get us more wine. Henry?"

"No, thank you," he said. "I should probably get going. Thank you for a wonderful dinner."

"I'm so glad you could join us," Dad said. "It was a pleasure meeting you."

"Same to you."

We all stood from the couch. Mom and Dad shook Henry's hand, then Mom went to get more wine and Dad slipped into my room for an early bedtime.

"Thanks for coming over tonight," I said. "It was nice to see you."

"You too."

I walked him to the door, but before he could leave, I called his name. "Can I ask you something?"

"Of course."

"Why did you call Felicity the night I killed Anton?" I had replayed that night a hundred times, and with every rewind, I wondered why he'd called Felicity instead of my parents.

He sighed. "Because I didn't want you to have to tell her what had happened."

"Right," I said, though I was still confused. Why hadn't

he done the same with my parents? Having to explain every-thing to them had been awful. Before I could ask, he answered my question.

"And I knew Felicity would call Holt and he'd come to you."

"You did? How?"

"Because that man loves you, Sabrina. Which is why I'm surprised he isn't here."

Beau loved me? Then why wasn't he here with me? Why had he left weeks ago without a trace?

Curses.

Because I'd pushed him away.

I was such a fucking moron.

Henry chuckled. "I can see you've got a few gears turn-ing. I'll say good night."

"Oh, sorry," I said, snapping out of my head. "Thanks again for stopping by."

He bent to kiss my cheek. "Good-bye, Sabrina."

"Bye, Henry."

When the door clicked shut, my hands immediately went into my hair.

"Uh-oh," Mom said when I walked back into the living room.

"I messed up." I sank onto the couch and pressed a pillow over my face.

She jerked the pillow away and handed me my wine instead. "Would you like to talk about it?"

I nodded and took a healthy gulp. I had told my parents about Beau and my time at the outpost but I'd kept it fairly vague and PG-rated for my dad. Now that it was just me and Mom, I spent the next hour giving her the full story, all the way from meeting Beau in Silas's kitchen to the bomb Henry had just dropped.

"There. That's the whole story. You don't need to read my next novel because I basically just recited it for you, except I gave my characters a happy ending."

She laughed. "I'm glad you shared with me, dear."

"Me too." I was still upset but it had helped to talk it over, especially with Mom. "I'm glad we're closer these days," I admitted. "I've really missed you and Dad. Kameron and Kellan too."

"You have no idea how happy that makes me." She sniffled and wiped a tear from her wet eyes. "I hate all of the bad things that happened to you over the last year but I can't regret them. When Janessa died, you built these walls to shut everyone out. I think it was your way of keeping your heart from being broken. Nothing we did could get through. I'm just so glad to see you're starting to take those walls down."

"I'm sorry."

"You don't need to apologize. You were so young and what happened with Janessa was so traumatic. She was the Kameron to your Kellan back then. I just wish we had known what to do to keep you from pulling away."

"I don't know if there was anything you could have done." They had always been there for me; I just hadn't let them in.

"Most of the time, I don't even think you know you're pushing us away. So many people love you and want to be close to you, Sabrina. You just don't always let them. The only person I've seen you really let in since high school is Felicity."

And Beau. Being with him at the outpost, stripping away

all of my comforts, he had opened my heart. He had broken through my walls and helped set me free.

"I don't want to shut people out anymore," I whispered.

She reached out and grabbed my hand. "Then don't. You can't let what happened with Janessa all those years ago define how you're going to build relationships. Your guard isn't just keeping out the bad. You're blocking the good too."

"Why do you think she killed herself?" Never, not once had I asked that question.

Janessa had left a note for her parents but no one had ever told me what she'd written, and I'd been so angry with her at the time, I hadn't wanted to hear any excuses.

Mom pushed out a deep breath. "She was pregnant."

My jaw fell open. "Pregnant? We pinkie promised to stay virgins until college. And she didn't just kill herself but her baby too? I can't—" I took a long breath and stopped my rant. "Never mind. Getting all worked up isn't going to bring her back."

"No, it's not."

I shook my head, dumbfounded at her choice. "I wish she hadn't been able to buy that gun."

"Is that why you went after the Federovs?"

I nodded. "Kids shouldn't be able to buy illegal guns off the street. Without that pistol, she would have had to commit suicide some other way. If she'd taken pills or even cut her wrists, I might have been able to save her, Mom. I could have gotten there in time."

"No, dear. You wouldn't have. She had been dead for hours by the time you got there. No matter what, there was nothing you could have done."

"Maybe you're right."

"Oh, Sabrina." Her head fell. "I wish I had known you

felt this way. I should have forced you to talk about this a long time ago."

I shook my head, sending a couple of tears down my cheeks. "I probably wouldn't have listened but I'm glad you told me. Now I can let it go."

We sat together in silence, holding hands and finishing our wine until she gave my fingers one last squeeze and stood from the couch. "I'd better get to bed. We can talk more tomorrow if you'd like."

"Okay. Thanks, Mom."

I was emotionally drained but doubted I'd sleep much. Instead, I'd be thinking about the serious life changes I was going to make, starting tomorrow.

No more pushing people away. I was done working from sunrise to sunset and most of the hours in between. I was done using sex as a way to keep men at a distance. I was done living a solitary existence.

I wanted to be close to my family. I wanted to build life-long friendships. I wanted to surround myself with people who loved me unconditionally.

"Mom?" I called before she could slip into the bedroom.

"Yes?"

"I think I'm going to move home."

CHAPTER TWENTY-ONE

SABRINA

"Miss Sabrina," my doorman answered the phone.

I smiled. "Hi, Tim."

I always smiled when I talked to Tim. He was more like an uncle than a doorman. At nearly sixty-five, he had been in this building long before I'd moved in and he'd be here long after. This place had become a part of his soul just like the outpost had imprinted on mine.

"What can I do for you today?" he asked.

"I wanted to let you know that my movers should be here within the hour. You can just send them up when they arrive."

"I'll see to it but are you sure that you really want to move? It's a long way away."

I smiled wider. "I'm sure."

For the last two weeks, Tim had been relentlessly trying to convince me to stay in Seattle. He'd written me a note that summarized all the negatives of moving. Every time I came in or went out, he'd remind me of all the wonderful things about the city. He'd even had my favorite Thai food delivered one evening with a red circle on the attached menu showing its Washington-only locations.

"All right," he muttered. "I'll expect you to come back and visit."

"You can count on it. Thanks, Tim." I hung up and swiped through my contacts, pressing Felicity's name next.

"Hey, hold on one sec," she answered. In the background, baby Victoria was wailing like a banshee. A door clicked shut and Felicity sighed. "There."

"Um, maybe you should call me back. Don't you need to get her?"

"She's fine. Silas is with her."

"Is everything okay?"

"No. Yes. I don't know." Her voice cracked as she started crying. "We're trying to get her to drink from a bottle so that Silas can get up with her at night too. My nipples need a break and I am just so tired. I've barely slept in two weeks."

"It will get better. I promise." I had no idea what else to say to a new mother.

She sniffled. "You're right. I keep telling myself that too, but it's just been a rough couple of weeks."

"Hang in there. She'll probably be sleeping through the night by the time she goes to college."

"God, I hope so." Felicity laughed and sniffled again. "How's the packing going?"

"All done. The movers should be here soon and my car is all loaded up with the stuff I'm hauling myself, so as soon as they're finished, I'm out of here. Good-bye Seattle."

"It's a long drive so please be careful and call me if you

get tired. No matter what time it is, I'm sure I'll be awake. Victoria and I can keep you company."

"Sounds good."

"Good luck today."

I smiled. "Thanks. Give my girl a hug and a kiss for me."

"I will. I'd better go rescue Silas." The sound of Victoria's screaming got louder as Felicity went back to the nursery.

"Okay. Bye."

Tossing my phone on the couch, I scanned the stacks of boxes in my living room. My movers would be packing up the rest of the apartment but these boxes were all going to charity along with most of my furniture. Where I was going, I didn't need a bed, couches or chairs.

Beau's house already had it all.

Felicity thought my plan to show up on Beau's doorstep tonight was romantic. I'd thought so too, at first, but now I was starting to think it was foolish and impulsive. What if he turned me away? Or worse, what if he was with another woman when I showed up?

The thought made me nauseous so I went to the kitchen to get some water.

Chugging it down, I willed myself to stay positive.

Besides, it was too late to change my plans now. For Beau, I'd take the risk. He deserved to see how far I was willing to go to keep him in my life. He deserved this grand gesture.

With nothing left to do but wait for the movers, I stood by a window and took a few moments to appreciate the city. The street below was bustling with cars and people walking by. The tower across the street was mostly office space, people working away at their desks. There would certainly be things I'd miss about Seattle, but mostly, I was glad to be going home.

Even though I'd only spent a few days in the actual town of Prescott, I knew without a doubt it was the place for me. Montana had won my heart.

Just like Beau had.

The nervous energy in my stomach swelled when a knock sounded at the door.

This was it. I'd spend the morning hours watching the movers wrap and box my belongings and then I was leaving. I'd lock up and give Tim my keys. By this time next week, this place would be home to someone new. I just hoped that during their residence here, it included far fewer traumatic moments.

I rushed to the door, forgoing a check at the peephole, and swung it open wide, smiling and ready to greet my moving crew.

But my movers weren't on the other side of the door.

Beau was.

My smile dropped and I gaped at him, using the door to balance my swaying feet.

"Hi." One hand was in his jeans pocket and the other was holding a small black bag. His jeans were newer, not the faded and worn pairs he usually wore and he'd traded his normal plain T-shirt for a deep green button down with rolled up sleeves.

He was breathtaking.

This rugged, sexy mountain man was every one of my lost hopes and forgotten dreams come true.

The shock of seeing him finally wore off and I found my voice. "Hello." I wanted to scream and jump into his arms, to kiss his face a million times, but first, I wanted to know why he was here. "Would you like to come in?"

"No." He shook his head and dropped his bag so his hand could stroke his beard. "I want to say a few things before I come in."

"Okay." The excitement I'd felt a moment ago was now tied in an anxious knot.

He sucked in a long breath before launching right into his speech. "When you left, you said you didn't belong."

"Beau, I—"

"Please, let me get this out."

I nodded and whispered, "Okay."

"You belong right here." He held out his arms, making a circle in the space between them. "You belong with me. Right here. No matter where we live, whether it's Montana, Seattle or Timbuktu, this is where you belong."

My breath hitched and my heart started racing. Was this really happening? He'd really come for me?

He'd come for me.

He was willing to give up his home, the town he loved and being close to his family, Coby, just to be with me. Any doubts I'd had over the past two weeks vanished. Henry had been right. This man loved me completely.

I opened my mouth to tell him that I was moving to Prescott but the stairwell door flew open with a loud bang and I flinched.

"Oh, Sabrina," my neighbor sneered. I'd nicknamed him The SOB in 5-1-3. "Don't tell me we're back to having federal agents roam our hall." He eyed Beau up and down.

I shook my head. "No. No federal agents. Excuse us, we'll go inside."

I wouldn't miss this guy when I moved.

"Should I expect to hear gunshots later?"

Asshole.

I wasn't the only one who thought that was a rude question. Beau did his jungle growl and turned to loom over my young, arrogant neighbor. SOB's face paled when he realized he'd gone too far.

With clenched fists, Beau ordered, "Go."

SOB scurried to his door down one from mine, fumbling with the keys as he cowered away from Beau.

The second his door clicked shut, I started giggling. SOB had completely ruined our moment but I did love how Beau was first and foremost my protector. "Come inside." I reached out to tug Beau's hand.

He grabbed his bag, then walked past me and down the hall. I dragged in a huge whiff of his amazing pine smell as I closed the door and followed him inside. When I got to the living room, he was staring at the boxes stacked on my couch with his hands planted on his hips. "What's all this?"

"I'm moving. Those are the boxes going to charity along with my furniture."

"You're moving?"

"Yep. The movers should be here soon."

He ran a hand over his beard as he walked to the windows on the far side of my apartment. "Where are you going?" he asked the glass.

The smile I'd been fighting let loose. "Montana."

Beau spun around, his eyes wide.

"You kind of stole my sunshine here, Goliath. I was going to show up at your house tonight and ask if you felt like having some company."

A sexy grin replaced the shock on his face. "Does that mean you're smitten with me, Shortcake?"

I shrugged. "You're just okay."

"Yeah," he whispered. "You're just okay too."

I smiled. "You need to come over here."

"You come here."

"Meet in the middle?"

He nodded and I took a running leap as he bolted across the room to catch me. My legs wrapped around his waist and my arms banded around his neck as our lips crashed together.

Our mouths and tongues moved frantically but neither of us could get enough. We were desperate to get as close as possible and erase the distance of this past month.

I squeezed my thighs, pulling my center closer to Beau's waist, hoping for some friction to dull the throbbing ache under my jeans. He groaned as his big hands jerked my hips even closer, positioning me lower so his erection was pressed right against my core.

I tore my mouth away from his lips and trailed them up his jaw. "Bedroom," I panted against his ear before running my tongue along his earlobe and then down the muscled cords of his neck.

Beau didn't waste any time hauling me to the bedroom. All of my bedding had been folded up in the corner and the mattress was bare, but thankfully, the bed itself was still intact.

He planted a knee on the edge of the bed and threw me down in the middle of the mattress. His fingers fumbled with the buttons on his shirt while I started stripping. My clothes, bra and panties came off with reckless speed and were scattered across the floor by the time Beau managed to shed his shirt.

I sat up and reached for the button on his jeans while he

tugged off the T-shirt he'd been wearing under his button-down. My hand dove inside his boxers and wrapped around his thick cock, my thumb circling the tip to spread the drop at its end around the head. I ached to have him inside.

Beau stopped undressing for a moment to suck in a sharp breath and mutter, "Fuck." I only stroked him twice before he pulled my hand away. "I'm going to have trouble making this last as it is, angel. If you keep drooling over my cock while you're sitting there naked, this will be over before it starts."

I smiled. "We don't have much time anyway. The movers are coming."

"They can wait outside." He stepped out of his jeans and laid them carefully beside me on the bed before kicking off his boxers. His long fingers trailed up the inside of my thighs as he came down on top of me, his light touch leaving a trail of goose bumps on my skin.

My hips bucked and I gasped when his thumb strummed my clit twice. When two of his fingers slid inside my wetness, I closed my eyes as he rocked them in and out. It was amazing but it wasn't enough. "I need you inside."

He dipped his fingers one last time before positioning the broad head of his cock. "Your wish." With his elbows bracketing my face, his hands dove into the masses of my hair splayed behind me on the mattress.

With a slow and deliberate push, he buried his huge cock, connecting us so completely I knew we'd never drift apart again.

"I love you," I whispered.

His smiling eyes locked with mine as his hips kept thrusting. "I love you too."

Beau's strokes sped up and my empty bedroom filled

with the sound of our bodies colliding. One of his hands left my hair and came down to my breast, rolling a nipple and sending a whole new wave of heat to my core.

"Yes," I moaned.

"Say that again," he whispered in my ear as his cock kept stroking and his hand kept working my nipple.

"Yes."

He kissed my neck, thrusting deep once more but then stopped.

"What?" I panted. "Did you hear something? Is it the movers?"

He didn't answer me; instead he lifted up and leaned over to rifle through his jeans pocket.

I listened for noise but the apartment was silent. "Beau?"

He still didn't answer. *Seriously?* What was so important that he stopped fucking me? If he came back with his phone, I was going to kill him.

"Beau!" I smacked him on the arm, causing him to chuckle. "This isn't funny." I tipped my hips up as a silent reminder that he had much more important things to be doing right now than messing around with his pants.

"I'm glad you said yes." His torso came back to mine and he grinned. His right hand reached for my left and slid a cold metal band past my knuckle until it rested perfectly at the base of my ring finger.

"Wha—"

He interrupted me by slamming his mouth down on mine and kissing me deeply. I didn't kiss him back, I just lay there, stunned.

Did he just propose? I ripped my lips away from his and turned my head to the side. He had my wrist pinned, a diamond ring sparkling brightly against my skin.

"Oh my god," I gasped as I stared at the ring. I wasn't sure whether to laugh or cry so I did both, hiccupping sobs as a wide smile split my face. Blinking away tears, I turned my head, needing Beau's eyes. They were waiting for me, bright and full of love.

"I love you, Sabrina," he whispered. "Be my wife?"

I nodded, unable to speak because I was crying again.

Beau swiped my tears away with his thumbs as he peppered kisses on my nose, chin and cheeks. When I finally got ahold of my emotions, I lifted up to kiss his lips. My legs wrapped around the back of his thighs and pulled him closer, burying his cock as deep as it could go.

He smiled against my mouth before sliding his tongue inside. Our kiss started out sweet but quickly turned hot as Beau's long strokes resumed. My body ignited again and my legs started to tremble. Beau started going faster, pounding hard and deep, until he gave me an intense orgasm. I was so consumed with the explosion, I vaguely registered Beau telling me he was coming too.

My entire body went limp as he slid out, letting me go to collapse by my side. When my racing heartbeat and labored breathing started to subside, I lifted my left hand in front of my face.

"Wow." I was mesmerized by the jewel on my finger. Set in a thin, white-gold band was a square-cut diamond. The ring was simple but exquisite. Exactly what I would have picked out for myself.

"Do you like it?" Beau asked, propping himself up on his side.

"It's beautiful." I turned my head to give him a kiss but the second my lips touched his, a knock pounded on the door.

"Ahh! The movers are here and I'm naked!" I scrambled off the bed, scooping up clothes and nearly tripping as I rushed to the bathroom to clean up. By the time I emerged, Beau had gotten dressed, sans the button-down, and was showing the crew around my living room.

"Hi." I waved and shook hands with the foreman, who immediately started walking me through the moving process and introducing me to his team.

"We should be done before lunch, ma'am," the foreman said as his crew dispersed to bring in flattened boxes and tissue-paper rolls from the hallway.

"Sounds great. Thank you."

Beau tucked me into his side as we stood in the living room and watched the movers get started.

"Shit!" I planted my face in his chest. "The bedroom smells like sex."

He started laughing and hugged me tighter.

"It's not funny," I hissed, which only made him laugh louder.

Still laughing, he called to the foreman. "Do you need us to stay or can we step out for a while?"

"We're all good here. You just need to sign off on everything once it's packed."

"Come on, Shortcake." Beau steered me down the hall. "Let's take a walk."

Hand in hand, we rode down the elevator, waved at Tim as we passed the front desk, then walked outside. The mid-morning air was fresh and cool as we strolled down the sidewalk. The diamond on my finger glittered in the sun and I kept twirling it with my thumb to see it sparkle.

"We're getting married." I'd probably keep saying that all day until it really sank in.

Beau smiled. "Damn straight."

Everything had happened so fast this morning I realized there was still a lot to talk about. There were things I needed to say.

I took a deep breath and started with an apology. "I'm sorry I pushed you away when you came here last month." I never should have told him to leave.

"I'm sorry it took me so long to come back." There was regret in his voice too. "I tried to get back sooner but it took longer than I thought to wrap up stuff in Prescott. I had to train a guy to take over the search-and-rescue team and find someone else to take my job, and I wanted to spend some time with Coby before I left."

"You quit your job?"

He nodded. "Yeah. But I think they'll let me have it back."

I smiled and rested my head on his arm, glad he was here now even if it had taken him a while to get back. "I missed you."

"I missed you too."

"Whenever I thought about you, I sent you these good thoughts."

"Yeah?" he asked. "Like what?"

"Just little things. I'd wish you a good day at work or a nice dinner. I'd ask you to give Boone a hug for me."

He grumbled. "Don't get me started on that damn dog. You've ruined him. He's been moping for eight months."

"Really?" I smiled. "He missed me?"

"Almost as much as I did." He bent and kissed the top of my hair. "I meant what I said earlier, Sabrina. I've thought about it a lot. I don't care where we live. As long as we're together, I'll be happy."

"Me too." It meant the world to me that he'd make that kind of sacrifice but it didn't change my decision. "I choose Montana. I want to take Boone for walks down the street by our house. I want your family to invade our privacy and I want to become Coby's favorite aunt. I want to take our kids camping at the outpost. Just promise me I'll never have to shovel snow."

"You're sure?"

I looked up to him and nodded. "I'm sure." I'd have no regrets about trading my busy, whirlwind lifestyle for a simple country life.

After walking for a bit, we started making our way back and I started making a mental list of everyone I wanted to call on the drive to Prescott. We had a lot of exciting news to share. My family and Felicity would be over the moon when they learned about our engagement.

I was sure Mom would want me to tell her how Beau had proposed in detail, at least twice.

My feet stopped dead as realization dawned.

"What?" Beau asked when my hand slipped out of his. "Are you okay?"

I shook my head. "What are we going to tell my parents when they ask how you proposed? Or our kids? We can't tell them the real story. It will scar them for life!"

He stepped into my space and smiled. "You're the story-teller, I'm sure you'll think of something."

Maybe I could tell them that he surprised me. Just keep it vague. That would work, right?

Right.

EPILOGUE

BEAU

E *ight years later . . .*
   "Daddy?"

"Ella?" I tucked my six-year-old daughter under her dark purple quilt. Everything in this room was purple. The walls. Her bed. The chair in the corner. Sabrina had even found a round rug that was entirely swirls of purple. Because Ella loved it so much, it had become one of my favorite rooms in the house.

"I'm not very happy with you," she declared for the fifth time tonight.

I grinned. "I know."

"Mommy's going to be really mad at you too."

I leaned down and kissed her forehead. "Probably."

"I still can't believe you did that."

I tried not to laugh but her stern expression was too cute and one slipped out. Ella had my dark hair, but other than that, she was Sabrina's tiny clone. Personality and all.

"It will be fine," I told her. "Now did you get the rest of your clothes picked out?"

She nodded and smiled, revealing two missing front teeth. "Mommy said I could have my own suitcase this time."

"Okay. We'll load it up tomorrow."

"And you'll remember to bring my book?"

I nodded. "Yes, I'll get your book."

"And the picture I drew for Grammy and Grandpa?"

"And the picture."

"And my movie for the plane?"

"Yes, and your movie. We'll get it all tomorrow. Now, time for bed."

"Okay, Daddy." She tucked her hands under her cheek as she sighed. Her beautiful green eyes looked at me like I had hung the moon. Even when she was grown, I hoped she'd always look at me like that.

"Night-night, princess." I gave her another kiss. "I love you."

"I love you too, Daddy."

I shut off the purple lamp next to her bed and pushed up off the floor, closing her door before walking down the hall to the boys' room. I loved that the kids were all downstairs these days. They had been upstairs when they were babies but now the upstairs extra room was for guests. It gave the kids more space and Sabrina and I more privacy.

"Peyton, Tanner," I called as I walked into their room. "Time for bed."

The twins were nowhere in sight.

"Boys. Stop hiding." This was their new thing. They couldn't sit still or stay quiet at the dinner table to save their lives, but when it came to hiding, they were as silent as the dead.

I gave them a minute, but when they didn't emerge, I started counting. "One. Two. Th—"

Two little four-year-old boys started laughing. Tanner popped out of the suitcase on the floor. Peyton sat up from the gap between the bottom bunk's mattress and the wall. I shook my head and looked to the floor to hide my smile.

My boys were not small for their age, but to hide, they could contort themselves into the tightest places imaginable. Sabrina didn't like that they hid from her so I didn't want to encourage them, but at the same time, I was always impressed with their new hiding spots.

"Who's on the top bunk tonight?" I asked.

"My turn!" Tanner yelled, scrambling up the stairs to the top bed. I had built them an elaborate bunk bed last year, complete with stairs and an iron railing, but because they both loved the top so much, we made them switch off every night.

"Daddy?" Peyton asked, climbing under his blue comforter. "When's Mommy getting home?"

"Later tonight, bud. She's out with your aunts."

Once a month, Sabrina met Felicity, Maisy and a whole group of women at the Prescott Spa for a girls' night. She'd come home with fancy toenails and a wine buzz, which meant I was getting lucky later. I got lucky most nights, but when she was tipsy, she'd let me get creative.

"Ella says Mommy's going to be mad at you," Peyton said.

"I know," I muttered.

"Tomorrow is our baycation!" Tanner cried as he bounced in his bed.

"Vacation. With a V. *Vay*-cation."

"Vvvacation."

"Good job." I tucked him in first and then bent down to tuck in Peyton. "You guys be quiet and get some sleep so you've got lots of energy for the trip tomorrow. Okay?"

"Okay, Daddy!" both chimed. There was no chance of them staying quiet tonight. They'd talk to each other for hours, only stopping when their little bodies physically shut down to sleep.

"Love you, Peyton. Love you, Tanner."

"Night-night, Daddy!"

I closed the door and the giggles started. "We're going on a roller coaster!" one of them yelled at the same time the other said, "Grandpa said he'd take me on a saffrari!"

Shaking my head, I let them be and went to the kitchen for a glass of water. Boone was lying on his bed, his eyes locked on the door to the garage. He'd stay just like that until Sabrina got home.

"More moping?" I asked him.

He didn't move, not even to blink.

I huffed, scowling at my former dog. He'd abandoned me completely in favor of my wife and kids. *Man's best friend my ass.* Boone didn't give two shits about me anymore. If Sabrina wasn't home, he was all about Ella and the boys.

After turning off a few lights, I went back to the boys' room, reminding them to be quiet before starting up the stairs. Making my way to our bedroom, I took in the framed pictures along the hallway. Sabrina kept growing the collage Maisy had started, replacing older pictures with new and adding a couple more rows of frames. But even with the additions, the black-and-whites still centered around one color photo.

Our wedding picture.

Besides the pictures of her in the hospital on the day the

kids were born, there wasn't a picture on this wall where she looked more beautiful than at our wedding. We'd gotten married in an open meadow not far into the mountains with close friends and family looking on. Sabrina's long hair had been curled and left free to flow down her back. Her delicate lace dress had hugged her top and flowed to her feet. And her smile. The photographer had captured her breathtaking smile after I'd slid my ring onto her finger.

I touched the frame then kept walking to the bedroom to do some packing of my own.

Tomorrow, I was finally taking Sabrina to Disney World.

The day after she'd moved here from Seattle, I'd offered to take her on vacation, but she'd jumped right into wedding planning instead, insisting we save money and focus on the wedding. Then I'd pitched the idea of Disney World for our honeymoon but she'd nixed that too.

She'd wanted our honeymoon to be at the outpost.

I had argued at first, but when she'd pointed out that there would be no distractions from a week of sex, I'd immediately shut up.

After the wedding, we wasted no time in getting pregnant with Ella, then again with the boys. Disney World with a two-year-old and twin babies sounded more like torture than fun so we'd kept pushing back the trip.

But now the kids were old enough to have a blast and we were leaving in the morning. We were flying to Florida tomorrow and spending a day at her parents' house, and then we were all going to Orlando. Her parents, brothers and their families were coming along too. We'd all be wearing matching *Holt-MacKenzie Clan* T-shirts that her brother Kameron had designed.

The family time would be great, but more than anything,

I couldn't wait to give Sabrina this trip. She was more excited than Ella, Peyton and Tanner combined.

My phone chimed in my pocket as I pulled a suitcase from the top shelf in the closet.

Shortcake: Just leaving. I'm kissing the kids and then we're locking the door.

Hell, yeah. Packing would have to wait until the morning.

Stripping down to nothing, I slid into bed to wait for my wife. Propping myself up against the headboard, I reached for the book on my nightstand.

I had read every single book that Sabrina had written. Romance novels weren't my thing but hers were the exception. I'd reread most of them more times than I could count. I swelled with pride whenever I read something written by my talented wife. I loved finding hints of Sabrina in her main characters.

The one I held tonight was my favorite, *Holt's Compass.* This one was *my* book.

Flipping to the beginning, I read the dedication.

To Beau.
The hero who stole my heart.
The man of my dreams.
The love of my life.

She'd written that when we were apart, which made it all the more special.

I read it again then heard the garage door open downstairs. Setting my book aside, I grinned and stared at the door. The kids had been right earlier. She was going to be mad. Lucky for me, it wasn't the real kind of mad. She'd do her best to put on an angry face—it was cute as hell—but with one kiss, she'd be all smiles again.

When her bare feet padded down the hall, I dropped the grin and rested my hands behind my head.

"Beau, you should see the boys. They're so cu—" She crossed through the door and stopped dead, her eyes widening as her jaw dropped.

"Hi, angel."

"What. Did. You. Do?"

I grinned. "It gets hot in Florida. I thought this might be cooler."

"We're taking pictures, Beau!" She fisted her hands on her hips. "When I bring them back and show everyone, no one is going to recognize you. They're all going to say, 'Who is that strange man holding Ella's hand?' "

That or they were going to ask why she'd taken Michael to Florida, because with my hair buzzed off like his and no beard, I was my brother's doppelganger.

"It's not that bad," I said. "Besides, now the boys and I have matching haircuts."

"Where are those clippers?" She sprinted from the door toward the bathroom.

I whipped off the sheet and ran after her, barely rescuing my clippers before she could take them apart.

With her pinned in my arms, my cock getting hard against the top of her ass, I bent down to kiss her neck. "I'll grow them back."

"Yeah, you will." She was still pretending to be mad but I could feel her shiver when I kissed her again.

"Do you still love me even though I look different?"

She huffed. "You know I do."

"Do you still think I'm sexy?" I slid my fingers into the waistband of her jeans and fingered her pussy.

"Obviously," she panted as I rubbed her wetness up to her clit.

My fingers kept working and she started to melt in my arms. "I'll make you a deal, Shortcake. I'll promise to let you dictate the length of my hair in exchange for a new puppy."

"You jerk!" She laughed, yanking my hand out of her pants and spinning around to playfully smack me on the bare chest. "This was your plan all along, wasn't it?"

I shrugged. I'd been wanting another dog for months but she had always refused, not wanting Boone to be put out by a puppy. I admit, this negotiation tactic may have been extreme but I was pretty sure she wouldn't say no this time.

"What do you say? Have we got a deal?"

She sighed. "Fine."

Damn, I love this woman.

"Good." I smiled and wrapped her in my arms, lifting her up to carry her to bed.

The next morning, the bags were loaded, the kids were arguing over puppy names in the back seat of our car, and Sabrina's hand was holding mine as I drove us to the airport.

I'd told Sabrina once that I wasn't a dreamer. That was still true. I'd leave the dreams to her and to my children.

Because I didn't need to dream.

I already had everything I could ever hope for, right here in my car.

THE JAMISON VALLEY series continues with *The Bitter-root Inn.*

AUTHOR'S NOTE

Last summer, my husband was invited on a hunting trip to Idaho. He went with a friend of his that has a couple of small planes, so rather than drive, they decided to fly. On their flight out, my husband kept spotting these small strips of bare land in the mountains and asked his pilot friend what they were all about. The pilot shared that those strips were actually U.S. Forest Service outposts spotted throughout the mountains. The open fields were for small airplanes, like his, in case they needed to make emergency landings. When my husband came home and told me about his trip and the flights, I was instantly fascinated by the idea of these outposts and knew it would make a unique setting for a novel. I have taken some fictional liberties with Sabrina's outpost but I hope you've been able to picture it as a place where she was able to fall in love with Montana and with Beau.

ACKNOWLEDGMENTS

I am incredibly, *incredibly* lucky to have such an amazing team of women who add their special touches to each of my books. To my editor, Elizabeth Nover. My cover designer, Sarah Hansen. My proofreader, Julie Deaton. Thank you!!!

Also, a huge thanks to all of the amazing book bloggers who have been so wonderful in promoting this series.

And a special thanks to you. Thanks for reading *The Outpost*.

ABOUT THE AUTHOR

Devney is a *USA Today* bestselling author who lives in Washington with her husband and two sons. Born and raised in Montana, she loves writing books set in her treasured home state. After working in the technology industry for nearly a decade, she abandoned conference calls and project schedules to enjoy a slower pace at home with her family. Writing one book, let alone many, was not something she ever expected to do. But now that she's discovered her true passion for writing romance, she has no plans to ever stop.

Don't miss out on Devney's latest book news.
Subscribe to her newsletter!
www.devneyperry.com

Printed in Great Britain
by Amazon